*Torres Strait Islander Women
and the Pacific War*

To all those Torres Strait Islander women who experienced the trauma of evacuation and removal to an alien mainland Australia and those who experienced isolation, desertion and fear on their small island communities in Torres Strait during the Pacific War, 1942–1945.

*Torres Strait Islander Women
and the Pacific War*

Elizabeth Osborne

**Aboriginal Studies Press
Canberra
1997**

FIRST PUBLISHED IN 1997 BY

Aboriginal Studies Press for the Australian Institute of Aboriginal and Torres Strait Islander Studies, GPO Box 553, Canberra, ACT 2601.

The views expressed in this publication are those of the author and not necessarily those of the Australian Institute of Aboriginal and Torres Strait Islander Studies.

© ELIZABETH OSBORNE 1997

Apart from any fair dealing for the purpose of private study, research, criticism or review, as permitted under the Copyright Act, no part of this publication may be reproduced by any process whatsoever without the written permission of the publisher.

NATIONAL LIBRARY OF AUSTRALIA CATALOGUING-IN-PUBLICATION DATA:

Osborne, Elizabeth
Torres Strait Islander Women and the Pacific War

Bibliography
ISBN 0 85575 313 7

1. World War, 1939–1945 – Queensland – Torres Strait Islands – Personal narratives. 2. World War, 1939–1945 – Women – Queensland – Torres Strait Islands. I. Title.

940.5426092

COVER PAINTING: Ellen Jose *Reach Out and Touch: Distance and Time* (courtesy William Mora Galleries and Ellen Jose)
PRODUCED BY Aboriginal Studies Press
FORMATTED in Palatino 11/14 using Macintosh QuarkXpress
PRINTED IN AUSTRALIA BY Ligare Pty Ltd, Riverwood, NSW

2000/09/97

Contents

Abbreviations   vi
Torres Strait Island names   vii
Acknowledgments   ix
Maps   xii

Chapter 1	Introduction 1
Chapter 2	'We didn't know we would be evacuated' 15
Chapter 3	The mainland experience 35
Chapter 4	'It was all of a sudden' 61
Chapter 5	'Leave the Islanders where they are' 87
Chapter 6	Enlistment and the quest for freedom 103
Chapter 7	The enemy at the front door 123
Chapter 8	Fear and faith 157
Chapter 9	Hard times 183
Chapter 10	'The people had to do it' 211
Chapter 11	Breaking down barriers 233
Chapter 12	Reflections 249

Notes   256
Bibliography   266

Abbreviations

AA	Australian Archives
ABC	Australian Broadcasting Commission
AIF	Australian Imperial Forces
AR	Annual Report
ARP	Air Raid Precautions
ATSIC	Aboriginal and Torres Strait Islander Commission
AWM	Australian War Memorial
Board	Island Industries Board
CCC	Civil Construction Corps
CMF	Citizen Military Force
CPA	Chief Protector of Aboriginals
Department	Department of Native Affairs
Director	Director of Native Affairs
DNA	Department of Native Affairs
JOL	John Oxley Library
LMS	London Missionary Society
MAC	Medical Aid Centre
MAP	Medical Aid Post
QPP	*Queensland Parliamentary Papers*
QSA	Queensland State Archives
QV&P	*Queensland Votes and Proceedings*
RAAF	Royal Australian Air Force
TISHSS	Thursday Island State High School Students
TSIMA	Torres Strait Islanders Media Association
TSIRECC	Torres Strait Islander Regional Education Consultative Committee
TSLIB or TSLI	Torres Strait Light Infantry Brigade
US	United States
VDC	Volunteer Defence Corps

Torres Strait Island names

Badu	Mulgrave Island
Boigu	Talbot Island
Dauan	Mount Cornwallis Island
Dauar	Dauar Island
Edgor	Nepean Island
Erub	Darnley Island
Gialag	Friday Island
Keriri	Hammond Island
Mabuiag	Jervis Island
Masig	Yorke Island
Mauar	Rennel Island
Mer	Murray Island
Moa	Banks Island
Muralag	Prince of Wales Island
Nagi	Mount Ernest Island
Nurupai	Horn Island
Palilag	Goode Island
Purma	Coconut Island
Saibai	Saibai Island
Tudu, Tut	Warrior Island
Ugar	Stephens Island
Waiben	Thursday Island
Waier	Waier Island
Waraber	Sue Island
Yam	Turtle Backed Island

Source: Anna Shnukal (1988, 249–50).

Acknowledgments

The writing of this history was made possible only by the willingness on the part of over 150 old Torres Strait Islanders to share with me, an outsider, their present recollections of the women's experiences during the Pacific War from 1942 to 1945. Throughout, every one of their voices is heard. However, as some historians requested anonymity, I chose not to reference individually any of the almost 200 oral testimonies used in the writing of this text. Nonetheless, in recognition of their contributions, the name of each person is recorded in this acknowledgment. And I say to all of the old Torres Strait Islanders, with whom I seemed to have had daily intercourse through their words for seven years, the biggest ESSO (thank you) it is possible to say.

Thank you:

Jaub Agie, George Ahmat, Petrie Ahmat, the late Benjamin Alfred, Gainu Anau, the late Jerry Anau, Florence Anderson, Imasu Aragu, Kales Aragu, the late Lota Asai, Perelina Bagie, Ephraim Bani, Philemon Barbari, the late Cec Baruna, Noah Batu, Mena Bennefather, Tapim (Binny) Bennefather, the late Ezekiel Billy, the late Margaret Billy, Panai Billy, Hagiga Bindoraho, Betty Binjuda, the late Saia Binnawell, Guneuro Blanco, the late Lui Bon, the late Mabagie Bon, Mary Bowie, the late Kaupa Cook, Robert Cook, Gorpie Cowlie, Maloko Daia, Annie Day, Francis Durante, Selina Dorner, Tegani Epsig, the late Flora Filewood, Grace Fischer, Betty Foster, Romina Fuji, Russell Fuji, Miriam Fukamura, Ellie Gaffney, Zilla Garnier, Retemoi Gela, Cedric Gisu, Betty Harris, Carolus Issua, Keru Issua, 'Aiai' Kaigey, Umbra Kaigey, the late James Kanai, Flo Kennedy, Lorita Ketchell, Wilson Kris, the late Tataka Lee, the late Maggie Lewin, the late Sam Lewin, Sadie Loban, Maleta Lota, Elizabeth Lui, Getano Lui, Snr, the late Murray Lui, Nancy Lui, Akoko Mabo, Bua Mabo, Pennino Mabo, Bethel Mairu, the late Jo Mairu, Steve Mam, Zanobeza Mandi, John Manus, Megina Marau, Nauma Mareko, 'Auntie' Marou, the late Father Ibigen Mene, Louisa Mene, the late Alam Mene, Teisi Mene, the late Ella Mills, Harriet Mills, the late Salome Mills, Sammy Mills, Gabai Min, the late Siai Min, Bessie Missi, Gwen Moloney, David Mooka, Kitty Mooka and interpreter May Au, Sarbie Mooka, Angela Morrison, Dan Mosby, the late Canon Eddie Mosby, the late Elda Mosby, Jo Mosby, Masibar Mudu, George Mye, Cessa Nakata, Col Nakata, Martin Nakata, Tom Nakata, Naila Namoa, Eselina Nawia and interpreter Ron Wasaga, Lizzie Nawia, the late Daisy Noah and interpreter John Noah, the late Kaba Noah, Harriet Nona, Irad Nona, Walter Nona, Francis Oba, the late Waidorie Oba, Dana Ober, Kawie Panuel, Neliman Panuel, Yupeli Panuel, Etta Passi, Father Dave Passi, the late Lena Passi, Olai Passi, Rotana Passi, the late Sam Passi, the late Ettie Pau, the late Philemon Pearson, Wais Pearson, the late Pali Peter, James Rice, Jianna Richardson, Camilla Sabatino, Eddie Sebasio, Elsie Smith, Laura Soki and interpreter Mario Soki, Billy Shibasaki, Jamel Shibasaki, Seriba Shibasaki, Joseph Stephens, Lency Stephens, Pedro Stephens, Sammy Tamwoy, Alo Tapim, the late Seriama Tapim, Thelma Tapim, Ina Titasy, Vera Toby, Isobel Tom, Sania Townson, Dora Uiduldam, Jeffrey Waia, Diwai Waigana, Father Maleta Waigana, the late Koko Waigana, Kada Waireg, Father Napoleon Warria, Peter Warria, the late Sister Peta Warusam, the late Selopi Whap, John Whop, Myra Wigness, Dulcie Williams, Ethel Williams, the late Seppie Woosup.

To everyone else who contributed to the writing of this history, I also say thank you. Among them were three army signallers: Paul Barlow, Merv Nargor and Randy Williams; Catholic nuns: Sister Sylvia Cleary, Sister M Gemma and Sister Jules Hogan; and old residents of Cooyar: Mrs Barron, Gwen Just, Charlie and Thorene McNalty, Cyril Petersen, Killian Scherber and Mick Shick. The few old people who recalled the Thursday Island evacuees coming to Cherbourg were Tolly Collins, Marjorie Law, Charlie and Nerida Renouf, the late Eileen South and Les Stewart. Others who shared general insights about that period in Australia's history were Audrey Elliot, Bill and Janet Cummings, Dolly and George McKay, Vivian Robson, Matron Mary McLaren and Jim Mangan. The late Jerry Langevad assisted me in my search for old Department of Family Services and Aboriginal and Torres Strait Islander Affairs' records, and he introduced me into Cherbourg. I am grateful to JF McMahon, the Catholic Archivist, Kensington, Sydney, who provided much valuable data on the evacuation of the Hammond

Island mission. Two former Anglican priests on Thursday Island, Tom Dixon and the Reverend HE Palmer, kindly contributed their recollections. Thank you, Bishop Tony Hall-Matthews, for enabling me to access Anglican records in the John Oxley Library.

Thanks also go to those readers who waded through manuscripts at various stages of the writing of the history: Romina Fuji, Edward (Rocky) Nai and Jeremy Hodes. I am deeply indebted to my doctoral thesis supervisor, Dr Noel Loos, and to my husband, Dr Barry Osborne, for their tireless support and direction over the years since the work began.

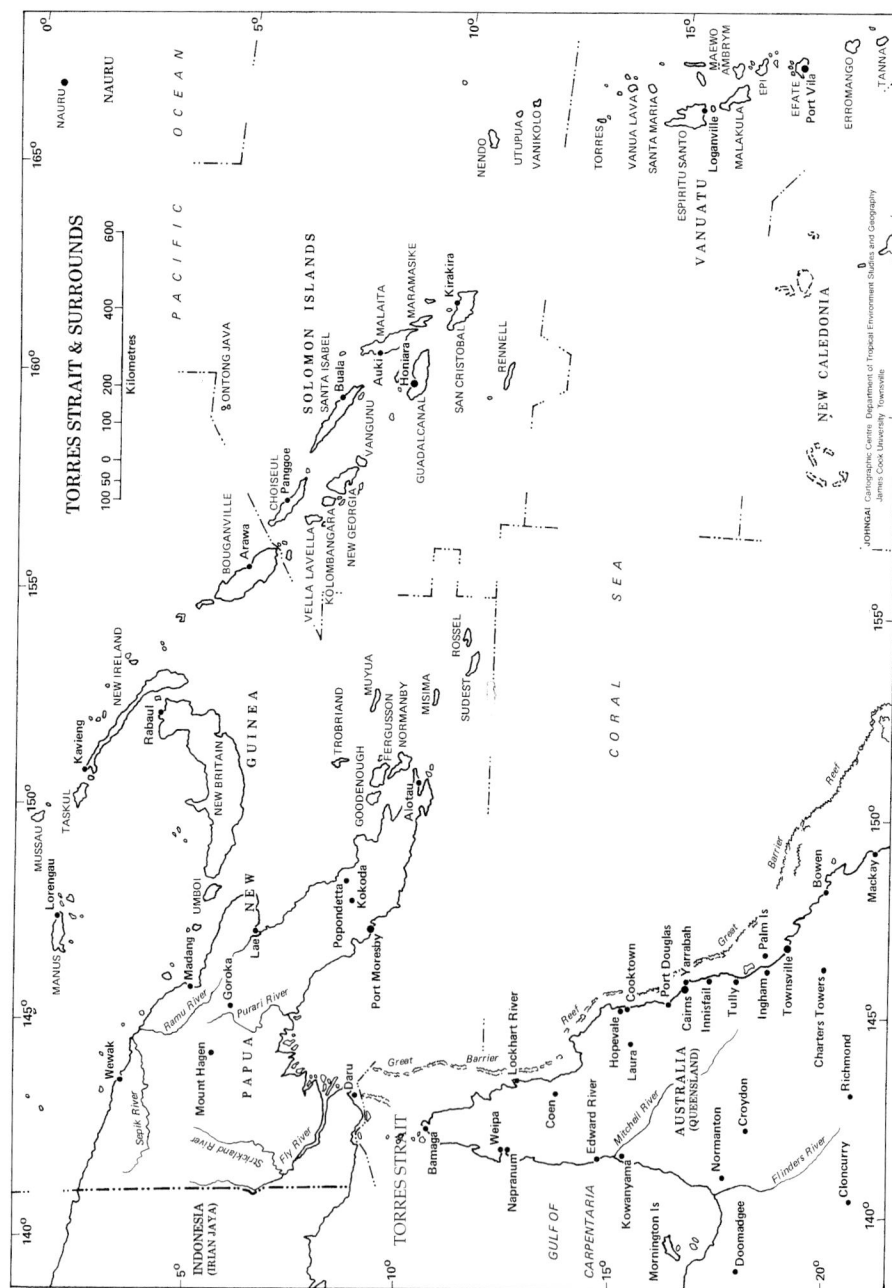

Torres Strait and surrounds

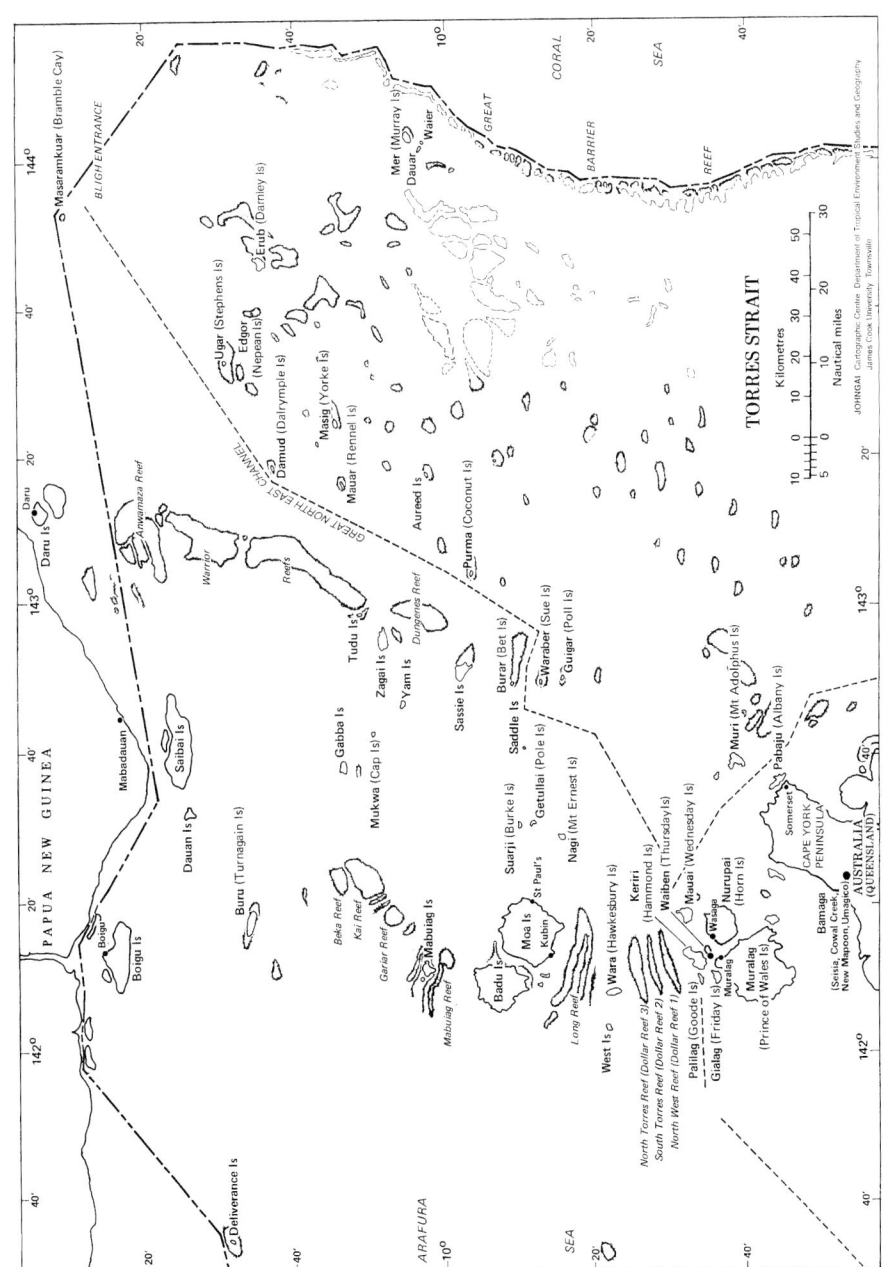

Torres Strait

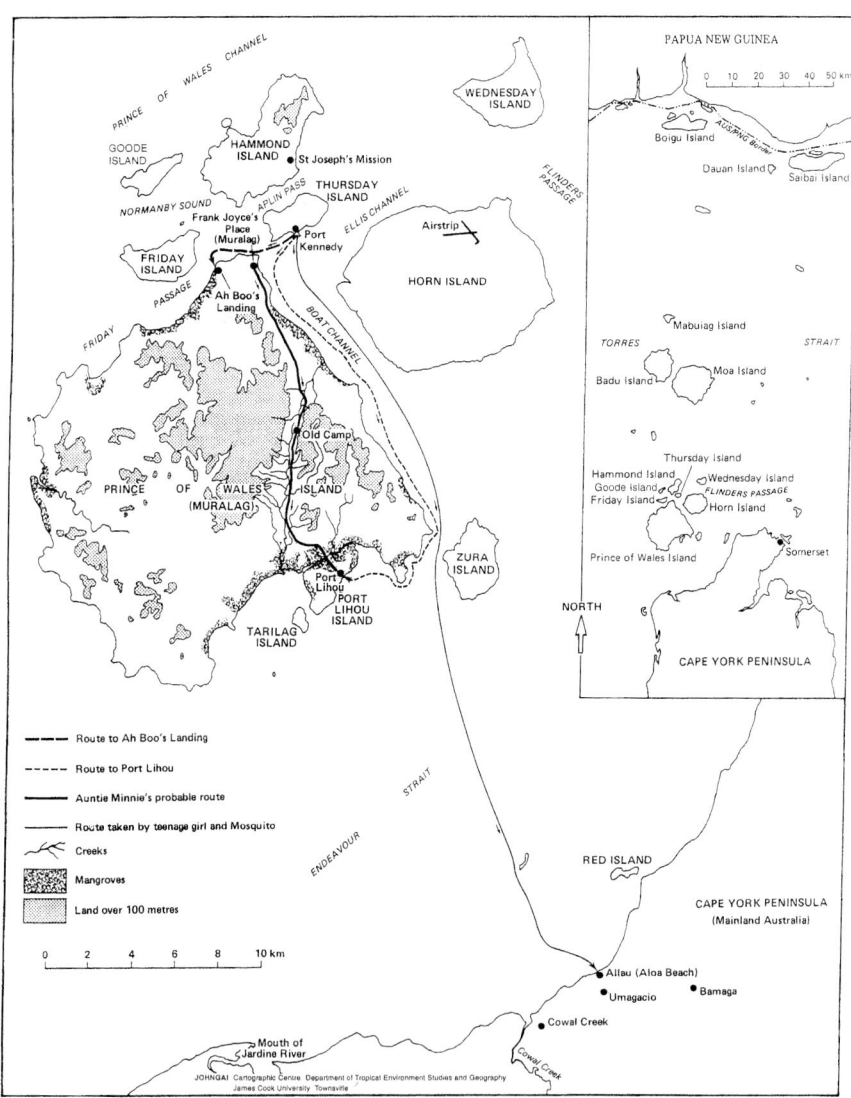

Muralag, with routes taken by fugitives to escape evacuation, 1942

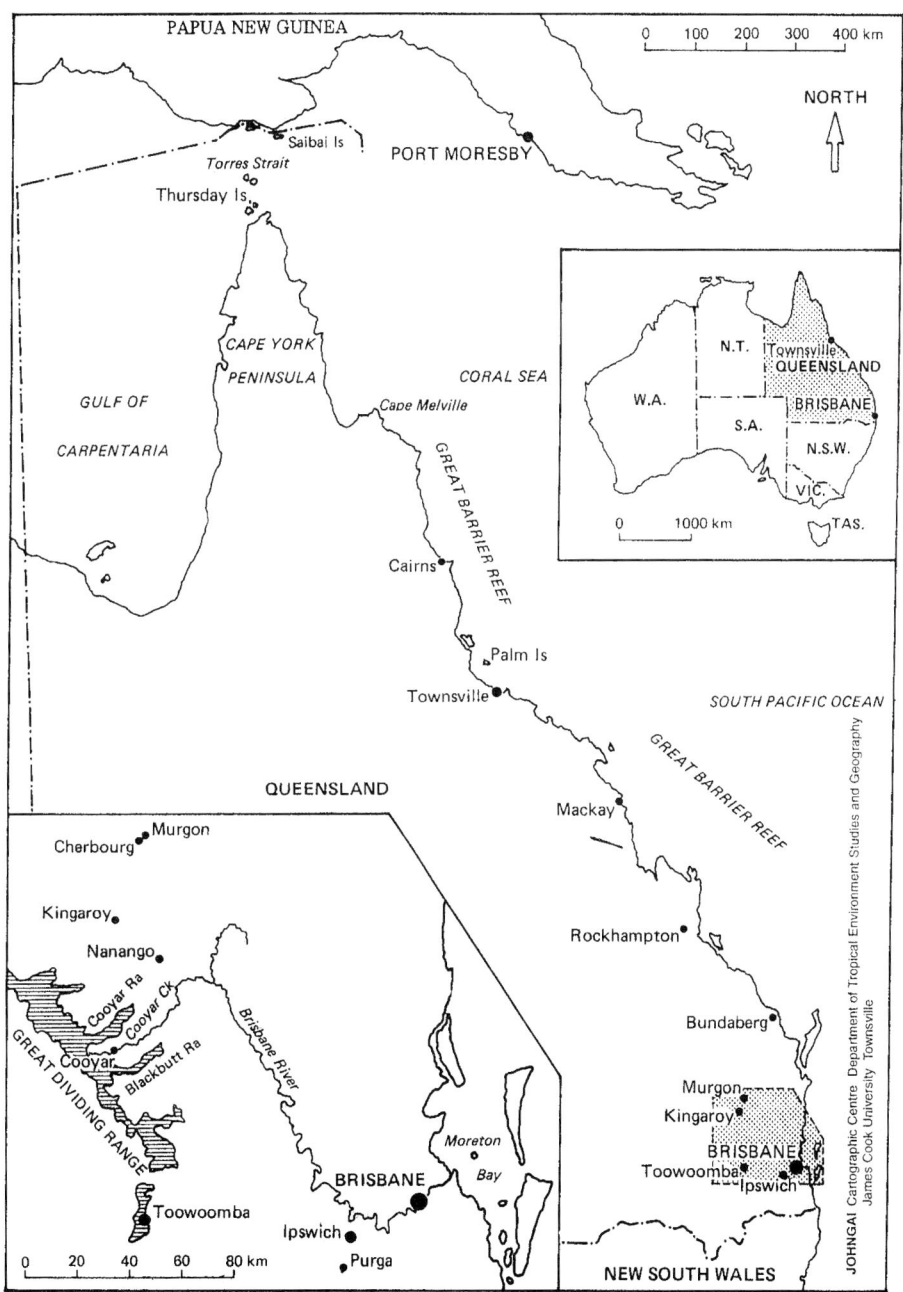

Queensland, with insert showing where Thursday and Hammond Island evacuees were sent in Southern Queensland

Chapter 1

Introduction

> Sadie and Bessy Delany's lifelong insights provide us with a priceless oral history of our nation's past century. And what they 'have to say' shows us, as no one else can, where we've been, how far we've been, how far we've come ... and how far we have to go.[1]

This review comment refers to the Delany sisters, two Black American women, both over 100 years, who are, in their own words, 'having our say'. In doing so, they have articulated a dimension of American society to which members of the dominant culture had no access, or chose not to, or could not, look at. Moreover, while they subsequently expressed surprise that people would be interested in what they had to say about their lives, their words help to break down barriers which continue to keep white Americans ignorant of not only Black Americans' experiences but also of their own. Both women claim that their life stories were not meant to be black or women's history but a history that belonged to all Americans.

Marginalised groups of women in different parts of the world today, like the Delany sisters, are wanting to have their say. Daphne Patai, a literary theorist who collected life stories of both women of colour and white women in Brazil, was told by one of the marginalised women she interviewed: 'I'm glad you're doing this. We need to know one another.' Julie Cruikshank, who worked with Athapaskan (Athabaskan) women in northern Canada, said that they had a 'commitment [to] document their past in their own voice'. Australian historian Ann McGrath interviewed Aboriginal women as well as men in the Northern Territory who believed their 'pioneering role in building up the cattle stations' should be recognised.[2]

The women belonging to Australia's smaller Indigenous black minority, the Torres Strait Islanders, also want to speak out: 'Well, at last someone wants to know about us' was the response from several women when asked if they would talk about recollections of their wartime experiences. It is only by the 'speaking out' of marginalised women that members of the dominant western societies will be better informed about the histories of their own nations. Thus, in the pages of this history, old women belonging to a little-known group of Indigenous Australians speak out for the first time to an outsider audience about a most poignant period in their history, the Pacific War.

Lost identity

For many white Australians, the identity of the Torres Strait Islander people is still in the process of emerging from its obscurity. From the turn of this century, governments continually lumped Torres Strait Islanders in with Aborigines and outsider perspectives of them were that they were indistinguishable. Martin Nakata, a Torres Strait Islander academic, articulated the situation which had pertained for his people for almost four decades before the war: they were a 'minority within the Indigenous minority in Australia ... not only were they spoken about as "Aborigines" but always by people other than themselves'.[3] An old Meriam woman's recollection was: 'In 1936 I was thirteen. Everyone was angry. We are not Aborigines; we are Islanders. They fought for that name.' By this she meant that seamen from the diverse island communities in Torres Strait formed a cohesive group in 1936 and refused to work the shelling boats in demonstration of their dissatisfaction with the Queensland government's treatment of them and their loss of identity. In 1983, Torres

Strait Islander leaders were still concerned about the erosion of their identity. Three political activists, the late Ted Loban, the late Seppie Woosup and Benny Mills, complained: 'For far too long the wording "and Torres Strait Islanders" has been a quote and not supported by fully recognising the Torres Strait Islands, its people and their culture.'[4]

This loss of identity contributed to the Torres Strait Islanders' invisibility to the majority of white mainlanders, with the consequence that they had, and many continue to have, no informed perceptions about this unique group of Australians. Moreover, this invisibility extended to the international scene. At the First International Indigenous Conference held in Adelaide in 1989, island delegates found that 'most people have not been aware that Aboriginal people and Torres Strait Islanders are two distinct races within Australia. As a result, our delegation came as a surprise to many people.'[5]

Prewar life in Torres Strait

While the name 'Torres Strait Islanders' suggests a homogenous group of people, it is the case that there have always been differences between the island communities. There are also different names to describe the different areas in Torres Strait to which these island communities belong. The Eastern Islands comprise the Murray group (Mer, Dauar, Waier), Darnley and Stephens Islands. The Central Islands are Masig, Purma and Waraber. Among the Western Islands are the Prince of Wales Group (Nurupai, Muralag, Hammond, Thursday Island), Yam, Nagi, Moa, Badu, Mabuiag and Dauan. Saibai and Boigu are referred to as the Top-Western Islands and Dauan is generally associated with this group because of its location and traditional language rather than its typography. The term 'outer islands' is used to describe the inhabited islands in Torres Strait that are situated beyond the Prince of Wales Group. Generally, the traditional names of the islands are used in this book, exceptions being Thursday Island, the administrative centre for the area, and Hammond Island where the Catholic mission was known by that name.

Their physical environments range from volcanic and hilly, rocky formations to coral cays and swampy islands. Thus, there were different food sources and methods of cultivation. On the volcanic islands, gardens flourished. On less fertile islands, there was heavier reliance upon seafoods and garden produce was obtained by the people on the swampy Top-Western Islands from their Papuan neighbours during the wet season. There were variations in the men's and women's roles. An old woman said that on Muralag, where traditionally food was gathered rather than sown, 'women had all the chores, looked after the baby, went hunting for food ... fished, got wild yams or fruits, they did all the work ... They were strong and they did the lot.' On Masig, it was suggested, 'it was traditional [that] women did the same as men' and, on Mer, where gardens flourished in the volcanic soil, the roles were said to be 'not much different'. On the flat muddy island of Saibai, the division of labour was described as more clear-cut: '[The men and women] got a different life. When every work is done, finish ready for sleep, the man and wife sleep together but when the sun comes up at six o'clock they spread out; man did his work, woman did her work.' Indeed, Nakata points out that his people still see themselves as 'a complex and diverse heterogenous group of people with differing needs'.[6]

After colonisation, island men working in the marine industry in Torres Strait were absent from their islands for long periods. However, in their evolving semi-subsistence societies, the women continued to be the major food producers: 'For the food line, women had to work and make gardens; at the same time they used to go fishing. They had to plant food and vegetables because the men would be out on the boats.'[7] (Old Torres Strait Islanders use the terms 'food line' and 'money line' when talking about how much food or money they had.) It was a matter of survival that every girl learned good gardening skills:

> I always went with my mum and grandparents and they had to teach me, show me the way they worked — how to garden, how to plant, when to plant when it's ready and like everything, yam, taro, cassava, sweet potatoes. Well, that's the main diet, that's our staple foods.

Gardening was a daily chore: 'We got no refrigerator then ... We walked for two hours to our garden and came back. We had to get fresh food every day and be busy to keep our garden going.' Gardening was a 'back-breaking' job: 'You don't plant on top of the soil but arm's-length deep we plant our yams and bananas.' On most islands, when the men were home they assisted the women to break up the hard soil in readiness to plant. However, without a husband, a woman's work was exceedingly hard:

> When *baba* [father] been dead there's no one to help *ama* [mother] and we were small ones. She had to climb up the hill, she took our big sister with her, to dig yam. They were very tired when they come back from the top of the hill, it's not near the village and you have to climb up and then go down. We were looking for Mum. Poor Mum came down when sun been on top with two baskets, firewood, water.

From traditional times, Torres Strait Islander men were deep sea fishermen and dugong hunters, but it was the women who ensured their families' daily fish requirements were met. Before they had stores which carried fishing tackle, the women made nets and lines from bush materials, such as guinea grass and coconut fibre, and later from embroidery cotton; hooks were made from pearl shell or pieces of metal, even a crochet hook. They fished from the shoreline and the reefs and in the lagoons around their islands. Fish were caught in stone traps, *sais*; the smashed roots of a plant called *sad* dropped into the traps made the fish 'blind and drunk' and easier to spear. The women speared crayfish, caught crabs and netted sardines. Torres Strait Islander women were strong swimmers. Two Nagi women described how they swam to the reef each day and returned with a full basket of fish held high above the water in one hand.

These island societies had no wheeled transport; the women were the main carriers: 'We came from the hills and carried down loads of wood on our backs. We had to have firewood every day for cooking and washing ... That's our life, carry wood on our backs.' The women remembered that carrying water for all their needs was the 'worst chore of all'. On Purma, they frequently transported water from a nearby island: 'Come summertime there's no rain water ... we went over in the dinghy, sailing to Waraber, and got the water.' The Saibai women went in rowboats, 'six miles by sea', to Dauan to get water or walked 'probably about three miles [across the island] to Mag' for supplies in the dry season.

Women were co-workers with the men in the construction of new houses and in the maintenance of older homes. Women collected and plaited coconut palm leaves for the walls of the houses. They cut grass for the thatched roofs and, after leaving it to dry in the sun, they carried bundles of the dried grass on their backs to the construction site. Thatched roofs had to be replaced every year or two because the grass rotted. This job generally fell to the women. They were also manufacturers of household goods. Mats were essential items in island homes and they were made in all sizes and for many purposes, 'for sitting and shelter, roofing and interior decorating, sails for canoes and most important ... [for] the burial and wrapping up of the dead bodies'.[8] If the woman was quick, an old man explained, she made 'a fair-size mat ... about ten feet square [in] a couple of days ... She would work late at night with only a lamp.'

Other items manufactured by the women were pillows, flour bags stuffed with fibre from the 'cotton trees', plates and spoons from coconut shells and brooms from the dried thick veins of the banana leaves. They made their own soap, dye and coconut oil. They produced sago by treating the huge palms that washed down from the Fly River in New Guinea onto their beaches. *Gusi*, a kind of arrowroot, was manufactured: when boiled with coconut milk, an old woman explained, it was 'as good as porridge'. Nuts from the *eger* (tar) tree were roasted and the prune-like fruit from the wongai tree dried. Both were stored for when other food was not so plentiful. From the outsiders, the women learned dressmaking, embroidery, crochet and lace-making. They made their own jewellery by threading crimson seeds, red and black *gidee-gidee* berries and fine shells.[9] Perfume was manufactured from *pas* (basil) cooked in coconut oil.

Even though Torres Strait Islander societies had been semi-subsistent for some time before the Pacific War, the survival of those who were left on their island communities in 1942 was greatly dependent upon these sorts of traditional skills. By this time, too, all communities had monetary economies. Money was needed to buy and maintain clan boats, to pay for basic store items on which they had become dependent and to support the church. However, because of the men's low wages, women were also forced to engage in paid work.

When Papuan Industries Limited, a private company which conducted a store on Badu, and the Queensland government assisted some clans to buy boats in the 1890s, women were apparently recruited as divers to help pay for the boats:[10]

> In the early days of the pearl-shelling industry the women had to help and they were considered better divers than the men ... men who were fishing for shell to pay for boats or canoes generally tried to get women friends to help them.[11]

Other women supported their breadwinning husbands on the boats. An old Meriam (Murray Island) woman remembered being told: 'My mum went with my dad. She was diving for three years. She stayed with Dad and we were not born yet. Then he said, "That's enough. You stay home now", and she had babies.' Women who had married Malay or South Sea divers might go on the boats to guard their breadwinners' lives:

> If they were boss of their own boat, well their life was mostly in danger, so always their wife held the lifeline. So they carried their wives on the boat when they dived. Children too, oh yes. She handles his lifeline because it was dangerous in those days; if you didn't like anybody you just killed them when they were down. A lot of that went on.[12]

In 1914, when the war in Europe forced the closure of the shell market and drastically affected their men's employment, the women gathered trochus and bêche-de-mer from around the home reefs and sold small quantities to the store.[13] An old woman's recollection was that it was little bit deep when you dive. Your eyes nearly burst. But we try our best for our living. We get *tet*, it was big bêche-de-mer, prickle one. We cut it and take all that stuff out and put it on a stick and dry it. We made a fire and smoked it. We got good money for that one. Trochus, we got to boil it, wash those shells, pick the fish out and we packed the shell in bags and sent it to TI [Thursday Island].

After the shell markets were revived, the women continued to collect shell until the Pacific War broke out. By this time too, a few Meriam women were working for a white capitalist enterprise on Dauar. A sardine processing factory was established there in the late 1930s: 'The company took a lease of the island and they brought big machinery there to can the sardines ... I don't know how much wages they got. They were under the Act, so I suppose it wasn't much.' There was a certain resignation in her tone. She knew how the men's work in the marine industry had been devalued under government awards. The value of women's work was hardly likely to attract more. In any event, any move to pay them more would undoubtedly have been quashed by the Protector.

In 1938, wolfram was discovered on Moa. This discovery opened the way for further paid employment for the women. They mined the ore with their husbands and children. Old people recalled families came from 'everywhere', Kubin, St Paul's, Mabuiag, Mer, Boigu, Saibai, to dig: 'The men were at the top and they had to blast it with dynamite, then dig, like you dig for gold, and the women were on the creek side where they washed it out and you got that pure stuff that ran down from the hill.' The heavy ore from the mine at Eet Hill was transported to St Paul's, 'maybe three or four hours walking time' away from the village, on 'the backside, like a horse', and sold to the store. An important outcome from their mining was that the women could keep powdered milk tins of wolfram in the house and, when the men were away and they were short of money, they sold it.

On the communities, there were 'few [paid] jobs for girls when they left school'. Some found employment as domestics and cooks in the white teachers' homes. The elders on the communities were not opposed to the young women learning European skills and earning the small incomes paid for such work, but any suggestion that they should work away from Torres Strait was strongly opposed. The elders feared that it was not so much the girls' domestic skills which were in demand as their services for immoral purposes. Nevertheless, some did go to Thursday Island. One old Kubin woman said that she had worked in the Grand hotel before the war: 'Mr O'Leary [the Local Protector] sent me in and I was a house girl, I looked after the children and I did the housework.' Her widowed mother was a domestic in the home of the sergeant of police.

When Papuan Industries Limited was sold to the Protector's Office in 1930 and renamed Aboriginal Industries Board, avenues of paid employment in this retail industry opened up for female school leavers on Badu. A former employee recalled that a few young women worked as seamstresses in the small clothing industry set up in the store: 'They got a wage and they used material from the store ... it was cheap ... the material was one shilling a yard in those days.' Anyone with 'good schooling' might be employed as the cashier and ledger-keeper. She said she handled the money which came to the cashier's box via a 'monkey chain, one of those things you pulled the string and the money goes along the wire'. Other young women took shop assistant positions working the grocery and drapery counters. However, these store jobs were not available on other communities until the late 1930s. A Masig women recalled being very happy when a store was set up on her island and she obtained a position there: 'Out from school there's no job. You clean the road. I didn't have to do that because I have the job in the store.'

Store work resulted in a change in the way some women thought about themselves. A former Badu shop assistant said that she married a Nagi man and went to live with his family. There she was struck by the roles played by all of the women in her husband's family: 'They all worked for their living in the garden or swam for trochus.' Fifty years later, her recollection of these women, probably influenced by the role she had played as a functionary in a capitalist enterprise and in words couched in contemporary terminology, was that they were 'working-class' women:

> In the morning when they got up, one went out fishing and brought home fish for lunch and the rest went to the garden. They never stopped working and when it was hot in the day, they sat out in the shade mending clothes and weaving mats. They were very busy women.

Another Badu woman who had worked in the store made a similar comment about her mother: 'She was a working woman, she did the gardening and fishing — she was a hardworking woman.' Both women were suggesting that work in this western enterprise was easier than the traditional-type work most Torres Strait Islander women did, probably a reflection of their perception that white women's work was not as demanding. Nevertheless, two Nagi women who, at that time, had had no experience working in a store described their own busy lives without labelling themselves as 'working-class':

> Some go to the garden. One stays home, and the others get fish and she cooks it. We work all day until sunset. We take a piece of damper and we eat fruit from the tree and continue with our garden. Come sun up, we go to the garden and go back when sun sets.

While change was occurring for some women, the Nagi women's daily routine was still typical for most. If they can now be described as working-class women, that designation had little meaning for them before the Pacific War. What they did was women's work and it would remain so for many for a long time to come.

For about five decades prior to the Pacific War, the traditional work roles of Torres Strait Islander women were being affected by outsider intervention, although the new knowledge remained complementary to the old. Survival without the women's traditional skills would have been impossible. In this way, semi-subsistence societies evolved on the outer island communities. However, after the arrival of men from the South Pacific and Southeast Asia to work in the marine industry, some intermarried with island women. Together they might leave their outer island communities to live on Thursday Island and, later, Hammond Island. They took with them the knowledge passed down for generations, as well as the new knowledge. Much of the new knowledge helped them to adjust to the mainland once they were evacuated there in 1942 but, for the women who spent the war years on their outer island communities, their traditional knowledge was essential to their survival.

Under the Act

Torres Strait Islanders were virtually invisible to the outside world in 1942. Moreover, they were, in their own words, 'innocent' of that world. Four decades of internal colonialism had contributed to this condition.[14] Their affairs had been rigidly administered by officers in the Protector's Office in Brisbane under the provisions of Acts of Parliament initially passed for the 'protection and segregation' of Aborigines, the *Aboriginals Protection and Restriction of the Sale of Opium Acts, 1897 to 1934*. 'You couldn't do what you wanted to do ... it was very bad, everybody seemed to be mastered by the Protectors ... very similar to slavery.' The feeling was that 'the government treated them as natives'. They saw proprietorship in their pearling and trochus boats as diminished by the absolute control which paternalistic Protectors exercised over their affairs. 'The Islander boat owners were only boss of the wood, just for the timber of their boats, but somebody else had all their takings', an old island woman remarked.

In 1936, the people's anger boiled over. The men boldly told the Protector: 'You can anchor up the boats and sail back to TI; we refuse ... we can stay on the land doing gardens'.[15] Seventy per cent of the island seamen refused to work the boats. The outcome was a setting up of a 'partnership of non-equals with a right of veto by the self-appointed senior partner [the Director of Native Affairs]'.[16] Moreover, the Director continued to control their money: 'DNA, you know, has power over every money going through the account. So, any money you want, you go there and then you ask for money. "How much money you want?", an officer would say.' More often than not the specified amount was reduced. The people were indignant: 'It was not right ... one of our own people should have been appointed to care for the people, good sensible person — it was okay if [the Island] council controlled it but not DNA.'

Importantly, too, the people were still totally dependent upon the official guidance of the Department as it related to their interaction with the outside world. And, after radios were installed on the larger islands in 1937, its benefits, for example medically, ranked alongside of more direct control of the people, particularly those seen by the outsiders as troublemakers. Any grievances still could not be heard beyond their own islands:

> The only means to get to the outside world was to go through the office here on Thursday Island and it was under the Department's control and you had nothing, only a smoke signal, and it could not be seen by the outside world.

Thus, when that Department's officers were withdrawn from the outer islands in March 1942, it was not surprising that the people, who had had no preparation for their desertion and abandonment, felt 'helpless — everybody did not know what to do'. When everybody had left, it 'gave them a feeling of being very worried'. Situated between Australia's front line of defence to the south and the rapidly advancing Japanese forces to the north, they described themselves as the 'meat in the sandwich', 'a precious bait for the enemy'.[17] For years, as wards of the Protector, Torres Strait Islander women were given virtually no opportunities to experience the world beyond their own island communities. They entered the Pacific War years as innocent victims of a war beyond their comprehension.

In early 1942, there were about 3,000 Torres Strait Islander women and children and old people in the Torres Strait area. The majority lived on the outer island communities controlled by the Director (formerly the Protector) of the Department of Native Affairs in Brisbane. Others, not under the Act and free to some extent from this control, were Torres Strait Islander wives of South Sea, Southeast Asian and Filipino men and their families and descendants of those unions. They lived on islands in the Torres Strait bottleneck directly north of the tip of Cape York Peninsula. From mid-1940 there had been a build-up of defences on these islands, including the construction of an airstrip on Nurupai. When it was feared that Japan was about to attack or invade Australia, all white and 'coloured' women and their children on Thursday and Hammond Islands were evacuated to the mainland. Those on the outer island communities were left where they were.

The experiences of Torres Strait Islander women from Thursday and Hammond Islands and the outer islands of Torres Strait during the Pacific War have been pieced together from the historical 'scraps' gleaned from old island women and men and a few outsiders.[18] Although this history is based on the recollections of events recalled after almost half a century, and notwithstanding that they do not represent events just as they were, they are historically important because they make possible a more meaningful interpretation of the Pacific War. Moreover, old Torres Strait Islander women have, for the first time, had their say to an outsider audience. Their hitherto devalued and suppressed knowledge can no longer be regarded as such.

Chapter 2

'We didn't know we would be evacuated'

On 12 December 1941, five days after Pearl Harbour, the War Cabinet ordered the evacuation of certain women and children from Darwin. Darwin was strategically vital to the defence of northern Australia. It also complemented the major British defence base at Singapore until it fell to the Japanese on 15 February 1942. Forces in Darwin were heavily dependent on supplies from southern states being transported through the Torres Strait bottleneck. In early 1940, plans were made for an air base on Nurupai in the bottleneck. During the ensuing eighteen months it was constructed and military installations and personnel numbers were stepped up in that area.

As early as 1938, with fears of war in Europe growing, representations were being made to the government on behalf of an elite section of the European civil population on Thursday Island about the unsatisfactory military condition of this northern outpost of Australia. By late December 1941, the group was deploring the fact that the government was making no provision for the evacuation of civilians, despite mounting military activity in the area and Japan's rapid southward advance. Meanwhile, the military was advising civilians to voluntarily evacuate and, despite the risk of cyclones, some white lugger owners sailed south with their families.

Others bought passages on southbound coastal vessels or, if wealthy and lucky enough, left on a small plane which serviced Thursday Island weekly. But there were many working-class families, white and non-white, who had no boats and no money to pay fares for large families. It would be impossible for them to leave without a compulsory evacuation order from the Commonwealth government. That order was not made until 24 January 1942, by which time the enemy had moved its forces much nearer to Australia. Three days later, the *Torres Straits Daily Pilot* carried the following notice:

> TO THURSDAY ISLAND PUBLIC
>
> Decision has been given that the women and children of Thursday Island be compulsorily evacuated.
>
> All women and children, white and coloured, will therefore be prepared to leave Thursday Island by ship at 6 p.m. on 28 January.
>
> Suit cases and personal effects only may be taken. Further notice will be given if additional belongings are later allowed.
>
> Port of disembarkation will be notified later.
>
> T.J.R. Hurst Lt.-Col. Staff Corps,
> Fortress Commander, Thursday Island.

Compulsory evacuation is a traumatic experience in anyone's terms. A working-class white woman, from a family with eleven children who had lived on Thursday Island all of her life, recalled:

> They came around in the morning and told us to be ready by 10 o'clock. We had no idea this was going to happen. There was washing on the line, meals being cooked, clothes being boiled on the fire in the backyard, there were chickens being hatched. It was a hell of a mess ... We didn't think about being evacuated. We didn't want to leave, we cried.

This was one of the white families not privy to the elite's press for evacuation. Nonetheless, the present concern is with the effect of the evacuation on the lives of those non-European women living on Thursday and Hammond Islands whose roots ran deep in the soil of the outer islands of Torres Strait and who also had been unaware that evacuation was on the agenda.

The establishment of lucrative fishing industries in Torres Strait from the 1860s attracted men from the South Pacific, the Philippines (more particularly Manila) and Southeast Asia. The first to arrive were the men from Samoa, New Hebrides, New Caledonia, Niue, Guam, Rotuma, Vanuatu and the Loyalty Islands (South Sea Island men). Later arrivals were from Southeast Asia, more particularly the Malayan Peninsula, Malacca and some of the islands in the Dutch East Indies (Indonesia) and the Filipino or 'Manilla' men. As already indicated, a number intermarried with women from the outer islands of Torres Strait. By marriage the women became eligible to apply for an exemption from the Protector's control and move away from their home islands with their husbands. Some moved to the mainland or Thursday Island, while others remained on their island communities with their husbands. Subsequently, many of the Catholic families, mainly Filipino, relocated on a Catholic mission set up in the early 1930s on Hammond Island. When the Pacific War broke out, there was, however, a substantial population of Southeast Asian men with their Torres Strait Islander wives and children living on Thursday Island.

The women in these families (referred to in this history as the TI women) had little or no social interaction with the white elites. Their children were not permitted to attend the state school; a separate school for 'coloured' children had been set up in 1913 in response to white agitation. Whether they went to this school or to the Catholic convent on Thursday Island, the children were 'only allowed to go to grade five'. They were told they did not 'have the brains to go further ... That was it, you had to leave school because of your colour. We weren't allowed to sit for scholarship.' An eighty-year-old woman recalled that they had had no say in their children's education: 'That time [the white authorities] don't have school meetings — we were not involved in school.' There were entertainments, which were also segregated. There were dances for whites only and the upstairs seats in the open-air theatre were reserved for them. If the 'bank boys' were caught associating with 'coloured' girls, they had to pack up and leave the island. When the white soldiers began arriving, 'the rule was not to go to the darkies' houses or the Japanese'. The 'navy boys' were not permitted to talk to 'half-caste girls', and if there were girls on the beach when they went swimming the boys were required to leave. In this segregated town, it is little wonder that the TI women were totally unaware of agitation on behalf of an elite white group for the evacuation of their women and children: 'We didn't know anything about that. We weren't told anything.' This was true also for the poorer working-class whites who were generally more comfortable associating with the 'coloured' people.

Looking after their own safety

It is difficult to gauge what understanding the adult members of the TI families had regarding their vulnerability in the Torres Strait bottleneck in late 1941 and early 1942 when a Japanese attack on Australia was by then more than speculation; it was, as far as most whites could see, on the agenda. Few TI families had electricity connected to their homes and only one woman said her family had a radio. Her father, she recalled, was a 'crank for the wireless' and had it connected to a battery. This family was probably one of the few able to follow the war news consistently. Nonetheless, she remembered that they had all begun to notice 'strange things happening, like planes going over', more white soldiers arrived and a camp was set up on the golf course where the TI children played. A woman said that it was then that her father 'pleaded with the captain to give us a passage [on a] passenger ship that used to come up ... we didn't know they would evacuate us all'. However, as suggested, this solution was not a viable alternative for most families. Moreover, many felt so strongly about staying on in Torres Strait that they were prepared to do whatever was necessary to ensure their own safety, even if it meant running away to Muralag, the large island adjacent to Thursday Island.

The son in one TI family, who was a teenager when the Pacific War broke out, recalled his white employer telling the men working in the pearl shell sheds: 'Everybody look after yourself, we can't help you. When the Japanese come we can't do anything.' He further recalled how his family 'simply packed up the boat and ran away' to

Port Lihou Island, off the southeast coast of Muralag. A woman who was also a teenager in 1942 recalled that her family also went to Port Lihou where they had a 'weekender'. They thought: 'Oh well, we'll be safe [here]. There's lots of food. We won't be in danger.' More TI families followed. Some had inboard motors on their clinker dinghies; others rowed down Boat Channel to Endeavour Strait, taking advantage of the wind by fixing sheeting between upright oars attached to the sides of the boats.

Muralag is one of the largest islands in the Torres Strait, with an area of about 3,108 hectares. Much of it is stony ground with low scrub. The coastline is marked by white sandy bays and mangrove swamps. At the southern tip, an area known as Port Lihou is cut off from the main landmass by a narrow waterway, or creek. Overhanging mangroves obscure the fact that it is actually a small island. Here it was that one group of TI families established themselves, just beyond a sandy bay lapped by the waters of Endeavour Strait, with coconut palms forming a backdrop to their new home. There was plenty of 'lovely sweet water' in wells and running creeks just beyond the beach. A few old South Sea Island men had built their homes in this location many years before when they were working the pearl and trochus shell. These old Port Lihou residents welcomed the fugitives. Apart from the one family who had a weekender, the remaining new arrivals set about constructing grass houses. They anticipated that they would be there for some time: 'We made big gardens, planted cassava and sweet potatoes. We intended to stay there. There was a lot of fish, crabs and everything to eat.' However, it was soon realised that this idyllic location was under the path of fighter planes.

The old people were constantly and nervously on the alert. Only recently had they become accustomed to the appearance and noise of the small weekly plane which serviced Thursday Island. The daily roar of large numbers of fighter planes, flying low over Muralag at great speed with guns which seemed to be pointing ominously at them, was a different matter:

> When we were over there the planes pass over ... we're frightened. It was our planes. We didn't know ... There were a lot of

> planes. We made a big garden ... and ... old grandmother goes in there and puts a white towel on her head and hides in the garden. She didn't think they would see her. We made fun of her. We go up the hill and hide in the bush but she goes in the garden with the white towel.

The younger ones, one woman recalled, put their fears on hold in order to have some 'fun': 'It was good. In spite of the war there was a lot of noise, the old-time gramophone playing, people singing, everyone enjoying themselves, we forgot about the war ... The young women sang and the old ladies got mad.' On Saturdays, the men rowed over from Thursday Island where they were employed by the Civil Construction Corps (CCC) on essential work associated with the defence of the area. The children looked forward to a weekly treat of lollies and biscuits, and fresh supplies of flour meant their mothers could make coconut-milk damper in the earth ovens. There was no school for the children, no books to read and no toys to play with. They helped with the gardening and went fishing, crabbing and hunting. They swam and explored the bush. When it was dark they sat around in their mothers' makeshift kitchens or curled themselves up on their sleeping mats, hoping that someone would tell them stories.

One woman still remembered the stories told by an old Aboriginal woman, Auntie Minnie, who lived with one of the South Sea Island men. She told them tales about the ghosts of children who played in the creek at a place on Muralag called Old Camp. She slept there on her two-day trek north across the island to buy stores from Frankie Joyce, an old stockman who lived across the channel from Thursday Island. At night, when everything was quiet, she said she heard children 'laughing, screaming and crying'. Auntie Minnie did not identify her ghosts, but she would have known about the Kaurareg people who had been brutally slaughtered by whites at the end of the last century.[1] Whoever the ghosts were, the woman remembered the stories as convincing: 'Even if you thought you didn't believe in ghosts, you were never quite sure.' Despite her belief in ghosts, Auntie Minnie impressed on the children that she read her Bible every night; her new spiritual beliefs had not totally overridden the old. This was also the case for other Torres Strait Islanders.

The location at Port Lihou was indeed idyllic compared with that of another group of TI women, children and old people. They chose to hide in the mangrove swamps at Ah Boo's Landing, across the channel from Thursday Island. Ah Boo's Landing was reached from the beach by rowing a dinghy up a narrow creek into the mangroves. The heat was unbearably oppressive in this swampy environment with its myriad of interlocking mangrove roots clawing for a hold in the black oozing mud. The children had no sandy beach to play on and there were no shady palms for the women to rest under. Nonetheless, like the Port Lihou people, they believed they could continue to ensure their own safety on Muralag. Some 'built up little humpies out of old sheets of iron'; others simply lived under the mangroves on a platform with no roof.

In the weeks that followed their arrival, the group's endurance was sorely tested as they sought to avoid detection from the enemy and from their own military authorities. Every day an old man, referred to as 'Grandad', led the group inland as far as possible away from the camp. His grand-daughter recalled:

> We left about 4.30 in the morning and come back just on dark. This was so they could not find us. We took a bit of water to boil for tea. We mainly lived on Sao biscuits ... you know, the tin with the cocky on it. Everything was covered up so the planes could not see us.

Another woman's memory of their fugitive days: 'We walked with a bare amount of food, no thongs, no sandals or shoes. It was rough and we were wet, we stayed in those clothes until we got back. No school ... We had to keep moving.' There were the march flies, the mosquitoes, the mud, the mangroves to contend with: 'I don't know how we survived the mosquitoes and the flies and near the mangroves. We don't have Rid, we burnt ant nests to keep mosquitoes away.' It was particularly hard for the pregnant women and the old people. They, too, travelled every day into the bush with the others, walking for miles in the belief that this was how they could remain invisible to both allied and enemy airmen. An old former fugitive sighed as she recalled her experience: 'It was awful.'

When the group returned to their camp just before dark, the women set about preparing supper on small open fires in the bush, camouflaged as best they could. They ate fish caught by the old men, and rice when available. The women tried to encourage gardens to grow under the mangroves, with little success. Back at camp, they did their washing in the running creek. Their only night light was a burning strip of calico in a bottle of kerosene. The little makeshift shelters were camouflaged by the mangrove trees and the children were kept away from open spaces. They had to constantly worry about detection, although it has been suggested by an outsider that 'the authorities knew exactly where they were as they saw them light their fires at dusk'.[2] Seen or unseen, the fugitives' testimonies were: 'We stuck in there ... we hear the planes but we never come out'; 'It had to be done, there was no choice'; 'It was a really big experience for us.'

The first contingent to leave

While the two groups of fugitives were on Muralag, the first contingent of 459 evacuees from Torres Strait (159 whites, 280 'coloureds' and 20 Chinese) sailed out of Port Kennedy harbour, Thursday Island, on 29 January 1942 aboard the SS *Ormiston*. And, even though they were not 'wards' of the Queensland Director of Native Affairs (the Director), his department coordinated the reception and accommodation of the 'coloured' evacuees after disembarkation at Cairns.[3]

However, while the ship was still at sea, the military authorities were advised that the chamber of commerce was objecting to the disembarkation of the 'half-caste evacuees' in Cairns for 'military and other known reasons'.[4] Fear of invasion or bombing attacks in the north were such that Cairns people were certainly being urged to voluntarily evacuate the town for their own safety, but no one was forced to leave. It was a time of general confusion: people were said to be 'rushing hither and thither', with many going to the more thickly populated coastal areas further south rather than inland.[5] Nonetheless, the *Townsville Daily Bulletin* ran an article on 29 January, the day the *Ormiston* sailed from Thursday Island, pointing out that the tableland area of North Queensland was also feeling the impact of the voluntary evacuations. Thus, it was suggested that to land the TI families in Cairns at that time would embarrass the authorities who knew that they would have no jurisdiction to then remove the evacuees compulsorily. Ultimately, a resolution to what the intelligence officer in Cairns described as 'hostility' to the landing of 'coloured' evacuees was made without consultation with the people: they were to be housed in a local school until accommodation could be found for them on local mission stations.[6] Even if such paternalism could have been justified for 'military reasons', references to 'hostility' and 'other known reasons' for the opposition to their landing suggest that their presence may also have been objected to on racial grounds.

It is difficult to recall, after almost fifty years, the intensity of racial feelings throughout Australia in the early 1940s. Many white Australians were still obsessed with the threat of colour, and Aborigines on the mainland were, for the most part, invisible in towns and cities. Two Cairns people recalled that 'the Aborigines lived in a couple of camps on the fringe of the town but they weren't seen around too much, not like today ... you only got the odd black or "half-caste" child at school in the early 1940s'. Racist attitudes were not without precedence among those who were in control of Indigenous affairs. In 1933, the Protector of Aborigines claimed that the 'crossbreeding' of 'free' mainland descendants of the indentured black labourers brought to Australia in the latter part of the nineteenth century presented 'a serious social evil, especially around certain Northern coastal towns, because of their freedom from protective control'.[7] There is little doubt that this sort of attitude was still prevalent in white communities in the north a decade later. Moreover, protective control and segregation were seen as essential to the maintenance of a white Australia. Nonetheless, whether or not the authorities wanted to keep the TI women and children out of Cairns for military or racist reasons, they did not succeed in removing this first group to missions. The evacuees, probably unaware of the opposition to their disembarkation at Cairns (although one woman remembered there was a dispute on the wharf when they arrived), quickly dispersed with relatives:

> I went to Cairns on the *Ormiston*. Most people had somewhere to go ... We stayed at a staging camp, Cairns Central school. Our relations came to see us and offered us accommodation and we picked who we wanted to go to.

Another evacuee recalled: 'I knew I had relations ... in Bloomfield and Mossman. We went with them.' Relatives helped either by making room in their own homes or assisting in the search for rented accommodation. Because of the large number of voluntary evacuations from Cairns, for a short time, accommodation was relatively cheap and plentiful.

Apart from a rare exception, like a young woman who was sent to the mainland in the late 1930s to live with a white family while she studied, the TI women had not travelled far before the Pacific War: 'When we born here we stayed here all our lives. It was only that war move us away.' Indeed, the world view of most of these women was very much limited to Thursday Island:

> To tell you the truth I didn't know the outer islands existed. I didn't know Badu existed. I didn't know there was anything out there. Sometimes we saw Saibai people and they would come down and we were frightened of them.

It is not surprising then that they said: 'When we arrive on the mainland everything was so big and we got frightened looking at all the two-storeyed buildings and they were like skyscrapers to us, and the wharf was so big.' The wartime environment added to their fears: 'Everything was so frightening with all the negroes [American servicemen] and the army being there ... and I was going on fifteen and my mother used to keep me close, cannot go anywhere, you had to have escorts.' For these island women, initially, the mainland loomed large and formidable.

Fear of a Japanese invasion caused Australians in possibly vulnerable areas to act quickly. Many had no time to think about how they would manage financially. At its meeting on 20 January, the city council discussed the financial position of the voluntary 'coloured' evacuee families in Cairns. Some of the compulsory evacuees also had little money when they subsequently arrived on the *Ormiston*. One woman remembered that, because they were rushed away, her mother 'had only a few shillings to her name'. It is understandable that the desperate situation in Torres Strait and the women's hurried departure caused monetary problems for them. These families, it was suggested to the Premier of Queensland, were 'destitute and without housing accommodation and furniture'.[8]

How widespread this situation was is conjectural. The women who arrived on the *Ormiston* claimed that their relatives came to their assistance and, as it was their custom to look after one another, few would have been absolutely destitute. Moreover, these women were accustomed to hard work, thrift and contributing to the family income and they were loath to accept charity: 'When we went down we still work for ourselves. We don't want that government money.' Generally, it was the younger women who took paid employment outside the home. One young girl put her age up from twelve to sixteen to get a job as a pantry maid: 'This brought into our household an extra and much-needed income.' Mothers did laundry and ironing at home in order to pay the rent and 'help the money along'. However, for any who needed government assistance, adults received a pound a week and five shillings was paid for each child. Where families shared accommodation, the maximum payment for the household was five pounds a week. The payments for a man or a man and his family were paid for one month: for women and children, the period was three months. However, if a comparison is made between these amounts and what white evacuees received — a weekly allowance of two pounds, with ten shillings for the first child and five shillings each for subsequent children per week— the TI families were certainly being discriminated against.

The government's attitude was expressed in a letter from the Queensland Premier to the Prime Minister: 'Their standard of living and general circumstances are little different from the better type of half-caste [Aboriginal].'[9] Such a comment reflected these men's own ethnocentrism, which stereotyped Indigenous people. They had no first-hand knowledge of the actual standard of living of these proud TI women. A former soldier who spoke from his own experiences on Thursday Island said: 'I went to their houses and I'd say their houses were a lot cleaner than the whites. You would go to the dance in the Town Hall and they would come up beautifully dressed.' A daughter recalled her mother as always being 'very house proud'. The house, with its corrugated iron walls, was painted every Christmas and new frilly curtains hung at the windows. She wove the coconut mats that covered the wooden floors and everything in the house 'was in order'. There should have been no suggestion that their standard of living was lower than that of whites. Moreover, on the mainland, their commitments were no different from those of the white evacuees: they paid the same for food, clothing and rent. Social justice would have demanded equal monetary assistance.

Forced to 'walk away from it all'

While these first evacuees settled on the mainland, the fugitives on Muralag carried on their lives in the hope of remaining there. However, that was not to be. They too were forced to leave Torres Strait.

With the fall of Singapore on 15 February 1942 and the bombing of Darwin on 19 February, white Australians feared the worst. How realistic this situation had become to the fugitives on Muralag is difficult to know. Their strongest recollections were that they just wanted to stay in Torres Strait and look after themselves, however naive that may have seemed to anyone else. But the final choice was not theirs. On a day late in February, the Port Lihou people were carrying on their lives as normally as possible: 'We were making a feast: the chooks and the pig had been killed.' Without warning, the army launch arrived. Everyone was ordered to pack a suitcase and board the army boats. Back on Thursday Island, they faced the reality that Torres Strait had become a war zone; there were no civilians, only soldiers and sailors on the island. On 24 February 1942, the little band sailed out of Port Kennedy on the schooner *Goodwill*, accompanied by a launch belonging to a white family. No one knew how long it might be before they could return, or indeed if they ever would.

A day later, the fugitives at Ah Boo's Landing were also forced to leave. The moment they dreaded was recalled by a woman who, as a young girl, witnessed the heartbreak of her grandparents and parents as they were forced to 'walk away from it all' with only a little bag of possessions. She saw 'how hard it was for them ... rushed like animals to the boats ... "Hurry up, hurry up". ' They left their houses on Thursday Island just as they were. There was little time to make safe their few treasured possessions. Added to the trauma of evacuation was the thought of what it would be like on the mainland: 'We don't know what city life is like until we move down there.' One old woman remembered she was worried about not having 'a very decent dress — you live here, no trouble'. Somehow she visualised people dressed differently there and her pride did not want her to be seen as an unkempt island woman in the city. But going to the mainland certainly closed the chapter on the hard times on Muralag. These fugitives were among the eighty-nine evacuees who sailed out of Port Kennedy on the SS *Katoora* on 28 February 1942.[10] They too were left to wonder whether they would see Thursday Island again.

A TI family who had earlier sought refuge at Allau (Umagico), on the tip of Cape York across Endeavour Strait from Port Lihou, was picked up by the *Katoora*. The father had taken his family there soon after Japan's entry into the war when, with so many soldiers coming in, it became 'unsafe for any female to walk the streets ... after dark' on Thursday Island. Family members supported themselves by fishing and hunting. Each weekend the eldest daughter and an Aboriginal friend, Mosquito, braved the elements and the dangerous sea journey in an old launch to get store supplies from Thursday Island and to bring her father back for the weekend. The family was finally ordered to leave. The daughters remembered the night they left on the *Katoora*. The moving ship widened the distance between them and their father and they strained their eyes in the dark to get a last glimpse of him on the customs vessel.[11]

Another TI family who had gone to the Aboriginal reserve at Cowal Creek near Allau to live with relatives, in the belief that they would be safe there, was also taken away on the *Katoora*. The relatives, an outer island school teacher, his wife and children, were not evacuated nor were the island priest and his family and the Aborigines living on the reserve, despite the danger associated with their close proximity to airstrips and thousands of Australian and American troops stationed nearby: 'At night ... you could see searchlights all over and see Japanese planes ... Planes shoot and it was scary ... we see the Japanese plane, that red dot ... They come very low and people run and hide in the rocks.' In addition to the fear of enemy attack, the Aboriginal women were fearful of the Black American soldiers: 'The negroes ... took women and women went running off when they came. They marched in the house and take the women.' The school teacher soon relocated his family nearer to the army camp for protection. All of these people were Indigenous Australians under the Act. Decisions about who would be evacuated were obviously made in a discriminatory fashion, otherwise it made no sense to take one or two families and leave others.

The Ah Boo's Landing fugitives recalled the voyage on the *Katoora*: 'Everyone got sick ... we were offered food but everyone was too sick to eat it.' A pregnant woman who had only recently trudged every day into the bush in the hope of escaping this fate had back pains during the entire voyage. It was only a small vessel with not nearly enough cabins for everyone, so people were 'on the deck or down below, all crouched up, where you sat you had to stay ... oh, it was terrible'. The ship berthed in Cairns on 28 February for a brief stopover before continuing on to Townsville.

The schooner *Goodwill*, about the size of a pearling lugger, transporting the Port Lihou fugitives to Cairns was old, unseaworthy and much slower than the *Katoora*. 'She was not too good and leaking bad', an old woman remembered. In the early 1900s, the boat had commenced service with Papuan Industries, carrying supplies to Badu Island, along the New Guinea coast and to the Gulf of Carpentaria missions. It was licensed to carry twenty-seven people, but with her human cargo of ninety-seven evacuees everyone was so crowded together there was barely space to move: 'If you wanted to go to the toilet you had to walk over everybody.

Mostly where you sit, you did it there.' The expected date of arrival in Cairns was 3 March, an eight-day sea voyage on an overloaded, unseaworthy and undefended boat. Each family was told to take their own food and the cooking was done by the younger women on the schooner's stove, a wire grid over a fire in a cut-down drum. A woman who has been one of these cooks almost fifty years ago explained: 'We have to serve the old women sitting down ... them small kids we have to worry to feed them ... half the time you don't have anything for yourself [so] that escort boat they sometimes gave us food, usually something nice like biscuits.' The little ship encountered rough seas. However, one woman recalled that, even though she had always been a bad sailor, she was not sick on that journey: 'God must have been with us.' Her companion laughed: 'You were too frightened to be sick.' They certainly had reason for fear.

Out on the ocean, everyone knew the little boat would be an easy target for enemy aircraft or submarines and they had no means for defending themselves. Frightening too was the fact that they had no wireless to radio for help if they were spotted by the enemy or if they got into trouble in a cyclone. In 1899, two cyclones had converged at night in the area of Cape Melville, destroying 100 boats of the pearling fleet with the loss of 300 lives.[12] And, it was here, inside the reef, that the skipper anchored the *Goodwill* late one afternoon. Forty-three years later, this great tragedy had not been forgotten: 'We been worried because it was a cyclone place. That was where the cyclone sunk all the boats.' And, as if the knowledge of this disaster was not enough, in the fading light there was a visual reminder of it: the evacuees could see the skeletons of luggers perched on the hills high above the shoreline where they had been washed up and left by great tidal waves.

The little band of evacuees huddled close for warmth and security and dozed; there was not a sound as the anchor dragged on the sea floor. Then, with a thump and a grinding, scraping noise, the old hull was lodged by the receding tide on the reef:

> We were on top of the reef ... The boat tipped over and we got to jump off onto the reef ... We had our grandfather and he was old

> and they had to carry him and jump ship and go on a little island and wait for help. It was dark when it happened, no moon, nothing, and my grandfather was blind ... all those kids we had to worry about them.

In the inky blackness, old people, pregnant women, and small children trying to cling to their mothers, sisters or aunties stumbled barefoot over the sharp and slippery reef to reach the shore. An old man cried for help. A woman had to reply: 'We can't help you. We have children to look after.' Someone had to carry the old blind man to safety. Without a radio to call for help, the accompanying launch sailed on to Cairns. Meanwhile, one woman recalled, 'we refloated the boat ... but it really got wrecked and we had to wait for another boat'. She talked about how inhospitable the place was:

> We waited on shore cooking tea and there were a lot of dingoes and we had tea, pancakes with flies. There were no trees, only boulders ... When we go for a bath in the creek you had leeches on you and you had to pick them off. We took water with bucket to bath then.

Then she remembered the noises in the bush and how frightened they were: 'You know, we believe in ghosts. We were doing washing in the creek and you can hear someone walking, crackling in the branches. We never wait to see. We take off and leave the washing behind.'

They had no way of knowing if or when help would arrive. Unbeknown to them, however, the non-arrival of the *Goodwill* in Cairns by 4 March had aroused concern. Had the enemy attacked the boat? Had it got into difficulties because it was an old boat carrying far too many passengers? The survivors, unaware of the authorities' concerns and with no guarantee that the launch would reach Cairns safely, made a desperate, but unsuccessful, attempt when a plane was sighted to attract the pilot's attention by waving sheets and lighting fires. Finally, the rescue ship, SS *Britha*, arrived and they continued their journey south.

Just prior to the *Britha*'s arrival in Cairns, the *Katoora* contingent of evacuees from Ah Boo's Landing had disembarked despite further local objections to their landing. It was suggested that the previous contingent of 'coloured persons' had left a plague of dengue fever. This time the evacuees were kept together in the disused Gaiety theatre in Cairns until they could be sent on to the quarantine station at Townsville (349 km south). Even so, there were doubts amongst the government officers whether they would be able to stop the evacuees from returning to Cairns. It was thought that they would make their way back if they were released from the quarantine station without some restriction placed on them. Thus, the decision was made to keep them in Townsville until other suitable accommodation was found. The authorities refused to consider that these people had relatives and friends who had arrived earlier in Cairns aboard the *Ormiston* and who could have accommodated 90 per cent of them.[13] The people had no choice.

On arrival in Townsville, the women set about making the quarantine station habitable:

> Actually, the place had not been lived in for years, the doors and windows banged, and it was dirty and terrible. All the adults and us kids cleaned it up with brooms and swept it out. They supplied us with food ... They had the doctors out there to give us injections. I don't know what for but we all got injections.

Many of these women, like those who had arrived in Cairns on the *Ormiston*, were frightened: 'We didn't know how to go into a big city. We had lived in the bush, not the city — we would get lost.' It was all, in the women's terms, 'a very big experience'.

The evacuees who had left Torres Strait on the *Goodwill* subsequently sailed into Cairns harbour on the *Britha*, but it seems the authorities took even more care to see they did not go off with relatives: 'We didn't get off at Cairns. We just stayed on the boat and went to Cape Pallarenda [Townsville].' By the time they arrived at the quarantine station in Townsville, the decision had been made to send the *Katoora* contingent on to a destination selected by the army in collaboration with the Deputy Director of Native Affairs, Cornelius (Con) O'Leary. That destination was the Aboriginal reserve at Cherbourg. O'Leary was at the quarantine station when the *Britha* contingent arrived and advised them that they too would be transported to the reserve. A couple of women said that Mr O'Leary was helpful but there was no suggestion that he gave them a choice of where they could go on the mainland. He suggested that the reason for sending them to Cherbourg was that they were 'practically destitute' and that the majority of them had no friends in North Queensland. Therefore, he concluded, they were ready to accept relocation on the reserve until their men were released from the CCC and found work on the mainland. If O'Leary believed this, he was not very well informed about the people he was making decisions for. And, while it is conceded that it was a desperate time, that decisions had to be made in a hurry and that O'Leary saw his involvement as being in the evacuees' best interests, by denying them any choice the Director was treating them in the same paternalistic manner in which he controlled his 'wards' under the Act.

Cherbourg, 272 kilometres northwest of Brisbane, was much further from Torres Strait than the women could have imagined. Distance aside, they were island people with strong ties to the sea. Their new home in a rural setting was to be far from the sea. The reserve had been set up in 1907 for the containment of detribalised Aborigines and was given the name Barambah after the cattle station from which the reserve land was resumed. In 1931, the name was changed to Cherbourg. By 1942, a profitable cattle-breeding industry was operating on the reserve. Cherbourg may not have been a location these island women would have chosen for themselves, but it proved to be a place of many experiences they have not forgotten. Moreover, they were able to appreciate that they had a much freer life than the Aboriginal women on the reserve.

The Ah Boo's Landing fugitives arrived at Cherbourg on 11 March 1942, five days before the Port Lihou survivors of the wrecked *Goodwill*. Some of the women in this first contingent spoke of their initial experiences on the mainland:

> We had never been south before. We packed all our stuff and I remember there were buses to take us up and they took us to the railway station and we got in; [it was] the first time we ride in a

train. They were good to us, the Red Cross, and they said, 'Are you warm enough?' The cold, we cannot get used to it, and they gave us blankets, hot soup and milk and we had lunch, sandwiches and rolls. Then we got to Murgon and Mum said, 'Where are we?'

At the end of the train journey, trucks took them on to Cherbourg: 'It was cold. Where are we going? In and in and just all trees and fog ... and we come in and first thing we see was this old hall for evacuees to live in and they took the girls to the dormitory.' This was only March and everyone was already feeling the cold, something they had not experienced before.

Meantime, the Aboriginal women had heard about the pending arrival of the group who, they thought, were 'wild people coming in from Palm Island' and they all turned out to see for themselves when the evacuees actually arrived. The younger evacuees confessed that, despite their fears, they felt a sense of adventure and excitement about everything that had happened to them since they ran away to Muralag. But mothers with young children and the old people were constantly fearful, heavy-hearted and disoriented. On arrival at Cherbourg, a mother sat amongst her ports and refused to eat. She sobbed, 'Where are we? They take us away from our home and we don't know where we are.' Cherbourg proved indeed to be remote in every respect from their island way of life. And, in the days to come, they sang about home many times:

> Old TI, my beautiful home
> It's the place where I was born
> Where the moon and stars that shine
> Makes me longing for home
> Oh, TI, my beautiful home.

Chapter 3

The mainland experience

The TI women had always been treated as if they were socially and intellectually inferior to the elite whites on Thursday Island but they valued their freedom from the legislation which controlled the lives of relatives on the outer islands of Torres Strait. Indeed, when 'there was talk about putting everybody under the Act' in 1935, the Thursday Island Half-caste Association was formed to fight the move. Thus, without knowing it, the evacuee women who had believed they could ensure their own safety on Muralag were to be sent to the sort of protective environment they had been, in principle, so strongly opposed to in 1935.

Many mainland Aboriginal people experienced the extremes of the repressive Queensland legislation to 'protect and segregate' them. It was estimated that 5,762 removals of Aborigines were made to settlements, such as Cherbourg, from 1911 until 1940.[1] The government had no qualms about breaking up Aboriginal families. A man from Cherbourg recalled: 'I was originally from Camooweal. They grab me from my mother when I was about fourteen, and my brother and sister and took us off the land and put us on the reserve.' Girls of white fathers and black mothers were taken and housed in dormitories on settlements. Here they were trained in domestic work to purportedly fit them for marriage to a certain class of white man or 'higher grade half-caste males'.[2] More often than not, they were the virtual slaves of white pastoralists' wives and objects of white men's sexual desires. Young Aboriginal males were sent to settlements as punishment for minor wrongs, to hide the fact that white men slept with black women, or on the pretext of teaching them trades.[3] A Cherbourg man was able to say: 'I came to learn a trade ... but they never gave us a ticket. I finish my trade ... you only work for tea, sugar, rice, not pay.' He remembered they were 'treated like animals', and that they were fearful of white men: 'Being a black fellow [we thought] they were going to send us out and shoot us.' The superintendent was 'judge and jury ... he could inflict anything on an Aborigine'.

During the 1930s, a few anthropologists, parliamentarians and concerned white Australians were disturbed by the way Aboriginal people were being treated. They conceded that Aborigines had not received a 'fair deal' and that something should be done to 'preserve the remnants of the race'.[4] However, whatever changes were being mooted in the latter years of that decade were certainly put on hold when the European war broke out. Moreover, many people were still contending that 'the "uncivilised" full bloods were dying out' and that ultimate absorption into the white population was the only solution to the part-Aboriginal problem.[5] But absorption was not a sufficient alternative in some minds:

> We must be careful to see that the half caste is not given the same liberties that are enjoyed by the white man. We do not want any further mixing of the population. We want to keep the white race white ... The half caste is a danger to the population. He has already got his leg in (laughter) and we want to see that position does not get any worse. We do not want to see any more half blood people born into this world.[6]

With such ethnocentric attitudes in high places, controlling the lives of Aborigines on reserves was easy to justify. In 1942, when the Thursday Island evacuees arrived at Cherbourg, they experienced, first-hand, the same repressive paternalistic measures. Unlike their

Aboriginal counterparts, however, the island women opposed the system.

Cherbourg

While the TI women knew they wanted no part of such policies, they did not know how such a repressive system worked on the reserves. They soon realised that the Aboriginal women had none of the freedoms they were accustomed to and the island women were struck by the differences in the lives of the two groups: 'Why those women like that? They not like us.' The initial living conditions of some of the evacuees were a far cry from the homes they had left: 'We slept on the floor with our own mats in one big open hall with toilet ... There were bugs in the timber ... and each family had a torch to kill the bugs.' The TI women were totally unfamiliar with living conditions which broke up families. At Cherbourg, there was separate dormitory-like accommodation for some men and women: 'Like you married [but] your husband can't stay with you.' Young Aboriginal people were separated from their parents: 'As soon as you were fourteen they stuck you in the dormitories and the boys too', the Cherbourg man recalled. Boys could only visit their families at certain times of the day. Young unmarried Aboriginal mothers were put in 'baby dormitories'. This was all bad enough but not to be able to complain, as was the case for Aboriginal women — 'we were not allowed to talk back to people, you couldn't stand up for yourself' — would have made life intolerable for the TI women. They soon showed the superintendent that they would not live like the Aborigines had to and that they could stand up for themselves. Old Mareja Binjuda was their spokesperson and she was not afraid to 'growl' at him. She 'tackled him ... and blew him sky high' whenever the younger women came to her with complaints: 'She fought for the other women.' About the housing of their children she told him in a very direct way: 'We can't have our kids like that.'

While they lived in the dormitories, meals were served in a long dining room. For breakfast,

> you lined up and ... sit along army tables and they said, 'Bring in the bread', and two big dampers as big as bicycle wheels would

come in and they would cut them up one half inch thick ... We said, 'Where's the butter?' But there was no butter, you have syrup.

One woman remembered: 'From the first day we went we could not stomach the food they cook in a big saucepan, like dog spew. We don't like that.' Totally unfamiliar dishes were served, such as brown rice and stewed fruit. Tea, brewed in an enormous vat from tea leaves used two or three times over, was served to the people in individual billies. Mareja told the superintendent: 'We not pigs. We don't like that. We never been grow up that way.' Their diet had been very different on the island: sweet potato, cassava, fresh fish from the sea, turtle, crayfish and white rice cooked in coconut milk. However, after some agitation from the TI women, a truck arrived twice a week from Murgon with fresh milk, butter, fruit and fish: 'There was a rush for that fish. We love fish.' Fish reminded them of home and they sang about it:

> We have missed the palms and fishes
> Which surround our island home
> And never more we'll dream
> Of leaving dear old TI.

Initially, some of the TI women lived with their children in one room: 'We had a big room and five children there with us. We cook ourselves. We only had one kitchen and we take it in turns to cook.' Pressure for better family accommodation resulted in the construction of small wood and iron cottages into which the newcomers moved. In some instances, two, or even more, families were housed in them:

> We had a kitchen and a bedroom and in the middle a sitting room and a verandah. Some slept on the verandah. We had little four-gallon drums and pieces of firewood stuffed in and lit for warmth. They made covers out of bags sewn together onto canvas to cover us up on the verandah. We had a blanket but the bags kept us warm.

On the island, their houses had also been small, but the weather there was hot and they had been able to live outside most of the year. Sleeping on verandahs at Cherbourg certainly added to the painful experience of their first winter. It was something they have never forgotten: 'The winter — don't even talk about the winter!' The cold penetrated their poorly constructed cottages; their skin dried and their lips cracked: 'It's cold. We can't bear the cold.' The only good thing about it, one old woman recalled with the sense of humour typical of these people, was that, 'if you want to make a jelly, just put it on the roof to set'.

The women learnt to cope with their new environment. They queued with the local women for rations of basic foods, such as flour, rice, sugar, tea, jam. Vegetables and meat from the settlement's garden and herds were handed out on certain days. Eggs could be bought from the Cherbourg farm and, as an old Aboriginal woman they called Granny recalled, she would 'sell them a fowl occasionally'. Household water was pumped up from the Barambah Creek without treatment, even though the children swam in it. It was also used by the sawmill on the reserve as an outlet for effluent. In 1942 there was an outbreak of typhoid fever and one young evacuee was seriously affected, others less severely.

Any money earned by the Aboriginal people was closely supervised because, according to the Cherbourg man, the superintendent maintained they 'couldn't manage money', a consequence of which was that they never knew if they were 'being taken down'. They were simply issued with just about all their needs, including clothing and blankets. If they wanted to walk the seven kilometres to Murgon, a permit was necessary before leaving the reserve. In contrast, the TI women were free to make the trip to Murgon to spend whatever money they had. The evacuee children attended the 'school for Aborigines' on the reserve. However, attitudes towards the local children's education were just as negative as they had been on Thursday Island:

> They didn't think the Aborigines' brains or minds could function the same as the whites, or they didn't think there was any reason to give them a first class education ... By the time we reached

fourth grade we were about fourteen years old and there was no further to go. Once you got to fourth grade you had to leave school, you couldn't do anything else, you had to go to work.[7]

Here, as in Torres Strait, the island children continued to suffer inequality in their education.

The costs associated with all compulsory evacuations were borne by the Commonwealth government. The evacuees' living expenses were also paid by that government until the men arrived from Thursday Island and found employment cutting cane, pulling peanuts, and picking cotton, corn and arrowroot. Then a contribution of seven shillings a week was made for each family member. The older boys were offered work in the rural school on the reserve at £1 a week, but, unlike their Aboriginal counterparts, they could choose to go with the men to cut cane for £15 a week. It was more difficult for young women to get suitable work in the area. The superintendent attempted to send them out to the stations under contract to employers for twelve months, as he did the Aboriginal girls. An old Cherbourg woman recalled what that was like:

> You name it, I milk cows, pick pumpkins, everything. We were supposed to be the housemaids but we did all that. We were getting 2s 6d a month. I don't know where the rest of the money went ... If you came back before twelve months, you had to go back.

But the TI women would not have their girls sent away and Mareja 'growled' again at the superintendent: 'We never come here to send our girls out to work. You send them, they come back in this baby dormitory.'

A time of discovery, cooperation and making new friends

With all its difficulties, the time at Cherbourg was a further step in the women's 'really big experience'. Their philosophy became: 'We got to be happy. We don't know how long we got to stay there.' Indeed, the time spent at Cherbourg was one of discovery, cooperation and making new friends for both groups of women and children. Out in the bush with their Aboriginal friends, the boys roasted witchetty grubs which they 'reckoned were juicy', while their mothers shuddered at the thought of eating them. Granny remembered that the island women taught her how to make blachan, a Malayan savoury sauce for stews and fish, and to cook rice 'Malay fashion'. Sometimes she took them out in the bush to see what they could find: 'We found pie melons. But they cooked them like marrow.' All the women and girls, Aboriginal and island, worked together to make hessian-bag bed covers, or waggas, for the cold weather. An old Cherbourg woman remembered how beautiful the island women's voices were: 'I could have heard them sing all day.' The Thursday Island girls nervously staged a concert in Murgon to benefit servicemen. They remembered how entertainment on Thursday Island had been segregated and they were also aware that some locals were hostile about their coming to the Cherbourg area. Therefore, they were amazed when 'all the soldiers ... and all the people came to see ... the TI girls'.

Women from both Indigenous groups commented on the differences they saw in each other's cultures. For instance, an Aboriginal woman compared their death customs: 'They were different ... They took out food, wine, cigarettes to the grave.' For Aboriginal people, she continued,

> death is sacred, you don't go near there ... you could hear a pin drop if anybody died ... [You] had a Christian burial but there was the Aboriginal part of it, you had respect with that. Sometimes an old woman would hit herself on the head and make a scar to remember that person.

Another woman remembered that the TI people 'took the body from the hospital home to the house and had the body in the middle of the room and sat around and had a party or something and did this crying'. She also recalled how curious the young Aboriginal girls were when they first saw a healthy ten-pound island newborn: 'They had never seen such a big kid. They used to go and peek at him in the hospital through the window.' The TI women were struck by the hardness of the Aboriginal women's lives: 'We felt sorry for them and made cigarettes for them.' One of the young evacuee men, Jeffrey Doolah, who became very friendly with the local people and stayed on the reserve after the war, occasionally took some of the TI women to church on the reserve. Granny recalled that the island women 'jumped in and did the corroboree' with them. On Christmas Eve 1942, both groups joined in a big party and Jeffrey Doolah played his guitar. And, despite their differences, the old Aboriginal woman reminisced: 'There was no trouble with the islanders when they were here. It was very peaceful.' However, three island women, who were teenagers at the time, remembered that the Aboriginal men fought amongst themselves: 'We used to like Saturday and Sunday afternoon. We would watch. They fought with sticks and stones ... with spear. They fought ... they have a row between themselves, go kill themselves.' They also remembered that problems arose if Aboriginal men 'looked at certain island girls; then it was on'. The superintendent was opposed to the island girls wearing shorts because it caused undue attention from the Aboriginal men. Generally, however, the old Aboriginal woman said, the bottom line was that the evacuees were 'black like us ... we just took them as we find them and they took us as they find us', although an understandable separateness was maintained: 'We sort of got mixed up, but not much.' Nonetheless, Cherbourg proved a time of new insights for the evacuee women: 'It was a really big experience for us to see how the [Aboriginal women] lived.'

In nearby Murgon, some whites were not so accepting. As already indicated, in 1942 most mainland Australians knew little, and in Murgon probably nothing, about the Torres Strait and its diverse people. An early reaction to the newcomers' presence in the district was: 'We don't want them here. They can't speak English and they live in grass huts.' Fights occurred when the men went into the town:

> The whites they call us black bastards ... when we walk into the shop it was same thing. If they see us standing there they would not come in, they would wait till we come out ... We boys used to get into fights. They insult our family ... When we went to the pictures we could hear them talking about us.

Such encounters decided a father to take his family away from Cherbourg as quickly as possible. His daughter remembered that,

> when my father and uncle came [to Cherbourg] and went into town ... and they tried to go in the pub and get a haircut, they couldn't. So my father said it's best thing to get a job outside and make enough money to get out, and my uncle decided to go to Brisbane and my eldest brother went ahead.

However, she recalled being pleasantly surprised by a white girl's attitude towards her on a farm where her father took a job peanut-picking:

> Mum and I went and did the cooking ... Mum would say, 'You better take the billy tea to [the men]' and while they were having morning tea I'd eat the peanuts, and I got friendly with the owner's daughter my age, and she took me horseback riding and showed me how to milk a cow and she wanted to take me shopping but Mum didn't want me to. We stayed there until Dad got enough money.

The family eventually moved to Brisbane and she considered herself lucky because a friend was able to get her a job 'peeling spuds and washing up in a fish and oyster bar'. Away from Cherbourg, at only ten years of age, she was contributing to the family income.

More families moved away before Christmas 1942. By 19 February 1943, the last family had left. For some there was the sadness of leaving a place where they had buried a member of the family. Others would remember Cherbourg as the place of the birth of a new family member. The Battle of the Coral Sea in May 1942 and the Battle of Midway in June gave the allies an edge on the Japanese southward advance and, as the Australian troops began to push the enemy back along the Kokoda track over the Owen Stanley Ranges from September, most mainland Australians began to look to the future with more optimism. But going home for the TI families was still a long way off.

Back to the coast

Eventually, the evacuees asked to speak with O'Leary: 'All the families want to go out because we are not under the Act and we are free people. Everyone talk, "I want to go, go find a job".' They had not lost the sense of the importance of their freedom. However, leaving Cherbourg meant the splitting up and dispersal along the Queensland coast of a group of people who had always lived in close proximity to one another. Only a few families stayed on in the rural area because they had jobs there. One young woman married an Aboriginal man and established a permanent home in Murgon. However, it is probably true to say that the majority of families moved nearer to the coast, to Brisbane, Bundaberg, Mackay or Townsville where the weather was warmer. In these places, the Manpower Directorate deployed the men into jobs.

One of the first families to go to Brisbane was assisted by a son who had recently returned from the Middle East with severe war wounds. Another family had to wait until 'Dad made enough money to take them out'. In Brisbane, an older daughter took employment as a housemaid for whites and, later, she worked in the kitchen of a popular restaurant, Davey Jones' Locker. The important thing about leaving Cherbourg, according to another woman, was to get enough money:

> You had to have some money and they could leave [Cherbourg] ... We had no relations or friends. We don't know anyone. Mum's sisters were in Cairns. They got away earlier on their own accord. Dad went to Bundaberg to look for a house and work ... he worked there for a while at the sugar mill. He went cane-cutting. It was good money ... Dad made money to get us out ... found a house and job and took my grandfather and grandmother too ... I went to school there and the other children were born there.

Moving away from Cherbourg also meant that the TI children were finally able to attend state schools where they were taught the mainland curriculum. However, older children were sometimes denied this opportunity when it eventually came because they had to find employment to help pay the cost of supporting large families.

Employment for working-age girls had been an incentive for families to move to the larger coastal towns and cities but, like their counterparts who arrived on the *Ormiston*, they can look back and express how limited their work horizons were: 'We scrubbed floors and polished for white people, what else! ... That's all for us black people. That's all we were fit for. We didn't have the education to go any further.' They worked as housemaids, kitchen hands, waitresses and domestics in hotels, restaurants, cafes and private homes. Factors which contributed to the ready availability of such jobs were that white working-class girls had, for some time, been finding better paid jobs in the clothing and textile industries. For a time, immigrant women took their places. But, with the advent of the Pacific War, the work horizons of both of these groups of women were expanded. They became process workers in munition and aircraft factories, postal workers, ticket collectors, conductors, to name a few wartime occupations available to white and immigrant women. Moreover, with thousands of men enlisted in the armed services, Public Service jobs, previously reserved for men, were also taken up by white women. When it became possible for women to join the three armed services, there was a further drain on workers in essential industries. By March 1944, 49,000 women had enlisted in the armed services and a further 3,000 joined the Australian Women's Land Army.[8] Thus, the focus of white working-class and immigrant women had been drawn away from domestic-type work, which made it readily available to young evacuee women who were eager enough to take the jobs if it meant they could bring home a much-needed extra income.

Manpower regulated the employment of all eligible white women, but there was no evidence to substantiate whether or not island women were required to register for employment. From their own stories, it seemed that they generally found employment through wide family networks and friends. No one mentioned obtaining work by any other means. Three women recalled that, in Brisbane, they had been waitresses in the Valley: 'We knew a lot of people, Indonesians there and they told us about jobs. The men lived at the hotel. They were in the merchant navy.' One of the women said, with pride, that when the white cashier left after a row with the boss: 'I ended up getting the job. I was the cashier in the hotel in the Valley.' She had reason for pride because she would never have dreamed of getting such a job on Thursday Island before the war. Another domestic position was secured by a young woman who had known the white employer from Thursday Island. Moreover, it was not uncommon to find two or three girls working at the same restaurant or hotel because they looked out for jobs for one another. Such networks of families and friends were important to female job hunters.

The war years gave a great many married white women of all ages a feeling of emancipation. They were no longer confined to their homes, housework and the care of children. The experience of the married TI women was different. In many cases, the number of children in their families, and quite often the size of the extended family, made it impossible for them to contemplate employment outside the home. Moreover, the older women continued to be more nervous about city life than the younger ones. In some cases, if the male breadwinner's income was sufficient, younger women also chose to stay at home. However, for any island young woman, 'there were jobs if you wanted them', and, as one discovered, 'as long as we do our job properly [employers] treated us good'.

To some extent, employers were forced to treat their workers well because of the drastic labour shortage, particularly in domestic employment. However, while some members of the public treated the evacuees with respect, they encountered others with racist attitudes. A male evacuee's perception was that they 'didn't see racism much in Brisbane ... In the cities it was all right. It was in the suburbs the trouble was ... they called us black bastards.' Young women, however, remembered that they were confronted with racism in the towns and cities. An incident in Townsville was recalled:

> We did housework, working in hotels as housemaids. We used to cop it ... We had to go across the bridge to get into the town section and Australian soldiers were on convoys and they would

say, 'Look at all the dark clouds. I think it's going to rain today.'
It hurt too.

Dark clouds comments, another woman said, 'seemed to be the favourite'. An American sailor with his white girlfriend stared at a group of island girls as they walked into a cafe. The girlfriend commented loudly, 'Dark clouds about ... it's going to rain.' In anger, an island girl responded, 'Come on, come on, fight, white girl!' Another woman remembered that, 'as soon as we pass, everyone turned around and looked at us and I said, "What are you looking at?".' An American serviceman stared at a mother sitting with a group of island girls having a meal. To his embarrassment, the woman returned his stare, opened her mouth to its fullest and poured spoonfuls of soup down her throat. American sailors in Brisbane sniggered at the girls and called them 'fuzzy wuzzies', which resulted in one sailor having an icecream thrown in his face. There were also racist attitudes amongst school children:

> I remember the white kids called us 'fuzzy wuzzies'. It hurt. I remember having a fight with one girl ... I remember Mrs Villalba [an ex-Thursday Island resident], she saved me. She had a fish and chip shop in Mulgrave Road and we would go there and buy lunch and the white people ganged up on us and when I went to fight she would call me and say, 'Now, Mary, cool down'.

Travelling on public transport could also be embarrassing: 'The people used to just stare at me. You would be sitting there, your head down, not game enough to look up and say "hello". I felt really homesick. I just think that I should go back home.'

While such attitudes and comments were not new to the island people, there was always the hurt associated with them. However, as time went on, the younger women who were away from the home more than the older women grew in confidence in the dominant white society. They lost their fear of travelling on public transport and ignored the stares of other passengers. One woman recalled how she and her friend explored Brisbane on the trams: 'We got excursion tickets for about one shilling and you can go from two to ten or ten to two on Sunday.' Younger women occasionally established friendships with white people with whom they worked or with friends their brothers brought home. Again, it was more difficult for the older women and women with children: 'We never went out. We stayed at home. You didn't have babysitters then.' A Thursday Island Association was formed in Brisbane and monthly dances were held at which island young people and Aborigines who had moved to the city when the war made it easier for them to do so became friendly. There was, however, a handful of TI women for whom the war years held few opportunities for interaction with anyone outside of their own group. These were the TI women who had married Japanese men before the war. They, together with young women who had only been friendly with the Japanese, lived out the war years under a cloud of suspicion.

TI wives of Japanese divers

The establishment of Thursday Island as a base for pearl and trochus shelling operations from the mid-1800s attracted people from Southeast Asia, the Philippines, the South Pacific and Japan. In the early 1900s, under the White Australia policy, the flow of non-whites into the country was slowed down and many already residing in the country were expelled. Nonetheless, Japanese divers came in increasing numbers. European pearling companies convinced the government that their operations were dependent upon these men because they could not get good white divers. By October 1941, there were 301 male and sixteen female Japanese on Thursday Island.[9] One island woman's recollection was that the different ethnic groups generally kept themselves separate, although the Japanese 'mixed in better than some of the other groups — they joined in parades and celebrations'. Another woman thought that, 'from [the Japanese] point of view, they were too good to marry any of us. They thought they were above even the white people. But they lived their own culture. You couldn't fault them. When they came they still lived like Japanese.' The Japanese lived in an area of the town known as 'Jap Town' or 'Yokohama'. There 'they had their own stores ... their own women and boarding houses. They had communal baths.' But there are always exceptions to rules and, in this instance, four young TI women married Japanese nationals and another handful were friendly with them. Japan's entry into the war put these women in an invidious position.

On 8 December 1941, soldiers from 49 Battalion, the Volunteer Defence Corps, Navy Intelligence, local police and outer island men in the Torres Strait Infantry in a combined operation located and interned all Japanese on Thursday Island and at sea. A former soldier in 49 Battalion recalled:

> What I could make of TI it was just a normal life in early 1941. When the Japs came into the war there was an urgency then. They put machine guns on army trucks to round up the Japanese and put them in a concentration camp on the island. The Japanese had shops; you just went in, 'We have got to take you, the Japanese are in the war' ... A couple may have tried to get away in boats, but they were brought back.

One man, who resisted strenuously because he claimed that 'the war was nothing to do with him', was shot in the leg before his captors were able to remove him from the boarding house where he had taken refuge.

On the first day of the round-up, 110 Japanese were interned. Army boats searched for luggers at sea and a further 200 men were apprehended; their island crews were ordered to return to port. By 15 December, 300 Japanese had been interned. Jap Town was converted into a concentration camp. The triangular-shaped area, bounded by Victoria Parade, and Milman and Hargraves Streets, was surrounded by barbed wire, mounted with machine guns and guarded by armed soldiers. Island wives and their children were not interned but were permitted to visit their husbands and fathers while they remained on the island. Any gifts they brought were carefully examined: 'cakes were cut open to see if they contained knives.' An island woman recalled: 'Many people felt sorry for them. They were really good people.' She remembered how the Japanese had helped her family: 'When we were kids we had lots of chooks and we tried to sell the eggs to the Japanese boarding houses and they always took them.' Just prior to Christmas 1941, 315 Japanese men, women and children sailed on the SS *Zealandia* for camps at Hay, in New South Wales, and Tatura, in Victoria.[10]

Wives of seamen throughout Torres Strait were accustomed to the absence of their deckhand husbands for months at a time. However, a diver's wife had good reason to be greatly concerned about her husband's safety. The son of a Japanese diver explained that his mother 'lived with the knowledge that he might not come back home'. There was the constant fear of the bends. The Japanese tombstones in the Thursday Island cemetery testify to the reality of this fear. With the internment of their Japanese husbands, the island wives were confronted with new fears as well as financial hardships. No longer did they have a breadwinner for the family. Moreover, they found the small sustenance allowance of £1 5s a week for a woman and child quite inadequate for their needs on the mainland. The son of a Japanese internee and an island woman remembered that, after their evacuation, his mother 'washed and ironed twenty-five long-sleeved shirts a day' for money to support them. But, even worse, she, like each of these wives, had to keep a low profile to avoid people discovering she had a Japanese husband. There was a lot of anger in Australia against the Japanese. The man recalled how his mother was constantly fearful that people would hear their names: '[She was] afraid someone might kill them.' They told their children: 'Keep away from trouble, avoid it, don't go mix, don't start making trouble.' He said some sympathetic teachers controlled potentially ugly situations, but virtually their only reliable support came from close family members. This man's grandfather looked out for him. As a young teenager, the boy worked alongside the old man doing the 'back-breaking' job of cutting cane, always with the thought of his father's release and 'getting back home one day'. Covering up the identity of their children was difficult. One of the Aboriginal women at Cherbourg said that when the evacuees were there the people 'put two and two together' and thought one of the women was married to a Japanese internee because 'the kids were squinty-eyed'. She was not sure and they said nothing.

Not only were the women under the constant suspicions of white people, they with their children were liable to be taken to a staging camp for prisoners-of-war at Gaythorne in Brisbane, where the women were interrogated before a military tribunal. A single woman might also be taken into custody just because of a prewar friendship with a Japanese man. These were particularly harrowing experiences for the women and their children. While in the camp, they were housed in army huts and cooked their own rations. The picture of the camp, imprinted on the boy's mind almost fifty years before, was of

> guards ... posted up all around the camp. It was fenced in with barbed wire ... There was movement of people all the time. They had Malays and Chinese because they didn't want to work the ships. They went on strike so they were in camp ... talking about prisoners of war, there must have been 200 come in every third day. Most of them didn't stay long.

He remembered the sergeant coming around, perhaps once a week, saying: 'Mrs so and so, and so and so, the commandant wishes to see you.' The mothers were taken off for hours at a time, leaving the children in the huts. The boy had no idea what was happening to his mother; she returned fearful and confused and, when he questioned her about what had happened, all she could tell him was that it was 'all about things having a connection with Japanese men and with ... being married ... to them, and they wanted all the information they could get'. They could be kept in the camp for up to three months. After their release the women were more fearful and everyone stayed close to their relatives. They were the only people who could possibly have some understanding of the women and children's situation. There was certainly little opportunity for the women to have any sort of social life outside of their own group.

The long wait

Regardless of whether the evacuees came to the mainland independently, dispersed after arrival on the *Ormiston* or after their sojourn at Cherbourg, they had similar experiences with accommodation. Generally, they looked to relatives and friends to help them. However, as the war progressed, building programs were put on hold and any sort of accommodation became more expensive and harder to find.

Even when rented accommodation was not too difficult to find in early 1942 because of the many voluntary evacuations from northern coastal towns like Cairns and Townsville, the problem was that the evacuee women had no knowledge of how things worked on the mainland and certainly no idea how to go about finding accommodation. As already indicated, one of the earliest families to arrive on the mainland stayed with relatives in Mossman until another family connection helped them to find accommodation in Cairns: 'It was hard to get a house ... They sort of gave us a pretty good idea how to get it.' Another family with a number of children was assisted in Brisbane by a white family. The TI mother had looked out for their son when he was on Thursday Island in the navy. However, by October 1942, the increasing lack of accommodation, particularly for young white women who had become more independent of their families because of the wartime environment, was brought to the attention of the Queensland parliament. It was pointed out that residentials and boarding houses in Brisbane and northern coastal towns were being taken over by the military, as were other properties. For those evacuee women who had to find independent accommodation, the rental situation was also difficult; a TI woman remarked on how lucky she had been when a friend got her one room to live in.

This trend was evident in northern newspapers from mid-1942 until 1945 when offers to rent accommodation fell off dramatically. Moreover, as the demand for accommodation increased, greedy landlords began asking for 'key money'. Evacuee women and families could not compete for accommodation with people like the American soldiers. This situation resulted in island families crowding into small houses: 'We had a two-bedroom house [in Townsville] ... we all had to fit in ... some on the verandah and on the floor and in the middle room. We were lucky to get that place ... we were all over the place. Sort of crude but we made room for everyone.' In Bundaberg, an extended family moved into a worker's cottage with two bedrooms, a sitting room and a kitchen: 'In that house were my grandmother and my grandfather and my grandmother's sister and my family [mother and four children] and one of my aunties.' When the situation in Brisbane worsened, the Department of Native Affairs helped a few families in desperate circumstances. Some landlords turned a blind eye to overcrowding. A family from Hammond Island moved in with a TI family with the landlord's approval. The latter family subsequently found a house with 'two bedrooms and a big verandah' and three generations of that family occupied it. However, another motive was suggested for overcrowding in small houses: 'I don't know about other people, we sort of wanted to stick together ... We were dead set on getting back even if we had to come back in canoes.' It is understandable that such support in an alien environment curbed the loneliness they felt and served to keep alive their vision of returning home.

Scarcity and the cost of housing were not the only factors which militated against Torres Strait Islanders and Aboriginal people obtaining suitable accommodation. Because of the desperate need for labour early in the war, Aborigines were permitted to come into the cities and towns. Working side by side with white Australians, they began to gain confidence and their hopes and expectations were raised. Nevertheless, their presence in the towns and cities was met with reactions from white racist landlords. An Aboriginal woman drew attention to this in the media: 'We are banned from decent accommodation by our colour.' Not only was there discrimination against them in the renting process, the perception of this woman was that they were also charged higher rents if they were lucky enough to get even a room. White people, she claimed, 'can get accommodation at a first class hotel for much less than we are paying [for a room]'.[11] In this environment, there could be no doubt that, whether the evacuee families knew it or not, they were likely to be discriminated against, particularly as they were sometimes erroneously identified as the 'despised' Aborigines.[12] Indeed, they were described by a member in the Queensland parliament in 1939 as 'aboriginals who live on the Torres Strait Islands'.[13] The member may have meant that the Torres Strait Islanders were the first people in that area of Australia. Nonetheless, the name 'Aborigine' was all too frequently used to refer to the island people in a derogatory way. It was said that Aborigines were too uncivilised to live with

European amenities. That myth was challenged and found wanting for many Aboriginal families when army settlements were set up for them after the bombing of Darwin and they lived in European-styled houses.[14] However, the strong family networks among the TI evacuees sometimes served to show landlords that they could be good tenants, such as the family which took over a lease from a cousin married to a white man: '[The landlord] came once [to check the house] and didn't come to see the house again. Everything was clean and tidy. We only went down to pay the rent then.' But, once a house was rented, there was no guarantee that the neighbour would be friendly. An evacuee family in Brisbane was repeatedly harassed by a drunken neighbour hurling stones at the house and calling out: 'Why don't you go back to the river bank?'

In December 1944, the housing demand in Cairns was described as exceeding anything that the authorities could have contemplated. Three months later, the Queensland government proposed plans for the building of houses in Mackay, Townsville and Cairns to relieve the acute shortage in North Queensland. How far this building program went towards alleviating the overall housing shortage in Queensland of 33,000 is conjectural, particularly as it continued to grow.[15] In any event, it was getting too late to help the TI families because peace was imminent and they were anxious to get back home to Thursday Island.

It was not unusual to find extended families living in relatively small houses on Thursday Island. The white perspective was that the houses were overcrowded but these people looked out for one another and this was particularly so when it came to the totally inadequate housing available to them on the island. As one woman said: 'We always look after one another.' It was, nevertheless, such overcrowding of rented accommodation in Brisbane, an example of which was twenty-one adults and nine children living in one small dwelling, that finally aroused the Health Department's fear of disease and raised the question of sending the evacuees home. In November 1944, various government bodies, including the Department of Native Affairs, concluded that the only answer to the evacuees' accommodation problems was to return them to their home islands. However, this was not a viable alternative, which the

Director well knew. The Torres Strait bottleneck was still under military control and the facilities for civil resumption of the island did not exist. There was little doubt that the evacuees would have willingly returned home in late 1944. Indeed, when peace returned in the Pacific in August 1945, the majority of TI families waited impatiently to return. However, government authorities were indecisive about the future of Thursday Island. Questions were being asked. Was it to be essentially a defence base? Could the people be allowed to return if no civil industry was to be put in place? The future of the TI evacuees hung in the balance until 25 March 1946, when military control finally ceased and the prohibition on their re-entry to Thursday Island was lifted.

The *Wandana*, bringing the TI families home a few weeks later, was overcrowded: 'There were five people in a cabin, they slept on the deck, anywhere, they did anything to get home. They sang "Old TI, My Beautiful Home" as they came near the wharf.' An old woman remembered that it felt as if the boat would roll over because everyone was on one side to get their first glimpse of home after four long years of uncertainty about whether they would ever come back. However, the civil authorities had made no preparations for their return and, in September 1946, the Bishop of Carpentaria complained to the Premier about the situation. There were housing and food shortages and no schools for the children to attend. They had nothing better to do than run wild in the streets, he said.[16] A member of one of the first families to return told her story:

> We just lived on bully beef and fish and after all those things we had in the city, and we came back and there were no lights in the street. Everyone started to come back and they formed the tennis club and no coloureds allowed ... the theatre started and then it was that coloured business again, coloureds not allowed upstairs.

But the 'coloured' people were no longer willing to acquiesce in the rule that only whites sat in the upstairs seats. They picketed the theatre and refused to patronise it. Management had to change the rules but, as one recalcitrant recalled, 'we all stayed downstairs'.

They preferred it that way, but they had made their stand, something they would have been hesitant about doing before the war.

The war had positive effects on some aspects of the women's lives. A whole range of jobs became available to young TI women, such as in stores and cafes: 'After the war my first job was serving behind a counter and I thought I was made. Here I don't have to scrub, polish silver for white women and, oh, I thought it was wonderful.' The convent school's response to the need for office training set the few island girls whose parents could afford the fees on new employment paths: 'Before we didn't have that education to apply for a job in an office.' A more respectable wage enabled young women to purchase fashionable dresses by catalogue from Brisbane. At the weekly dances there was always an air of excitement amongst them to see their friends' latest selections from the catalogues. One young woman remembered how she purchased her whole wedding regalia — her dress, veil and bouquet — in this way.

Almost half a century on, old TI women have looked back and told the story of their 'really big experience' during the Pacific War. It was a time of sadness, upheaval, apprehension, fear and uncertainty. But now that they have looked back, perhaps the words of one old woman sum up the present attitude of the evacuees to that experience: 'Sometimes when I think about it I cannot believe what we went through. Funny, eh!'

Nazareth Ansey with Jeennie Bon, both from Mer (courtesy Elsie Smith)

Lizzie Nawia plaiting a basket

Margaret Abednego (from Mer) with Japanese friend (courtesy Elsie Smith)

Graves of Japanese pearlers, Thursday Island

The SS *Ormiston* (courtesy John Oxley Library)

The sailing vessel, *Goodwill* (courtesy John Oxley Library)

Evacuation notice, *Torres Straits Daily Pilot*, 27 January 1942

Chapter 4

'It was all of a sudden'

Across Aplin Pass, a narrow sea channel, lies Hammond Island, to the north of Thursday Island. The Torres Strait Islander women living on the Catholic mission there were also ordered to evacuate on the *Ormiston* in January 1942.

Hammond Island mission

The slaughter of many of the Kaurareg people at the instigation of government officials forced the survivors to leave their mother island Muralag. They scattered to other tribal lands, including Keriri (Hammond Island).[1] In 1881, an area of two-and-a-half square miles of the northern half of the island was gazetted by the Queensland government as an Aboriginal reserve. A remnant of the Kaurareg people lived there until 1921, when the government forcibly removed them to Adam (later named Poid) on Moa Island. The reserve was subsequently converted to a grazing lease.

When Father John Doyle arrived in Torres Strait in 1927 to take up his post as parish priest under the patronage of Our Lady of the Sacred Heart, Hammond Island was without a resident population. He was moved by the plight of the Catholic Filipino and South Sea men's families on Thursday Island. The men earned little money and their homes were substandard. Immorality was rife on the island and, like the families of the Southeast Asian men, they enjoyed no social status in what was a decidedly hierarchical society. Father Doyle saw their futures as bleak unless they were given opportunities to possess their own homes, cultivate gardens and bring their children up in a more congenial environment. Hammond Island seemed just the place and the priest approached the Local Protector. As a consequence, in August 1928, the government terminated the grazing lease and an area of land was set aside for a Catholic mission.

In 1929, Father Owen McDermott came to Thursday Island to take up the post of resident priest on the fledgling Hammond Island mission. Francis Durante was thirteen in 1928 when he was brought from Edgor to Thursday Island by his Catholic Filipino father to receive his first communion. He subsequently became the first boy to go to the new mission with Father McDermott. In those days, he said, 'people were short of money and they cannot look after [their] children and parents take them up to Father and make the orphanage.' The two were soon joined by a dozen boys from the orphanage. The mission took shape:

> A house of second-hand galvanised iron was erected near the beach to shelter the priest and the boys ... The priest taught school on the house verandah each morning and afternoons were devoted to gardening, care of poultry and pigs and the erection of a school-church ... The presbytery was built in 1932 and a new church was erected ... A comfortable house was built for the boys ... and the mission school housed over forty pupils.[2]

'There was nothing there', Francis remembered, 'we used mangrove wood to build. Father used to go to town and there were auction sales, iron, timber. He got it from them Jap and issued it out to the people and they make their own homes out of it.' Mangrove wood, secured locally, was used for the uprights and beams of the houses; the walls and roof were of corrugated iron. Packing cases were used for flooring. The people had little money when they arrived on the mission so it was not unusual for families to get sheet iron from the dump and make 'a sort of humpy' until they were in a position to build better homes. The houses generally had three bedrooms, depending on the number of people in them, with an attached kitchen. Cooking was done in an open fireplace.

The mission also attracted Catholic families from outer islands where there were no Catholic churches or schools. In 1932, the first marriage on Hammond Island took place between a young man from the mission and a girl from the orphanage on Thursday Island. However, according to JW Bleakley, Chief Protector of Aborigines from 1914 until June 1942 and a supporter of the mission, a 'large slum population of cross-breds' belonging to the Catholic faith still resided on Thursday Island. This prompted the state government to provide the money to set up an industrial school on the mission in the hope of drawing these people there.[3] Most of the mission men worked on pearling and trochus boats: 'The boys reach an age they had to go out and work ... The men would go three weeks and come in for two or three days — never stay long'; some might be away as long as ten months at a time. Their wages were £3 a month or £4 if shell prices were high.

Seamen's wives supplemented their husband's incomes with money from the sale of garden produce. They planted and harvested the crops, loaded the surplus into their twelve-foot wooden dinghies and rowed across Aplin Pass to Thursday Island 'once or twice a week', where the produce was sold to shop-keepers and white housewives. To maintain their supplies, gardening was sometimes given priority over a girl's schooling: 'I went over to the convent school when I was very young. My bigger sisters had to go back to help Mum and Dad to garden.' Unlike the situation for their Thursday Island counterparts who might get domestic employment in white homes, generally, the Hammond Island women relied on their gardening enterprises for extra money. One old woman thought that gardening was 'the hardest time of all' but, she conceded, it was at least a means of 'helping the money along'.

Men not working in the marine industry were totally dependent on gardening and fishing:

> We had to have gardens. That was your living. If you didn't you don't have any money. Before we had no social pension, we worked for ourselves. You go fishing night time and take it to TI and sell it ... My old man was a hard worker. He didn't go on the boats when he got married. He did the garden. We sell fruit, walk down town (Thursday Island) with basket on your shoulder, sell banana, paw paw. We walked around and go to different houses ... They order more and you come back.

Both the men and the women fished and speared crabs and crayfish; boiled crayfish sold on Thursday Island for 1s 6d each. The men hunted dugong and turtle, the meat from which was shared generously in the village. Those who were industrious and careful with their money gradually bought china, linen and furniture for their homes; some experienced for the first time the luxury of a bed with a mattress or a cot for the baby.

An old nun, recalling life on the mission, said that for everyone life had been very basic: 'Even the chooks wouldn't lay because we could not feed them at times.' Nonetheless, she said, the island women cared for their families with pride: 'They were very clean and their houses were very clean and tidy, and they swept everything every day with those brooms that they made ... no one seemed to wear "rags" or was allowed to look uncared for ... Despite the size of the family, all were well fed and clothed.' The mission had its own little church and, according to an old Hammond Islander, the people 'had to go'. Otherwise, there was a freedom about their lives which relatives on the outer islands could not enjoy: 'We were not like the outer islands ... You could do anything. You could go to TI, stay two or three nights. You didn't have to get permission.'

Initially, the girls attended the convent school on Thursday Island. Catholic girls from the outer islands of Nagi, Edgor and Erub also boarded at the convent. But, like the children who attended the 'coloured school' on Thursday Island, they were 'not permitted to sit for scholarship'. Only the white children at the convent school could do that. The old nun explained that the island children were taught 'the basic three Rs' and that the aim of their education was 'to make them good citizens'. A woman who had lived at the convent for a number of years was able to say, almost fifty years after, that 'it was good that we learn something while we were there'. She said she learnt 'how to cook, wash, sew, iron, everything ... we chopped firewood ... we go out and get it ... and I was in charge of the chickens and goats and we had our own milk'. It is true that such skills were important in her semi-subsistence society. It might be argued that the curriculum taught to white girls was also designed to prepare them for marriage and homemaking. However, while these were white society's expectations, a girl did not have to leave school with such a low level of education — choice was involved. Before the war, a girl on the mission had little choice about her life. An old woman said that only two girls left with the help of the church: 'They went to New Guinea and became nuns. My eldest sister became a nun ... second from Torres Strait to go.' Even so, the nuns on Hammond Island were loath to see any girl denied the basic education they taught. By the late 1930s, these women had saved enough money from their own meagre allowances to build a small corrugated-iron school house on the island so that girls who might otherwise have had to leave school to help in the gardens were more likely to be able to attend classes.

Within a decade the number of people on the mission grew from a handful of boys to 130.[4] Francis Durante remembered the building of the mission as 'very struggle days'. Nonetheless, as Father Doyle had hoped, the mission gradually provided a better environment for his flock. But he could never have visualised in 1929 that the work of the church on Hammond Island would fall victim to a war. Even prior to Australia's declaration of war against Japan, the Hammond Island people's lives were being affected by the military build-up in their area. In late 1940 most of the men were employed on the construction of the airstrip on Nurupai, for which they received, for the first time, 'white man's wages'.[5] On these wages frugal families were able to build up savings but Father Flynn, the new resident priest, saw a down-side to this new affluence: 'At present my biggest problem is that too much money is spent on drink.' However, two months later when Australia was on the brink of the worst period in its history, he was faced with a much bigger problem: the evacuation and relocation on the mainland of all of the women, children and aged on the mission.

'It was really hard to leave'

The one-page daily newspaper published on Thursday Island carried very brief articles on the progress of the European war, while current southern papers with long reports and pictures, widely read by white mainlanders, were unlikely to fall into the hands of the Hammond Island women. Father Flynn operated the only radio on the island and passed news of the war on to the people. However, what was happening in Europe and the aggressive actions of the Japanese in China in the early 1940s were difficult for them to comprehend. Father Flynn commented to his Superior that there was plenty of talk about Japan among the people but that their notions of what the war was about were vague. From early 1941, when the Hammond Island men began working on military projects on Thursday Island and Nurupai, they had opportunities to interact with white soldiers. Father Flynn also allowed them to visit the mission. In talking with the outsiders, the men were in a position to gain a somewhat more acute awareness of the war's progress. For the nuns, and the women with big families of five to twelve children, however, their busy lives allowed little time to contemplate the war; in the words of one of the nuns: 'I don't think we [women] fully realised the danger we were in.'

Mounting tensions in Torres Strait caused the Hammond Island men to become concerned for the safety of their women and children. One man told his wife: 'If they come around for you to sign a paper to go, sign it.' But, when they were ordered to leave, 'the women resisted the authorities with all their might ... saying they would never leave', an old nun recalled. Francis Durante remembered that his wife 'didn't want to leave ... They just force them to go. The army came over and start to gather you up.' The old people were worried. They feared that if they died on the mainland they would not be buried with those loved ones who had gone before. One old woman made her son promise that if she died there he would bring her back for burial: 'She died during the war and I cannot go back ... I say [to the authorities], "When can I take her back?" They say, "About three years". I dig her up and take her back after the war.' Some old people attempted to hide in the bush. Married women with families found it hard to leave their homes, their possessions and their animals. However, they were given little time to think about it: 'It was all of a sudden ... we got word today and leave the island tomorrow and leave everything behind and just take what we can carry, our suitcases ... We were sad.' The daughter in a family of nine boys and three girls remembered: 'It was really hard to leave, leaving everything behind. I remember seeing all our animals run wild, pigs, fowls and duck ... We had a day to walk out and leave all our beautiful linen and beautiful china.' There was confusion: 'We don't know what was happening, something bad ... something just hit all of a sudden.' Like the TI women, going to the mainland was a totally new experience for them: 'We didn't go to the mainland. I had never been there before the war. None of the women [had].'

Despite the urgency of the situation, the evacuees' departure from Thursday Island was delayed. The harbour master had been hopeful that the evacuees would sail from Port Kennedy almost immediately on an American ship. His hopes were soon dashed. An old nun recalled: 'The American boat was supposed to come in at 6 pm but the harbour master came and he was irate and he could not get over that they would not take the half-castes.' Meanwhile, twenty-three adults and seventy-one children were fed and accommodated on the convent verandah on Thursday Island while they waited for the SS *Ormiston* to dock.[6] When they finally boarded the ship, the men could only watch and wonder about the future:

> Oh, we feel upset when they leave. The guards stand at the end of the jetty with a bayonet, you take your wife that far and the guard let them through the barricade and you stay behind. You cannot go on the boat. We never knew if we would see them again. We write letters but they were all censored.

The poignancy of the departure was etched on the memory of a nun who sailed with the women:

> The scene I remember best was the actual departure of the *Ormiston* from TI jetty. Mothers and children on board the *Ormiston*, the fathers standing on the jetty as we pulled out. All, both men and women, were in tears. They made no effort to hide their tears, they couldn't. These families from both Thursday Island and Hammond Island had never before been separated from one another. Some would never meet again.

This was true for the old parents of one woman. They chose to return to Edgor where they had lived, without the company of other families, for about thirty years. It was where the woman had given birth to several of her many children with only her husband's help. She died in 1945 and her husband in 1947.

The ship, designed to carry 200 passengers, carried in all 459 evacuees away from Thursday Island. The island women were scheduled to disembark at Brisbane.[7] One evacuee recalled they were 'put down steerage' and that only a few 'coloured' families were given cabins. They thought the white women had been 'favoured' with better cabins on the upper decks. One woman remembered how she and her four children, a sister-in-law and two other children occupied a small cabin and that the sister-in-law's baby girl died during the night. Whether she died of heat exhaustion or because someone had rolled on her, the woman was not sure. Those without cabins huddled together in corners and hallways with their few possessions. They tried to comfort the children. The nuns were in charge of a number of orphan girls but they assisted mothers with big families by bedding down as many children as possible in their own cabins.

Strict rules were imposed: they were to keep quiet, not smoke, and no lights were allowed to burn. They heard that a submarine was following the boat and everyone was frightened. The weather worsened. The order was to keep all portholes closed but, below the deck, it was stifling and many were seasick. Too sick to eat the ship's food, they survived on Sao biscuits. The nuns remembered that when the heat became unbearable the women opened the portholes slightly: 'Big seas arose and water came into the cabins. The stewards were angry — it meant pulling up the carpets.' Finally, Father Flynn complained to the captain about the women's accommodation, but it was not until the TI families disembarked at Cairns that the situation eased somewhat.

On to Cooyar

Father Flynn's intention was to keep the group together once they reached the mainland. However, the suddenness with which the evacuation had been carried out had allowed him no time to find suitable accommodation. He sought O'Leary's assistance. By the time the ship arrived in Brisbane, O'Leary had located an old, vacant and delicensed hotel for rent at Cooyar, a small town on the Darling Downs. The women were offered no alternative: 'We were from the mission so we had to go to Cooyar.' The old hotel was certainly not constructed to house 100 people but Father Flynn was desperate and agreed to lease it.

Cooyar, about 209 kilometres from Brisbane at the end of the northwest rail line out from Toowoomba, was a very small town in 1942. It lies in a valley between the Blackbutt and Cooyar Ranges, part of the Great Dividing Range. Through the town run two ambling creeks, which turn into raging torrents when heavy rains fall on the range. The buildings of the town clustered between the two creeks: a bank, baker and butcher shops, two stores, a police station, a hotel, a school, two churches, a few houses and the old disused Royal Mail hotel in which the evacuees took up residence. The industries which supported the town were dairying and logging. A retired local and his wife recalled that, in the late 1920s and into the 1930s, there were a lot of dairy farms in the area. Anyone could make a living on the smallest farm if they had property with good grass and a separator; the factory bought any quantity of cream. At that time, about sixty bullock and horse teams brought timber into Cooyar each week. The logging industry reached its zenith between 1934 and 1940 when it supported two mills and there were three hotels in the town. Fourteen motor trucks were contracted to cart logs into the railway yard.

When the evacuees arrived in 1942, it was a much sleepier town, with only one mill operating and one hotel open. The Royal Mail had served as a boarding house for loggers and travellers from very early in the century. Later it had been converted to a hotel. It fell into disrepair after some years of no occupancy but its proposed demolition was deferred when Father Flynn negotiated a lease of it.

The children's excitement on the train journey to Cooyar was recalled by a nun:

> [They] had never seen a train before and in their excitement lost all sense of fear. We spent our time up and down the carriages endeavouring to save heads and limbs. They couldn't see the danger of leaning out of the carriages — not just arms but the whole body from the waist up was extended as far as possible.

But the women remained sad. The Pacific War had forced them to leave their island homes for a rural destination far from the sea.

On the evacuees' first night in Cooyar, the local Catholic women prepared supper and left a good supply of foodstuffs in the kitchen. These women had little or no knowledge of the culture of the Hammond Island women. An old resident remembered a reference being made in a geography class to Thursday Island but admitted that he really knew nothing about Torres Strait. Not surprisingly, the common misconception that Torres Strait Islanders were 'like Aborigines' manifested itself on that first night. One evacuee explained: 'I think when we first got there they were frightened or something. They thought we were like Aborigines and we eat snake. The white ladies who got our tea said, "We couldn't get any snake", and some of our women were mad.' In their ignorance, the local women had touched upon the painful issue of the Torres Strait Islanders' loss of identity. Nonetheless, with the passing of time, the locals proved to be generous and friendly. But, at dawn on the morning after their arrival, the unfamiliarity of their new surroundings became all too clear: 'There was nothing to see, no sea. The kids too, they missed the sea.'

Finding accommodation for his flock was not an end to Father Flynn's dilemmas. Now he was a priest without a parish. At its inception in 1884, the Sacred Heart mission on Thursday Island came under the administration of the Vicariate Apostolic of Papua but, because of its remoteness to that diocese and because it was on the shipping route to Darwin, in 1938 its operation was transferred to the diocese of Darwin.[8] With the evacuation of Darwin in 1941, Father Flynn was left without a bishop. The war had turned his world upside down, something the Father Provincial in Sydney, to whom he subsequently became subject, recognised: 'Yours is an unusual position ... in days gone by you little thought you would [be] a pastor of a wandering flock, with an hotel for a home.'[9]

Nevertheless, the Father Provincial pledged his support for the idea of keeping the Hammond Islanders together as a mission. The dilemma then became how to find enough money to support such a venture. As priest-in-charge of a mission, he would have access to the child endowment for each child as well as some government support for them and allotments for the few orphan boys in his care. Moreover, he could expect contributions from each family with a breadwinner and money from masses. His basic outlays were for rent, council and sanitary rates, food for 100 people and clothing for some. While being aware that he would have to work on a slim budget, his belief that God was on his side finally overrode any doubts he had about the economic viability of his vision. During the ensuing months, the old Royal Mail hotel took on a new character: 'They made it like a mission, like a convent', was how one old woman described it.

With 100 people in residence, the workload for every woman was heavy. They were responsible for their allotted rooms, they cared for their children and they worked in the kitchen, dining room and laundry. A few young women obtained domestic employment for short periods outside the mission, but generally they were needed to help their mothers with the endless tasks in the hotel. In the early days, the cooking for 100 people was done on 'a little fuel stove no more than 36" x 24",' and all water was carted by the bigger boys from the creek. The nuns rapidly organised schooling in the hotel for fifty children, ranging in age from eight to fifteen years. Initially, they had no teaching materials and aids. The situation on the island had been too desperate to think about such things and a request to the Department of Education for second-hand books and some furniture was rejected. Later, the old butcher shop next to the hotel was converted into a schoolroom.

A nun remembered how quickly the women resigned themselves to life at Cooyar, made the most of it and constantly found something to laugh at. Nonetheless, they also lived in the hope that the war would soon end and they would be able to return home. An old nun said that it was when they sang 'TI, My Beautiful Home' that you knew they were really homesick. When the day's chores were done, they sat on the hotel verandah overlooking the little town and embroidered or they went fishing in the creek. Like all Torres Strait Islander women they loved fish, but, 'Yuk', the freshwater jewfish and eel they caught were not at all palatable. For the first time they tasted the stone fruits which were in abundance in the area: cherries, apricots, peaches, nectarines, plums. These were more to their taste.

Another recollection of a nun was that the women, whose only experience of motor transport had been cars, trucks and boats in very small numbers, adjusted quite quickly to their 'totally new and fast-moving lifestyle ... They used the motor train, visited large shopping complexes ... In Toowoomba they coped with crowds, traffic, trains and bustling highways.' If anyone was seriously ill they were sent to the hospital in Toowoomba. On Hammond Island, the women had had their babies in their homes with their own midwives. An old woman talked about that:

> She delivered the baby and she is like [a] nurse for the mother, she cooks for the mother, bath for baby, stays for week until mother well enough now to handle herself. [The mother] has it in her own house. [The midwife] comes back home and she goes and checks the mother. If there's a problem they have to go to TI.

Old women remembered their midwives as 'very good' at the job. They delivered the babies without the aid of any modern medicine; if the mother was in long and heavy labour, the only relief she was offered was a 'sip of brandy — it helped the mother off to sleep'. They received no monetary reward: 'No, it was all done free — only gifts. She received material and they just give it to her.' A new and more comfortable, although awesome, experience for the evacuee women was having their babies in sterile labour wards at the

Toowoomba hospital. Here, however, the women were sometimes subjected to the sort of racist attitudes they did not experience in Cooyar: 'It was awful in the ward with all those white women. Some were very nice, [but] when we went to sit on the verandah, some of them got up and walked away.'

With so much to be done around the hotel, Father Flynn made a request to his Superior for a Brother to be sent to Cooyar. Brother Carter had been appointed the trades instructor to the boys on the Hammond Island mission in 1937 when the government gave the church the grant to set up the industrial school. His trade skills had been invaluable in the development of that mission. His appointment to Cooyar was welcomed by Father Flynn not only because of his trade skills, which were desperately needed around the mission property, but because the priest regarded the older boys as 'a bit of a problem'. They needed constant supervision, he thought, and this was another job he allotted to Brother Carter. Father Flynn suggested that he had tried to get the boys jobs around Cooyar but this, it seemed, had been difficult. Why this was so when there were drastic labour shortages in the rural sector was not made clear. Mothers may have opposed the idea of their young sons being sent away from the mission to live on farms with total strangers. When some of the men arrived at Cooyar after being released from work with the CCC on Thursday Island, the bigger boys did accompany their fathers on work such as peanut-harvesting at Kingaroy. There was, however, plenty of unpaid work around the mission for those a bit younger. They chopped wood, cut grass and tended the vegetable gardens. One of Brother Carter's innovations was a pump to bring water up from the creek to a tank near the hotel, which meant the boys no longer had to cart the many buckets of water needed every day. They were rostered to pump it in the morning while the girls did it in the evening. After the winter rains there was plenty of water and the gardens produced an abundance of vegetables, a big saving on the budget.

By the end of the first year, the young women were confident enough about their new surroundings to stage a financially successful dance in the town. Father Flynn was impressed when £50 was cleared for the night. In the past, it seemed, Catholic dances in

Cooyar had not been so well supported. The tradespeople, Catholic and non-Catholic, proved to be generous. They made donations of food and fuel, even though their generosity was exercised at some cost to themselves because, as an old Cooyar man remarked, 'nobody had much money then'. There was one incident where the people's concern for the women and children almost cost the life of a farmer and his son while delivering a load of wood to the mission. The creeks were in flood but, because the farmer thought the wood was urgently needed, he drove his horses into the creek to get into the town and the cart tipped over.

Father Flynn, in the belief that he could keep the people together for the duration of the war, acquired a motorised means of transport by manipulating a Melbourne priest to divert the £5 donated by his concerned parishioners to transport a piano to Cooyar towards the cost of a truck. The concern of people farther afield and the local Cooyar people assisted the priest to balance his slender budget. Brother Carter set up a chapel in the hotel. As a consequence, the evacuees rarely worshipped with local Catholics, although occasionally the baptism of one of their babies in the hotel chapel brought the town and mission people together. Occasionally, too, some of the evacuees were taken to Nanango for mass.

The school children spent their free hours down by the creek, sliding on their bottoms from the top of the bank down into the water. One resident recalled that this was where they were most visible to the town people. Because they did not attend the state school, they had few opportunities to become friendly with the local children, although occasionally the two groups competed on the mission's sports ground developed by Brother Carter. A few young boys, while roaming around the town, formed friendships with locals. An old Cooyar resident especially remembered a boy called Jackie who found a friend in a local railway employee named Norman. Norman jibed the boy by calling him 'Jackie Combo' after a black boxer. The lad responded by calling the man 'Norman Combo'. Naming in this way was not foreign to Hammond Island children. The names stuck and the old resident recalled that the boy often wandered down to the railway yard to see his friend.

The younger children walked about the town and down by the creeks with their mothers and it was then that brief communications between the adults and the local people might occur. A Cooyar woman recalled: 'That was really all I saw of them. The women and girls, they would go for a walk down the creek or up the other side ... When we went into town they were there ... but we didn't get to know them much.' Another recollection was that 'if you walked down the street you might meet half-a-dozen women taking kids for a walk and you talk, but no long conversations, just recognise them ... they seemed to do a lot of walking'. The wife of the local butcher employed a girl for two weeks to help her with the children but she admitted she was 'busy and didn't have much to do with them. My husband had more to do with them.' He employed some of the lads in his butcher shop from time to time. Farm people, too, said they were always busy and had few opportunities to socialise with the women. One evacuee recalled her friendship with a couple of the local families and said she even attended a party held in one of their homes. She agreed that this sort of interaction was not common, and anyway 'you had to have the priest's consent to visit'. She and another girl had worked for a while as domestics at the convent in Nanango where there was a shortage of local girls after they took jobs to help the war effort. Living away from the mission had helped her to make other friends. Nonetheless, for most of the evacuee women, she said, they only 'had the company of one another'.

Unlike in Murgon where the TI people were subjected to racist comments, there was no suggestion this was so in Cooyar. An old resident said it may have been because of the history of black–white relations in his town: 'Years before us there must have been black people here. We find stone axes and Aboriginal tools.' However, in the 1920s, there were only four or five Aboriginal families in the town and a few Aboriginal men from Westbrook rehabilitation centre working as stockmen on Cooyar station, the only cattle property in the area. Sometimes, he said, Aboriginal people passed through the district in about January to meet up with one another and go to the Bunya Mountains to collect nuts. Others came through to go to the Nanango forest to get wood for their boomerangs. He expressed how he remembered feeling about the Aborigines in the town:

> [They] got jobs all round. It was not unusual for the dark people to marry whites. We played with the black kids. We liked them. Those Williams' were just as good as us. I don't think as far as I can gather that there was any discrimination. They got work and they were good workers. They were good horsemen. Black and white worked side by side and there was no trouble ... They went to the dances and pictures.

Another oldtimer said the Aborigines were respected and trusted: 'We kids were left with Combo, a black Aboriginal. Mum and Granny would go to meetings and Combo would look after us. There was never any trouble. There were black men camping across the creek from us and we never had any trouble.' A decade later, he recalled, fewer Aboriginal people were seen about the town. Once Cooyar station was sold and cut up, stockmen were not needed in the district. Aborigines did not work on logging, and the work on the small dairy farms was done by members of the generally large families who owned the properties. Moreover, the government was rounding up Aboriginal people and putting them on settlements like Cherbourg. Some gravitated there to their own people, particularly during the 1930s, the depression years. He could remember only the occasional black man amongst the many white stockmen on the road, collecting the dole at one town and moving on as they had to do. No longer were there 'black kids' at the school. From these perspectives, the Aboriginal presence in and around Cooyar in the decades before the war does not seem to have been a contentious issue.

Another local perspective on why the people of Cooyar were so accepting of the evacuees was that many changes were taking place around the town in 1942. The young men were enlisting, Australian and American military camps were being set up in the bush, and 'lots and lots of army vehicles, tanks, whatever' were being off-loaded at the rail terminal to be driven north. Thus, the arrival of the evacuees could be seen as just another change due to the war; everyone 'knew the Japanese were coming in, and they had to bring [the evacuees] from the island ... it helped people to be more sympathetic or willing to share'. These attitudes were demonstrated in what old Cooyar residents remembered about their initial reactions to the arrival of the women and children: 'They seemed to come overnight — we just accepted it'; 'They just came in there and they were accepted, just like you move into next door and we talk to you ... Nobody seemed to have anything against them.' Friendly exchanges occurred in the town: 'If they came along and said, "Good day", we would say it back. They were very friendly, the Islanders. They would say, "Good day" ... You would see them at the post office or in the street and they would say, "Hello".'

An old resident of Nanango, however, made it clear that there were negative attitudes towards Aboriginal people amongst people living in his town, not far from Cooyar. Country people in an isolated town like Cooyar, he suggested, might have been tolerant but in nearby Nanango, 'a city for those going north ... where you would get a different type of people ... who thought they were someone', there was racist talk. He recalled the mildest language used to refer to Aborigines by the white men he worked with on the roads was that they were 'black bastards ... to most people ... they have no recognition of them being human beings. They think of them as being closer to the apes.' He expressed his interpretation of black–white relations in his poetry:

> Who is he who seeks my friendship,
> Asking me but for a sign,
> But my heart is cold, unmoving,
> For his skin is not as mine.[10]

From what the evacuees said, such a negative attitude was not met with in Cooyar.

By early 1943, with the physical, spiritual and educational needs of the women and children being met on the hotel premises, Father Flynn was satisfied that the group would stay together. He brushed aside signs that it might not.

'They wanted to be free of the mission'

A nun, while telling her story, conceded that the memories which stood out for her were 'the best side of the experience'. However, it would be naive to suggest that there was no friction in the hotel even though the women gave no details of the problems raised in

Father Flynn's correspondence with his Superior. Perhaps their most vivid memories were also of the positive side of their experience. Initially, Father Flynn suggested that the women's crowded circumstances in the hotel were conducive to disharmony. Nonetheless, he indicated he was confident that things would settle down. Whatever rumblings there were amongst the women, he suggested, were brought about by the few who would complain no matter what was done for them and he was prepared to live with that. Even when the first family left the mission in May 1942, he saw no reason for concern. At the end of July when another group left, he said it was because of an upset over his outspokenness about the conduct of one young woman. He attributed the exodus to a strong clan spirit: when the mother decided to go, the daughters-in-law conformed. Whether this was the case is conjectural. Two evacuees remembered that Father Flynn had been freer with the young women than was proper. But, in a letter to his Superior, the priest said he refused to let this little episode shake his faith in the work of the hotel mission; he was sure God was in control. He expressed to his Superior, in ethnocentric and paternalistic terms, his view of the situation:

> The remainder will stick I think. I suppose I will always have my troubles as the half-caste is rather a problem. When it is all said and done, even if only a few lead really good lives, our work will be not in vain. Like the poor, the sinner will always be with us and we must be patient and kind with them, but at times it is hard. Even among the consecrated of the Lord, there are sinners, so I suppose we must make allowances for these people who are only a couple of generations removed from barbarianism.[11]

Expressions of this nature were still not uncommon in white Australian society in the early 1940s, although such a strong written statement from a man of God to his Superior may have raised some eyebrows even fifty years ago. Indeed, his attitude and behaviour towards his flock seem to have eventually sealed his fate at Cooyar. His successor, while not disclosing reasons, subsequently stated that it would have been most imprudent to allow Father Flynn to return to Cooyar, even as a relieving priest: 'If you wish for my reasons I will readily give them to you ... my wish not to have Father Flynn [return] is from a well considered judgement, from no personal antipathy, and from no criticism of his work ... he did a whale of a job.'[12]

On his arrival to take over the leadership of the Cooyar mission in April 1943, Father JM Docherty conveyed his first impressions of the people to his Superior in typically paternalistic terms: 'I liked the job from the start ... They are the easiest crowd of natives I have ever had to handle. I find them most responsive.'[13] He enthusiastically set about improving practical aspects of the work, again as a man with an eye to the cost. The chapel was upgraded, and a new bathroom, proper clotheslines for the daily loads of washing and a regulation urinal were installed. Furthermore, he fought with the local council and succeeded in having the rent and sanitary rates reduced, both worthwhile savings, he suggested. The priest was sensitive to the living conditions of the nuns; he saw them as having no comforts whatsoever and suggested that, for a few pounds, he could make their lot better. For himself, he found it impossible to live in the crowded conditions in the hotel and, again at a small cost, established himself elsewhere.

Because of his concern about the small children whose attention he could not maintain in church, he used 'half-caste talk' to keep them from fooling around, an innovative idea in an era when the emphasis was on getting children to speak English. He, like Father Flynn, found the older boys restless. At home they would have spent most of their day fishing, crabbing and hunting. At Cooyar, catching a few eels and jewfish in the creek was less exciting. Father Docherty decided to expand the garden area to two acres to increase the production of vegetables and to give the boys more work to occupy their days. Other responsibilities given to the boys were the care and milking of four cows and the running of the poultry yard. He received some support for his expansion program from the local people, who donated the fence posts. The priest was satisfied that the bigger boys now had more to interest them and that he would always know where to find them. Moreover, the produce from what had become a mixed farm greatly reduced the food bills during most of the year. There is little doubt that Father Docherty's determination to have such a well-run establishment supported his intention also to keep the evacuee families together until they could return to their island.

In December 1943, when it was suggested to Father Docherty that, because of a general shortage of Brothers, Brother Carter would be more gainfully employed elsewhere, the priest was alarmed. He could not run the hotel mission without this man. The two husbands living at the mission were in full-time jobs outside. This left only Brother Carter to supervise the two-acre farm, oversee the poultry run, effect repairs and do the carpentry. He also saw to the cutting and carting of the large amount of wood needed daily. Moreover, Father Docherty knew he could not do without Brother Carter's supervision of the bigger boys. To relocate this man might prove to be at the expense of the mission's survival. Of this, Father Docherty successfully convinced his Superior in Kensington.

Like the Thursday Islanders who had been at Cherbourg, the mission evacuees found the cold weather hard to bear. According to a local, the old hotel was located between the two creeks, where it was particularly cold: 'They got a lot of frosts there.' The women had never experienced frosts. A nun remembered that it had been a painful experience for the evacuees: 'They had warm clothes and blankets but no heating ... I never heard them complain. They asked for what they needed, then coped with the discomfort.' The first winter was so cold that Father Flynn said he was amazed some had not died of pneumonia. The second winter was no less severe and it was a particularly bad year for frosts. The women's memories of the cold were: 'It's cold there'; 'We could not stand it ... the place was really cold ... our lips split and cheeks'; 'That place was really cold.' The extreme cold was one of the reasons why some evacuees began to move away from the mission. A father who had been working on Thursday Island recalled how he was given three weeks' leave to see his son who had become sick from the cold: 'I came to Cairns ... I sent for [my family] to come to Cairns. It was too cold for Mum, too, she was very old. I brought my mum, wife, child, two single brothers and three sisters from Cooyar ... to stay in Cairns.' When the third winter came around, the continued existence of the hotel mission at Cooyar was in doubt, but for reasons other than the cold.

By May 1944, the little hotel mission was not running smoothly. Nevertheless, the priest continued to believe that the group could be kept together until they returned to Hammond Island, hopefully in the not-too-distant future. If this became impossible, he told his Superior, he hoped something could be done for them elsewhere and that the church would then achieve what it had failed to do at Cooyar. By October, however, only thirty people remained; the other families had joined their men working in towns along the coast. Father Docherty was finally faced with the demise of the mission, something both he and Father Flynn had not wanted to believe could happen. Its doors closed on 15 November 1944.

Earlier, of the first men released from work with the CCC on Thursday Island and Nurupai, three joined their families at Cooyar where they secured jobs in the district, wood-chopping and charcoal-burning. One man who later found employment as a slaughterman stayed on with his family until the mission disbanded and all the property was disposed of. Others went to coastal towns and cities where Manpower put them in jobs: 'Manpower was very strong ... you had to work so they found you work ... I join up [with the] Gas Works in Brisbane ... this is Manpower. I got good wages, I was a fireman.' They also worked in glass and can factories and for the Americans, 'splicing wire'.

Once families joined the men, the younger women, like their TI counterparts, looked for paid employment to 'help the money along' and it was again friends and relatives who assisted them to find their first jobs. In Brisbane, an evacuee said, 'I worked at a laundry ... It was run by a white lady but this coloured lady ... got me the job. She was Murray [Meriam] Islander married to a Greek man. She lived near the laundry and the lady wanted more girls and I got the job.' Later she worked for 'Mr and Mrs Penfold, you know, Penfolds Wines, as a housemaid. I stayed with them. I used to cook.' She was friendly with the young people in the family but her status remained that of a servant: 'The young boy had friends in and had parties. I was friendly and helped but I never joined in.' When she moved to Mackay she obtained a job in a cake factory, icing and creaming cakes. Her domestic training at the convent on Thursday Island, she said, enabled her to do that job. However, even though they were away from the demands and controls of the mission, the younger women had little time to socialise with whites: 'We were allowed to go to pictures and other outings ... but not often. There was work at home ... and we stayed in our own group.' For older women, their lives were dominated by domesticity and they had even fewer opportunities to widen their circle of friends: 'Generally they stayed home. It was hard for them to meet white people.'

As the war wound down, the Hammond Island men found it harder to get jobs, a fact recognised by the government in November 1944. 'In view principally of the improved war position, there does not appear to be the same avenues for employment of these men as there were in the early part of the war', an officer wrote.[14] A Hammond Island woman remembered that, when her husband left his job in Brisbane and the family moved to Mackay, he found it hard to get work. A local council report disclosed opposition to the employment of 'coloured men' by sanitary contractors, even though white men were hard to find. It seemed the average housewife viewed with intolerance the weekly visit of 'coloured' men to their homes.[15] Moreover, some employers paid 'coloured' men lower wages. The slaughterman at Cooyar recalled that this happened to him but he was philosophical about it: 'In those days it was like that. Look at the soldiers' [pay]!' In the merchant navy these men were also discriminated against by the boat owners until they were forced to pay equal wages by the union in 1943; then they were replaced by cheap Indian labour. Under Manpower, at the height of the war, there had been not only jobs but also an acceptance of these men: '[At the Gas Works] I was the only coloured man. They treated me good.' However, by the end of the war, employers were no longer under the same compulsion to employ non-white labour while increasing numbers of discharged servicemen were seeking employment. A ripple effect from this marginalised island men as a potential source of labouring work.

Nonetheless, many Hammond Island families were optimistic about a future for themselves and their children on the mainland. They thought about the job prospects back home and concluded that they would be no better there: 'On the island you got no job there ... or I join up [on the luggers]. I [am] paid £3 10s a month. No good!'

Both the men and the younger women were willing to take whatever jobs they could get on the mainland. Moreover, there was a growing attractiveness about getting away from the constraints which were part of mission life. 'I guess they wanted to be free of the mission now', one woman reminisced.

Returning home

A Hammond Island woman who, with her mother and eleven brothers and sisters, had been evacuated in January 1942 recalled that, after leaving Cooyar,

> we made our home in Mackay. We had our brothers working for the army and sending money for us ... Some of us went out to work and my brother went droving cattle and it was a help and another two sisters [were] out working. Most of us [had] work. The youngest brother and sister ... [were] going to school. Most of them had a small income.

She married before the end of the war and subsequently returned to her island home. Other members of her family, however, decided to stay on the mainland:

> My mother didn't want to come back. We already bought a house there in Mackay. All the boys and girls were out working. We saved the money. You didn't waste money. She had daughters down there married and the boys married. We had word to say we had nothing, only poles standing up, back home. My mother was a widow and she was old and the life was down there and everything there now.

The father in another family got a job in the railways as a fettler and was supplied with a house. Along with better jobs and housing, their children could attend state schools. Here they received the same education as white children, instead of the low standard maintained even by the nuns: 'On the island just everybody knew coloureds didn't go past grade four.' Jobs, housing and a higher standard of education for their children on the mainland added up to a better life for the majority of Hammond Island families. For a few, and for almost all of the TI families, the desire to go home was stronger. But what was in store for all of the returnees they could not have realistically foreseen.

Camilla Sabatino and her husband Hislo and children were the first to arrive back on Hammond Island, in July 1947. Almost six years had elapsed. Camilla had one child when she was evacuated. She returned with four and pregnant with another. Her recollections best tell the story of that return:

> We were walking up the path, we could see nothing. We can see pig tracks, wild pigs ... Mr Killoran [postwar Local Protector, later Director] brought us over [from Thursday Island] ... I start to clean up and I was carrying with another, and in September I had another one. Mr Killoran was shocked when he [saw] the place. You could not see the school, it was full of wild passion-fruit vine. It was all covered and all the roof and we cleaned up that place, the presbytery and the convent and the dirt in the convent. We had to carry water, we had no hose or tap. The well was down bottom [of the hill] and we carried it up. We carried two buckets on sticks [across our shoulders]. The boys were only five and seven and had to carry water. We made the convent fit enough to sleep with blankets on the floor ... All the mess the army made, they didn't clean up ... There was not one house in the village, everything was down. There was no house at all. We expected to come back to our houses.

Mary Durante and her family were the last to leave the old hotel at Cooyar. They stayed on until all remaining property was removed or auctioned. Mary's return home with her husband Francis and their six children was via Palm Island. O'Leary had come to Cooyar and told them, 'We send you all to Palm Island now'. Francis replied, 'What for? I didn't do anything wrong.' He knew Palm Island as the place where Aborigines were sent when they were in trouble. On Palm Island he worked for the Catholic church doing carpentry. Later he was sent to the leper colony at Fantome Island to build a church and presbytery. When he finally finished his work on Palm Island, he asked O'Leary: 'What you going to do with me now?' This man was not a 'ward' of the Department of Native Affairs but, because he had been the first boy to go to Hammond Island and had witnessed the growth of the mission with the support of the Department, his acceptance of O'Leary's paternalism is understandable. The family's next move was home. Father McDermott, who had been involved with the Hammond Island mission from its inception and knew Francis well, had requested this family's return. But, like Camilla and Hislo, they were saddened by what they saw:

> All the houses just about all gone that belong to the people but presbytery and church still standing ... lieutenant, sergeant and all them take our stuff ... About 200 over here, American and Australian [troops] ... We had six horses ... and they said no, they shifted them to Badu. Looked for the milking cow, she was a bit wild. Everything had gone ... It was five or six years before it got established again.

The rebuilding of homes and the replacement of household goods were at the people's expense: 'We never got a penny [compensation] ... They said it was a mission and we couldn't get anything.' The daughter of a former midwife said her mother had received many gifts for her services before the war and was very saddened by the loss of these treasured possessions: 'My mother had a wardrobe full of material not used, lovely bedspreads, everyone had their own bedspreads with beautiful designs and we packed it away behind the wardrobe. We had to start again to get things.' The returning TI families had also to start again. A woman who returned to her home on Nurupai said: 'When we came back it was all flattened. The army destroyed everything, our little boat, filled our well up with all sorts of rubbish. Everybody had to dig their own well ... it sort of wasn't the same.' Some returnees received war damages while others were told their property was too old to be worth anything. All the evacuees had left with sad hearts and they returned to have their hearts saddened again by the scenes of devastation on their islands.

Despite the heartbreak, the few families who returned to Hammond Island faced stoically the task of rebuilding the mission.

Sidney Williams huts were purchased from the army and served as their new homes. The sturdy frames of two huts were used to reinforce the structure of the beautiful stone church which stands in a commanding position on a hill overlooking Aplin Pass. However, the evacuation in 1942 foreshadowed the end of an era for these Torres Strait Islander women. With so many new experiences behind them, their lives and the lives of those who remained on the mainland could never be quite the same again.

Chapter 5

'Leave the Islanders where they are'

For those on the outer islands of the Torres Strait, evacuation played no part in their experiences of the Pacific War. Vulnerability alone, it seemed, did not determine who would be evacuated. In early 1942 the women and children on these islands were left beyond the front line of Australia's defence, with no fixed defences and their able-bodied men in the army on Thursday Island. They were deserted by the whites upon whom they had been made reliant.

Evacuation policies

Plans for the evacuation of white children and non-essential citizens from vulnerable zones around Australia were formulated by the six Australian states well before Japan's attack on Pearl Harbour on 7 December 1941 and Labor Prime Minister John Curtin's announcement that the nation was at war with Japan. A general policy was that removals would be from areas at potential risk of aerial and naval attack or where invasion might be anticipated. Towns and cities along Queensland's northern coastline came within these guidelines. Nonetheless, in August 1941, EM Hanlon, Queensland's Secretary for Home Affairs and Health, suggested that the evacuation of coastal towns would be 'tantamount to complete surrender to the enemy'.[1] Once war with Japan was declared, Curtin reiterated this policy. But, in a matter of weeks, Australia was faced with imminent invasion and the states moved quickly to formulate plans to meet their own anticipated evacuation needs.

New South Wales, which had fully supported the national policy and was opposed to mass evacuations, bent under public pressure in late December 1941 and made plans for the removal from the coast of 100,000 school children and adults.[2] In the same month, Victoria raised its figure from 90,000 to 300,000 removals from vulnerable areas.[3] In Western Australia some Perth children were relocated to safer zones. Farther north, the Geraldton high school was evacuated inland. At the southern-most extremity of the nation, fear of attack or invasion prompted the voluntary evacuation of children from one primary school in Hobart.

In early 1942, Queensland's coastline was highly vulnerable. A central evacuation committee had been established in Brisbane in February 1941. Evacuation and accommodation committees were set up in cities and towns along the coast. However, mass evacuation posed a severe problem in this state as 80 per cent of its population lived along the coast. Thus, government reaction in January 1942 was to declare compulsory evacuations would be carried out in grave emergencies only. It did, however, close schools in all coastal towns and cities and inland north from Townsville. Nonetheless, local authorities along the northern coast were urging voluntary evacuations. The government virtually placed the people's safety in their own hands. Simultaneously, there were Indigenous women and children across the north of Australia for whom no official evacuation orders were made, even though they were potentially in as much danger as those who came under evacuation orders for Darwin, Broome and Thursday Island.

With Japan's entry into the war, the fear of an imminent attack on Darwin was heightened. Evacuation plans were made as early as June 1940 and, in December 1941, compulsory evacuations of the women and children were carried out. The first evacuation ship, the *Koolinda*, sailed from Darwin harbour, via Torres Strait, on 19 December 1941. By 15 February 1942, four days before the first bombing of Darwin, a further five evacuation ships had sailed and by 13 July the number of evacuees who had left by ship, plane, train and road convoy totalled 4,274.⁴ Both non-Aboriginal and 'half-caste' women who were reluctant to leave Darwin were told that they were being evacuated 'for their own protection'. However, 'full-blood' Aboriginal women, without white husbands to press for the right to be evacuated, were told to go bush or to labour camps. In *Australia's Pearl Harbour*, Lockwood succinctly described the government's position: 'Official gallantry had decreed Women and Children First, but not black women and children.'⁵

The tiny picturesque pearling town of Broome on Western Australia's far northwest coast had become a staging point for supplies from Perth to the American-British-Dutch-Australian command forces in Java. When the allied resistance there was on the verge of collapse in February 1942, Broome provided a stop-over haven for an estimated 8,000 refugees. Sometimes there were fifty flying boats refuelling simultaneously in the harbour. After the first bombing of Darwin, it was realised that Broome's involvement in the refugee operation had put it at risk also. On 27 February 1942, sixty-three white women and sixty children embarked for Fremantle on the SS *Koolinda*.⁶ The remaining white women and children left a few days later on American aircraft. Within two weeks, on 3 March, the Japanese made a vicious aerial attack on the fifteen flying boats lying in the harbour packed with refugees about to leave Roebuck Bay for Perth.

While discrimination was undoubtedly an element in the formulation of policies on the compulsory evacuations of Darwin and Broome, there were white women and children as well as mixed-race women and children in other remote parts of Australia's north who, although they were ordered to leave and wanted to get out, were left to their own devices to do so. One such group comprised seventy-seven white women and children from missions along the Arnhem Land coast. They looked to the military to assist them but were told the army had slender means at its disposal in early 1942, with most of the Second AIF troops overseas. A request for naval assistance was met with the reply that there were higher priorities than theirs. Moreover, only light aircraft with minimal passenger capacity could operate in these areas and airstrips were frequently unserviceable at that time of year because of heavy rain. The small mission lugger was their only hope. Finally, with the assurance of some fuel from a RAAF refuelling base on Groote Eylandt, the party set out on its nightmare trek of 6,500 kilometres to safety by mission lugger, a police officer's truck, a mission car and a derelict car resurrected from a rubbish-tip.[7]

There are other stories, recorded and unrecorded, of the determination and stoicism of people from isolated communities across Australia's northern coastline. Perhaps the most memorable recorded story is that of the epic journey of ninety-six 'part-Aboriginal' children, under the leadership of Margaret Sommerville and the Reverend Leonard Kentish, from the Croker Island Methodist mission northeast of Darwin, by foot, in trucks, on horseback, in canoes, on trains and in lorries to Adelaide and on to Sydney. Seventeen children returned to the Wyndham school on 10 February 1942. What happened to them and their families after a Japanese raid on 3 March 1942 has still not apparently been disclosed.[8] For many black women and their children, the bush was to be their only protection.[9]

The situation which existed across the north of Australia in late 1941 and early 1942 was extremely desperate and prompted government action to evacuate certain women and children from both Darwin and Broome. However, what was for the protection of white and 'half-caste' women and children in these towns was not applicable to their Aboriginal counterparts. And this, too, was the case when the evacuation order was finally made for 'whites and coloureds' in the Torres Strait bottleneck. For the Torres Strait Islander women and children living on even remoter island communities, although directly under the path of enemy aircraft and with no certainty of immunity from a Japanese landing for almost two years, no order was made for their removal. Can the Commonwealth government's order to evacuate only those women who were not under the Act be seen as other than discriminatory, particularly in the light of evidence which indicated that some military men wanted the women and children evacuated from outer

Torres Strait? Perhaps their situation may have been different if the final decision had not been left to the Director of Native Affairs in Brisbane.

The Director's decision

Until mid-March 1942, about 3,000 Torres Strait Islander women, children and aged, living on remote island communities in what was, by then, a war zone, awaited a government decision about where they would spend the war years. Military personnel on Thursday Island did not discount the possibility of an invasion of Australia via Torres Strait, in which event, they suggested, Torres Strait Islanders might be used as a labour force by the Japanese. After discreet talks with the island councillors, the army intelligence officer on Thursday Island was satisfied that these men would welcome an evacuation of their women, children and aged people. Moreover, he saw such a move as practical and advisable. It was subsequently suggested to the Director that the people be moved south where they could work in primary industries for the war effort. The Director's reply was: 'Leave the Islanders where they are.'[10]

His reason was not made clear but subsequently he indicated that a large pool of labour would be needed in Torres Strait after the war to re-establish the marine industry, a lucrative enterprise for both the government and private enterprise. By not evacuating the women and children, he may have believed he was ensuring this outcome. The men would return to where their families were but, if evacuated, many may have chosen to stay on the mainland rather than return to live under the Director's control. Whatever his reasons were, in early 1942 his decision meant that outer island women and children were to be left in the same unique position vis-à-vis Australia's front line of defence as the 'full-blood' Aboriginal women and children on Melville and Bathurst Islands adjacent to Darwin. On all of these islands there were Indigenous Australian women and children who were nearer to the advancing Japanese forces than their defenders stationed at Australia's northernmost fixed defences. To leave these women and children in such potentially dangerous locations must be seen as blatant disregard for their lives at a time when the worst wartime scenarios were being considered: the bombing and invasion of Australian soil or even a surrender of the Far North to the enemy.

Unlike some groups across the north who evacuated themselves, this was not a viable alternative for these Torres Strait Islander women and children. There were no airstrips on the islands and a lift of the number of people in Torres Strait by seaplanes or ships would have been impossible without a government order. It appears, however, that they could have effected their own evacuation. 'It was wartime. We could go if we wanted to', an old Ugar man recalled. The irony was that it took a war to move the government to allow them to leave the islands. In such circumstances, however, their only means of transport would have been by sail-powered luggers and, even though the men's seamanship was unquestionable, out on the open sea there would have been the constant danger of detection by enemy airmen. Moreover, naval resources were being stretched to the limit and there was little chance that a ship would have been made available to escort their craft, a procedure deemed necessary for all civilian shipping along the northeastern seaboard. In any event, an escort ship would have given no guarantee against submarine attack, subsequent proof of which was the attack on the MV *Malaita* just outside Port Moresby on 14 August 1942 while it was being escorted by the HMAS *Arunta*. Seven days prior to that event, the same submarine had sunk the MV *Mamuta*, 200 kilometres northeast of Thursday Island, with the loss of over 100 evacuees fleeing from Port Moresby in the wake of the enemy's advance.[11]

There were other factors which militated against self-evacuation. In the early months of the year, cyclones and angry seas are prevalent. Overloading of sailing vessels also would have put the people at risk on such a long sea journey. And where were they to get enough seamen to man the boats? Until Nurupai was bombed on 14 March 1942, many able-bodied men were on luggers and cutters, working away from their home islands. Over 100 had already enlisted and were serving on Thursday Island.

And, once further extensive recruitment of the men began in early 1942, the outer islands became bereft of nearly all of their seamen. In April, all seacraft in Torres Strait came under military control.

The women knew nothing of the world beyond their own islands, so it is unlikely that they would have contemplated leaving without the men, particularly if no government agency was involved. Some may have had relatives on the mainland with whom they could have stayed, for instance any of their women who had married alien seamen and acquired exemption under the Act to leave their communities. For most, this would not have been the case. Moreover, the people's history of relations with whites suggests that they would have been nervous about fitting into a dominantly white society. Also, an incident recalled by a Meriam woman raises some doubt about what would have become of them if they had self-evacuated in large numbers. By December 1942, submarines had been sighted off Mer and the people heard bombs exploding out to sea. Everyone was very frightened. It was then that the only two women to get away were persuaded to leave by a relative in the army. Their cousin, an 'intelligence officer' on the army boat *Reliance* which had come to Mer, obtained permission for them to travel to Thursday Island. They continued on to Cairns on a vessel carrying evacuees from Timor. On arrival in Cairns, their presence was reported to the Director. He ordered them to go to Cherbourg Aboriginal reserve where many of the evacuated TI families had already been taken. Fortunately, the three women had a male relative who was not afraid to tell the Director that the women would not be leaving. The women were not destitute, so why was he so anxious to get them out of Cairns? Perhaps he was still sensitive to the hostile reaction there to the earlier arrival of the 'coloured' women and children. Nonetheless, while these Meriam women got away, it is doubtful that any other 'back door' of escape for the rest of the women, children and old people left on the outer island communities would have presented itself if the enemy had advanced through Torres Strait.

In hindsight it is easy to say that such a strategy would not have been used by the enemy. But, in early 1942, no one knew what

Japan's intentions were towards Australia. Her rapid and ruthless southward advance left military strategists with no absolute answers and the chances of defeating the enemy along Australia's northern coastline were very slim indeed. Harold Thornell, missionary and wartime coast watcher at Yirrkala, wrote:

> Whatever politicians have subsequently said, the north of Australia was to be abandoned in a mood of near panic. Coded messages the coast watchers were receiving hinted that invasion was considered inevitable. And indeed, in the circumstances, no doubt the north would have been beyond defending, no matter how willing anyone may have been to try.[12]

War historian Paul Hasluck recorded a similar assessment of the situation in the north:

> At this time there were marked differences in the experience of war between various parts of Australia. Northern Queensland, the Northern Territory, and Western Australia had an experience of the crisis different from that of the rest of the continent. They were the areas nearest to the advancing enemy and, despite any policy of resisting the Japanese wherever he attacked, they knew that they were in fact practically defenceless. For the people of Southern Queensland, New South Wales and Victoria, talk of invasion meant a fight with some prospect of success. People in the more remote parts of Australia knew that, though they would fight, they would be certain to be overwhelmed.[13]

These subsequent assessments were in line with military thinking at the time. The concept of a 'Brisbane line', which was the allotment of the bulk of the land forces to defend the main areas of industry and population from Brisbane south, was never officially sanctioned by the government. Nonetheless, Australia's 'crippling' defence limitations forced the Australian Chiefs of Staff to adopt an initial plan based on the most effective deployment of the troops then available, which meant that the remote areas of northern Australia for the time being would be inadequately or, in some places, totally undefended. The situation, it was hoped, would be rectified as soon as the 6th and 7th Divisions of the AIF returned from overseas and American forces arrived. Thus, it cannot be contested that in 1942 these Torres Strait Islander women, children and aged were left in a highly vulnerable area of Australia. However, the Commonwealth government did not see fit to override the Director's decision.

War historian David Horner has suggested that, by mid-March 1942, there was an 'air of panic or desperation' on the mainland.[14] Perhaps the Torres Strait Islander women's initial reaction to their circumstances was less traumatic. They had no realistic understanding of modern mechanised warfare. They probably could not have conceived that it threatened their continued existence as a unique group of people. Their small communities could not have survived ruthless bombardments. One old man who lived on Hammond Island at the time of the First World War remembered seeing German warships passing through the Prince of Wales Channel north of that island. Their presence, he said, generated fear amongst the people and they fled into the bush: 'We saw a lot of warships ... which made everyone frightened so everyone fled the villages and went into the bushes.'[15] Even so, none of the people on Hammond Island from 1914 to 1918 had reason to fear the Germans to the extent to which the outer island people would come to fear what the Japanese machines of war could do to them. In the beginning, however, those fears were clouded by what they termed their 'innocence': 'We didn't know what this war was about, only that people were being killed'; 'We don't know what the enemy is like, only that he comes to destroy our life.'

The women's fears were heightened after the bombing of Nurupai and their men's subsequent rapid recruitment and relocation on Thursday Island, which may just as well have been a million miles away as far as the women were concerned. Moreover, their desertion by the Director's staff and the white priests left them without those who had controlled their lives for four decades. What else could the men conclude but that the women would have to get through the war by themselves: 'They leave the women, nobody to protect them, only old men and wives and children left ... They don't worry about us when white people are gone.' The men had good reason to worry: 'We were too far from our wives. Everybody left. How they going to get out? No ammunition, nothing!'

Deserted and abandoned

Graphic pictorial reporting of the European war brought home to all white Australians the stark realities of modern warfare. Apart from such reporting in newspapers and magazines, cinema news bulletins captured the suffering of people in other parts of the war-torn world. The cinema was a great attraction for Torres Strait Islander seamen when they were on the mainland and Thursday Island, so they too were exposed to moving images on a large screen depicting the horrors of modern warfare. Their women at home were isolated from all media reporting and they gained their impressions of the war second-hand through stories the seamen told.

However, when Nurupai was bombed, modern technological warfare was no longer something they just heard about. Within a range of forty kilometres, on the nearby islands of Badu and Moa, the bombing was visible and audible, and vibrations from bomb blasts were felt on Nagi. For about two years, both allied and enemy planes were visible phenomena in the skies over Torres Strait. The people saw dogfights between these planes, and Yam Island was strafed. Allied warships passed close to some islands on their way to and from New Guinea. The women on the Top-Western Islands heard about mines: 'Yeah, when the army boys came back to Saibai they talked about all kinds of things and we listened ... They tell us something like a buoy, it floats on the water and it bursts if something hits it.' Submarines were reported in the deep waters of eastern Torres Strait. Here, too, the women were in the 'grandstand' of the Battle of the Coral Sea when, as a signaller described it, 'thousands' of allied planes flew over their islands for days and nights.

Torres Strait Islander women had had no preparation for this type of warfare. Nor were they prepared for their abandonment by the Department and the Church, which occurred before they had even had time to recover from the shock of the first bombing attack.

Eight days after that attack, the Local Protector's personnel were ordered to leave. WC (Wally) Curtis, manager of the Island Industries Board (the Board) at Badu, refused to follow the lead given by WT Pryor, the Board's chairman and also the Local Protector, and other government officers who left Torres Strait. Of the five European teachers on the outer islands at the beginning of 1942, only one chose to remain in the Strait, and of him an old Torres Strait Islander said: 'The white teachers walked off the job when the Japs came into the war; Charlie [WCV Turner, commonly called 'Charlie' in Torres Strait] elected to stay ... He was doing the right thing.' Another recalled: 'That's the one good man that didn't go. He spent his life for the Torres Strait.' Otherwise, the widespread perception was that: 'When Japan declared war against Australia, all our European leaders of Torres Strait ... escaped for their lives, leave us helpless. There was no word of evacuation';[16] 'The government they run away, on all islands the white teachers they all run away, frightened from dead and leave us.' The men were angry, one island man recalled: 'That's the way they treat us that way ... Like a dog, let them eat the bone. It was an act of Grace we didn't starve.'

There are outsider perspectives which support the people's feelings of desertion. The Governor of Queensland suggested, after his visit to Badu in April 1943, that for the people to 'see the white man "running away" from the Jap' had an effect on them which mainlanders would find hard to understand.[17] A signaller who arrived on Masig shortly after the evacuation of government men and white priests said: 'I believe the reason for our welcome and ready acceptance was that [the people] felt that they had been completely deserted.' It has also been suggested by a contemporary researcher that many Torres Strait Islanders were so 'disgusted' with the Local Protector for 'running out on them' that they did not want him to return after the war.[18] Even so, an island priest's contemporary view is that: 'The feeling of desertion you could not generalise.' He saw the more isolated communities like Mer as less affected than Badu where there had been greater interaction with whites. Nonetheless, the Director's stand in 1946 was that it was the government that was most concerned for the people and fed them during the war years.[19] But his claim does not negate the recollections of feelings of abandonment and helplessness expressed by many old Torres Strait Islanders today: 'We felt helpless when the white people went.' The feeling expressed by old people who had been on the Anglican mission of St Paul's in 1942 was also that they had been deserted: 'The Church just left us.'

Throughout 1942 and most of 1943, Curtis attempted to maintain some semblance of administration of the Department's affairs in the Strait under unprecedented circumstances. In this he was helped by RW Stephenson who made visits to Badu until he joined up in mid-1942. To add to the problem of a drastic lack of staff in the Board's store, transport around the Strait and from southern ports became increasingly chaotic so that irregular shipments of inadequate store supplies were commonplace. In those early months of the war, O'Leary conceded that Curtis and Stephenson had accepted an enormous responsibility. He also suggested that, in their desperation, the people on the outer islands had had no alternative but to throw themselves on this depleted Badu administration. That would have been difficult to do during 1942 and well into 1943.

The Protector's vessel, QGV *Melbidir*, was withdrawn to a safer anchorage on Palm Island a week after the bombing of Nurupai. Curtis, on Badu, was then without a vessel to visit other islands, which meant that he was unable to administer effectively the Board's business beyond Badu. Indeed, the women on all islands were frequently without even the most basic store supplies. Colonel HR Langford, commander of the Torres Strait Force, made food available on occasions from army supplies. The people's luggers and cutters were impressed by the army, and they were ordered to beach their dinghies. All movement around the Strait was severely restricted and totally controlled by Langford. An Erub man recalled that 'nobody was allowed to sail across to Mer, Ugar, Masig, TI ... If you want to go, like you are sick, you must get the war boat to come and get permission to be picked up and taken in.' There is little doubt that the remnant of the administration which the Torres Strait Islanders believed had abandoned them proved hopelessly inadequate to give more than minimal support to the women. After the worst was over and in an about-face, O'Leary conceded this when he stated that, because of a breakdown in the transport system, 'the

Islanders were on many occasions deprived of even adequate food supplies ... until towards the end of 1943'. Moreover, he recognised the fearful situation in which the women and children had been left: 'Torres Strait was under enemy fire and continuous enemy air activity and the Islanders were on the verge of panic.'[20] Thus, by his own admission, there was little support for his prior notion that the people had thrown themselves upon the Badu administration during 1942 and 1943.

Dire circumstances pertained in the Strait for up to two years, during which time most of the women, children and old people were remote from the Department's one-man operation on Badu. Torres Strait was declared a military zone and priorities were geared to maintaining the effectiveness of that status; civilian needs were not the army's first priority. Thus, it was not difficult for the women to conclude that 'everybody had left' and that they had to 'do it themselves'.

'We were innocent'

The women and old people's feelings of desertion and abandonment were compounded by their lack of a realistic perception of the world beyond Torres Strait, a world which had burst in on them with hitherto unknown fury, and because they had no understanding of modern warfare at all. They had been drawn into a war being waged between societies whose ideologies and technology were incomprehensible to them: 'We were innocent. We don't know what's going on in the outside world', an old Saibai man explained. Another man put it this way: 'We are still learning before the war. We don't know anything about these things.' And if this is how the men felt, how much more keenly innocent of these things must the women have been.

From their own oral historians, Torres Strait Islanders knew about the wars which had gone on for generations between the different islands and between their peoples and the tribes from the southern coast of New Guinea. On Boigu the people have a constant reminder of the wars of their forefathers in the form of a very old and revered fig tree called *dhani* or the Tree of Spy. From high up in this tree, the first coast watchers in Torres Strait kept a look out for their worst enemy, the 'Tuger' (Thuger), a tribe of people who lived at Tuger in the Moorehead River area near the West Irian border with New Guinea. Another reminder of those wars is the Tree of Skulls. After successful battles with the Tuger, the warriors returned with the heads of their enemies. A most-loved sister would be given a head which she hung on a branch of the tree.[21] However brutal and bloodthirsty these wars may seem to the outsider today, bows and arrows were the only weapons used until about 1887 when the fierce Saibai warriors met for the last time in battle with their dreaded enemies, the Tuger.

Just prior to that war, the government had entrusted a gun to the Saibai leaders, Alis (of the cassowary clan) and Anau (of the wild yam clan). That gun was used against the Tuger who, being totally unfamiliar with firepower, were too afraid to attack the village of Saibai again.[22] The old man Aniba from Saibai who told this story to Margaret Lawrie in 1967 would have been no more than a young boy at the time of that war, so he probably learnt these things from his father or other elders in the community. Ugari Nona, who lived on Badu in 1942, was a young woman of about twenty-four when she resided on her home island, Saibai, in 1887. She was born when the custom was to wear a nose ring, a custom predating the London Missionary Society's arrival in Torres Strait in 1871. She is reputed to have been about 105 when she died in 1968. Ugari Nona and Aniba may have been the only persons in Torres Strait in 1942 who had a living but dim memory of the last war with the Tuger when one gun gave the Saibai warriors their victory. From 1942 until 1945, both Aniba and Ugari experienced a war 'different altogether' from the traditional wars of their people.

It is difficult to gauge the degree of understanding Torres Strait Islander women had in early 1942 about whether the modern enemy was more formidable and merciless than the dreaded Tuger in the 'before-time'. They knew the stories of inter-island wars and the wars with the Tuger. They were feats belonging to the oral history of the Torres Strait Islanders: 'They know the war, you know, civil war ... between Papua New Guinea and Torres Strait Islands, and that was with bow and arrows.' The Saibai woman who said this also indicated that the people knew these wars were 'scary' but that their enemies then had 'nothing like planes' and, of course, nothing like warships and submarines. Such destructive aerial and naval technology were absolutely new phenomena.

Modern warfare too was no respecter of the traditional ways of life which the Torres Strait Islanders had maintained, despite the 'civilising' influences which had been imposed upon them. For generations they had taught their children to read the sky as a white person reads a calendar or a clock. An old man explained: 'I can tell you very straight, before-time they don't know what this is [pointing to the watch on his wrist], they are living by the stars.' So, the chief said to his son:

> 'Go and find out the position of the star *Waisu* the younger of two *Meur wer* constellation.' The son told his father the position of the star the next morning and the father said that it was not yet time to rain. One morning, the son told the father the position of the star and the father said, 'Go and plant your crops now as it will soon rain'. The son did as he was told, and several days later heavy rain fell.[23]

They taught their children to respect the moods of the sea: 'Ailanman never growl the sea or anything. Not say anything bad about the sea when you're on it. Because the sea we treat like a polite thing like you say, not criticism.'[24] Getano Lui Senior, an old Torres Strait Islander leader, explained the spiritual and historical meaning his people placed on the sea: 'Our spirits live in our seas and our people sailed them in our war canoes, our trading canoes and our fishing canoes.' Seamanship was 'the test of [the] young men's manhood', and the seas were their highways. He spoke out about these things in the early 1970s when the Australia–New Guinea border issue was being debated: 'We came from the sea; our history and culture is tied up with it. Even winds, tides, currents, the air, the cays and reefs are part of our culture.'[25]

When the LMS missionaries and the pearlers introduced a monetary economy and it became imperative for many men to participate in the capitalist enterprise built on the marine industry in

Torres Strait, their relationship with the sea did not change: 'We have always grown our children from the sea and the sea-beds, and they have continued to work in the sea.'[26] But, in 1942, outsiders came in planes, warships and submarines and the Torres Strait Islanders' sky and sea space were made areas of great fear. In this environment, the women, children and aged became potential victims of the hostilities.

Chapter 6

Enlistment and the quest for freedom

> When all that was going on, it brought a lot of sadness ... they had never seen anything like that before, seeing all the men and young boys taken away ... to defend their country and their islands, their homes, their families.

For some time before the European war broke out, many Aboriginal activists hoped that, under political pressure from the Aborigines themselves, the Commonwealth government would change its stand on their citizenship status. In 1939, after realising this was not going to happen, the Australian Aborigines League, in anticipation of a call upon Aboriginal men to enlist, took the stand that there would be no enlistment without citizenship.[1] Nevertheless, by the end of 1939, at least twenty-two Indigenous men had enlisted in the Second AIF. Three Torres Strait Islanders who were not under the Act — Charles Mene, Ted Loban and Victor Blanco — were among these early recruits. However, Robert Hall suggests that it was because of a policy vacuum on non-European enlistment that these men were accepted for enlistment in that early period of the war.

Senior military officers were certainly formulating racist enlistment policies by early 1940 without investigating whether

Indigenous servicemen were accepted by their white counterparts. No account was taken of the experience of other countries, such as New Zealand where Maoris were enlisted freely. The military simply maintained, apparently as an axiomatic truth, that to force white and black soldiers to live in close proximity would result in racial difficulties and affect the men's performance. Moreover, it was deemed neither necessary nor desirable to draw Indigenous men into the army. While the war remained in Europe and the Middle East and Australia was not directly threatened, it was relatively easy to adopt such an ethnocentric approach. Thus, on 5 May 1940, the army entrenched its discriminatory policy in Military Regulation 177:

> Every person before his enlistment in the Military Forces will be medically examined, and no person is to be enlisted voluntarily unless he is substantially of European origin or descent and reaches the standards of medical fitness, age, height, chest measurement, eyesight and teeth authorised by the Military Board.[2]

Less than a year later, the army was forced to recant on its opposition to the enlistment of Australia's first inhabitants.

Inferior conditions of service

Despite the military's racist mindset, in early 1940 the Local Protector and the Bishop of Carpentaria had discussed with a visiting army officer the possibility of enlisting Meriam men. These men had withdrawn their labour from the company boats after the 1936 maritime strike and were without employment.[3] However, the Director indicated that enlistments from one community only might result in dissatisfaction amongst the men on other communities. Thus, on 17 January 1941, in the hope of freeing a company of the white 49 Battalion for service elsewhere, authorisation was given to raise a company of Torres Strait Islanders from all islands for service on Thursday Island.[4] By this act, the army's prior opposition to the recruitment of black men was negated. However, from the outset, their conditions of service set them apart from their white counterparts. For instance, a private's rate of pay was £3 10s a month, less than half of the £8 a month paid to a white soldier of that rank.[5] Discriminatory policies, it seems, were not necessarily the military's original intention. It was the Director who suggested that the island men's pay should remain in line with what they received in civil employment.[6] The army negotiators were certainly not opposed to this saving, even though they knew that to pay the men at this lower rate was illegal and 'serious repercussions might follow'.[7]

Not only were the island men paid at this lower rate but no allowance was made for their dependants and the Director did not press for equal treatment with white servicemen's families. In April 1941, this injustice was discussed in military circles. It was noted that, although the Torres Strait Islanders were 'the least known of the world's civilised natives', they had made 'extraordinary progress' under colonisation.[8] This degree of 'civilisation', it was further suggested, indicated that there should be some provision for the men's families. Nonetheless, a ridiculous counterclaim that some women were in 'paid employment' militated against the making of a firm policy, even though mainland wives of servicemen were eligible for allotments while employed.[9] In any event, the final decision rested with the Director. His advice was that the army follow the arrangement in force for men employed on boats away from their islands, which was that each man made an allotment of £1 or £1 10s for his dependants out of his monthly pay.[10] This was not only discrimination against the men but also the women. As will become apparent, the Director's decision drastically affected their monetary viability.

Recruitment

Recruitments on the outer islands began on 9 June 1941. Captain JH Cadzow and Lieutenants S West-Newman and HN Hockings, three white Thursday Island identities known to the island men, were commissioned as the company's officers. In total, sixty-one men were enlisted out of an anticipated 113.[11] The Local Protector suggested that, although it had been an inappropriate time to recruit because many eligible men were away on the boats, the opportunity to volunteer had been enthusiastically received, except on Saibai where, he said, enlistment was not favoured. Military officers put another interpretation on the result: the men were dissatisfied with the pay offered, especially when they knew that 'coloured' men serving in the AIF were receiving more. With further recruitments until October 1941, the total number of enlistments rose to 106.[12]

In December 1941, the question of the payment of allotments to the men's dependants was raised again. The Premier of Queensland, W Forgan Smith, wrote to the Prime Minister, pointing out that the low rates of pay of the island men were inadequate for the support of immediate families, not to mention mothers and fathers or even more distant relatives. 'It was characteristic of this race that they consistently support[ed] their dependents [sic]', he pointed out. Moreover, he suggested that the payment of allotments would be an inducement for more men to enlist if it became necessary to recruit again on the outer islands.[13] Once again, the final decision was made by the Director. He reiterated his initial directive: allotments were to be taken from each soldier's pay and transmitted to the outer islands through the Protector's accounts, as was the case with the civil employment of the men. Ironically, as late as August 1942, the women on the outer island communities were not receiving these allotments and the army was requested to give the matter its urgent attention. Urgent indeed! By this time many of the women on the outer islands were experiencing severe financial hardship. As early as mid-March, the intelligence officer at Thursday Island had drawn the army's attention to the people's financial plight: 'Since evacuation most of the Islanders [seamen] have returned to their respective islands, and are now without [paid] employment of any kind ... They are, in the main, living on the child endowment or rations.'[14]

The Japanese southward advance was alarmingly rapid. Prime Minister Curtin, frustrated by the British government's seeming indifference to Australia's desperate plight in late 1941, determined to link Australia's hopes and plans with the United States of America. On 27 December 1941 he announced: 'Without any inhibitions of any kind, I make it quite clear that Australia looks to America, free of any pangs as to our traditional links or kinship with the United Kingdom.'[15] The first American troops landed on

Australian soil on 5 January 1942, and General Douglas MacArthur arrived in Melbourne on 17 March to take up his position as Commander of the South-West Pacific Forces. He subsequently assessed Australia's position:

> The immediate and imperative problem which confronted me was the defense of Australia itself. Its actual military situation had become almost desperate. Its forces were weak to an extreme, and Japanese invasion was momentarily expected. The bulk of its ground troops were in the Middle East, while the United States had only one division present, and that but partially trained. Its air force was equipped with almost obsolete planes and was lacking not only in engines and spare parts, but in personnel. Its navy had no carriers or battleships. The outlook was bleak.

MacArthur quickly expressed his opposition to the purely 'passive defense' strategy for Australia which lay behind the 'so-called Brisbane line' concept. He formulated a new strategy. His forces would move forward into eastern Papua and halt the Japanese in the Owen Stanley Range — 'to make the fight for Australia beyond its own borders'.[16]

Simultaneously, the federal Labor government passed totalitarian regulations under the National Security Act, which had been amended in 1940 to give the government just such powers. No aspect of civilian life would be left untouched by these regulations, which Curtin saw as absolutely necessary to direct the whole community towards the 'essential needs' of the war. To him, the government's objective had to be to ensure that the resources of 'manpower and woman-power be appraised and applied in the best possible way' for the benefit of the nation, now on a total-war footing. Under the national security (Manpower) Regulations, adopted on 29 January 1942, a Manpower Directorate was set up. Labour was immediately transferred from non-essential to essential industry. Not everyone agreed that Curtin's far-reaching national security regulations were necessary or appropriate but he never wavered under this opposition. While the very survival of the nation was at stake, he claimed that the Australian people, their services, and their property should not remain inviolate.[17]

After MacArthur's arrival, the overwhelming demand for troops to take his offensive offshore made it imperative to draw every able-bodied Australian male, not engaged in essential civilian work, into the services. Japan's focus was fixed on Port Moresby. Major-General Morris of the New Guinea Force foresaw that whoever held Port Moresby would control the vitally important supply line through Torres Strait.[18] Not only would this close the sea lane to allied shipping but it would also place the small outer island communities in an extremely vulnerable position. Thus, soon after the bombing of Nurupai, the intensive drive to recruit all able-bodied island men began. Consideration of the moral issue of enlistment which continued to concern some Aborigines was not a stumbling block for most Torres Strait Islander men who, although daunted by the process, saw army service as a ticket to freedom.[19]

'They took all those men'

During 1941, approximately 500 Torres Strait Islanders were in employment in the marine industry. This number was considerably reduced when the 1942 season began. About 100 men found employment on master boats which subsequently transferred their operations to southern ports. Some company boats also located their operations away from Torres Strait. Thus, with these men absent from their home islands in early 1942, further military recruitment necessitated not only visiting all of the outer islands but also locating luggers working along the coast of Queensland as far south as Mackay.

Old island men remembered how recruitment was carried out. A Purma man recalled: 'An army launch called *Reliance* was sent to advise all fishing vessels to return immediately to their nearest port and report to army officials ... *Poruma* and *Caroline* were at Dugong Island and because the southeast wind was blowing they sailed to Cooktown for shelter ... At Cooktown they were told to sail to Cairns.' There they were told they were now 'under the authority of the army. After giving them some foodstuffs, the army ordered them to sail non-stop from Cairns to TI.' After four days sailing, they arrived at Thursday Island. There they left the boat and joined the army.

The crew on a Badu lugger was also sent back to Cairns: 'We were working on the coast outside of Palm Island and up to Cooktown way ... *we were caught* [emphasis added] by the Australian Army and ordered to go to Cairns ... later we went back to the Torres Strait.'[20] The boats were intercepted 'a long way away from home ... They never saw their parents and families. They reported from the working area straight to Thursday Island.'[21] Enlistment was not a matter of choice: 'They called everyone. They said, "Anchor your boats and go into the army camp". They never asked them, "Do you want to join the army?".' The men were afraid to disobey the officer's orders:

> The boat from TI, it was looking for trochus boats ... we were in there at Portland Roads cutting our firewood, then after that we had a big dance, Aboriginal and Torres Strait mixed up ... Mr Hockings was in the launch. Mr Cadzow was captain. They came in the dinghy, pulling Mr Hockings, and went up where we're dancing, all Aboriginal and Torres Strait Islanders ... and ... said to us, 'Take the boat back to TI'.

The men felt compelled to obey: 'They had machine gun on the boat and we don't disobey, we followed Mr Hockings. We go straight to TI and we signed on the army.'

The perceptions of the Torres Strait Islanders, after almost fifty years, were that recruiting on the islands was carried out indiscriminately and in such a manner as to arouse fear, particularly amongst the women:

> The army boat came, they grabbed those boys off the boats and what's left on the islands they went around recruiting. Just grabbed anyone. More or less they don't ask, grabbed them and sorted them out on TI. If they cannot go through the doctor, they send them back to the island.

Men who 'weren't suitable to be soldiers' were recruited.[22] Hall contends that, in their haste to recruit these men, the army relaxed medical requirements — chest x-rays and blood and urine tests, standard procedures for white recruits, were not carried out and men with flat feet were accepted.[23] They took children. A Masig woman recalled: 'They pointed to the boys and said, "How old are you? You go".' A boy of eleven or twelve was taken without his father's permission. One man recalled: 'They took him, put him in the boat and said, "You got to come".' He served as a batman and 'only got pocket money, no wages like the soldiers. He had to clean the boots, 1s 6d.' A Saibai woman recalled: 'Many of the young army fellows were very young, only seventeen or eighteen and some hadn't begun to shave. Some cried for their parents as they left.' There were mothers who hid their young sons. However, as was also the case on the mainland, there were the fearless, underage boys on the islands who wanted to join up. George Mye recalled that he was one such hopeful. He was on Thursday Island in early 1942: 'I thought it was a good excuse to put on a big pair of pants and I put my age on ... the day I went down, bad luck, don't get in. The corporal was a relation, "Go back home and look after *baba* [father] and *ama* [mother]", he said.' A couple of months later, while recruiting was taking place on his island, he saw another underage boy accepted without question.

There were many recollections of white armed soldiers arriving on the islands and recruiting the men 'at gunpoint'. One man said it was not like 1941 when the men were asked if they wanted to join; in 1942 the 'sergeant fired a pistol in the middle of the street and frightened the boys to join. After the 1941 and 1942 recruit, nobody's left except school children, women and more or less older ones.' A St Paul's man, Thomas Lowah, wrote in his biography that 'officers came with escorts and with fixed bayonets and revolvers. They asked who would join up. My people did not hesitate in putting up their hands, they were more scared than willing ... thinking they may get shot by the officers.'[24] However, George Mye's recollection was that, when the recruiting party came to his island, 'the sergeant wore a pistol [but] he didn't threaten anyone. They had the gun and bayonet to protect the officers.' An Anglican priest who went to Torres Strait after the war said that no 'press gang' tactics were used to recruit the men and he thought that underage boys may have been taken because they did not know their birth dates.[25] Nevertheless, the weight of evidence in the testimonies of the people cannot be discounted; nor can the strength of their convictions, after almost fifty years, be ignored.

A Masig woman recalled:

> They took all those men and never warn them. Just take them with the gun and bayonet and uniform and all Torres Strait women ran away. They pointed the gun, 'You got to go, you got to go'. The women ran away with the kids into the bush, everybody ran, all day and night they stayed in the bush.

She said that the men 'never talked with their wives, they just signed on ... the poor women cried, they were left on the islands, some had nothing in the house'. The women on Poid were very confused:

> The sergeant came out recruiting, taking all the men and boys to go over to Badu to recruit, but when they did go over they didn't come back. The wives cried when their husbands went and didn't come back. The women didn't understand what was going to happen to them.

A Saibai woman remembered that, when the recruiters came to her island, the women ran to the old trenches which had been dug during the First World War: 'They went inside the olden day holes because they were frightened. They all sat down inside, they didn't care what was inside the holes, snakes or anything.' Perhaps the major source of their fear was that they 'didn't know anything about the war. We were like the blind leading the blind. It was a sad time.' These were the recollections of old people about how they had been treated in the unprecedented circumstances of the Pacific War. Unlike their white counterparts, island men were denied a political stake in Australia. Nonetheless, in 1942, it seems they were expected to accept the same responsibility for Australia's protection and to enlist without question.

A few of the new recruits were subsequently returned home:

> Next morning after they arrived on Thursday Island, everybody was in camp. The officer asked the sergeant, 'Which people did you pick up from the islands? Put them outside.' They lined up Ugar and Erub men, and they asked what jobs we had been doing on the islands. I was chairman. 'All right, ship him out.' He told me, 'Tomorrow the truck will pick you up, straight down to the wharf and take you back to the island. The chairman got to go back; coloured teacher, you got to go back; policeman, you go back and the manager.'

For the men who did not return, there were mixed emotions. They recalled that there had been a lot of excitement about what they might learn in the army and how that would help them get what they wanted for their families when peace was restored. By the same token, they could not divorce themselves from the knowledge that their women and children had been abandoned by the white administration. The women would have to maintain their families under circumstances of terrible fear and uncertainty, with little outside help and money. Several veterans' reflections were: 'We were too far from our wives. They are lonely, no husbands, we are sorry for them, but it can't be helped ... That was cruel to take those men and leave all those women and kids'; 'My wife was told we were in army. You have to cry because you leave your mother and your wife'; 'Out on the island they felt insecure. How could a woman mind her family without the help of her husband? She believes that most of the support comes from her husband'; 'When we were on TI we always think about our mothers, fathers, sisters. We worry about them.' All around Torres Strait there was sadness:

> When all that was going on, it brought a lot of sadness, sorrow and even brought tears to the Torres Strait Islanders' eyes on that day because they had never seen anything like that before, seeing all the men and young boys taken away from their homes

to go and defend their country and their islands, their homes, their families.[26]

These men's recollections reflected the poignancy of the women's wartime situation.

Did the men join voluntarily or were they coerced? Beckett concluded that the TSLI men were all volunteers and a strong motive for enlistment was the belief they would receive a 'better deal' after the war. Hall also believed that the men 'enlisted voluntarily', although he suggested they had 'little alternative but to serve' given that the impressment of all luggers and cutters in the Strait meant that the seamen had lost their principal means of livelihood.[27] And, as George Mye poetically expressed it, the men 'hopped in to do their share ... to keep all Australia free'. There is no hint of coercion in these interpretations. An old TSLI man saw a distinction between volunteers and those recruited. He and a mate were on Thursday Island in late 1941 when Cadzow, West-Newman and Hockings asked them if they wanted to join the army. They said they did but were told to go home and wait for the army boat to pick them up: 'When the boat went out to pick us up, we were already volunteered ... I was not a recruit. I signed on. I was a volunteer here on TI, me and my mate.' Apart from this man, why did so many people talk about the men having no choice, being told or ordered to join up? In the people's minds, was there a distinction between volunteering and being recruited? Why was there such a consensus in the interpretations about the menacing manner in which the 1942 recruitments were conducted if, as suggested, the guns were part of military procedure only?

The Torres Strait Islanders seemed to be saying two things: the men wanted to join the army, but it was the manner of recruitment that angered and even frightened them and made them feel they had no choice. The adults would have known about white men who, in the past, had come to their islands in uniforms with guns to exert authority over them. The story of Captain Bligh's arrival at Tudu in 1792 and his use of firepower against the bows and arrows of Kebisu and his men is well known amongst the old people. In 1879, when the Queensland government completed the annexation of the Torres

Strait islands, Captain Pennefather of the QGS *Pearl*, on that government's authority, visited the communities to proclaim the people's new subordinate status. At Tudu, where Bligh had fired at Kebisu, ship's guns were again fired to demonstrate the power of the new masters. An old Kaurareg woman said that, while she did not see Frank Jardine, the police magistrate at Somerset, shoot Muralag people, she heard elders say that they saw him shoot six people. Frank Jardine, who died in 1919, and his father John were notorious for their treatment of Torres Strait Islanders and Aborigines around Cape York Peninsula. The same old woman was twelve years old in 1922 when Bleakley came to Hammond Island with policemen to forcibly remove her people to Adam (later named Poid) on Moa: 'My mummy told me, "Don't cry" ... I was frightened they would shoot us.' An old Kubin man recalled that incident too: 'I was only a kid ... I hid behind my mother and grandmother. When the police took the revolver out and try to make me frightened, I had never seen that thing before.'

It is likely that the recruiting soldiers' appearance and authoritative manner in 1942 revived in the people's minds such historical instances of violence against Torres Strait Islanders. Their colonial history had left them with gleaming constellations of this violence, still reflected through the clouds of past generations. Thus, it is understandable that even the men felt intimidated despite their willingness to join the army. For the women, their fears were further justified because they had always been isolated from the outside world. Their fears of white men were great and when those men were armed and in uniform they presented an even more fearful spectacle. And, because of their ignorance about Torres Strait Islanders, the recruiters were totally insensitive to the fears which had been nourished in the people's minds by a history of adverse dealings with white men.

It might also be argued that the Torres Strait Islanders' perceptions of recruitment were influenced by another four decades of struggle for freedom. No one would argue that the old people's memories were frozen in 1942, but it is also relevant that no one suggested that they were pressured to join during the first recruitment in 1941: 'They didn't force people to go then. They asked if you would like to join ... That was recruit time but we volunteered' (again, there is a suggestion of a distinction between recruiting and volunteering). The difference in 1942 was that there was an urgency about everything. Recruits had to be found quickly. In this context, and in the context of their treatment as second-class citizens under a paternalistic administration which determined what was best for them, the Torres Strait Islander interpretations are credible. Moreover, as has been demonstrated, the Director's influence with the army was persuasive and it is reasonable to suggest that, because he harboured his own postwar plans for them, choice was not an issue in his mind. Recruitment was yet another reminder to them of their subordinate status.

Between 1941 and 1945, about 800 out of approximately 900 able-bodied Torres Strait Islander men in a population of 3,675 served in the army on Thursday Island.[28] In the early months of 1942, not all men responded: 'Some didn't turn up. They hid in the bush. They didn't understand properly'; some were dissatisfied with the amount of army pay. These men were picked up in subsequent recruiting drives which resulted in an almost clean sweep of able-bodied men from the islands. Military reports corroborate this. For example, in July 1943 on a further recruitment drive, only about ten able-bodied men were found on Mer. In September, after four recruits were picked up on that island, 'practically nil' able-bodied men remained.[29] An army medical officer described the situation on Dauan in May 1944:

> I found the island to be peopled by approximately 70 natives, consisting of women and children, with the exception of 4 adult males, two of whom were aged and decrepit, and another, the local school teacher, to be in an enfeebled state of health. I was informed that all able bodied males of the island had been removed for military duties.[30]

The absence of so many males had been the case for a long time on all communities.

It has been suggested that, even though many more males were absent from the communities during the Pacific War than when the able-bodied men worked on the luggers, the absence of this larger number of men could not be seen as 'unusual or abnormal': it was a 'regular aspect of island life'.[31] It is certainly correct to say that all communities lost large numbers of able-bodied men to the marine industry for long periods of time each year. So long, as one woman recalled, that 'we don't see them from February to December. We had our babies and our husbands don't know.' It is also true that the women were aware of the dangers which constantly beset seamen: sickness, sharks, the bends. The wives were happy when the boats returned and there was no flag flying at half-mast to indicate that a crew member had lost his life.

But the two circumstances were beyond comparison. The war brought a totally new dimension to the women's lives. The peace and serenity they had known on the islands since their traditional wars had been rendered obsolete under the influence of the pearlers, missionaries and government men from the mid-1800s was disrupted. It caused their white administrators, upon whom they had been made totally dependent, to desert them and it took their able-bodied men away to a possible fate the women could not even imagine. Many women, quite justifiably, feared that something dreadful was about to happen to them, not because the Japanese people were the fearful enemy white women believed them to be or because they understood the intentions of those in power in Japan and the strategies of the Japanese high command, but because of those visible elements of modern warfare: the planes, bombs, warships, submarines and mines. And, even though the enlisted men on Thursday Island believed they were helping to defend their families on the outer islands, this was little comfort to the women who really did not know what the men were doing there. For a few only, there were other ways of seeing the situation. One woman said that her old father had a blind faith about their safety on Badu because the 'boys were in the army'. Therefore, he refused to let his daughters evacuate into the bush with the other villagers. Some old people were afraid but thought it did not matter if they were killed because they had lived their lives. Nonetheless, the reaction to their situation, recalled by a Purma woman after so long, must have been widespread amongst the women:

> My husband left me with a baby two months old and a boy. I got real cross. We ran inside the mangroves or the bushes when the planes come. The three of us, we sat together and we would die together if we were bombed. It was an awful life.

The women had to contend with the thought that, in their undefended state and without even the comfort of their men, they and their entire families might be killed. From whatever angle, the women's situation must be viewed as worse than when the men were pearling at sea.

Army time

The enlisted Torres Strait Islanders hoped to acquire practical and interpersonal skills in the army which they believed would give them a door into the wider, white Australian society after the war. They would no longer be dependent on 'boat' and 'shore' work on their communities. This was important because they wanted the freedom to move to wherever they chose. Army life would prepare them for just that, but the men increasingly resented their inferior status, their low pay and other conditions of service. In December 1943, they went on strike because they saw it as the only way to draw attention to their grievances, just as they had in 1936. The women were removed from the men's actions but what they did had direct ramifications for them.

On Thursday Island, the enlisted men embarked upon a whole new experience; they were excited to have a 'soldiers cap'. A white digger recalled their arrival in the camp:

> I could hear the thump, thump, thump of feet in the night. I felt sorry for them because half of them didn't know where the hell they were; just marched into camp, dead of night ... didn't know whether they were going to be slaughtered or not.[32]

They fell into army routine, but not without a sense of confusion, which an old Meriam man described:

> When we join the army we don't know anything. When he gives the command, we don't know about left-hand, right-hand turn. No savvy anything from A to Z — about turn, right turn, left turn, right incline, left incline. Strange, because we no savvy anything.

Army discipline had to be learnt and the old man's recollection was: 'That was very hard. We didn't think about the army before. The army taught us discipline. Our culture, white people's culture, they are different cultures.' Another veteran explained: 'I got everything from the Second World War, discipline of life, discipline of war, discipline of living ... to examine myself and the attitude of myself. I learnt a kind of respect for people, any person black or white.' Importantly, 'we joined the army and we learnt something about Europeans'.

The men were initially formed into a labour force for the army. Later, their skills were used in special ways. Sixty former seamen worked for a time at their old trade, pearling. During the New Guinea campaign, the army needed gold-lip pearl shell and cowries to pay the Indigenous people in their own currency. An old Badu man said the Torres Strait Islander had 'everything in his head': 'I don't use a chart ... because I have got the chart in my head. I know it to Swain Reef outside Mackay ... the last reef on the Barrier Reef.' A water transport company was formed and, with their knowledge of the sea, they navigated small craft around the treacherous waters of Torres Strait, along the New Guinea coastline and into the Gulf of Carpentaria.

However, the TSLI men were also given the opportunity to gain knowledge of things previously denied them. Before the war, the Department of Native Affairs had not trusted them to do such things as 'touch the knobs on the [island] radios'. An old man also recalled that the 'government didn't let [them] use a motor in the boat before-time' because they might burn themselves. In the army they became air compressor operators, bootmakers, crane drivers, carpenters, motor transport drivers, motorcyclists, plumbers and tinsmiths, pigeon handlers, signallers, tractor drivers and winchmen.[33] An old soldier recalled: 'We trained to be soldiers, and a carpenter, and any such work which we were given to do, even to do what engineers do ... then we started to learn about patrolling and all these things.'[34] And, even though the white teachers had thought they were not reliable enough to touch the knobs on the radios, the army gave some Torres Strait Islanders the opportunity to become wireless operators, at which they proved their reliability.

They also did jobs which were not strictly 'men's work'. A Saibai woman explained that 'all house cooking was done by the women' but that the men helped when there was a *kapmauri* (feasting with food cooked in an earth oven, *kapmauri* or *amai*) or when 'the woman was sick, he would cook'. The new recruits, however, did not envisage that they would have to cook and do mess orderlies' duties for a whole lot of men. Nonetheless, the problem was overcome when they realised that everyone in the army had to do that work at some time. Likewise, western-style medical care of the sick was not exactly men's work. In traditional times, the *maidelaig*, a specially trained medicine man, treated the sick. There were also bush medicines, used by everyone. But, when their 'colonisers' arrived, health care evolved as the responsibility of the outsiders. Army time, however, gave Torres Strait Islander men practical experience in European medical practices. A Meriam man, who subsequently supported his family for thirty years from income earned as a medical worker on his island, remembered that, although he was trained in the army to 'shoot and kill the enemy', he also 'trained for the medical aid force ... We learnt about medicines, bandaging and first aid, we worked in the Thursday Island hospital.' The work horizons of many of the men broadened and they were, according to an old soldier, 'very thankful' because they 'never learnt anything about these things before'. They were anxious to learn because they would need these skills in the new order of things envisaged for after the war: a better life for their families.

Army time also strengthened the men's resolve to stand up for themselves. A Boigu man recounted how initially they 'weren't being trained to do anything ... they didn't give them ammunition, all we did was labouring work'. He plucked up courage and talked with the major who said, '"Don't worry, you can have it". They gave us gear, and no worry', he said. Another TSLI man said: 'I know nothing. We were all frightened, very frightened. It was very hard to speak English to the officers but we tried and then we got action, we were allowed to use the rifle.' Moreover, contrary to army opinion in 1940, Torres Strait Islander men did get on well with their white counterparts: 'We were glad to work with white soldiers. We learnt things from them. They treated us well. We didn't fight with them.' A white digger's impression of the TSLI men was: 'I still think they're the equal (given the right weapons and further advanced training) of *any* soldier in the world. I had nothing but respect for them; I loved them.' He remembered talking to his officers: 'They took the same oath, they could be ordered to go anywhere same as me or the others and they weren't getting the same amount of pay; they were only getting a pittance in pay. I always have thought it unfair'.[35] Among the white troops they earned a 'reputation as the best workers in the Strait'.[36] Many of their new-found friends 'sympathised' with them and, it was suggested, 'tried to radicalise them'.[37]

In late 1943, seven TSLI men went on patrol with white troops to Merauke, an area in Dutch New Guinea disputed by the Japanese. Two were wounded. Thereafter, the TSLI men were absolutely convinced that they should be treated equally with white soldiers. Moreover, the men claimed that promises about pay increases had been made to them by their white officers while serving in Merauke. They had proved they were fighting men, not just labourers. As such, they also wanted the abandonment of island laws — those which prohibited them from drinking alcohol and gambling, for which they could be punished while white soldiers went unpunished. These were the grievances which forced the island men to once again act as a cohesive group. An Erub man said that, although the three groups of Torres Strait Islanders (eastern, central and western) were in their 'own battalions', they had 'no feeling of hate' towards one another — 'no growl now'. Whatever differences they had as separate island groups were put aside. On 30 December 1943, despite warnings that they risked charges of treason and that they could be shot, the TSLI men went on a sit-down strike. Their grievances aired, they returned to work the next day.

Following the strike, there were suggestions that the men had resorted to trade unionist tactics, while 'sorcery' had been used to force the participation of any who were hesitant. And, in words which smacked of the paternalism from which they had hoped to escape by enlistment, the army concluded that, like naughty boys, they knew they had done wrong and resolved not to be blindly led again.[38] Whether or not the men had adopted trade unionist practices or 'sorcery' had been used was not the core of the matter for them. As was the case at the time of the 1936 maritime strike, they were calling attention to what they believed were legitimate grievances, one grievance in particular, pay conditions, having direct repercussions for their women.

The sit-down strike precipitated a conference in Melbourne in early 1944 of representatives of all parties except the men. Recommendations related to rates of pay, deferred pay and dependants' allowances were formulated. However, even though the army preferred all soldiers to serve under the same conditions, the new rates for the TSLI men were set below those of their white counterparts. A private's rate of pay was raised to £6 10s a month, plus deferred pay at the rate of 1s 6d per day. Dependent wives received 1s 6d per day and a first child, 1s 0d; subsequent children received 6d per day. There were proportional increases for ranks above private. The new rates were made retrospective from 1 July 1943, with the exception of deferred pay which was paid from December 1941 or from six months after the date of enlistment.[39] These rates (just as illegal as the initial rates, a fact substantiated in the law courts more than forty years later) were once again determined on the Director's advice; if the enlisted men received a greater income than they were likely to earn after the war, 'they may be spoilt from the State point of view for times of peace'.[40] This was undoubtedly a compelling reason for his rejection of the higher pay scales from the outset. The army too had a motive: the greater 'sum involved' if these men received the proper rates of pay.[41] It seemed anything could be justified when dealing with Indigenous people.

O'Leary even expressed his reservations about the increases. His concern was that the men would buy more drink or gamble the money, whereas he wanted them to be encouraged to save their money to finance his postwar aspirations for them. To placate O'Leary, the army gave certain undertakings. It would discourage large withdrawals of money from the men's accounts, treat as a serious offence the supply of liquor to them by whites, constantly check that the prohibition on gambling was enforced and educate the men to improve their knowledge of the value of money. Such undertakings placed the army in the same paternalistic relationship with the Torres Strait Islanders as the Protector had had with them for four decades.

As in the late 1930s, the TSLI men's action in 1943 did not achieve the equality they sought. Their settled rate of pay was raised from less than half to about two-thirds of that of the AIF men, and their dependants' allowances and deferred pay were also less. Prohibitions on drinking and gambling were not abolished. Nevertheless, once the women's allotments intermittently flowed through to them in late 1944, these small monetary gains gave them a somewhat improved economic viability.

With the rapid enlistment of the able-bodied men during early 1942, there was the realisation that the women, children and old people had been left with no back door of escape. They turned to face a new dilemma. How could they best protect themselves?

Chapter 7

The enemy at the front door

> Dealing with the question of civil defence, the circumstances of the present war emergency are very different from the circumstances of any previous war emergency. On previous occasions the Commonwealth has never had to contemplate the possibility of attack or the possibility of air raids. The complete immunity of the Commonwealth from attack does not now exist, and less still is there complete immunity of the Commonwealth from air raids ... accordingly there has arisen a new problem — namely, the problem of civil defence ... Particularly do these possibilities concern Queensland with its great length of sea-coast.[1]

Indeed, no previous Australian government had ever been required to organise the civil defence of this country's vast and sparsely populated territory; it was a new problem. For a long time, the focus of civil defence was concentrated on cities and big industrial towns, from Brisbane south. How people and property in these areas would have fared, however, in a Japanese attack of the force and ruthlessness with which Darwin was bombed must remain conjectural. Across the north, it was a different story. The concerted effort in civil defence coordination seen in the southern areas was certainly missing, even in towns like Darwin and Townsville. On Thursday

Island it was only when the enemy was on the doorstep that something was done to protect the civilians. On the outer island communities, ad hoc preparations for the safety of the women, children and old people were virtually left until Nurupai was bombed on 14 March 1942. Thus, the civil defence measures finally adopted on these communities, as discussed in the wider context of the civil defence plans for Australia, suggest that there was indifference on the part of the government towards these people's safety.

At the outset of the First World War (1914–18), Australians responded with great enthusiasm for overseas service. It was the war to end all wars. However, only two decades later, Australia was again at war. On 3 December 1939, the conservative Australia Party Prime Minister, Robert Menzies, in his announcement that Great Britain had declared war against Germany, stated: 'As a result, Australia is also at war.'[2] Menzies 'passionately' believed that 'British institutions and the British way of life were synonymous with civilisation'.[3] Once they were put at risk, he did not hesitate to commit this tiny off-shoot nation, sitting precariously on the Asian Pacific rim, to another war. This time, many Australians were not so convinced that the war had anything to do with them. Nonetheless, because of the possibility that Australia would be attacked, the government set the wheels in motion for the civil defence of the country.

The problem of civil defence

In March 1941, state and Commonwealth representatives met to discuss uniformity and coordination in civil defence plans. Three months later, a Commonwealth Department of Home Security was created, with JP Abbott as Minister. Even so, different policies and practices between the states evolved, such as the codes for air-raid warnings — in Queensland the warning siren gave a 'fluctuating note', while in New South Wales it was sounded by 'intermittent blasts' — and states varied in their colour codes for warnings. Abbott subsequently attempted to unify plans and practices because of the potential danger, in the event of attack, for people moving from state to state.

In the cities and larger towns with multistorey buildings, industrial areas, wharves, airports, railways, and large populations, the civil defence problems were vast and complex. The efficiency of essential civil services, such as firefighting, ambulance, police, medical care and social services, were dependent upon finding voluntary workers at a time when enlistments were drastically depleting labour resources. Female air-raid wardens were recruited for daytime duty, while middle-class women everywhere emerged from their domesticity to be trained in first aid, the emergency care of children and Red Cross work. Air-raid warning systems were installed all around the states, with an emphasis on big cities and industrial areas. Firefighting equipment was upgraded and respirators for use by civilians in the event of gas warfare were ordered. Decontamination dressing stations were set up and provision was made for the demolition of dangerous buildings. Householders were instructed through the press and by air-raid wardens in how to construct their own garden trenches or refuge rooms; trenches were dug in streets and parks and building basements were converted to shelters. Practice raids were conducted in schools and children carried earplugs and a stick to bite on. Householders were required to obey brownout regulations, and enthusiastic 'foot-slogging' wardens tried to enforce strict compliance. These were some of the measures adopted to meet the new problem of civil defence in certain areas of mainland Australia.

While the war was in Europe, life in Australia went on much as usual, with many people enjoying a new economic prosperity; there was an air of unreality about it all. Thus, after an initial enthusiastic response in 1939, many air-raid wardens came to view their duties as onerous and irrelevant. The sceptics decided that the enthusiastic wardens were being misled by government and the whole business was a political ploy. Nonetheless, those who took their duties seriously continued to conduct air-raid practices, to encourage people to gas-proof rooms in their homes and to build shelters, as well as to brownout and shatter-proof their windows. Then, in late 1941, Japan's attack on Pearl Harbour brought the war closer and forced the stepping-up of civil defence. City buildings were sandbagged against incendiary bomb blasts and windows were taped to minimise the danger of splintering glass. Street blackouts were enforced. Cars crawled about the streets at night with headlights showing only a slit of light. Trench digging was accelerated. Sand was dumped in streets and parks ready to extinguish fires. Air-raid precaution drills were conducted in cities and towns. In suburbs, the impromptu wail of sirens sent housewives and children fleeing to backyard trenches, transport ceased and streets were graveyard still.

Despite these preparations, on the eve of what was to be the realisation of that recurring nightmare — 'Oriental' aggression against Australia — and after years of fearing the worst and planning for it, there were doubts all around the country about the effectiveness of the civil defence measures. In December 1941, air-raid wardens' posts in Sydney were crying out for equipment. Two months later, trial air-raid warnings failed because no more than a quarter of the wardens attended and shelter accommodation was inadequate. In Brisbane, air-raid tests were conducted on Sundays, leading to strong criticism that the worst possible scenario, an attack on a busy city, was not being assumed. North of Brisbane, in Townsville, the chief city on the threatened North Queensland coast, there were insufficient trailer pumps for firefighting, and fire-watching posts had no telephones. Ingham, the small sugar town further north, had only twelve whistles, and the list of wardens was constantly recast and shortened because of departures from the district.

The real test of Australia's civil defence came in towns across the north and northwest of Australia. In these towns, however, less emphasis had been put on civil defence preparedness. Two warnings of raids preceded the bombing of Darwin on 19 February 1942. On the first occasion, the town was blacked out, although wardens had to break the glass in a shop window to extinguish lights left burning, and the locals complained that sirens were not loud enough. A second alert was sounded in the early hours of New Year's Day 1942, but again no raid eventuated. The people lived expectantly. On 19 February, Darwin was devastated by Japanese bombs. Ironically, the sounding of the air-raid sirens was delayed because of the slow military response to the coast watcher's report from Melville Island. A Thursday Island man who was working in Darwin at the time commented:

> We had mock battles — lights went out, there were bags of sand all round the town. The whistle goes, we take a bottle of water to the trench, and the *Northern Standard* said, 'If the Japs come to Darwin the citizens are well prepared'. So, when they did come there was no whistle, no nothing.

Moreover, the civil defence force had been drastically reduced a month before the raid because of a lack of government support and because of civilian apathy. However, despite the devastation and a loss of 243 lives, the censor's pen made sure that the rest of Australia remained ignorant of the gravity of the attack.

There were further attacks on Darwin, although the Japanese did not confine their raids to this town. Many locals believed that Broome was beyond the capacity of a Japanese strike from Timor, so the sound of approaching planes on 3 March 1942 did not alarm them. They were accustomed to the daily roar of seaplanes carrying refugees from the Dutch East Indies (Indonesia), as they arrived to refuel. When the attack commenced, the townspeople fled to their trenches until they realised that the flying boats on the bay, filled to capacity with refugees, were the targets. The scene on the water was horrific — sinking flying boats, dead bodies, and people struggling to survive in a sea of burning oil. Seventy people died; it may have been more. Japan's aircraft range had been underestimated and the town's civil defence was little more than a few ill-equipped Volunteer Defence Corps personnel with .303 rifles.[4] It remains conjectural whether better civil defence plans might have resulted in less devastation and death in these towns. However, their potential vulnerability did not appear to be high on the civil defence agenda for the nation.

Townsville's vulnerability was also not high on that agenda despite vast numbers of allied servicemen in the town, naval shipping in the harbour, and airfields and army camps in the vicinity. As late as June 1942, air-raid precautions in Townsville were described as unsatisfactory:

> There was no clearly identified person to co-ordinate civil defence measures, no one seemed to have the power to enforce the blackout regulations, the press was 'unhelpful' and the essential services of supply were both strained and vulnerable.[5]

Nevertheless, when the first four Japanese raiders appeared over the town on 25 July 1942, unlike Darwin and Broome, the town was given ample warning; wardens moved quickly to their posts and the civilians to their shelters. The blackout was regarded as effective, although one resident told a warden to put an aerodrome light off before he would extinguish his. There was also a delay in extinguishing the lights on the wharf because the watchman had to walk some distance to secure the keys to access the switch. Some civilians subsequently recalled that the potential seriousness of their situation was not fully realised: 'We weren't in our slit trenches, we was out ... excited ... watching to see.'[6] There were two further raids on Townsville by single flying boats, within the space of three days. Fortunately, however, unlike Darwin and Broome, the test of Townsville's uncertain civil defence preparedness was no more than a practice run.

The bombing of Nurupai

Within the area of the vital Torres Strait sea lane, the people were excluded altogether from official civil defence planning. In February 1942, the Japanese planned to capture Port Moresby and the southern Solomons, and 'to isolate Australia' by seizing Fiji, Samoa and New Caledonia. Thus, unbeknown to the allied Chiefs of Staff, Japan had no immediate plan to invade Australia.[7] At this point, Japan was not willing to place excessive demands upon her military resources. Nonetheless, as early as August 1939, the Australian Air Board had recognised the vulnerability of the country's thinly defended northern coastline and recommended the construction of an air base on Nurupai, a few minutes flying time from the tip of Cape York Peninsula. The airstrip was constructed and became operational in late 1941. RAAF historian Robert Piper has suggested that the

> strategic importance of Horn Island [Nurupai], near Thursday Island in the Torres Strait, quickly became apparent to the Japanese in 1942. The new aerodrome there was a vital link for Allied aircraft flying in and out of New Guinea, maritime reconnaissance and airborne attacks against those northern areas that had already fallen to the enemy.[8]

Thus, the construction of this airstrip gave the Japanese every reason to have a focus on the Torres Strait area. On 14 March 1942, Japan made its first attack on the strip.

The population of Nurupai in March 1942 comprised army and air force personnel and island men working for the Civil Construction Corps. Air-raid protection was in the hands of the military. However, unlike in Darwin and Broome, the Japanese were seen before they arrived and the allied defence was ready. The Kerema coast watchers on the south coast of New Guinea radioed to the navy on Thursday Island at 11.15 am on 14 March that seventeen unidentified bombers and fighters had been sighted minutes earlier, headed in a southeasterly direction. The alert was given and all troops were ordered to dispersal areas at 11.45 am. The raid commenced at 12.15, by which time Kittyhawk aircraft were already in the air.[9] Simultaneously, two planes carrying sixteen young members of the Citizen Military Forces, who had volunteered for coast watching service in Torres Strait, landed on Nurupai: 'We landed in the middle of the raid. They riddled the office with bullets, the toilet got a hiding — they must have thought it was a radio station. There was no hope of going back, [our] planes didn't have enough fuel.' A TSLI man's recollection of that day was:

> I was sent over to [Nurupai] to defend the post over there, me and my mate, I am number one gunner and he is number two. The Japanese come over. When they come close, right up to Nurupai and we were looking after the post, they dropped a bomb — boom, boom. We were frightened, we cried, we never

saw a bomb in our life. They fired that machine gun on top of us. They fired one way and came back. Oh, very close up to that post, the fighter. I rang to signal to shoot that thing down. They said, 'Don't shoot until you get the command'. I had the machine gun ready to knock 'em down. Bomber goes up, fighter right down. The white soldiers ran away, went outside the trench and leave us. We black boys left. They go in the bush. Me and me cobbers were in a clear space just inside the aerodrome. We had no bush, camouflage was all we got. I told them, 'Don't lose your brain'.

For some inexplicable reason, however, the eight Japanese raids on Nurupai lacked the ferocity with which Darwin and Broome were bombed and the island was spared the severest test of its defences. Thursday Island, across the channel, was left unscathed.

Prior to the evacuation of the women, children and old people, the civil population of Thursday Island was about 1,600.[10] The island had no coordinated civil defence. It lacked air-raid shelters, and no practice drills were being conducted. 'They didn't do anything until the women were evacuated and then it was a bit late', a veteran AIF man recalled. On 27 January, two days before the sailing of the first evacuation ship, the town clerk made an urgent plea for volunteer air-raid wardens. Six weeks later, the formation of seventeen planes from the Japanese base at Lae in New Guinea, on its way to and from Nurupai, passed over Thursday Island. A Torres Strait Islander seaman who was on a lugger in Port Kennedy recalled that army men yelled a warning to the crew: 'So we jumped out of the boat and swam ashore ... and we got behind the Federal hotel ... inside those drains and hid ourselves.' From their hiding place, they saw 'bombs, big smoke and bong [on Nurupai] ... we thought that was the end of it. Calm down. We got out of the holes when the army told us it's all over.'

The army's immediate concern was to assess people's reactions to the alert and the civil defence preparedness. Reports indicated that the air-raid sirens had been inefficient, giving a local effect only. This was verified by a white soldier who was on Thursday Island during the period of the earliest raids on Nurupai: 'We couldn't hear the sirens for the noise of the cordial factory next door, so after the first raid we kept an eye on the luggers and if we saw the Islanders jumping into the dinghies and rowing madly for the shore, we knew it was on.' However, there was a military perception that the 'coloured' civilians were slow to emerge from their shelters after the alert and that they were likely to be 'frightened away' in future air-raid alerts.[11] Where these men could go on such a small island is hard to imagine. From their own perspectives, the 'coloured' men gave no indication that they wanted to run anywhere. The men hiding behind the Federal hotel were fully aware of the danger but told themselves to 'calm down'. They emerged from their hiding places when the army gave the okay. Another man's response to the raid was philosophical: 'I had to run up to the shelter on the hill. When we went up they said, "Hurry". I just said, "If I have to die, I may as well die here", and we saw that first bomb blast on Nurupai.' Indeed, death might have been the fate of many if Thursday Island had been bombed. A few bombs, true to target, could have devastated this tiny island of one and one-quarter square miles. Furthermore, it would have been difficult for anyone to flee from the island, as had been the case in Darwin and Broome. There were seven further raids on Nurupai but, amazingly enough, no attempt was ever made to bomb Thursday Island.

The Japanese had every reason to bomb this militarily strategic island. Moreover, they had the capacity to do so. When the eight T96 Japanese bombers returned to Lae on 14 March, they still had bombs in the aircraft holds. An old Thursday Island man who spent the war years on the island remarked: 'There was a lot of naval ships and cargo ships. I cannot understand why they didn't bomb the ships in the harbour. It would have cut our supply line.' Several reasons have been proffered by the Torres Strait Islanders for this. It was because of the friendships which had existed between Japanese skippers and the Torres Strait Islander seamen. A former crew member on the supply boat recalled: 'There's twelve Japanese planes above us. They look hard to see bottom of the boat. They pass ... didn't take notice because we black men.' It is understandable, too, that the Japanese would not have wanted to kill any of their own nationals who they may have thought were still under guard on the island, or to destroy the hundreds of Japanese graves in the cemetery; and people still talk about the 'legend' of a Japanese princess buried on the island and that her countrymen would not have wanted to disturb her grave. Others say that the TSLI men were spared by a divine manipulation of the elements: 'It was too overcast when the Japanese wanted to come in.'

Taking their own safety measures

Torres Strait Islanders under the Act, or in the case of St Paul's under the direction of the Anglican Church, were living on eighteen communities at the outbreak of the war but virtually no civil defence was instituted for them until the enemy was at their front door. Moreover, the responsibility for their safety finally came to rest not with any government agency but with the people themselves. And, while there were commonalities in the people's testimonies about the defence strategies they adopted, such as keeping a low profile and observing blackout procedures, their safety measures were also related to the geographical features of the islands and proximity to Nurupai. Thus, experiences from all communities have been included to gain the fullest understanding of the Torres Strait Islanders' perceptions about the civil defence measures they adopted.

The enemy's advance through Torres Strait could not be ruled out. Some thought there would be advantages for the enemy in capturing Thursday Island and that they might place outpost stations on the hillier islands to prevent a surprise allied counter-attack on Thursday Island. However fanciful this notion may have seemed to some at the time and even in retrospect, members of the Military Board did not rule out the possibility that Japan might attempt to seize Thursday Island. It was widely believed that the Japanese military authorities had been familiarised with the coastline, ocean currents and landfalls around northern Australia by nationals who had worked in the marine industry.

Old Torres Strait Islanders, too, were convinced that the Japanese knew about the area. One said: 'They made their own charts when diving around Torres Strait.' Another believed that 'the Japanese knew all about the islands'. Indeed, it would not have surprised some Torres Strait Islanders if the Japanese had landed in the Strait. They recalled Japanese skippers expressing views which were sympathetic to the people's desire for liberation from their colonial yoke: 'You see this Australia ... we are going to fight Australia, we are going to take it back, the land is wasting'; 'You know we are black, you are black, we are going to chase the white man from Australia and take this for you black people.' Therefore, it might be argued that the people had nothing to fear from the Japanese and that they had no need for any civil defence measures on the islands. Even if this had been the case and the government was aware of such promises, there could have been no excuse for the total lack of civil defence planning in outer Torres Strait. The Military Board indicated as early as 1938 that, in the event of war with Japan, Thursday Island would be at risk. Finally, it was left to the army, with few men to spare, along with Curtis, the white storekeeper on Badu, and Turner, the only white teacher to remain in Torres Strait, to give what assistance they could to the women in their efforts to ensure their families' safety.

Before the first attack on Nurupai, the people on the Anglican mission of St Paul's were the only ones on the outer islands receiving civil defence instructions. In January 1942, the white priest-in-charge, the Reverend Godfrey Gilbert, instituted air-raid drills. He believed the people were being well-prepared:

> We have been busy on ARP [air-raid precautions] and are all proud of our blackout and air-raid shelters — in fact I have just come in from a practice raid warning when everything went off very well indeed. The people are taking things quite quietly and in good heart, and they seem prepared 'to take it' if the worst does come.[12]

On the communities under the Director's control, it was a different story. 'No one came to tell us what to do if there was an air raid', an old Masig man recalled. In late January 1942, the army had suggested that the white teachers should act as air-raid wardens on the larger islands of Saibai, Badu, Mabuiag, Mer and Erub and that they should instruct the people in civil defence. However, the departure of four of the five teachers in March 1942 thwarted the military's intentions. Turner was the sole remaining white teacher. An old and revered leader explained why he became so important to them during the height of the danger:

> The people liked him and he could speak the native language. They could talk in Creole ... If anybody wanted something, they have to go to somebody who knows how to speak and help them to get over their troubles, and people knew him quite well and they wanted him to speak for them.

At great risk, Turner sailed from island to island, more often than not in the totally unarmed sail-powered supply vessel, to help the people. An old Torres Strait Islander teacher indicated how dangerous sea travel was: 'You can just imagine what it is like while you are sailing there and the Japanese bombers sailing overhead.' Two Saibai women recalled that in the early days they 'didn't know anything about the war' and when the planes came '*baba* [father] Turner was there. We had pegs hanging around our necks. We don't know what to do. This is what *baba* said, "Everyone wear pegs and if anything happens, bombs fall, you bite on it".' So they wore the peg on a string around their necks, 'like a necklace'. A Masig woman also recalled that 'nobody knew what to do, but *baba* stayed all the time, he looked after us'. Curtis, despite his heavy administrative load, did what he could to encourage and assist the women on Badu. The communities were also given basic information about air-raid precautions by army personnel. The local policeman assumed the role of warden. He passed orders, which came from the military via the chairman or councillors, on to the community and saw that everyone obeyed them. With a bell, a whistle, a drum, blowing a *bu sel* (trumpet shell) or even by running through the village calling to the people, he sounded the warning when enemy planes were sighted, and he called the all-clear.

On all of the small outer island communities, the people soon realised that being as inconspicuous as possible to the enemy was the best thing to do. Like their mainland counterparts, Torres Strait Islander women complied with strict blackout rules. The bright light of the pressure lamp was banned, although a Masig woman said that her mother painted the glass of the hurricane lamp black so she could have a little bit of light as she sat huddled with her family in their tiny bush house at night. Most families had only a flickering light from a thin strip of calico fuelled from a bottle containing coconut oil. The women's recollections were that: 'We only sit there at night with that small light and we hide it so nobody can see us'; 'We had to live in the dark'; 'You even had to put that cigarette out.' During daylight hours, fires and smoke posed problems: 'We were ordered [by the army] not to make fires, not to make smoke or light a torch [of dry bark] or a lamp.' The women did a lot of their cooking over open fires, with a pot resting on 'two irons across two stones'; only sometimes in their sand ovens (*amais*). The army had banned the use of *amais* because they made too much smoke, and they were hard to camouflage and to extinguish. Cooking was done during daylight hours and 'everyone had tea before it was dark'. Nevertheless, someone was always watching for planes while the fires were burning and, at the sound or sight of them, the order was swiftly relayed to everyone: 'No fire, no smoke, nothing.' Clothes were washed early in the day, hung under the trees and removed quickly because the 'planes might think we waved at them', a woman from Mer recalled.

The army told the people they could not wear brightly coloured lavalavas and 'Mother Hubbard' dresses because 'to walk on the street or beach in bright colours, something might happen'. The storekeeper on Yam shared a roll of dark-coloured cloth amongst the women. They quickly made clothes from the 'pale brownish material ... something like canvas, really strong but it was hot'. An old Mabuiag woman laughed as she mused about the time she disobeyed the army's orders. One morning she went fishing in the red silk dress her husband had bought her in Daru for the Coming of the Light celebrations. Soon a plane approached and she 'sat in the lagoon', believing she would not be visible from the air. The plane passed and she resumed her fishing. It returned. She went under the water again. It returned a third time: 'Now he came near', she said, 'I was frightened.' Back at her bush home, she quickly washed the red dress and hung it out to dry under the trees. To her amazement, a signaller arrived to tell her father: 'They are not to wear the red dress.' Initially, the women had no idea they could be seen from the sky when they were under the water.

In another such incident, two Nagi women saw enemy planes while they were fishing in the lagoon. They dropped the nets and lines and lay on their backs in the water with only their noses protruding, thinking they would not be seen. Little did they know that it was no guarantee of their safety. In this case, perhaps, the Japanese did not wish to waste ammunition on pointless targets or they just did not want to kill Torres Strait Islanders. The St Paul's women used perhaps a more effective tactic to conceal themselves: 'When we were out fishing and the planes — twenty-five, thirty — came over, we dig a hole and lie down in the sand and cover ourselves with our dress and put sand over us.' These are examples, however, of what the people called their 'innocence'. What an airman could see on the ground from his plane was impossible for the women to imagine.

Besides blackouts, restrictions on fires, the prohibition on bright clothing and avoiding the beaches, each community took whatever other measures were appropriate for their safety. The communities on Moa, Badu, Mabuiag and Nagi were within hearing or visual distance of the bombing on Nurupai. An employee at the Dogai store on Badu remembered that, when the bombs fell, they heard the explosions and 'felt that place shake'. On Nagi, the vibrations were also felt and 'things on the wall, some things on the shelves, fell on the floor'. The people saw planes fighting in the sky and said to each other: 'This is it. We're going to die.' From Mabuiag, too, allied and enemy planes fighting in the sky between St Paul's and Nagi were seen: 'We could see them, like white birds everywhere on top, and we can see the smoke when they fired the guns.' Because of the proximity of these islands to Nurupai, the army ordered the people to evacuate into the bush. A Mabuiag woman recalled that they were told: 'Move out from here quick. Make houses in the bush. Evacuate.' On Nagi the instruction was: 'Don't stay in the village. All Islanders must go into the bush.' The women, children and old people went a long way behind the village, up the hill, and built houses with plaited mat walls and sheet iron or grass roofs. Everything was camouflaged with branches and leaves. The old people found the disruption to their lives difficult to deal with. Two Nagi women recalled what happened when the alert was given:

> Our grandmother was a short little lady and she used to run in between us. She could not keep up. Her daughter said, 'Go on, go on, keep up, quick', and we used to shove her in the bush. She said, 'Next time they come, leave me. Let that bomb fall on me.'

Eighty-year-old James Morrison on St Paul's spoke for himself and his wife: 'Take these children in the bush, and we will stay. Let the Japanese come and kill us.' No one should underestimate how hard it was for the old people.

On St Paul's, Father Gilbert's air-raid drills were abandoned. On the day of the first bombings, the policeman rang the bell and 'screamed' to everyone to move out of the village because 'war had broken out on TI'. They ran into the bush, an old woman recalled, 'far, far away' from the village. The women were confused: 'Mum, she didn't know about the war and when they said "Raid!" she thought ... like the enemy was there, and she pulled us together and tried to take things with her, everything one time. I tried to help Mum, the young ones were too small.' Everyone sat under the trees to rest. They listened, 'Hey, something up!' Then someone came running, whistling, calling, 'Let's go back ... go home, there's no war, that's lightning'. There was a lot of confusion. On another occasion the people looked up into the sky and saw two planes. They said to one another, 'What are they doing? They are playing!' They did not know that the planes were fighting until the wireless operator came and told them, 'Head into the bush. See those two planes fighting over there? That's the enemy and our plane.' Finally, a soldier came around to all of the houses and told the women to leave the village. One woman recalled: 'Mum took a sheet and put everything in it and we went into the bush. We just slept in the bush, spread a mat out. We had to collect grass and build houses, cut the wood, everything.' Another said: 'Some broke their kitchens up and took them into the bush. We had iron on our house, we pulled the iron off and made a bush house, a sort of shelter.'

Lizzie Nawia, the widow of the wartime chairman of Poid and famous in her own right as a storyteller, recounted how the people in her village were ordered by the army on two occasions to relocate in the bush:

> It's been very strong, that Second World War. We all moved into the bush. We built these bush houses, some of them grass and bark skins, some of them irons ... Terrible, we had to carry everything. Terrible time, and all the planes flew on top.

However, it was not long before

> that war became very, very strong, and they sent out a white sergeant and moved us further into the bush. We had a big river on north side of Poid. We used to live inside there, but when the sergeant came, he said, 'This is dangerous. Big river barges can come in.' He told the chairman, 'Go further in, inside the bush'.

Wherever the people were forced to live in the bush, they were instructed to disperse: 'The army told us not to make one camp, make different camps so that if anything happened they might only destroy one village and another camp would be saved.' On Badu, across the narrow sea channel from Poid, all but a handful of the women, children and old people also evacuated into the bush where they spread out in small villages, identified even today by their American names: Bar Twenty, Wild India, Arizona, Blue Mountain, Hollywood, Atlas Bay, Silver Plains, Rocky Mountains. Local names were also used, such as Malay Town, Dobbie Town and Junglewalek (*walek* meaning lizard). Almost half a century later, one woman reminisced about the physical effect evacuation had on her: 'Oh, I can feel the tiredness, me with a big bundle and my four small sons. I was really tired that time when that thing happened.'[13] Indeed, many women who were by no means old at the time and who were accustomed to hard lives described their wartime experiences as 'hard times'.

The people on the Top-Western Islands, further away from Nurupai, took different measures for their safety. On Boigu, when the siren sounded, the women quickly gathered the children together, picked up the damper they had cooked earlier in the day and a mat for the babies to lie on, and ran into the mangroves. Once there was a fire on the island and everyone thought a bomb had been dropped. The 'people ran with a peg in the mouth to the end of the cemetery — no lights, just run in the dark'. They got a fright when they ran into somebody, but they kept on running to get as far away from the village as possible. Like Boigu, Saibai is a flat, muddy island, yet there the people dug trenches, 'straight ones and ones like the letter L'. Amazingly enough, there were some trenches in the village which had survived from the First World War when there was fear the Germans might land on the island. The trenches were covered and 'emergency supplies of food, water and firewood' were kept in them so that 'when the planes came over, they could just dive inside'. Until they learnt to distinguish between allied and enemy planes, that occurred frequently. Some of the women built 'huts in the bush as a precaution'.[14] Others made grass structures in the mangroves to which they intended to go if the 'worst came to the worst'. If they were working in their gardens, they simply 'crouched down among the plants, the bananas or cassava' when planes were sighted in the hope that they would not be seen. Japanese patrols eventually pushed into areas along the coast of Papua around Merauke. Fortunately, however, they were contained there in December 1943 by allied troops, including some TSLI men, and it was never necessary for the women to evacuate into the swamps for any length of time. Nonetheless, according to one old woman, when the policeman gave the warning, 'everybody must be ready like when there's a cyclone' to move out of the village. Then, she said, 'everybody grabbed the children and grandchildren and went underground [into the trenches], into the grass or mangroves. When the planes go by and no smoke comes down [no bombs], the policeman told everybody to come back home.' An old woman who lived on the rugged island of Dauan said that, for their protection, the people 'scattered in two camps, one each end of the village'.

The small size and the geography of the coral cays necessitated, yet again, different civil defence plans. On Purma, the people spent the daylight hours scattered in the bush and returned to the village when it was dark. Stumbling around in the dark without lamps resulted in many bumped toes. The boys had to go to the well after sundown to get water and, as they 'groped' in the dark, they splashed much of the precious water out of their flour-tin buckets. Purma lies along the Great North East Channel and ships of 'all sizes and shapes' constantly used the route. In this militarily strategic location, the people frequently saw dogfights in the sky and 'everyone ran everywhere' for fear of what might happen. Thus, with the potential for enemy attack always present, the people asked each other: 'Look at us, not many trees, how are we going to exist? There's no way we can survive.'

One of the first precautions adopted on Masig was the construction of 'L' and 'T' shaped trenches at opposite ends of the island. The plan was to run to them if the *bu sel* sounded. Within about ten days after the first attack on Nurupai, two army signallers were sent to Masig. They noted that the people were 'pretty well disciplined and quite well prepared' by then for whatever might happen. It seemed that, after the bombing of Nurupai, they were so afraid that they decided not to rely on the trenches for their safety. The signaller recalled that each family had built 'a fairly basic second house in the low bush ... and this was referred to by them as the bush house'. However, unlike on Purma, the Masig people spent the nights in the bush. During daylight hours, they remained as inconspicuous as possible while they went about their business in the village. Probably neither the Masig nor the Purma Islanders realised just how vulnerable they were on their small, flat islands with low vegetation. Nevertheless, the signaller concluded that, in all of the circumstances, the Masig elders had adopted the best possible tactics, even though he had little doubt that 'a couple of good-sized bombs' would have devastated the island.

The hilly nature of Yam afforded the people better cover from enemy planes and no attempt was made to move into the bush until the island was strafed by the Japanese. Along with the bombing of Nurupai, the experience of the Yam Islanders has been incorporated into each community's oral history of the war years. The majority of the oral historians made mention of both events even though many had not had a personal experience of either. The wartime Yam Island storekeeper gave his version of the attack:

> I was in the store, the people were out there and there were the Jap planes coming across to bomb Nurupai. The people said, 'I don't know what happened. Maybe some boys on the beach were saying goodbye to the Japanese planes with red lavalavas and then they turned and machine-gunned the village.' When I came out, the village was all smoke. I was lucky. There was a big mango tree and I ran straight up to it and hid myself. Lucky it was broader than myself and I got right behind it. When it was over, nobody was in the village, everybody was in the bush. Just the older people who could not run, they stayed back.

A Masig man who had been a seaman on the supply lugger *Mulgrave*, which was discharging cargo at the time of the attack, recalled:

> We jumped out of the boat and swam ashore. So we ran up to a hiding place but there was no time to hide. We could see the bullets whiz. When the bullets hit on the rocks we saw lights, the grass was burning. We ran for our life ... So we stayed in the bush the entire morning. When we ran when the plane dived, we could see a man sitting in the Japanese plane with a gun.

Another former crew member gave his personal recollection:

> People were screaming on the beach, 'Oh, this is enemy plane'. We looked up. We saw that enemy plane. We forgot about the dinghy. We swam under the boat. When we came up we heard machine guns, and we dived down again. Everybody was running to the mangroves. We were only in our underpants and we sat amongst the women and we saw bullets cutting off mangrove branches. We picked up babies, frightened mothers had thrown them on the ground.

Immediately after the attack, some women moved their families into caves near springs of water; others built thatched huts in the bush. No one offered any other explanation for the attack than the one given by the storekeeper. Perhaps the pilot interpreted the boys' actions as 'cheeky' and wanted to teach them a lesson, although there were boys on Saibai who acted similarly without reprisal. Perhaps the people were right when they said Japanese men did not want to kill them and, in a sense, the gunner was only playing a war game with them. Nonetheless, the attack on Yam was terrifying.

When the fighting in New Guinea worsened, the people on Ugar were considered to be 'too exposed to planes and ships', and they were evacuated to Erub and St Paul's. On Erub, the people built trenches near their homes and the school, but when the possibility of landings from enemy submarines was realised, some of the women, like those on islands nearer Nurupai, 'stripped' their houses in the village and carried heavy loads of materials into the bush and built shelters there. Others trekked across the island to the opposite shoreline, because 'the enemy might walk in that village but they won't know where you are ... it was safer'. One woman whose family remained in the village recalled:

> I used to hold my grandmother's hand and she walked all the way up to the back of the island and we sat there until we got news whether it's enemy boat or Japanese boat before we went back. We did that late at night too. It was dark, we had to run in dark because the enemy might see us if we do it with a light.

Another grand-daughter remembered that her grandmother, like old people on other communities, said to her: 'Don't worry about *Ate* [grandfather] and me, you go and save yourself. Never mind about us, God will look after us. If it's our time He will take us. Because you are young, you have a lot of years ahead of you.'

Several of the Meriam people recalled their wartime leader, Marou Mimi, when they talked about how they protected themselves. He, according to one man, was 'different' from the other Torres Strait Islander chief councillors. Back in the days before the people's movements were controlled, when Marou was a young man, he left the island and worked on the mainland, cutting cane. There he 'rubbed shoulders' with the Pacific Island men but he never abandoned his own culture; he loved Torres Strait. Indeed, he was 'an authority' on the tradition of his people.[15] His experiences made him unusually confident with outsiders. Thus, when the war broke out, Marou had no difficulty liaising with military personnel and his home was always open to them. Someone remembered how he personally instructed the women living near the radio shack in the middle of the village to sleep with relatives or friends at either end of the island because the shack would be a prime target in an attack. He also told them that, in the event of a surprise raid, they must 'move fast, go out and stand in the tree and not move, stand up straight and still near the tree and never move. Let the plane go past before you come out from that tree.' Here the people did not dig trenches or evacuate for any length of time into the bush. Thick vegetation covers Gelam Hill, which rises to a height of 230 metres behind the villages, from Webok to Babud. If the alarm was sounded, the people took cover 'on that high place or in some creek or cave … We just lived in our houses and ran into the bush.' Another said: 'Sometimes we spent one night in the bush. We just took a mat and slept there.' Older sisters helped the little ones to run and hide, but the very old people had to be left behind because Gelam Hill was steep and they 'slowed the others down'. The small population on Dauar moved to Mer at the height of the danger so that 'everyone could watch after one another'.

Coast watching

The army signallers stationed on the larger Torres Strait communities during 1942 and 1943 were not only vital to Australia's defence but they also assisted the women in diverse ways, filling, to some extent, the roles formerly played by the white teachers. One signaller remembered that the people called him 'tissa Mov', meaning 'teacher Merve' (Merve being his Christian name). The Masig leaders told him the people were 'proper glad' they had come and the signaller suggested that this was because the people felt 'completely deserted' by the government. Island leader George Mye spoke very highly of them. There was general consensus amongst the people that 'the signallers helped us a lot'.

The signallers were AIF men in a newly formed Northern Command Area Signals and when things were getting really bad, as one signaller recalled, there were

> calls for coast watchers to watch the coast around Torres Strait and down the Gulf and along the east coast. The navy did not have enough personnel to do the job, the air force did not want to have anything to do with it, so a call was made to provide a number of volunteers from the CMF who weren't going overseas, but to tropical islands.

Initially, two signallers were posted on each of the communities of St Paul's, Mabuiag, Saibai, Masig, Erub and Mer. Curtis was in charge of the radio on Badu, so that another responsibility in his already heavy workload was the surveillance of that island. The signallers went out with 'very little training':

> We had to know morse code ... I had been in the scouts and knew morse code and knew compass reading and map orienting. Another signaller had been a key operator in the post office and one was a post office worker ... We went out ... on the old *Paluma* and it was a rough trip. We had to be roped to the mast on deck. V2 [radio call sign for] the official navy station was only for emergency. If it was desperate we used normal language but normally we would use code. VKP2 was the [radio call sign for the] commercial station taken over by the army and it was the call sign to the main station on Thursday Island. They gave us instructions how to code and decode messages and we had pamphlets to destroy if anybody landed ... We asked the island people to look out for anything that floated, for any information.

Although some of these men were barely twenty in 1942, they adapted to their unique wartime situation in remarkable ways.

The people left on the islands had had no training in the handling of wrecked aircraft and dead crew, but on several occasions the old men were involved in the rescue of allied airmen after their planes crashed. The Dauan men assisted the signallers after they saw a plane come down over Papua New Guinea. They went by canoe to rescue the pilot but he was dead. In another incident, an American plane crashed on the New Guinea coast. After sailing from Boigu, the men found the pilot in the mangroves. He was taken back to Boigu from where he was picked up by a naval vessel. One night the lights of a plane were seen by the people in the bush on Moa. They smothered their small lights. The plane circled the island several times and finally crash-landed on the water. At daybreak, while the women were told to remain hidden in case it was an enemy plane, Wees Nawia and the local policeman rowed out to the wreck. However, during the night, the six allied airmen had reached the mangroves from where they were eventually picked up. In instances such as these, the people were assisting the allied cause.

Neither were the Torres Strait Islanders given any instructions about the dangers of explosives. Soon after the Battle of the Coral Sea, when a lot of debris was being washed up on the central and the eastern island beaches, an old Masig man and his wife made a find; the incident was recalled by a signaller:

> Dan Mosby, his eyes weren't very good and he was the only Torres Strait Islander I saw wear sunglasses. He was a great old roamer. He roamed around Kadal. He'd take a stroll with his wife and we'd asked the people to keep their eyes open for us because we were only two and we had a rifle and twenty-five rounds of ammunition each and the enemy were coming down in droves. Danny scouted around all the time. He also liked to sit and yarn. He would say, 'Give me a yarn'. One day he came up to the house and said he wanted to yarn.
>
> 'I want to report', he said, 'I find this bomby, bomby'.
> 'Where did you find it?'
> 'Along Kadal.'
> 'Sure it's a bomby, bomby?'
> 'Yeah.'
> I was a bit alarmed. 'I hope you didn't touch it.'
> 'No', he said, 'I told that old woman belong me, you poke that bomby, bomby belong that fish spear'.

On investigation, we found it was an aluminium crate with partitions to hold anti-aircraft shells or something and it was a floatable thing, and it had washed up on Kadal. If it had been a bomby, she would have gone up all right.

The women on Ugar, located on the Great North East Channel, had excellent boat-handling skills and familiarity with the reefs and currents around their island. Thus, before their evacuation to other islands, they were recruited to work for the civilian pilot service. Prior to the Pacific War, the channel had been poorly surveyed and charted. Its use was light and irregular, but, with the Japanese southward advance, it became a busy sea lane. The dangers of navigation in Torres Strait, with its maze of reefs and treacherous currents, necessitate the pilotage of ships. The Torres Strait Pilot Service had its own launch, the *Torres*. However, independent back-up boats had been necessary to meet even peacetime shipping needs in the Strait. Thus, after the impressment of most of the small craft in Torres Strait, the service was unable to meet the wartime demand. A handful of Ugar women came to the rescue. They volunteered to assist with the task at the northern end of the channel by using the small wooden dinghies they had been ordered to beach:

> Fortuitously, a completely unofficial, but most welcome, launch service was introduced at Stephens Island [Ugar], operated by a group of Torres Strait Islander women. When a ship arrived off the island and blew its whistle, this was a signal that a pilot was to be disembarked; the women rowed out in their open boat to the waiting vessel and collected the pilot. The fee [was] £2.10.0. Usually the pilot would be returned to T.I. by *Torres* or by light aircraft, but sometimes he would wait on the island to be eventually put on board a westbound ship by the same female-crewed boat.[16]

It was an awesome task. One of the women explained: 'We did it in a rowboat. Sometime we can't pull out to the boat. All depends on the weather, if it's calm the dinghy can go closer to the boat. We were out in the sea in the war and we were frightened.' Frightened indeed! One evening as the women rowed towards their rendezvous, the ocean ahead 'boiled' and, to their absolute amazement, a totally alien object, an allied submarine, surfaced and discharged a pilot into their care.

Twenty-four-hour daily surveillance in outer Torres Strait was a vital part of the defence of Australia. However, it was an enormous task for the few signallers responsible for that operation. They recruited the local people, including women and children, to help with coast watching. Wees Nawia and his sergeant of police on Moa kept the channel between Badu and Moa under constant surveillance. If they saw anything suspicious at night, they shone a torch in the direction of Badu, and Curtis radioed Thursday Island. During daylight hours, the signal was made by using a reflective mirror. An old Meriam woman recalled: 'In the afternoon [the school boys] watched the street and some watched out for boats, and some were watching for the planes coming.' Another woman said:

> Masig to Daru, that's only half an hour in a plane and the Japanese might come. You don't know. Any time the Japanese can land. The boys would watch from points on the island to see if they were coming, even at night. Anything can happen when you are asleep.

In an incident on Mer, women, children and old men responded to an emergency which was recalled by a signaller:

> We heard a noise and we could not make out what it was. It sounded like a diesel. It woke all the island, about 300, and they came up to the house. It was very clear and distinct and it was travelling the length of the island about four to five knots and we had Islanders, both men, women and boys, stationed on the beach and they would report back to one another or send messages to each other reporting on the sound location. It went up and down the island for an hour or so. I immediately reported it in plain language to V2 and they said to us, 'If you can't see it, it's not there. You are going native.' We got mad. It had woken the whole village.

A few hours later, just before sunrise, the signallers received a report that an allied ship had been torpedoed by a Japanese submarine north of Mer. The signaller who recalled the incident was convinced that they had been plotting the same submarine off Mer.

In another incident on Mer, old men and boys took up arms in preparation to meet the enemy and to protect the women and children after an old couple reported seeing an enemy submarine:

> [They] were making a sweet potato garden ... up the hill and they saw the submarine come this side of Dauar. A Japanese man knew Mer and he brought that submarine from Dauar and it ran out of water and it floated on top [surfaced] ... The old man and woman come down to the white signallers ... they told them of the Japanese coming up there to get water and they told all the people from Webok to Babud. The people grabbed their little children, called to them swimming in the water, 'Come on, Japanese submarine'. You should see all the people, they carried water, food, billy, clothes and ran into the bush. They thought they were being attacked.

The captain of the submarine is reputed to have been Otto (Ottosun), a former skipper on a bêche-de-mer boat. He had visited the late Geedie Williams when she was in charge of the sardine factory on Dauar before the war. So, Otto, once a welcome friend, was believed to have returned as an enemy:

> All of us with mothers and grandmothers, we went into the bush and hid ourselves. The old men took tommyhawks, axes. They went and grabbed hold of American coats with the US name and wore those coats, and the old fellow, Marou, went up Gelam with the other men, and hid themselves and waited for Otto, but he goes past.

A report was made to Thursday Island and American planes were sent out:

> The planes looked around and the submarine was under the coral; that Japanese man knew to go under the shelf, to hide

there. The plane ran about looking for them, went back to TI and after that they went out to the Barrier Reef and two planes came back next day and they found them and they bombed them. We heard the boom, boom, boom, and they told the people in the village they killed Otto.

After this incident, the people became supersensitive to the presence of any foreign object in the sea:

News came from village to village, 'Japanese submarine!' All our parents took us inside the bush, and all the old people and middle-age men they were walking around the street carrying axes, knives and spears to protect the women and children. They were marching around to kill the Japanese. They cannot do anything else. We were in the bush hiding and Mum was crying, 'Keep quiet!' All our parents told us, 'Don't make any noise because Japanese might come and kill us here'. Next day they told us they found that submarine — it was only a log. Those kids were playing and threw a log in the water and the people thought it was a submarine again.

Such was the pitch of the people's fears.

Late one afternoon, a radio message was received by Maxie, one of the signallers, that an unidentified boat was nearing Ugar and coming towards Mer. He was feasting at the other end of the island, some distance from the radio shack. Wearing the blue lavalava that the women had sewn and embroidered for him, he ran to the shack and grabbed his helmet, rifle and ammunition and made for the beach. The mysterious boat dropped anchor off the island. Maxie wanted someone to row him out to it. George Mye recalled that 'little Tony Durante from Nepean Island' said that he would do it for his *baba* (father) and *ama* (mother): 'I'll row Maxie out', he said, 'I will do it for Australia too.' Tony's traditional belief in the importance of family and great respect for his elders were undoubtedly welded to his patriotism. Maxie handed George and his mate a rifle and told the people who, by this time, had assembled on the beach, 'If I fire one shot and no more, go for your bloody life. If I fire in succession five rounds, it's a friend.' In the fading light, the mysterious boat became barely discernible on the horizon as the dinghy rowed away from the shore. George, who had never handled a gun before, recalled that, while he held it pointed out to sea as some sort of protection for the two in the disappearing dinghy, he shook so much that he had to rest it on the limb of an old almond tree. He and his mate listened for Maxie's signal: 'We were scared', George said, 'we didn't know what we'd do if he fired one shot.' The night was very still, and time dragged. Then Maxie's voice rang out over the water, 'Who goes there?' The answer came across the water, 'Launch plom Daloo [Launch from Daru]'. It was subsequently reported that a Japanese submarine had sunk the refugee vessel *Mamuta* in the Gulf of Papua and the launch from Daru was looking for survivors.

Mer was also visited by a number of men in green uniforms who landed on the beach from a vessel anchored off the island. Their appearance, from a distance, was suspiciously like that of Japanese soldiers. After consultation, the elders agreed that they would make the initial contact with these men. If they were the enemy, it was less likely that they would be hostile to the island men. Once it was apparent that the visitors were not hostile, the signallers joined the group on the beach. However, the only intelligible word spoken by these men was 'Ambon' [an island in Indonesia]. The signallers concluded that the visitors were escapees from there. They left as mysteriously as they had arrived.

Unbeknown to the Eastern Islanders, they were, in one signaller's words, 'sitting in the grandstand' of the historic Battle of the Coral Sea. Japan had planned to strike Port Moresby in early May, which augured badly for Australia. Fortunately, however, the Americans broke the enemy's naval codes and a good deal more was known by the allies about Japanese dispositions and intentions than they suspected. In addition, Australian coast watchers in New Guinea and their British counterparts in the Solomon Islands, at great risk to themselves and the local people who assisted them, were 'on the job'. They had the Japanese under constant surveillance. They reported that enemy cargo and transport ships were being massed at Rabaul and that there was a tremendous military build-up in the Solomons. Port Moresby was being attacked by air. By 5 May, the Port Moresby invasion force was at sea. So too was the American task force. The American and Japanese forces were converging and it was to be only a matter of time before the planes from one sighted the ships of the other.[17] For three days, allied and Japanese planes waged war in the skies over the Coral Sea but the aircraft carriers never met in battle. There were heavy losses in ships, planes and lives on both sides but no outright victory for either. Two signallers' recollections reveal how close the Battle of the Coral Sea had been to the eastern islands of Torres Strait. One remembered:

> There must have been a thousand planes. They were just coming over like a storm over the top of Mer. We thought they were Australian. We didn't know. It was dark. We could see flashes of gunfire all night. We didn't have a clue what was happening and about a week later a giant raft, big enough for fifty men, off the US *Lexington*, was washed up on shore. But we knew at the time that it was something big.

The other said: 'Wreckage from the American aircrafts *Lexington* and *Sims* were washed ashore [on Erub]. Also, bodies of servicemen from these vessels were washed ashore. We retrieved the dog tags and forwarded them to the US authorities.'

The Meriam people had no way of knowing that, after the Battle of the Coral Sea, the tide of war was turning. In the words of a US naval rear-admiral, the 'foe's drive south had collapsed — just as a wave breaks and falls back from a towering cliff'. Japan's 'aura of invincible power' had been shattered.[18] It was to be a long time, though, before the outer Torres Strait Islander women's fears of aerial attack or invasion were assuaged. Meanwhile, the women learned to live with their fears.

Hagiga Bindoraho serving Malay food at a festival

Col Nakata in Southeast Asian national dress

Young Hammond Island women evacuees: (l to r) Grace Nicholls, Dorothy Moyden, Sylvia Sebasio, Camilla Durante (courtesy Francis Durante)

Island Industries Board store, Badu (courtsey John Oxley Library)

Former storekeeper/teacher Sam Passi and his wife Rotana

'Charlie' Turner and his wife Elsie (courtesy Vickie Turner (Johnson))

Bakoi Baud, teacher and nurse (front row, right); Geedie Williams, manager, sardine factory (front row, second left); the others are, possibly, Mrs Grainger, Mr Hargreaves, Emily Agale and Edna, on Mer (courtesy Randy Williams)

Mitsubishi 'Nell' bomber used in raids on Nurupai, displaying the 'red dot' (courtesy RK Piper)

Japan reaching for Australia (*Bulletin*, 18 March 1942)

Chapter 8

Fear and faith

> So, suddenly, a very old Australian nightmare came to life. Throughout their history Australians had been given to bouts of fear that their remote, underpopulated coastline would tempt a foreign aggressor, probably Oriental, but this terror had been kept at bay by the naval supremacy of the British Empire. After December 1941 that supremacy was no more ... The year 1942 saw the greatest crisis in the nation's history.[1]

Virtually without exception, the oral testimonies of the old Torres Strait Islanders contained references to the women's terrible fears. These were not, however, consonant with those of white Australian women whose perceptions of the Japanese were influenced by the insecurity that all white Australians, as Europeans, felt living on the Asian Pacific rim with its teeming millions of people. Moreover, government propaganda depicted the Japanese as inhuman beings. For the island people, however, the images were totally different.

'He's coming south'

During the period of late colonisation in the South Pacific, white Australians, on their lonely outpost in a profoundly alien region, were suspicious of expansionist Russia and France. There were also fears that their white, British, democratic way of life might come under threat from the Chinese, a nation of allegedly land-hungry Asiatics, the 'Yellow Peril' of media and political debate. After Japan defeated Russia, readers of such journals as the *Sydney Daily Telegraph* were warned that they were 'slumbering beside a volcano'. With this victory, Japan proved that she was a strong military and naval power.

In 1901, the Australian government had articulated its White Australia policy in immigration laws which were especially directed at and most offensive to Japan. In 1902, after signing an alliance with Japan, Britain had reduced her naval force in the Pacific, which caused concern in Australia. She certainly could not afford to build a fleet of the capacity needed to defend the nation's extensive coastline. Japan had contributed to the allied cause in the First World War but at the Paris peace conference, Billy Hughes, Australia's controversial Nationalist Party Prime Minister, 'gave not an inch' in his opposition to Japan's efforts to have the principle of racial equality incorporated in the League of Nation's Covenant, the denial of which by the white powers humiliated Japan.[2] Moreover, Australia continued throughout the 1920s to make it difficult for Japanese businessmen to enter the country. During the 1930s, while offering goodwill with one hand, Australia implemented restraints upon Japan with the other.

When Japan annexed Manchuria (and renamed it Manchukuo) in 1932, Australian–Japanese relations became uneasy. That annexation demonstrated Japan's determination to use military might to satisfy her need for territory, materials and markets. Manchurians pleaded for food and weapons and reported Japanese atrocities but the Australian government offered no assistance. It feared antagonising an already aggressive Japan and the loss of important export markets at a time of deep economic recession. JG Latham, a senior federal minister, on a goodwill tour of Asia in 1934 assured Japanese ministers that Australia desired to continue trade relations. He offered to support Japan's reinstatement as a member of the League of Nations, from which she had resigned in 1931. On his return home, Latham warned parliament that, while Asia was the 'Far East' to Europe, it was the 'Near East' to Australia and that Japan was the 'key Asian state' with respect to trade and defence in the Pacific. For these reasons, he concluded, Australia's interests would be best served by doing everything possible to prevent war in the East. Moreover, it was contended that, if Japan succeeded in her continental policy in Manchukuo, this could encourage further territorial expansion. If she failed she would be even more determined to attempt to solve her population, market and raw material problems by occupation of islands in the Pacific and, eventually, northern Australia.

An Australian trade commissioner was appointed to Tokyo in 1935 but, almost immediately, the Commonwealth parliament introduced a trade diversionary policy which gave preference to imports from Britain over those from Japan. Thus, despite Latham's warning, 'at one blow, the Australian government ... offended both the largest trading nation and the largest military power in the Pacific'.[3] There were subsequent moves by the Australian government to appease Japan economically while simultaneously implementing diplomatic restraints on her. Australia made a proposal at the 1937 Imperial Conference for a non-aggression pact in the Pacific which would include the United States of America and Japan but be independent of the League of Nations. The conference left resolution of the proposal to the British government which allowed the matter to lapse, probably because it was aware of Japanese hostility to the proposal. By this time, too, England was preoccupied with events in Europe. In the same year, Japan launched a major assault against China which, in the eyes of many Australians, brought Japanese aggression closer to home and fanned fears about that country's intentions.

Politicians and military strategists were fully aware in the late 1930s that Australia would have to rely on the British navy for her defence. For that reason, at the 1937 conference, Britain had been urged to improve her relations with Japan to guard against the possibility of being faced simultaneously with hostility from Germany, Italy and Japan. Subsequent to that conference, the First Lord of the British Admiralty stated that 'Australia should not be concerned — there was Singapore' with its fleet of British ships.[4] His optimism was short-lived. Within five years that protection was no longer viable. The great and supposedly impregnable British naval base at Singapore fell to the Japanese on 15 February 1942, only four days before the first air raid on Australian soil.

There was a widespread belief on the mainland that Australians were living alongside a nation of people who had none of the refinements of modern civilisation. And, even after the tide of war had begun to turn away from Australia, the government kept this image before the Australian public. War production had to be maintained at full capacity and war loans filled. The people were subjected to a barrage of propaganda to promote these ends. Captions on posters plastered around cities and towns read: 'He's coming south', and everyone knew who 'he' was. Newspaper cartoons depicted the enemy as a 'grinning monster, with buck teeth'; he was a 'many-legged crab' clawing at Australia; a ferocious ape with a spiked baton, 'holding high the body of a white woman'.[5] As well as the propaganda, there were the accounts of refugees who had fled from Southeast Asia for the uncertain sanctuary of Australia, of 'beheadings, bayonetings, rapes, and other atrocities' committed by the Japanese.[6] Such images kept alive for many Australian women the fear of what they believed would happen to them if they were captured by the Japanese.

Torres Strait Islander women saw the Japanese in a different light. Their relations with Japanese skippers had been generally good, although outsiders have suggested otherwise. Bleakley claimed that the Torres Strait Islanders had no love for the Japanese.[7] After his visit to Torres Strait in 1943, the Queensland Governor stated that the people had a 'personal hatred' of them.[8] Gerald Peel, a communist journalist, claimed that an island man told him he hated the Japanese and that his wish was to be 'with the Yanks, at the death, in Tokyo'.[9] These outsider constructions certainly do not accord with the testimonies of many old Torres Strait Islanders today. Moreover, while the women expressed apprehension about men in uniform, guns, planes and submarines, no one expressed similar feelings towards the Japanese.

A St Paul's woman said that, although the people were 'angry with them because of the war, they did not hate them'. Fifty years later, Japanese skippers were remembered as concerned friends. One former seaman recalled: 'My wages were £3, sometimes £2 a month ... the Japanese skippers wanted to give us more but the government won't allow it. The law is there. Torres Strait Islanders get so much but the Japs gave us money out of their pockets.' An old man from

Purma recalled: 'We were friendly with the Japanese. They were good people. I was with them for a meal. We were always friendly to each other and that's how Torres Strait people learnt about pearling.' Two St Paul's women spoke of friendships with Japanese seamen: '[They] called in for food and made great friends with us. My mother gave them vegetables, pumpkin, sweet potato and they gave us rice and tinned stuff'; 'We were all good friends with the Japanese before the war.' Japanese skippers anchored their luggers off Mer while they waited for the neap tide. They ate with the locals, they went to feasts and learnt island dancing: 'They were one of us … They were good people, how do you say it, generous, yes, good people and not bad like they said. It was the war that made things go bad.' Beckett, too, found Torres Strait Islander men of that generation 'spoke well of their old skippers, who they suggested had dissuaded the Japanese air force from bombing their villages'.[10]

Faces of fear

The first sign of hope that the tide of war was turning came with the Battle of the Coral Sea in May 1942. But it was her losses in carriers and trained pilots at the Battle of Midway, fought in June, which forced a halt to Japan's expansionist program in the southwest Pacific. In New Guinea, where Japanese land forces came within fifty miles of Port Moresby in August 1942, Australian troops pushed them back along the Kokoda Trail and over the Owen Stanley Range from September 1942 until January 1943. On mainland Australia, voluntary evacuees began returning to their homes. Nonetheless, ongoing propaganda did nothing to help lessen women's fears which were compounded by the thought that they might learn that a loved one on service was missing or dead.

Many Torres Strait Islanders believed that the Japanese had no grudge against them: 'Japanese fight white man, not island man.' Theirs had been an uncomplicated trust in the Japanese men they knew, men who had shown personal concern for them. The political power structures in Japan were of no consequence in these relationships. Conversely, from their earliest encounters with whites, the Torres Strait Islanders had been demeaned and made fearful of them. In the 1860s many white pearlers and trepangers came to Torres Strait. These men forced both island men and women to work for them. To save their women from abduction, the men on Tudu 'buried their women and young girls in the sand with only their noses showing' when vessels were sighted.[11] In 1855, the South Sea Islander crew belonging to bêche-de-mer fisherman Captain Bruce's ship *Woodlark* went to Mer in quest of women and, when the village men resisted, the sailors returned with their captain and there were killings. The people's houses and belongings were burnt and those caught were 'hacked to pieces or disfigured'.[12] Fear of white people did not abate when the Torres Strait Islanders came under the internal colonial rule of the Queensland government.

John Douglas, Government Resident on Thursday Island from 1885 to 1904, once remarked that the Meriam people had 'unquestionably risen much in the scale of [what was called] civilization' in the fourteen years after the landing of the first LMS missionaries.[13] He had opposed any suggestion that Torres Strait Islanders be administered under the provisions of the Queensland Act designed to segregate and control Aboriginal people. However, his views were not the views of his successors. Under that Act, Torres Strait Islanders also became second-class citizens of Australia:

> We been work for JW Bleakley, you know. He come out all the island, he said, 'Oh, I'm your big *mamus* (chief), here are two sticks of tobacco, here are two blankets'. Oh, so we bend the knee and bow down to him because he's the big *mamus*.[14]

From 1911, the government's agents, the white teachers on the outer islands, with minimal supervision reduced the island councillors to puppet status: 'The teacher had more power than the council.' They were the government's 'right-hand man [sic]'.[15] One old man recalled: 'The way [the teacher] spoke to me made me think that she was a little god.' Another said: 'All the good things we needed we were too frightened of her to ask about.'[16] People from Badu, Mabuiag, Masig and Saibai recalled that 'everyone' was frightened to walk past the teacher's house because 'we weren't allowed to make noises around the house'.

In the 1930s, the then teenage Willie Thaiday was banished from Erub, not because he had done anything wrong but because, in his presence, a friend had put his arm around an island girl and kissed her at a dance.[17] Any kind of intimate relationship with a white woman, or crossing the 'caste' barrier, was punished. On Badu, a fourteen-year-old boy was gaoled for three months when the teacher 'blew the whistle' on him because he walked with a white woman when she asked him to do so and he did not like to say no: 'I was fright from her [frightened of being with her], scared ... We had a law about walking with white ladies.'[18] A Boigu man said that it was better for a young man to be out on the boats than on the island for any length of time: 'Staying on the island was a bad thing ... too many [men were] going around with girls. That's why I go out to sea ... They were very, very strict, DNA [Department of Native Affairs] ... very strict, one false move and you get about with girls and they say "Out!".' Sentences were severe. In the case of Willie Thaiday, it was banishment. Frequently, punishments were humiliating: 'Before-time they cut your hair on one side and make you shamed.' Councillors had no option but to go along with the outsiders' rules on such matters. They were under the teachers' supervision, and, as already indicated, they were seen as 'the law, terrible law'. Even after the 1936 maritime strike when the New Law was introduced which purported to restore local autonomy to the councillors, this, according to a Badu man, was 'in name only'; most Torres Strait Islanders continued to be 'frightened from the white man'. For the women, island custom made it even more difficult to build their confidence about strangers.

Traditionally, the women adopted an unobtrusive role whenever strangers appeared on their islands. In 1847, Jukes recorded instances of this. On Tudu they crawled into the bush when his party approached. On Erub he noticed that the 'younger women and girls kept in the background or hid themselves in the bush', and elsewhere he observed that they joined the men and visitors only after a 'little persuasion'.[19] The LMS missionary Gill described the women as 'excessively timid'.[20] An old Saibai man explained the tradition: 'From the time of our way, any aliens approach the island the women are the first to be hid; the menfolk are there to receive what's coming to them.' A Purma woman said:

> It's like a rule, it was passed on; whenever we come across strangers, we are not allowed to talk. If the husbands are around,

they can talk. When the husbands are not there, the women would not talk. If single or they got boyfriend, they still are not allowed to talk.

During the 1930s, the rigidity of the custom was being eroded on some islands and a few women gained a degree of confidence in the presence of white people. On Badu, for instance, there were women who worked with white government officers in the store as clerks, shop assistants and seamstresses, so that they were able to say: 'We Badu women, we were used to white people and we were not frightened of them.' Other young women from the various communities were sent to a teachers training college on Mabuiag and were instructed by Philip Frith, Charlie Turner and their wives. These women subsequently taught on islands, generally not their own, where they were supervised by other white government teachers. The presence of white teachers on the larger communities helped to erode the women's fears: 'Coloured people were frightened from white people; when the [white] school teachers came, everybody was frightened until you are friendly.' However, when a Saibai woman was taken by Charlie Turner and his wife on an unprecedented visit to Brisbane, it proved to be a terrifying experience for her even though she had lived with this white family for a long time: 'There were no Islanders when I went down ... no black people, only white. I was frightened of that place and when we go out they had to hold my hand.' From March 1942, white men came to the islands in army uniform and with guns. The women's fears were compounded.

When Japanese and even allied aircraft appeared in the skies over Torres Strait, new and terrifying experiences flooded in upon the women even though they had no realistic understanding of the full destructive capacity of these machines. A Badu woman remembered that, when the bombs were dropped on Nurupai, they heard the explosions and everyone was 'very frightened ... We don't realise that much that time. We hadn't seen planes. There were no planes around here. We travelled by sailing boats.' Another woman said: 'All the planes flew on top, they made me frightened and the children cried because we had never seen planes then.' The Saibai people recalled: 'We never saw that thing before and we were scared too much when we heard the noise'; 'It was war time, you know, we were very frightened. All of us were very frightened from that plane noise.' A Meriam woman's memory of it was that: 'We listened for the noise from the planes ... we were frightened from the planes ... We don't know if they will bomb our island.' Even when there were no planes in the sky, the fear persisted: 'We were frightened all the time planes might come.' Mothers were fearful when their children made noises and told them to stay quiet. Little children 'ran everywhere and cried' when they heard the noise of a plane and, like 'mother fowls', the women called them to come inside. A Purma woman told her story of fear: 'They said to me, "Don't look up". They took the baby from me and Henry, my two-year-old, ran along. I was frightened from those planes. I can't carry my baby.' So, 'fear was the problem', a Saibai woman recalled, 'I can still imagine those planes when they come in formation. We were scared.' Her people asked themselves: 'What's going to happen next?'

The nights brought no relief from the fear: 'We only sat there with a small light so nobody could see us and no noise, just kept quiet. We were frightened, frightened from the enemy.' Some families felt safer in their own homes: 'The planes went over. Yeah, we were frightened. Everybody liked to stay in their own home at night.' Fear drove other families closer together: 'We could not sleep ... we came together in one house and some sleep outside on the verandah. We felt safer together. We were frightened. Our brothers were away.' The women's fears were certainly accentuated because their able-bodied men were not there to support them through the ordeal.

Initially, the women and old people could not distinguish between allied and Japanese planes and this meant that they ran for safety at the sound of every plane: 'We did not understand where the planes were coming from.' On Mer, very early one morning, a woman was making 'damper dough' to put in her earth oven and the smoke from the fire wafted into the sky. When an Australian plane circled just above her to see what was happening, she thought it was an enemy plane and ran terrified into the bush. The enlisted men on leave talked to the women: 'We explained everything to them through our own language, like what is an Australian plane, an American, Japanese.' They told the women to look for the 'red dot', the insignia on the Japanese planes. That was the enemy.

The Saibai women experienced further apprehension when the first allied seaplane landed on the water out from their village. The older women ran away and the policeman called to them, 'Come back, come back. They won't hurt you. Don't be frightened, they are friends.' For the younger ones, their fascination overcame fear: 'They were like big shiny birds on the water. It was something different, a strange thing ... We were frightened but curious too ... We swam out to touch it.' A Meriam woman recalled: 'One time a woman died and that Catalina flying boat landed and all the people left the dead body and we ran out to see the plane — we had never seen one before.' Another fearful experience was seeing for the first time the intermittent sweep of light from searchlights. A Kubin man recalled that the women ran everywhere with their children because they thought a demon was causing it. It is generally accepted that by 1942 all Torres Strait Islanders were at least nominally Christian, but it had been only seventy years since they had accepted the new religion. Thus, it is not difficult to understand that recourse to old religious beliefs, which the missionaries had failed to stamp out completely, helped the women to comprehend the incomprehensible.

After the Japanese pushed into the area around Merauke on the southern coastline of Papua, aerial activity over the Top-Western Islands increased. One man recalled large formations — 'thirty-eight or forty-six bombers and fighters' — going over Saibai. He said the older boys had very little fear of the Japanese planes. It was an exciting time for them: 'We just enjoyed seeing Jap planes flying over. I was the ring leader.' With a smile on his face, he continued: 'We ran and waved to the planes. They were way up, but we could see the red marks on the tail. As children we weren't really aware of the danger. To us, oh God will protect us, we got nothing to fight with them.' However, their mothers were not so nonchalant about the danger: 'We got belted for it but a couple of days later I did the same thing again.' It was an exciting time for the boys on Masig as well. They watched dog fights between American and Japanese planes. One man remembered that when 'everyone fled into the bush he sat down on the beach and looked at the planes fighting, just like a movie'. There were girls too who threw caution to the wind, much to the old women's horror. 'We kids made big noises', a Badu woman said, 'we screamed, waved our hands. The old ladies said to us, "Don't make noise, they will come back and shoot you".'

Bearing in mind that the women had always adopted an unobtrusive role when outsiders, who were generally men, came to their islands, it was not surprising that many of the women described incidents which related to their fears of white soldiers. The women on Mer were frightened of the signallers when they were first posted there: 'When the signallers came ... we went inside and locked the door. They came around to make friends with us and we went and hid. Our Uncle Bon roused on us, "You are ignorant to run. They are people like us".' The old Kubin woman who had worked for whites on Thursday Island said that she had not been frightened of white people: 'But army white men, they leave us frightened. They looked different, they made us cry ... The people ran and cried everywhere.' Her husband called to the women when they ran away, 'Come back, they've got our Australian uniform'. The reactions of the women on Saibai were similar when the signallers hosted several American airmen, rescued after their plane ditched into the sea near the island: 'Everybody ran away in the bush, everybody was frightened.' One woman remembered: 'The signallers called to us, "Don't be frightened and ready a cup of tea for the airmen". They introduced me and I was scared.' A Badu woman, who had also worked for white people before the war, said she had lost her fear of white men until she was sent to work as a domestic on Thursday Island late in the war and there were 'army men everywhere'. One day the officer's wife said to her, 'We've got visitors coming, those head ones, they're coming to have a cup of tea. You look for flowers for the table.' She went out to pick the flowers and men in uniform came along. She dropped her flowers and ran: 'I was frightened from them', she said, 'I left the flowers until all the boys go by.' A Saibai woman who accompanied the old men in the long canoes on the dangerous sea crossing to Daru for trade during those years explained her fear of men in uniform: 'They got soldiers there too — white and black soldiers — some New Guinea. We were frightened, too many soldiers.'

Both men and women on the communities felt inhibited in their associations with whites because of their inability to speak what they now term 'proper English'. In the western group of islands, Kalaw Kawaw Ya and Kala Lagaw Ya were spoken and for most families English was only used by the children during school lessons. Over to the east, the language was Meriam and likewise it was spoken almost exclusively of English outside of the school room. Creole had become the primary language on some communities.[21] Thus, the people had little opportunity to practise their English and to feel confident speaking it. A Saibai man who had attended the Mabuiag teachers training college before the war was typical of many of his people:

> In 1946 I don't speak English. I read pretty good and write it down but I do not speak English. They taught English to us and they stopped us from speaking language in school — they tried to teach us, but English is just a word, no meaning to me in 1946.

A Meriam woman said that, although the women were afraid of the white teachers when they first arrived on their islands, they were 'more afraid because [they] couldn't speak English properly'. On the beach at Mer, an old woman spoke in language about her wartime fears which had been heightened by an inability to speak English. Her son interpreted:

> On their way back home from their gardens they saw some of the navy men on the island and they went up to the hills and when they saw them they went and hid in the grass ... They could not speak English, you know, so they were so scared: 'Stop, stop, white man, white man', they said. They had all those yams and bananas in this little basket and they dropped it and the navy went past and they saw the basket, 'No women!' They didn't see the women hiding there in bush. As soon as they saw the basket, they looked everywhere for people: 'There's no one here.' They just saw the basket.

An old Saibai man said something pertinent about why their inability to speak English confidently made them more fearful: 'The language is a very important thing. We were all frightened, very frightened because it was very hard to speak English ... We must be frightened unless we join in and understand. It's understanding that gets rid of fear.'

Spirituality — old and new

> In prayer ... we turn back to that source (of creative power) ... Prayer becomes a source of strength and certainty and not a mere sedative and tranquillizer.[22]

Michael McKernan, who wrote about the attitudes of mainland Australian clergymen to the European war in 1914, suggested that they drew on a basic Christian belief to explain why the world hovered on the brink of disaster: 'nothing happened unless permitted by God, who only sanctioned what was ultimately good.' Carried along by a surge of patriotism, overwhelming numbers of young Australian men enlisted and went to the front, while people at home attended church services 'as never before'. They flocked to processions of troops and attended fundraising functions. However, despite the clergy's warnings, religious zeal waned as the war dragged on.[23]

During the 1920s, Australians were swept along by a new, fast, free and even more materialistic way of life. Within a decade, the Great Depression reversed the fortunes of many and, in the latter years of the 1930s, war clouds gathered once again over Europe and finally over the southwest Pacific. Three days before the first bombs were dropped on Australian soil, one congregation was told that the present war was 'God's retribution for the sins of the world' and that materialism had made tremendous inroads into their spiritual life.[24] Churchgoers elsewhere were exhorted to place themselves and those on active service under the protection of God.

By early March 1942 a feeling of doom permeated mainland Australian society. The Catholic Archbishop in Brisbane echoed his 1914 counterparts when he challenged his congregation with the words: 'Might it not be that the danger now so imminent was permitted by God as a punishment and a corrective!'[25] Presbyterians heard their minister tell them that 'prayer is a force just as any of the other forces we know of in nature'. And the Prime Minister appealed to the people to repent and 'seek strength in prayer'.[26] Thus, while history repeated itself and nations went to war, so too did church leaders revive 'simplistic moral judgements' of the people. Congregations became somewhat bigger than before the war, but, as it dragged on, an ethos grew amongst mainland people which suggested that superiority and strength of arms, rather than prayer, would be the decisive factors in an allied victory.

The importance of the Torres Strait Islander women's spirituality during the Pacific War cannot be overlooked. The testimonies make it clear that they believed their faith and prayers carried them and their men through the war years. Old Torres Strait Islander men said it was the women's prayers that kept them safe and stopped the war. Christianity had been brought to the people seventy years earlier but, while the teachers of the new religion had done their best to eradicate the practices of the old spirituality, elements of it lived on. Thus, the people's testimonies about the women's faith and prayers must be read with a sensitivity to a Torres Strait Islander spirituality which incorporates both the old and the new.

Torres Strait Islanders are a Melanesian people cut off from their heartland by the Australian border. Traditionally, religious beliefs and practices permeated all aspects of the lives of the various groups of Melanesian people in the southwest Pacific, including the Torres Strait Islanders. The rhythm of their lives was dictated by the stars, moon, winds, tides and seasons, along with the supernatural powers upon which they called for good and evil purposes. Despite regional variations in their religions and practices, all Melanesian groups believed 'physical and spiritual realities dovetailed'. Plants, animals, inorganic matter and spirit beings all belonged to an integrated cosmos. The people relied upon supernatural powers to maintain the balance of their universe and its continued renewal.[27] Like other Melanesians, Torres Strait Islander groups had their own religious systems and practices. In Torres Strait they seem to have added to these systems or practices if they discovered a spiritual order which suited their purposes better. For example, Haddon suggested that totems on Mer had temporarily lost their eminence with the grafting on of new spiritual orders to their existing religious system.[28] In this way, a complex web of religious practices had been established throughout Torres Strait by the time of white intervention, the knowledge of which, generally, has been reflected to outsiders through the blurred lenses of white researchers. This section on the island people's traditional religions should be read with this in mind.

Torres Strait Islander and other Melanesian societies were kinship-based. Local groups were organised into clans with their own totems. Practices associated with totems assured good crops and plentiful supplies of fish, turtle and dugong. Supernatural power also emanated from inanimate objects. Practices associated with painted or anointed stones and carved images ensured good fortune in fishing. On Yam and Tudu, stone and carved pumice figures, a bullroarer and a wooden tablet with human bones and cowrie shells attached, when called upon, ensured an abundance of wongai plums, fertile gardens and increased yields of yams, sweet potatoes and turtle.[29] In response to certain practices, these inanimate objects unleashed their supernatural powers for the benefit of the people.

Warring was frequent in Torres Strait and strength and victory in battle were sought in practices associated with objects and legendary heroes. The fearless Saibai warriors adopted the Adi Buia stone as a means of tapping the supernatural for that strength and victory. A young Saibai man, who had been instructed by his elders, said that the warriors were imbued with power when they 'approached the stone naked', rubbed it with coconut oil, danced around it and touched it with their bows and arrows. Warriors on Mabuiag received their strength from the shell ornaments they believed were worn by their hero, the strong and fearless Kwoiam. The people on Yam and Tudu built shrines in the *kwods* (the men's place for religious rituals) for their heroes, the brothers Sigay and Mayawin. The figure of the legendary hero, or god, Waiet kept in a cave on the eastern island of Waier, a rugged horseshoe-shaped volcanic cone, was only removed from its eerie home for ceremonial purposes.[30]

Anthropological research in Melanesian societies suggests that their religious practices were concerned with 'life here and now': cosmic renewal, rites of passage and strength and victory in battle.[31] These practices were widespread in Torres Strait. However, the religion which has been the focus of much attention since white intervention is the Malo-Bomai Order. A brief encounter with this religious order confirms that the old spirituality in Torres Strait is far from lost. Bomai moved around Torres Strait in the form of different sea creatures. At Begegiz on Mer, he was recognised as a god: '*Keriba agud ged seker em* [This is our god and protector].'[32] The practices associated with this religion became all-pervasive in eastern Torres Strait. The laws of Malo, *Malo ra Gelar*, made possible unity between the eight clans on the islands of Mer and Dauar. So great was this religion that it still influences the beliefs of some Meriam Christians. The Reverend David Passi explored the theological implications:

> Malo was sent to Mer by God. He gave Moses to Israel ... God was working through Malo before the Light came to Torres Strait ... I am asking, is not Malo the same as the Great Spirit of the Red Indian, is not he the same as the One who appeared to Hagar in the wilderness, is not he the same as the missionaries brought to the Torres Strait, July 1, 1871? The reason for me saying this is that the eternal truths that emerged out of the savagery and heathenism, as we are often referred to, are not something that were created by the mask Malo. They are given by the true Malo. I would like to call the Great Jehovah, Malo. I would like that name to become the name of Jehovah for our people.

He calls all Christians to have respect for this interpretation: 'When I was in Rockhampton studying for the priesthood I did nothing to destroy what your people had developed over a long period. It was years of developing what happened here. I want that for here, not to be destroyed.' Father Passi's words make it clear that the old spirituality has not been totally dismissed.

Anthropological and other writings on Torres Strait Islanders in the nineteenth and early twentieth centuries do not make it clear whether the women played roles in what might be termed the public religious life of the communities. There are references to the women's exclusion from the *kwod*. Indeed, it is believed death was the punishment if a woman breached religious taboos, for instance if she recognised a *Zogo le* and divulged his name.[33] Contemporary anthropologist Maureen Fuary was told by island people that women on Purma and Tudu sang during rituals associated with the catching of the first turtle for the season. It is known that women had their own totems and they were inherited by their children, although the father's totem was the chief one. Whether the women called upon them to increase their garden produce or catch of fish is unknown. Haddon described the *maidelaig* as trained magicians, a powerful 'professional class', entry into which was by choice and was accompanied by stringent and physically terrifying instruction.[34] *Maid*, or the supernatural, it has been suggested, 'permeated every activity of the lives of the [people] from birth until death, and even thereafter'.[35] Again, however, there seems to have been no suggestion that Torres Strait Islander women entered this professional class, although an outsider who taught on Mer in the mid-1920s said there was 'woman sorcery' on that island.[36] An old Meriam woman suggested differently: 'Women don't use it, only men.'

Torres Strait Islander women belonged to societies in which supernatural and religious practices were associated with every aspect of their lives. It is to be expected, therefore, that there were religious practices which were associated with private aspects of the women's lives, such as to induce conception, to ensure the birth of a male child, at puberty and in the care of the corpse of a baby. Thus, spiritual significance must also be attributed to the women's practices. However, in their male-oriented societies, such practices might be described as private and on the periphery of the public spiritual life of the community, which was seemingly the men's responsibility. When the new religion was introduced in Torres Strait by white men in 1871, the women's spiritual roles were also peripheral to its functioning.

John Done, the first Anglican priest appointed to the outer islands, made his initial visit to Torres Strait in 1915. He described the people as 'religious in every sense'.[37] And, like the LMS before him, the Anglican Church gave the island men public spiritual responsibilities as church wardens. Moreover, men were trained at a college on Moa to be priests. Laymen, too, were permitted to preach.

The people on all communities were anxious to have churches which glorified God, and women throughout Torres Strait played important roles in the work of church building. The Saibai women dug coral from the reef and transported it back to the village in their dinghies. On Mabuiag they carried stone, sand and water and they made cement for the foundations from a mixture of crushed ant bed and water. In 1934 Tipoti Nona and fellow church warden Tamwoy gained village consensus to build a new church. The young women 'swam for stones' and collected coral to make lime. The old people broke the stones: everyone worked 'around the clock' to get the job finished. On St Paul's, the women crushed the stones, carried sand and raised money to buy cement. The women were not lacking in their physical support of the new religion but their hard work as church builders went unrewarded. They were not even given administrative or clerical positions.

However, in 1931, married women gained new status in the church. An Anglican Mothers Union had been founded in England by Mary Sumner and a group of churchwomen in 1887. In 1911 a branch of the union was formed by an all-white group on Thursday Island.[38] Its concerns were the sanctity of marriage and arousing in women a greater sense of responsibility in the training of their children. Women, too, were encouraged to unite in prayer. In May 1931, four Torres Strait Islander women were invited to attend a meeting of the Thursday Island branch; three of them were wives of 'native' priests. Mary Lui (Erub), Alice Passi (Mer) and Sepiama Min (Mabuiag) were elected to office. Within two years Alice Passi had formed a branch on Saibai and Joan Davies, the bishop's wife, had visited and addressed women on eight islands. By the end of the decade there were fourteen branches and just under 600 members in Torres Strait.[39] This new status for women was commented on by several old men. One said: 'That Mothers Union, they turned out very well, they worship God. Mothers Union everywhere in Torres Strait, they've done a good work.' Another also spoke approvingly:

> The women turned very bold when they formed the Mothers Union, that's their belief ... to women that's where they stand, that Mothers Union is the great thing in their life. It gave them a sense of caring for one another and prayer became bold and very firm in their lives.

A few old women spoke about their prewar involvement in this organisation: 'The Mothers Union just talked to the mothers. The men did their job and mothers had the Mothers Union and everyone worked together, they always cooked and worked for feast days.' A Badu women said that the Mothers Union was 'a very strong one' and that it was a 'very important thing' in the community. Another recalled that she was 'the messenger' for the Mothers Union, going to all the members' houses to tell them to come to the meeting. A former vice-president explained: 'We had our meetings, we talked to the women about how to live. We did plenty of fundraising and if any mother wanted help, we did it.' Members made and sold mats and baskets and embroidered pillowcases to boost church funds. The Mothers Union gave some women a say in family life in the communities as well as opportunities to learn about western meeting procedures and accounting. A few women went to meetings on other communities and on Thursday Island, one of the few reasons which permitted them to leave their own islands. This organisation, it was suggested by a former white Anglican priest in Torres Strait, brought the women together in a 'strong fellowship where they gained experience in leadership and in having a say'.[40] The new leadership, even if it was confined to family matters, gave the women a status within the male hegemonic church organisation they could not have previously dreamed of.

In late 1940, white members of the Thursday Island branch of the Mothers Union passed a resolution calling for a day of prayer:

> This Council feeling the need for the depending on the spiritual life in the Diocese requests the Bishops to sponsor a day of continuous prayer to be held in the Cathedral [on Thursday Island] and in island churches on behalf of peace.[41]

Understandably, the Thursday Island members wanted to draw the outer island women into their circle of prayer, but Germany's aggression in Europe was far removed from the thinking of Torres Strait Islander women. In another year, however, the tentacles of war reached closer to Torres Strait. The women were suddenly in a war zone and prayer became 'a big part' of their lives. Thus, in their recollections of the war, the women were extremely articulate about their prayer life. There can be no doubt, by reference to the old people's testimonies, that the belief persists that the women's individual and collective spirituality had been vital to the survival of the people during the Pacific War years. Moreover, it took the horrors of war to give them the opportunity to practise their spirituality in a more public and authoritative manner. They prayed for their own people, they prayed for the world and they prayed for peace. Moreover, with the realisation that so much depended on them, they prayed that they would be strong.

The women's peripheral roles in both traditional and Christian institutions are emphasised because of the connection between their traditional spirituality and their Christian faith. All around Torres Strait there are carefully preserved and revered reminders of the old — the great warrior Kwoiam's footprint in the rock on Mabuiag; Wasikor, the drum, which belonged to the *Zogo le* and was used in rituals on Mer. But perhaps the most universal and powerful reminder today of the continued existence of the old spirituality is the tombstone opening. The exact time of its inception is not known. A Masig woman said: 'I can't remember doing this thing when I was a young girl.' A Meriam man's first memory of it was about 1933. Perhaps it is significant that this ritual was not introduced until the 1930s when the people were being increasingly oppressed by the Local Protector. Underlying the tombstone opening are structures related to their traditional death practices: there must be a separation of the spirits which linger about the living after death. The tombstone opening is held at the graveside a year, or even more, after the death, at which a Christian priest officiates. Sharp describes it as a 'sign of cultural healing' of the 'cruel wounds' inflicted when the missionaries forced them to bury their dead in lieu of their own practices.[42] And, on Mer, a reminder of the old are the Si stones, reputed to still speak 'with the voice of *Malu*'.[43]

The Torres Strait Islander world was not suddenly converted to a compartmentalised 'rational' world after white intervention. The women's prayers then must be seen as those of a people who, for thousands of years, had relied for the renewal of their cosmos upon an absolute connection between every aspect of their existence and the supernatural. In their minds, victory was not related to superior allied military forces and arms; their faith lay in a direct supernatural interference in the affairs of human beings. So it was to the Christian God of their new source of all creative power, welcomed into their lives when the missionaries came to Torres Strait, that they prayed for that to happen.

The power of prayer

In January 1942, the Anglican Bishop of Carpentaria urged the faithful on Thursday Island to pray for the church's 'great mission development' in Torres Strait, that those who had been 'won to the Christian faith' would not be lost, that homes and parishes would be spared from bombardment and destruction.[44] JA Daniels, the Anglican priest on the island, reminded parishioners that these were 'anxious times' but that British people generally did not 'become unnecessarily alarmed but [would] maintain their trust in their leaders and faith in God'. He continued: 'We all realise the need more than ever for more work and more prayer if we are to accomplish our task of bringing peace to the distressed nations of the world.' He 'begged' mainland congregations, on behalf of the people of the Torres Strait, to pray for 'this outpost of the Commonwealth, that we may be consistent in things spiritual as well as things temporal'.[45] The priest on St Paul's, Godfrey Gilbert, did not doubt that right would conquer in the end no matter what anyone had to 'put up with'. Suffering, he assured Christians, would teach them 'all the better' to give glory to God.[46] There were exhortations for prayer in these words but no hint of the fire and brimstone preaching being heard in mainland churches where adherents' greater love of the temporal was loudly condemned. However, whether this softer line of preaching and calls for more prayer were adopted by the Torres Strait Islander priests is not known. There was no media coverage of their pulpits and Anglican records for the period threw virtually no light on the religious life of the people during the war. Only the women's recollections remained.

A Saibai Anglican nun recalled that, as a child in the late 1940s and early 1950s, she never heard her mother talk about how hard it had been for the women during the war: 'We grew up and we didn't know what the war was about. I didn't hear anything about the war from my parents.' She only remembered the women's laughter as they sat together, plaiting mats and baskets and yarning about the 'funny stories' associated with their wartime experiences. Then, years later, the 'television wars about Vietnam' set her thinking. She realised that the pain of war continued long after it was over and that many people did not want to look back at that pain. Indeed, it was on Saibai on Anzac Day 1989 that the women spoke publicly for the first time about their wartime experiences. Almost simultaneously, Torres Strait Islander women as well as many men shared, with me an outsider, their memories of those 'hard times' in answer to my inquiry.

An old TSLI man believed that God was 'the very important thing' in the lives of the Torres Strait Islander women and when the men joined the army and went away 'all the families ... they worshipped, went to church all the time'. Prayer was not confined to Sundays or even prayer meetings. It was frequently spontaneous in those awful early days. The women said 'a small prayer for the Japanese not come' when the noise of a plane was heard, no matter where they were or what they were doing. Children listened to their mothers pray, 'God, stop them coming', as they huddled together in the bush, caves, creeks, mangroves, anywhere where the Japanese airmen would not see them as they flew low over the islands. An old woman cried aloud to God as she ran for safety when Yam was strafed: '*Ngal mun, ngal mun, augud ngapayae, augud ngapayae, ngal mun, ebo poidan* [My God, my God, come on, come on, help us].' The women's prayers went beyond their own safety. They remembered their husbands, fathers and sons who had enlisted; they asked God to 'help Australia' and prayers were offered for a world about which they knew so little: 'The women prayed very strong prayer for the world to get peace.'

The Mothers Union members took responsibility for the group prayer life on the communities. They 'kept the church going ... they were very strong in prayer', a Masig woman recalled. On Saibai:

> The Mothers Union women, that was their job to pray all the time for the men on TI, for the war. That was when TI was saved when the Japanese men dropped bombs on Nurupai. They prayed and prayed all the time, proper hard, proper strong, the

> Mothers Union, and all the big men and women they prayed too, they prayed all the time for the army. The Mothers Union was strong. Getting the war organised, that's their job.

These women risked the dangers of leaving their bush homes to pray in the village churches. Prayer rosters were introduced on St Paul's and women 'prayed around the clock' every Thursday. They prayed 'two at a time'. A Badu woman recalled that they prayed 'very hard at night time' and that certain women were told: 'You go *poi piam* tonight', which meant that 'you pray night time and change over'. Some of the Purma women went to church at six o'clock in the evening and some were still praying at three or four o'clock the next morning; it was for them 'another thing to help the war'. The Meriam women formed prayer groups: 'They got to pray to stop this war', one woman recalled, 'every night they prayed, they just meet in the church and do it.' The recollections of a man, who was a boy at the time, were that

> the women were always in the church, In the dusk they don't sleep their head off, they cook our tea but their tiredness doesn't stop them. After that they come in to the church and stay until midnight and they come home again.

Someone else recalled: 'I was a little girl and we had prayer in the house first thing in the morning and last thing at night ... the only thing that saved the men on TI was prayer.' The people said prayer was without doubt 'a big part of their lives'. A Mabuiag man remembered his mother telling him most of the prayer groups gathered at night because 'there were a lot of other activities to be done in the day'. It would have been easy and reasonable for these exceedingly busy women to remain at home with their families at night instead of going out to pray. Moreover, there was always the fear that they might be seen moving about the island at night, not only by the enemy but by evil spirits which lurked in the dark.

Throughout all the islands, even at the height of great danger, the women congregated to worship the Christian God they had come to accept as the spiritual essence of their being. In the early months of the war, when it was too dangerous for everyone to congregate in the village on Badu, the church warden rang a bell and the people met in the bush in extended family groups. On Kubin the warden went to each bush house to give the women notice and 'everyone came together to make a service in the open air under the trees'. A Mabuiag woman said: 'Come nightfall, we cannot do anything, just sitting praying. We just want this war out quickly so the people can go back to the village.' Her godfather was crippled and he stayed on in the village. He prayed alone, she said: 'He was a good old man and asked God to finish this war so the people can come back in the village.' Two Masig women remembered that their old grandfather from 'LMS time', who also stayed on in the village, prayed 'day and night'. Another boyhood memory came from a Meriam man:

> Everyone got in there ... and they prayed for our islands, for the men on TI, the sick, the boats ... and all those things and they named them specifically and the most important one was that they would be brave from the time the war started until it ceased.

The island priests, Francis Bowie, Kabay Pilot and Poey Passi, went from island to island to take church services, give communion, baptise babies and officiate at weddings. Whenever and wherever possible, lay preachers and church wardens conducted services in the absence of a priest. There were no confirmations until Bishop Stephen Davies returned to Torres Strait on a visit in September 1943. The surviving wartime registers give no reliable information on church attendances during the war years but this is understandable in the light of the circumstances which pertained on the outer islands. It is reasonable to suppose that no one thought it was very important to count heads when they were able to congregate for worship. A Badu woman spoke as if there had been a strengthening of religious zeal on her island: 'Before we don't pray but when it was wartime we prayed', while a Meriam woman's recollection was that 'faith was not so strong on Mer'.

Another woman from Mer remembered 'a miracle from God' which had been witnessed by the people in the early months of the war. The store was empty and the vegetable crops had failed for want of rain, so her father, Poey Passi, the island priest, called the women together to repair the fish trap in the hope of getting a big haul of fish. As was their custom, some of the women prepared food for the workers. On this occasion there was no flour to make damper, so the women made *mabus*, mashed boiled bananas mixed with dry coconut and coconut milk:

> My father started to bless the food and he started to pray just like talking to God and all the people were watching ... they want Him to give them food. That night there were fish in the trap right up to the beach from the fence. His prayer was answered. Fish, so many, and the women said, 'Cargo boat coming', and they came and got the fish and the cargo boat arrived with food.

She smiled as she added after a pause: 'It was just like the five barley loaves and the two fishes, eh!'

Moreover, before the Battle of the Coral Sea, people on Moa reported 'a vision of the Lord in glory in the sky above Kubin, with His hands outstretched in blessing and protection'. As the news of the 'vision' spread, the people 'took it as a special sign to them that their islands would be safeguarded'.[47] The almost universal reference in the testimonies to faith and prayer, the recollection of a 'miracle of God', all after fifty years, and the 'vision' on Moa indicate the importance generally placed on the belief that it was the power of the supernatural that got them through the war safely, not the physical trappings of modern warfare.

An old man conceptualised succinctly his people's perception of the importance of the women's spiritual strength and prayers during the war: 'So much happened because the women had faith.' 'Their prayers', an island priest concluded, 'were a camouflage for us from danger and it was so great and big that faith stopped the war.' Since the Coming of the Light, the Saibai nun claimed,

> my people were very very devout to their faith in Jesus Christ and that when the women were expressing their faith when that

> ... unknown thing happened to them, their trust must have been very very strong in God ... Their own loved ones had been taken away from them to fight the war and prayer was the only thing left for them to do.

And an old woman's memory of it all was that: 'God is a true God, so we prayed to God until we won that victory.'

Only one Torres Strait Islander challenged the notion that religious zeal was strong amongst the women during the war years. Thus, the strength of the testimonies makes it difficult to reject an overall perception that 'faith and prayer carried them through that time'. Moreover, the Mothers Union women were adopting a new public image for themselves in the spiritual life of their communities. The war was drawing them away from the narrower focus on the family to pray for broader issues, such as helping Australia and the world and the return of peace.

Chapter 9

Hard times

Mainland Australians became more optimistic after the Battle of the Coral Sea in mid-May 1942. However, when two Japanese midget submarines slipped through the net into Sydney harbour on the morning of 31 May, the enemy showed he had not exhausted his potential for surprise and this was only the forerunner to further naval action. Twenty-two ships were sunk and seven others badly damaged along the eastern seaboard before the enemy was finally routed.[1] On 14 May 1943, the nation was shocked when the hospital ship *Centaur* was torpedoed with the loss of 268 lives. Nevertheless, in July, the lights in all town and city streets (except in the far north) and on public transport and motor vehicles came on again. In Torres Strait, the fear of enemy infiltration persisted until early 1944.

Japan had established the headquarters of her Southwest Pacific Force at Rabaul, from where she progressively occupied a wide arc of islands to the north of Australia on which sixty-seven airfields were constructed to accommodate 1,500 aircraft. Simultaneously, Japanese land forces were strengthened in these areas. During 1943, Prime Minister Curtin and General Blamey, the commander of the allied land forces in the southwest Pacific, feared that Japan would attack in force against Merauke (a desolate marshy little port on the southern coast of Dutch New Guinea), only 180 nautical miles from Thursday Island and just across the border from Saibai. Although there were those who believed in 1942 that a Japanese landing in Torres Strait would be suicidal, others maintained that the enemy still had the capacity and the will in 1943 to slowly occupy Papua, including Merauke. If this happened, no one could be certain that the Japanese would not take that suicidal step into Torres Strait.

To meet such a situation, defence of the Torres Strait area was strengthened. Further facilities and forces to defend the Merauke-Horn Island [Nurupai]-Thursday Island-tip of Cape York Peninsula area were augmented. The 7 RAAF Beaufort Squadron joined the 84 Boomerang Squadron on Nurupai in April 1943. Their instructions were to guard Nurupai, Merauke and the waters of the Torres Strait area. The Torres Strait Force was increased by two brigades which were concentrated in the Horn Island [Nurupai]-Thursday Island area. Thousands of allied troops were stationed throughout northern Cape York Peninsula. These forces provided a garrison against any attempted landing and the RAAF was ready to meet both sea and land attacks. From 8 May 1943, 84 Squadron was ordered to traverse Torres Strait daily and to maintain 'a standing patrol of two aircraft over Merauke during daylight hours', which continued even after enemy activity in the Merauke-Torres Strait area was reduced in September.[2] The increased number of allied planes over the outer islands during 1943 gave the island women no reason to think they were any safer than in early 1942. Moreover, without access to current news bulletins, the women were in no position to even try to grasp the significance of what was happening in the Pacific region and to realise that the tide of war was slowly turning away from Torres Strait.

Without their own radios, daily newspapers and magazines or cinemas, how did the women in Torres Strait hear about the war and what did it all mean to them? When the signallers arrived on the larger communities they replaced the vital radio parts, which had been taken away by the white teachers, and contact with the outside world was restored. Torres Strait Islanders had not been permitted to 'go to the radio room' before the war, but the signallers on Masig decided that the time was right for a new policy:

> The radio room was only small and we would invite several of the councillors to sit in the room and hear news broadcasts mainly from west coast stations in the United States ... sometimes other island folk would gather outside ... It was all very formal and attendance was only when approved by the island council. Sometimes they'd come to listen to music.

Another way of giving the people some idea of what was happening was to pass old newspapers and magazines on to them:

> The only newspapers despatched to the islands were sent by relatives and friends of the coast watchers or some of the other [white] soldiers on TI. We [signallers] made our newspapers available to the school teacher/storekeepers ... along with magazines that came to hand.

The old Masig men were particularly interested in magazines like the *Australian Post*. They were astounded when they saw images in them of huge cities like Sydney and New York for the first time. On Mer and Erub the signallers talked with the men in the village about the war:

> We got a lot of news from America and we would go down during the day and talk to the storekeeper or church fellow or older people. They would ask, 'How are things going?' There was not much local news to get. The Coral Sea stopped the Japanese for a time. We would tell them we were going into New Guinea. We would tell them we were doing all right. They asked us what their boys were doing but we didn't have a clue.

Daily handwritten news bulletins were posted on notice boards outside community stores and news was read aloud in church. In bush locations, other ways of conveying news were devised. The chairman from Poid went to each bush camp on Moa where he gathered the women together and told them what was happening. A Saibai woman recalled that the policeman got word from the signallers about 'what was going on' and he told the women. Another woman said: 'When the men came back from TI they talked to us and we listened about the war.' Thus, more often than not, the women heard the news belatedly and second-hand. However, even though the men had first access to the news, one signaller said he

> was never able to gauge just how interested [they] were in the news. It was more likely that they would have been upset to hear the Prince of Wales had surrendered to the Japanese than Singapore had fallen to the men of Nippon or that Britain had been attacked by one thousand planes overnight. It was difficult to judge just how concerned even the more enlightened and better informed people were.

There can be little doubt, however, that whatever the women heard about the war beyond their own communities gave them no more than a sketchy and unrealistic picture.

The Torres Strait Islander women's window on the world was small for various reasons, such as their remoteness from the mainland, their inability to go there and their enforced low educational standard. Moreover, their understanding of local politics was limited by custom. They had been given the vote in local elections but did not stand for election. Generally, too, it seemed that the women did not contribute to public political discussion. If they sat with the men while village business was discussed, they 'only listened ... they did not contribute ... [women] did not talk about things men discussed, they talked about gardens, weaving, fishing and baskets, feasting', which was natural enough seeing that their lives were fully occupied with such activities. A Saibai man said that, in the home, the women 'might be boss altogether, the mother was responsible', but when she sat with her husband the decisions were 'with the father'. Another man said that if a woman was told: 'You don't go to that house', she would obey him. And it was the men who volunteered their perceptions about whether the women had any sort of political role in the communities. One said that the Mothers Union was the only outlet for any political thought the women might have had: 'Every woman was on the same boat and had one political mind, it was the Mothers Union.' Another comment was that some women on Badu were 'very politically aware' and they had leaders who 'pulled together to get the job done'. The latter comment was probably made with reference to the Mothers Union or in recognition that the women had always done much of their village work in groups. The response of a St Paul's man was that 'on all those islands you cannot say one woman is stronger than the other'. If the women on Badu had been politically stronger than on other islands, 'Why didn't they have a woman councillor?' he enquired. These perceptions, and that the men were expressing them rather than the women, are not surprising when it is remembered that the women's roles during the Pacific War were still largely determined by the traditional values of the male hegemonic societies in which they lived. The men's testimonies were reflections of that bygone era.

'It was very hard time' was the phrase used repeatedly by the old Torres Strait Islander women. Occasionally these words seemed to be in substitution of an experience they did not want to talk about. Nonetheless, just as most of the women spoke enthusiastically about their faith and prayer, they were nearly as enthusiastic when they spoke about the personal hardships of feeding and clothing their families. Curtin's 'season of austerity' was sharply felt in Torres Strait.

The demands of war reached into every home in Australia. In mid-1942, Prime Minister Curtin called on the people to observe a season of austerity for the sake of the war effort. On the mainland, rationing and shortages became commonplace. Petrol had been rationed in 1940 and car tyres and tubes were only available to people classified as 'essential users', but this affected relatively few ordinary wage earners because most did not own a car. Shortages of tobacco and beer were another matter. A Victorian woman remembered that her brothers kept their cigarette butts and 'when they were short they would come up with about two very thin cigarettes'.[3] A Townsville man recalled that the shortage of beer touched soldiers and civilians alike. Home refrigerators were virtually unheard of, so there were long queues at the ice works in summer in the hope of getting a block before supplies ran out. Tea was brought under the coupon system in July 1942, sugar in August and meat in January 1944. Many items which were not couponed were frequently in short supply or temporarily absent from store shelves. In the southern states, gas restrictions and shortages of firewood made the winter months bleak; children queued hopefully with carts of all descriptions at wood yards. The shortage of vegetables in the cities prompted suburban gardeners, who had previously concentrated on flower growing, to grow vegetables.

In May 1942, the Prime Minister called upon all civilians to make do with what they had in the way of clothing, declaring: 'The darning needle is a weapon of war.'[4] Clothing quotas were introduced and many women rushed to stores and selfishly purchased whatever they could whether they needed the item or not. Others dug into their family wardrobes for discarded clothing, and invisible-mending firms did brisk business. In mid-June 1942, the government introduced what it envisaged was a fairer system: the issue of an equal number of coupons for the linen and clothing requirements of each civilian. Hints were given on the radio on how to get the print out of unbleached calico flour-bags which could then be used as dress material. And, although there were complaints about couponing, at the end of the first year some families returned their surplus. Curtin's season of austerity certainly was not a time when mainland people went hungry or were too cold. It was probably better described as a time of inconveniences and irritations. However, on the outer island communities in Torres Strait, the absence of store goods made it very difficult for the women to clothe their families; at times, some also went hungry.

'I only had two dresses'

The semi-subsistence lifestyle of the Torres Strait Islanders was a far remove from the consumer society of mainland Australia. Nevertheless, these women, too, had to contend with shortages and, at times, the lack of the basic store foods they had become accustomed to buying: 'Sometimes there was no flour, no rice.' Stores had been established on the larger communities since 1932, but, from his own observation in 1942 as a mainland consumer, a signaller concluded that 'the island folk did little shopping either before or during World War Two'. He gauged this from the sorts of goods he saw in the store on Masig which 'consisted mainly of calico of various colours ... cotton threads, white mainly ... embroidery cotton ... flour, rice, tea, sugar, jam, tinned milk, tinned peas, tinned meat, that sort of thing ... some maritime supplies ... like rowlocks and anchors.' There is no reason to believe that the situation would have been any different on other communities because many were less affluent than Masig. Only one woman indicated that her family had been able to stock up on any essential item before the war: 'We had five brothers. They had been working on the pearling boat for many years ... they went to TI with shell and they bought everything cheap. They bought material and they got one big roll and gave it to our mother. We had material when the war started.' Most families had little money to dress well: 'When the war started we did not have much clothing, we were already poor, we had only bad clothing.' An Erub woman described what it seemed was the content of most wardrobes: 'I had only two dresses in the war, two white dresses made out of that calico ... they lasted me all the war ... we had no shoes, nothing else.'

A woman from Dauan remembered that there was 'no material in the store'. Her mother made the boys' trousers out of flourbags. They were washed white and sometimes coloured with homemade dye. Hessian bags, softened by soaking, were also used for clothing. Women went to their gardens in 'bag dresses' so that they could keep their one good dress for church. As soon as they returned from church, the bag dress replaced the Sunday dress: 'We had to take very good care to look after that dress.' Most of the old men were reduced to two calico lavalavas. When these wore out, the women made lavalavas for them from the hessian bags. Singlets could not be bought so the women improvised by making them out of the sleeves of old shirts. Early in the war, there was a supply of men's trousers in the Meriam store which the women purchased to make skirts from the leg pieces. The skirts were stitched to bodices cut from old singlets. Children's clothes were made from the stronger bits of material in worn-out garments. Those who had old sheets and pillowcases transformed them into 'island drawers'. Indeed, every scrap of old or spare material was used to make clothes because, as a Saibai woman remarked, probably as a reflection on the changed culture: 'Well, what can you do? You have to cover up.' The Nagi women disclosed with grins on their faces that they were not so modest in their solution: 'We walked around with skirts and no tops when the men weren't there.' Most of the sewing was done by hand as there were few sewing machines on the islands, although a couple of grandmothers insisted on carrying their heavy hand-operated machines into the bush where they sewed and mended for large families.

Dinghy sails were fashioned into garments by these resourceful dressmakers and the cloth was 'good for patching'. The darning needle was certainly a weapon of war in Torres Strait: 'We had to look after those dresses ... mend them when they got holes.' On Nagi, the afternoons were set aside for mending: 'Every little hole was darned so neat and all by hand' and every bit of material was valuable. 'Now we are so spoilt; our grandmothers would have loved every scrap of the material wasted today', the women reminisced. A Saibai woman recalled that she never had to make clothes from flourbags because she managed to keep her family's clothes mended: 'If I went to the store I looked for a man-size shirt and I took it. I used that shirt to mend other clothes.' When darning thread disappeared from the store shelves, she said that a next-door neighbour sometimes helped out: 'Bit by bit you fixed it up.' An old storekeeper reminisced:

> No clothes came and the women had to cut down all the old lavalavas to make kids' clothes, and dresses with flourbags. Anything that could be useful you had to use ... Everybody had to be a bit clever in your head to look at things, otherwise you go without.

By sheer hard work and resourcefulness, Torres Strait Islander women kept their families clothed throughout the war.

'We had to rely a lot on bush tucker'

Even of more concern to the women was how they would feed their large families. An immediate reaction on some communities to the attack on Nurupai was to take whatever goods were in the store into the bush for distribution amongst the families. Everyone thought that Torres Strait was about to be invaded and good business procedures seemed superfluous. However, once the people felt reasonably confident that there was to be no immediate enemy invasion, the stores resumed business operations in the village. In some cases, stores were set up in the bush to service those who had evacuated there. But from then on, the problem was that supplies came irregularly. One storekeeper recalled: 'The boats just dropped them and off again. They were not very regular and the people had to depend more on their gardens. You did have times when you ran out of food altogether. Then they lived on coconuts.' In May, when the coupon system was introduced on the mainland, it was not extended to the outer island communities. The storekeepers just monitored the quantities the women purchased. A former store worker on Masig said:

> We only had a little bit of food. We had to wait a month ... You buy a bag of flour but you have to go steady. Tea was no problem because we had lemon grass [tea]. Sugar and butter were hard and Sunshine or condensed milk. If we had two or three cases every family had to get a tin of milk, so we had to make it go around.

Storekeepers introduced a 'loose quota system' on all goods received into the store. 'Everything was half', a Saibai woman recalled. 'If you want a bar of soap it was half, tea, small tin jam.' A St Paul's woman said: 'They rationed us and we had to depend a lot on bush tucker.' This was the situation everywhere. Moreover, even if there were stocks in the store, the women might not have the money to buy the food. Conversely, if anyone was lucky enough to have 'a bit of money', they could buy 'what was left over', although the general impression was that on most communities only 'so many bags of flour, rice and tea' would come into the stores and they were measured out to the people. One woman remembered that they only got 'bad food', that the flour and rice were mildewed and contained weevils: 'We got to wash the rice and my grandmother picked the bad ones out ... we got to sift the bad flour too.' As late as September 1944, Charlie Turner said that store goods were still 'none too plentiful' on the islands. He grew tomatoes, cucumbers, melons and lettuces beside the Masig hospital verandah and exchanged them for tinned foods with crew members on launches using the Great North East Channel. And, when the SS *Kintour*, on its way to Port Moresby, ran aground on Tudu, eighteen nautical miles from Masig, the captain gave the people permission to salvage it. The haul of tinned foods was very welcome.[5]

Torres Strait Islander women were unaware of the austerity measures which were operating on the mainland. Nevertheless, their exclusion from the coupon system is further confirmation that, not only in theory but also in practice, they were not regarded as full Australian citizens. Indeed, if they had come under the coupon system and goods to the coupon value and money to buy them had been available, Torres Strait Islander women would have seen that as a luxurious oversupply. However, at times, welcome relief came when commercially packaged goods from other sources were given to the women. American ships on their way to Port Moresby frequently anchored off Purma: 'They supplied us with food, milk and even trousers. We were short of water and, when the chairman told the sailors the problem, they supplied us with water.' A special treat for the children was ice-cream, something they had not previously tasted. The army signallers gave the children sweets from comfort parcels and the army assisted families desperate for store goods. Lime juice became a popular item of exchange for work done by the women or for produce from their gardens. And, as an old woman from Poid recalled: 'When the army boys come on leave, they bring plenty of food. We got something like meat or tinned fish.' The women on Moa were especially appreciative because their wartime gardens struggled under the camouflage of the trees.

However, some of the items were not palatable to families who had lived in slightly more comfortable circumstances before the war, such as the Masig Islanders. One woman suggested that tinned beetroot was so unpalatable to her family that she had no alternative but to 'open them and throw them out and use the tin for a cup'. Brown rice was not eaten on the islands but it was more acceptable than the beetroot. The women would have preferred white flour for dampers to those 'big dry biscuits' the men brought home. However, the Saibai women devised a way to make them more palatable: 'We scraped the coconut and when the milk boiled we put the biscuit inside the milk and put a little bit of salt on it. It was a good one.' However, no amount of juggling of the commercially produced food from all of the sources described could have ensured that large families would be fed each day. All families were heavily dependent on their own 'bush tucker', and that is why 'the women worked hard in the garden'.

In their stringent wartime circumstances, the heavy dependence on bush tucker meant a lot of work for the women. In the early months of the war, the Meriam women were faced with the added problem of a drought: 'There was no rain and all the coconuts were only little coconuts ... The people made the gardens but they didn't grow.' They were forced to make provision for their families by roasting the nuts from the *egere* tree. It was explained that this nut was always eaten by the people in 'bad times', and drought and war were 'very bad times [so] when we've got no food, we live on that tree'. The worry was always that 'it was very hard, very hard to feed all the kids'. The women who evacuated to the bush dug the virgin soil with crowbars: 'Oh, very hard work'; 'We camouflaged everything under the bush, don't leave any clear ground so the Japs couldn't see the gardens.' These gardens needed much encouragement. The women who went to their old gardens had to 'go quick and come back quick again so the planes don't see [you]'. Some days they could not go at all.

Women on the Top-Western Islands risked exposure to the enemy when they crossed to the southern coast of Papua to get food:

> If the supply boat did not come in, they've got no radio and there's nothing and they are short of food and they have to go. New Guinea people have always got food; they have good gardens. We still got the outrigger and they need people to sit on the outrigger, they had to balance it, so they need women for the crew.

The women did not say what was given to the Papuans in exchange for their garden produce. Before the war, old clothes and store goods were exchange items, but they were hardly in a position to make those exchanges during the war. Acting as crew members on the long outrigger canoes was not new to these women and they were good at it: 'We sailed those canoes, real fast.' A signaller vouched for this:

> In the *Reliance* coming back from Saibai to Moa, we saw a women's crew in a dugout or cut-out canoe and they raced past us. I think the *Reliance* was about forty feet and the canoe would

have been forty-five feet or longer and it just went past us. They were sailing and singing like mad. There were six, seven, eight women singing away and having a good old time. We had a motorised launch and they just slipped past us.

A Saibai woman explained why the old trading networks could not be abandoned:

It's hungry time, January/February. You cannot get anything. In the wet season we could not get to the garden. Cassava is our main food. You can eat it all that time but it went watery in hungry time. What we did was get yams from New Guinea and save them to help us go through hungry time.

The Boigu women were also exposed to the dangers of sea travel in their attempts to obtain food from gardens on the other side of the island. 'I was a small girl ... got no *susu* [breasts]', one woman remembered. She said that one day her family left the village in their paddle canoe to collect watermelons, about a day's journey. They paddled close to the shore: 'That plane was flying very near the water ... It was Japanese with a round dot ... we just put the canoe in the sand and leave Dad there and we ran into the mangroves ... then that plane went behind the other side of the island.' The plane circled them three times before it turned toward the New Guinea coast: 'We were really frightened, we never got those watermelons, we went back home.'

There were also difficulties in providing ample fish and in carting water and wood. When the people were ordered to keep away from the beach and all seacraft were removed from the islands or beached, it became extremely difficult for the women to obtain sufficient quantities of fish, a very important staple in their diet. A signaller recalled that one day, despite the danger, the old men 'gave the signal' to the women to go out in the dinghy to net the silver mullet that had begun to run. Old Barney Mosby had told him that the women were 'number one for fishing, much better than the men'. He was left in no doubt when they returned with a 'boatload' of fish, which was, according to island custom, shared amongst the people and even the signallers got much more than they could eat.

Each family's surplus was cleaned, spread flat, smoked and hung in the houses to dry and be eaten when other fish was in short supply. A Badu woman explained that all the fish caught were 'really cared for, then no one went hungry'. The Meriam women fished daily, while other members of their families kept a lookout for planes. The Nagi women went every day to the lagoon for fish and crayfish; no opportunity to get food was missed. On Saibai when a huge flock of ducks, like a 'big black cloud', came towards the lagoon, a signaller watched as a group of women waded into the water swirling sticks, three to four feet long, above their heads; they then let fly with them across the swamp, killing several ducks with each blow. Women stalked the huge mud crabs in the murky mangrove swamps, home to crocodiles, and searched for edible grubs in these eerie muddy places. They frequently ignored orders meant for their safety, but families had to be fed.

The women forced to live in the bush talked about looking for suitable drinking water and running creeks with 'good stones' for washing. Some dug new wells and kept them free from whip snakes and rats that fell in. They maintained the wells: 'We took the sand out every month and when you cleared it out it filled up with nice clean water.' The Saibai women, despite the danger, continued to cross the channel to Dauan for water, and the Purma women went to an old well on Waraber. On some islands where the women were relocated in the bush, they had to carry water even longer distances than they had before the war. However, for the Mabuiag women, moving into the bush was a blessing in one sense: 'It was hard because we shifted out from village and stayed in the bush, but it was good for us, easier because we were near the water. We were satisfied because we don't have to carry it so far.' Ironically, this ancient labour of third- and fourth-world women had been alleviated temporarily by the war.

Fuel for cooking and washing had to be collected daily. On Badu they searched along the beaches, where they were exposed to enemy aircraft. A signaller, on his first expedition to collect wood, recalled seeing a party of a dozen or so women with bundles on their hips. 'They seemed to be checking me out with some sort of expression of disapproval', he recalled. Later, the Chief Councillor told him that that 'wasn't the way it should be done'. It seemed wood gathering was the 'responsibility and duty of island ladies and they were very good at it'. From then on, the signallers' wood heap was quietly replenished every morning with 'beautifully cut sticks, eighteen inches in length'. Thus, in performing this customary role, the Masig women exposed themselves to possible Japanese fire for the sake of the outsiders as well as their families.

The 'money line'

An old Masig leader recalled that the 'money line' was very low, especially during the first two years of the war. He said the cessation of the marine industry and the subsequent impressment of their vessels was tantamount to taking the people's 'bread and butter' from them. Consequently, most women's economic viability was reduced early in 1942 to whatever child endowment and allotment moneys they could access.

The receipt of child endowment in late 1941 had suggested something to Torres Strait Islanders about their aspirations for equality with white Australians. It was the first Commonwealth government benefit to be extended to Indigenous Australians. Prior to the war, that government had been urged, without success, by people like anthropologist AP Elkin and Protector Bleakley on the grounds of 'social justice and practicality', to extend old age, invalid and maternity benefits to Indigenous people.[6] When the Child Endowment Bill passed through the Commonwealth parliament, it provided that payment would be made to Aborigines if they were living 'under conditions comparable with those of the people generally'.[7] Although Torres Strait Islanders were not specifically named in the Act (which is not surprising considering their lost identity in, among other places, the Commonwealth sphere), they did receive the benefit. But it is difficult to understand how Aborigines' or Torres Strait Islanders' living conditions could have been seen as comparable with those of even the poorest white mainlanders. Moreover, during the debate on the Bill, Sir Raphael Cilento, a leading doctor in North Queensland, said: 'A nation is dying which has not an average family of 3.6 children. It therefore behoves the government to encourage in every way possible those who are bringing families into the world.' It was argued that everything possible should be done 'to encourage the peopling of

Australia with *native-born* [emphasis added] persons'.[8] During the 1930s, the assimilation of Australia's Indigenous people was being mooted by anthropologists and concerned white citizens. But the opinion was still being espoused by many that the Aborigines were a dying race; Torres Strait Islanders were an invisible race. It is hard to imagine that the term 'native-born' referred to either group, particularly in view of mainstream thinking about Indigenous populations and miscegenation. Moreover, Indigenous women needed no incentive to have large families. From the women's testimonies, the average family had well in excess of 3.6 children. However, without any clear reference in the debates on the Child Endowment Bill as to why the Commonwealth government ultimately decided to pay the benefit to Torres Strait Islanders, it is reasonable to suggest that people like Elkin and Bleakley finally had some impact on the government's thinking. Furthermore, the Commonwealth government was aware, by 1941, that there may have been a need to placate disaffected Indigenous people living in the weakly defended north, many of whom had had close working relationships with Japanese divers.

This unexplained inclusion of the Torres Strait Islanders in the latest Commonwealth benefit had a dramatic impact on them. When the women received their first child endowment in late 1941, there was great joy in the villages. One old man said: 'The women came back and told us, "We got some money, the children are getting money". From that day to this, the people lived happy. We got child endowment.' On St Paul's, the women 'jumped for joy ... "Look at all the money we've got" ', they said. It was almost inevitable that the people personalised child endowment, seeing it in terms of their traditional gift exchange. Thus, the grant of this first benefit was subsequently interpreted by one Torres Strait Islander leader as putting the people in a new, and welcome, relationship with the Commonwealth government. The Torres Strait Islander economy was based on kinship rights and obligations. This leader saw the government's act as putting itself in a similar relationship with his people: the people's full allegiance by army service was being reciprocated by the payment of child endowment. He described the Commonwealth government as his 'friend':[9]

> All the councillors talked to this chairman ... He said, 'When I was a boy I had no friend. When I came to be a man I had many friends.' Then these people asked him, 'What was that, why you tell us that way?' He said, 'When I was born my mother had no child endowment, my father had no pension, but when I came to be a man, the war came and made me sign in the army' and they said, "We're going to give you that one that's been coming in the middle of the war, child endowment".'

But could the people construe this new relationship to mean full equality with all Australians after the war? Only time would tell.

For a month or two, child endowment was paid directly to the women on the basis that it would give them 'a chance to learn how to handle their own business affairs'.[10] By the time the men enlisted, the system of payment had been changed because the outsider perception was that the husbands took the money and the children received little benefit from it. This act demonstrated an insensitivity to the fact that island men were accustomed to shopping because, until the mid-1930s, few communities had stores. Nevertheless, subsequent child endowment payments were made through a passbook system over which the Director had absolute control. Problems with this method of payment soon arose. Almost three months elapsed before the teacher from Erub, on a visit to Thursday Island just before the evacuation, was given authority to enter child endowment in the women's passbooks. Moreover, on the eve of the Department's withdrawal, the women were being told how they should spend their child endowment. The moneys would be withheld, the white teacher warned, if they bought large quantities of materials instead of spending it on the children.[11] However, the women were not stockpiling materials but, in retrospect, it may have been in the children's interests if they had. In any event, as the war progressed, the women's spending capacity was drastically diminished through no fault of their own.

A Badu woman was sure that child endowment did not come regularly in the early period of the war and, according to the Meriam women, even if they got child endowment, it seemed, it was not their full entitlement. However, even with money, some women had problems spending it. A former Yam Island storekeeper said:

'Women sat outside the store and called to people who understood about money, "Would you do this shopping for me?".' Even on Saibai where there had been a store for a number of years, there were women who asked their children to help them make their purchases; some could only put their mark on withdrawal slips. This seems surprising when it is considered that western education had been introduced in Torres Strait four decades prior to the war. A St Paul's woman clarified the position. Her family left Erub in 1929 because, she said, 'DNA grabbed' all the people's money. During the year, the men bought such items as flour, rice, sugar and kerosene on a credit system called slopchest. 'Slopchest, it's a white man's word', an old island storekeeper explained, 'I give them something from the store ... they sign for it ... when they get their money they pay it back.' After repayments to slopchest and deductions for contributions to the Island Fund, boat repairs and seamen's insurance, there was little and sometimes no money left. Moreover, they had no way of knowing if they had been cheated. When they went to St Paul's, she remembered that her brothers came home with money in their hands and the women were surprised: 'We don't know about money ... What's that? Oh, that's money ... That's why my father went to St Paul's. On other islands [under the Department] they don't know anything.' Thus, without the opportunity to gain practical experience in handling their own money on many of the communities, there were women who entered the war years with little or no working knowledge of how the capitalist monetary exchange system worked.

As late as January 1944, even though transport around Torres Strait had improved somewhat, army intelligence officers listened to allegations, particularly those of the more politically aggressive Meriam men, that child endowment payments to their wives were 'irregular and unsatisfactory'.[12] They also complained that, if their wives did not withdraw the full amount of any month's child endowment which had been entered in their passbooks, they could not subsequently use the balance. Charlie Turner, who liaised with the government on behalf of the people, was told in April 1943 that endowees did not need to draw all of their monthly payments so long as the children were well provided for. It seems the Director had little realistic understanding of the women's position. Moreover, did this account for the credit balance in the Department's Child Endowment Account which increased during the war years?

In July 1942, the auditor drew the Department's attention to the balance and predicted that the undrawn balance would increase. And it did. On 11 January 1943 it was £4,325 8s 2d; by December 1945 the figure had risen to £6,185 7s 2d; and a year later it was £10,287 16s 1d.[13] The Meriam accounts had a credit of £2,279 13s 6d, by far the largest amount of undrawn child endowment for any community by the end of the war, and yet the Meriam men were complaining about the non-receipt of the full amount of the women's entitlements.[14] Clearly the Department held considerable child endowment funds throughout the war period, even though there were times when the women were without money to pay for store food for their children. The Director subsequently justified the withholding of money on the basis that the women were his wards and, like a good father, he was protecting their money: 'A close check is made on every individual account to which child endowment is credited to ensure that the expenditure by parents is in keeping with the purpose for which the payment is made.'[15] White endowees would not have tolerated the abrogation of their rights in this way.

The island women were further hindered in accessing their moneys by the Department's inefficient and poorly kept accounting system. The April 1942 audit report indicated problems with the Local Protector's accounts even before the evacuation. The Director responded to the auditor's suggestion that the accounts were in a 'most unsatisfactory' state by pointing out that the accounts had to be 'thrown to the four winds' in early 1942 in an attempt to help the people, who, he finally admitted, felt they had been 'deserted to the enemy'.[16] The situation was made worse by the inability of board manager Curtis to keep the accounts up-to-date because of the lack of support staff. Moreover, internal audits were not carried out on the books of the branch stores for at least three years. It was through these accounts that the women's entitlements and sales to them on credit were recorded. Therefore, if the Department's and the Board's accounts were not up-to-date, no one could be sure what moneys were due to the women at any particular time. The evidence corroborates the women's claims that they received little money.

As already discussed, prior to 1944 the women were not entitled to independent military allotments, only the allowances paid out of the enlisted men's pay or cash received from them, but this was not always forthcoming. One veteran recalled that he did not have money deducted from his pay because it was 'too little' to send any home. A Stephens Island woman said: 'Yes, yes, some women didn't get allotment. They had to make something like to sell. They support their own selves by selling coconut oil, mats. That was proper hard.' An Erub woman said: 'The allotment — the women never got it ... only once and that's it ... when the men came back home they gave us money but when they went back, my mother didn't get any allotment.' On Dauan, a woman also remembered receiving an allotment but it was 'very small money'. A Meriam woman thought the only money she received was some child endowment. Other recollections were: 'Dad sent allotment to Mum'; 'The boys used to give little allotment for us'; 'We got allotment, very small money.' A Boigu woman remembered that they had to 'wait for the boat to come with child endowment and that money from the army'. These testimonies indicate that allotments, like child endowment, were received irregularly and in small amounts. Even when the women became entitled to independent dependants' allowances in 1944, whether they received their full entitlements is conjectural. There had been no reconciliation of the Director's military allotment accounts for most of 1945 and, even when this was done, the number of errors in postings made it impossible to say whether the final balance was correct because it entailed 'hundreds of entries ... *over a number of years* [emphasis added]'.[17] Were the moneys taken from the soldiers' pay prior to 1944 included in the 'number of years'? The audit reports on allotment moneys do not support any contention that the women received what was due to them, even allowing for unavoidable delays in transmission of credits from Brisbane.

A further consequence of the paternalism of the Department and its mismanagement of the women's money was that they were forced to buy from the government stores on 'slopchest'. Slopchest had been a source of concern to the people for some time because their history of buying on credit had clearly demonstrated to them that they were, more often than not, left with no money once the amounts owed were recouped from the men's wages. Moreover, they were never sure whether they had been cheated. Thus, its use was being discouraged. 'No one here is satisfied about this slopchest; we all want to draw money', the Erub leaders complained.[18] However, one wartime storekeeper said he was forced to allow the women to use slopchest: 'I don't think it was easy for them to turn me this way and that way. I did my own thinking but if the women needed money, I paid them this way and I did it happily to help my people.' By March 1945, there was a debit balance of £3,038 in the account. The auditor stated that this was very unsatisfactory. He suggested little control had been exercised over the amount of credit extended to the women and that no attempt had been made to recoup the moneys. The auditor obviously had no appreciation of the economic corner into which the women had been forced. (Slopchest was discontinued altogether in early 1946.)

Another factor which contributed to this negative picture was that all the women's monetary transactions were passed through a local system of accounting which was time-consuming and complex. A former storekeeper talked about the system:

> In those days we had a double-entry system of bookkeeping. They had books in the branch stores but all records were sent to the Badu store; but the real ledgers were in head office and we had to allow credit sales on slopchest to all of the people on the islands and we had to get them to sign and we kept the books for that too.

Also, store work was frequently performed by island teachers whose workload was already heavy. Another old island teacher/storekeeper recounted an average day's work for him:

> The head told me to run it like this, eight o'clock and nine I did the store work in the morning and 9.30 I go to school. From that time to three o'clock in the afternoon I closed the store, then I went to carry on the store work and I served people until they were all satisfied and then I closed, sometimes at six o'clock, and every day in the week. There were preparations

of lessons for school, get ready for the store in the morning and I
did my books.

Moreover, during the war, many men were put in charge of stores without training, there was no supervision and internal audits were not carried out for almost the entire war period. The incentive to work hard at the job diminished for some when they found themselves working long hours with no arrangement for payment of their wages. The evidence supports the contention that the women's money line was low, indeed much lower than it should have been. Moreover, any accusation that storekeepers lacked control when it came to the amount of money the women spent on slopchest was totally unjustified in their desperate situation. As a storekeeper's wife commented: 'Yeah, but they had to eat something.'

Added to the problems associated with accessing child endowment and allotments, the full benefit of wages earned by Torres Strait Islander government employees in the latter part of the war was also denied families. From late 1943, some reconstruction had begun on the communities. In mid-1944, the wages of the growing number of people engaged in government positions — school teachers, storekeepers, nurses and police — were increased to provide a 'decent standard of living' on the communities.[19] Nevertheless, anomalies occurred in the payment of these wages. For instance, Abui was appointed a sergeant of police on 19 June 1944 on a wage of £2 10s per month, but was credited with only £1 5s per month until 30 November 1944; Mary Apai and Takata Bani (teachers) commenced service on 22 February 1944 but received nothing until 30 November 1944; and hospital nursing staff did not receive their increase of 10s per month for three months.[20] Meanwhile, prices in the stores continued to soar.

Thus all of these restrictions on the women's economic viability added to their struggles to maintain families in already austere circumstances. To alleviate the situation, many women looked for ways to resume earning their own money.

Paid employment

White women were a valuable pool of labour in the nation's attempt to maintain mainland society and promote the war effort on every front. That society's prewar expectations for thousands of middle-class white women had been that they would marry, leave the paid work-force and become mothers. Thus, in tune with this general view of the women's roles, their own earliest expectations of participation in the war effort were confined to voluntary caring-type work. However, some women were dissatisfied; wanting more involvement in the war effort, they formed quasi-military auxiliaries. Their members were ridiculed for 'playing soldiers', and governments did not support their ideals until forced to do so in 1941 with the formation of the women's services.[21] Women flocked to join. An old bearded critic remonstrated with a young woman in her overalls: 'A woman in trousers', he bellowed to the delight of passers-by, 'is an abomination unto the Lord.'[22]

In January 1942, however, the government had to acknowledge that Australia's human resources were totally inadequate for a country on the verge of invasion. Thus, new manpower regulations forced thousands of women out of their domesticity into jobs where they learnt new skills. Many 'lower class' women who were in employment as domestics, factory workers, shop assistants, kitchen hands and in the clothing industry retrained. A female textile worker, receiving £1 8s 6d a week, took on a job in an aircraft factory where she learnt welding and was paid £6 18s a week.[23] And, to meet the desperate need for rural workers, privately sponsored land armies emerged until they were given official status as the Australian Women's Land Army. One city girl who joined said she increased her skills by learning to prune, spray and plough and to handle animals. In the munition factories,

> young girls and white-haired women and women who had lived sheltered lives mingled with women who had only known lives of hardship and deprivation and were quite overwhelmed at the contents of their pay packets which, while not overly lucrative, were adequate to pay rent and ordinary daily needs.[24]

At all these jobs, women were judged as 'efficient and as good as any man' and their earnings gave many of them an improved economic viability after the stringent depression years.[25]

Torres Strait Islander women, unlike their white mainland counterparts, needed few new skills in the fight for the survival of their semi-subsistent societies:

> Things were no different for women work-wise in the war as they had always had to do the bulk of the gardening, they had to help with building housing, they did the housework and they could make a feast and sail the dugout canoes.

For a time after the evacuation of the whites and the cessation of the marine industry, avenues of paid employment for island women were few and often potentially dangerous. However, of necessity from early 1942, they were forced to resume collecting trochus shell from the reefs, despite possible exposure to the enemy. The shell was sold in small quantities to the stores, the monetary value of their wartime yield being an impressive £13,290.[26] Some families returned to mine wolfram on Moa. A Ugar family which had lost its main source of income when the marine industry ceased and was later forced to evacuate to St Paul's worked together at the mine. 'They said you make a lot of money on wolfram', the father recalled. But it was hard work for everyone:

> Six o'clock we drank tea ... walked up a big hill and I am not going to make it, and ten o'clock we got to the top of the hill. We started work and left at three o'clock and went down the hill and got home at six. We stayed for two years and the people worked hard every day until Sunday.

Everyone was constantly on the alert for enemy aircraft: 'We were working wolfram and we heard the noise of five or six planes, and we ran into the bush.' The miners' wartime yield of the mineral was 76,000 pounds [34,545 kg].[27] Apart from mining, and collecting trochus shell, women on all islands baked bread, washed clothes, ironed and did housework for the signallers and military visitors. By the time some young women became employed in the hospitals set up on Badu and Masig in late 1943, others were earning a small wage as teachers.

Sharing and not sharing

The longstanding Torres Strait Islander custom of sharing contributed to the survival of these island communities during the war. Reciprocity, based on the obligation to share with kin, was the people's own 'social security' system. Besides serving to 'validate and maintain social relationships and roles' amongst kin, reciprocity also ensured that with the sharing of food people did not go hungry. In traditional times, after a dugong hunt, the meat was apportioned out to those entitled to receive it.[28] First responsibility was to nearest kin: 'Look after mother and father, never mind if you and your wife have to go without', the young hunters were told.[29] Theirs was a world based on giving and receiving, not buying and selling.

During the war, the custom was extended: 'Instead of sharing with [kin], we shared out with all villages, all houses'; 'We have got that sharing thing really strong, that is we always distribute little bits to everybody ... people just helping each other — everyone put their heads together, stay together, eat together and share.' Thus, a former Yam Island storekeeper was able to say:

> The only thing that I appreciate about our people at that time they were never greedy. If I had nothing and I asked you for something, you always shared. That was one good thing ... it helped our people to survive because they were never greedy. Even when they got fish, turtle, they just shared it with everybody. Because we could share we survived. If you shared with somebody, that person would share with you.

Palmer, the white priest who went to Torres Strait after the war, suggested that 'no woman would be left to fend for herself if her husband had enlisted [because] the family and clan systems were such that [each island] was a single integrated and inter-dependent community'.[30] While this was true, the impact over time of their extenuating wartime circumstances was such that instances of self-interest were reported to army officers.

In late 1943, army reports indicated that self-interest or individualism on St Paul's was causing distress for the army wives: the TSLI men reported that their families were not being helped by the rest of the community. Moreover, it was claimed that the wolfram miners were being privileged in the distribution of rations from the village store when a store had been set up at the mine site in the latter months of 1943 exclusively for them. A St Paul's man made it clear that sharing had been practised amongst his people: 'We got fish and what we got we shared ... My father was a good turtle spearer and we shared out with the village.' Therefore, the soldiers' expectations that the men at home would look out for their wives was not without foundation. Self-interest, however, which it was said produced 'a crop of Army Wives [versus] the Councillors and the Rest', crept into the St Paul's community. It was thought to have been imported from Mer and Erub. Thus, it seemed, the problem was not confined to St Paul's.[31] In the light of the people's claims that they survived because they were willing to share, it is difficult to understand what caused these pockets of self-interest. Hall suggested that the removal of the very large number of men from each village for such an unprecedented time was bound to give rise to more self-interest than was the custom amongst them.[32] Self-interest, or individualism, however, is fostered in the western capitalist system. On the mainland during the war, its darker side was also demonstrated by the operation of thriving black markets. Those who had the money could always get what they wanted. In the latter part of the war, the miners on Moa were earning better money than the TSLI men and they probably wanted to give their families more after the period of severest austerity which had existed during 1942 and most of 1943.

Other social problems were reported to the army. Marou, the Chief Councillor on Mer, was accused of beating a woman with whom he had quarrelled over a land boundary when he tried to fence off part of her husband's land. A Badu soldier, separated from his wife for fifteen years, was reputed to have refused to let her transfer a house owned by his mother to Yam. Two men from Poid were granted leave to give evidence of their wives' immorality before the island court. Trouble arose on St Paul's when the community became divided on whether it should remain under the control of the church or come under the Act, like all of the other outer island communities.[33] None of the women spoke about these or any other social problems, but that is understanable. Even if they did remember them, they were issues that had been resolved a long time ago and the women may have thought they were of no interest to an outsider.

Council elections

The matter of council elections on the outer islands is raised because of the attitudes of military outsiders who claimed there was a need for more disciplined leadership of the women. After his arrival in Torres Strait, Colonel Langford, who quickly gained the people's confidence after the Protector had been discredited by his desertion of them, appointed councillors on some communities. He emphasised to them that the women's gardens had to be maintained at a high level to offset their dependence upon store goods. Nonetheless, in December 1943, it was suggested that the women were almost entirely dependent on store goods. Grievances mounted against Mareko (one of Langford's appointees on Saibai) because of his strong handling of them and in late 1943 the women told their husbands they wanted Mareko ousted. Simultaneously, elections were being demanded by TSLI men from all communities under the Director's control.[34]

The elections were a year or more overdue and the men feared the loss of the political autonomy they had fought hard for. Moreover, the TSLI men's army experiences had strengthened their resolve to take leadership roles in the anticipated new postwar order. They persistently enquired of their white officers when the elections would take place. Would they be eligible to vote? Were they going to be allowed to nominate for office? Because the latter two questions were not answered when early elections were held on the Anglican mission of St Paul's, the TSLI men from there had no opportunity to vote or to stand for office. Their concern had been that a faction in the community was tending 'to swing toward government control' and they were totally opposed to that.[35]

Langford finally realised he would lose the confidence of the people if he did not set a date for the elections. When they were finally held on 24 July 1944, the TSLI men were allowed to vote and stand for office.[36] Marou, the man respected by so many for his strong leadership on Mer, his vision for the freedom of Torres Strait Islander people and his ability to liaise with Langford and his officers, was not amongst the newly elected councillors. He had been dismissed from office shortly before because of the violent quarrel previously mentioned. Mareko lost his place as Chief Councillor on Saibai. Loss of the women's support undoubtedly influenced that result. Nevertheless, Langford probably felt satisfied with the overall results as many of the new councillors were men with army discipline and he thought it was men of this calibre who would see that the women worked harder in their gardens.

Langford, whom the people had welcomed as the Protector's replacement, proved to be no less paternalistic, particularly of the women whom he judged on the basis of his officers' ethnocentric observations after brief visits to the communities. None of the outsiders had a realistic understanding of what gardening on the outer island communities entailed nor could they adequately comprehend the problems associated with the women's wartime environment. Moreover, the comments of the white officers who reported on the newly elected councillors reflected their own officer-class mentality, which was also rampantly paternalistic. Thus, they were able to say of the new councillors on Saibai that they were 'a good young team, imbued with a desire to take back to the island all the useful knowledge they ... acquired in the army'. Aragu retained the chairmanship on Dauan. He and the other two members of the council were seen as having 'drive and initiative ... very health conscious'. Three soldiers, seen as 'an extremely professional triumvirate' with 'good army training', were elected on Ugar. On only two communities were the elected councillors, some TSLI men, viewed by the outsiders in a negative light.[37] Most of the newly elected councillors were younger TSLI men. In that respect, the 1944 elections broke from the custom in Torres Strait Islander politics whereby older men took the leadership positions.

Unfortunately, many of the foregoing events and circumstances, as important as they were to the women then, were not recalled by them. Thus, what their perspectives might have been are not known, but it is unlikely they would have seen events in the same light as the outsiders, who had none of the esoteric knowledge necessary to translate what they heard and saw from the women's perspective. However, it is paradox which makes history what it is — representations of the past. Paradoxes demonstrate the ways in which the world is viewed through the discourses of different groups of people and individuals. A sensitivity to this is necessary when reading this history.[38]

Chapter 10

'The people had to do it'

Parents, relatives and elders on the communities instructed the young in the traditions of their culture. From the turn of the century, their children's education became two-edged: they also received a western education based on a curriculum approved by the Queensland Protector. The government's attempts to outlaw all customary health care practices failed and old people continued to pass on some of this knowledge. However, a western health care system was introduced and also supervised by the white teachers. Both institutions were grafted onto the island culture and became important to the people. With the evacuation of the white teachers, a vacuum in both education and health care was created that island women filled as best they could.

'Parents tried to teach'

In 1982, RW Connell made the claim that in schooling on the mainland before the Second World War 'social inequality was hardly a problem: it was built into the system'.[1] Prewar working-class students recalled: 'Higher education was not something you thought about ... you had to come from moneyed families to go to university.' Thus, government policy and the inability of the majority of state school children to go on to higher education ensured the maintenance of the large pool of low-paid labour essential to Australia's developing capitalist system. Educational policy and the lack of opportunities for a 'proper education' kept Torres Strait Islander children from also contemplating higher goals in life.

The ethnocentric thinking and paternalism of a succession of officers in the Chief Protector's Office, later the Department of Native Affairs in Brisbane, supported long-time Protector Bleakley's notion that Torres Strait Islanders should develop as a 'race apart' and be kept separate from the white Australian community. Furthermore, he was convinced that it would be futile to try to extend their employment opportunities beyond 'boat' and 'shore' work. Thus, under the Department's umbrella, a school curriculum was set which he maintained suited the people's 'native circumstances'.[2] A ceiling, or mark as it became known, was placed on the level of education island children could hope to attain: 'The teaching was very bad because we only went up to grade five ... the government said [the teacher] couldn't go over grade five and if they do they will be sacked, so when we reached grade five we would have to leave school.'[3] The situation was no different at the Anglican mission school on St Paul's: 'You got no proper school. When you come to grade four when you are fifteen or sixteen, you leave school and go on the boats or in the garden'; 'Not a lot was taught to us ... Most of the time we'd spend doing work for the priest. Our parents always had bad feelings, but they couldn't do anything about it.'[4] Girls from Nagi who boarded at the convent school on Thursday Island were no better off: 'We came out of school in fifth grade. That was all, that was the end of our school.'

In the early 1930s, the Anglican Church attempted to redress, for brighter students, this low standard of education when it opened a 'high' school on St Paul's for boys and girls from any community. But parents were loath to send their young children away, particularly their girls. 'I finished schooling ... eighth year, doing fourth grade work. I was going to go to St Paul's but Mum wouldn't let me. She thought I might run away with boys. She wouldn't sign the papers', an old woman recalled. Simultaneously, the government recognised the need to do something about the increasing number of island young people being pressed into the classroom as monitors and teachers:

> Mr Agnew told me to be a teacher ... I was twelve years old when I became a teacher [1926]. I had a class of big boys. I had finished seven years. I was top scholar so he gave me a class ... The boys were older than me. Oh yes, they were naughty. I reported it to Mr Agnew and he gave them a hiding.

A teachers training college was set up on Mabuiag under Philip Frith. He tried to give the students a better understanding of things they had never seen: 'We did one year's training. Mr Frith was the only teacher. There was one big room, ... he made little tables and put everything there and he showed us things like animals, trains, boats. He had little models of them.' The college also offered in-service training: 'We once went to a seminar on Mabuiag in Mr Frith's time, that was everybody from all the islands, all the teachers. We had to go out the front and we had to talk and tell the other teachers where we were from and that.' Furthermore, both Frith and Charlie Turner refused to be bound by the mark. They did their best to raise the standard in their classes, something former students have not forgotten: 'These two gentlemen were working very, very hard, trying to [give] the children the same sort of knowledge that the white children got.' But they reached only a few students. And, even though those trained at the college on Mabuiag went into their classes a little better equipped, their own knowledge by its omission from the curriculum was being depreciated. If it had been taught in the children's first language, they undoubtedly would have achieved higher standards. More importantly, they would have developed greater confidence about their own identity which would have assisted them in their interactions with white Australians.[5] However, the changes implemented in the 1930s were still directed at maintaining a cheap pool of labour for the marine industry in Torres Strait. It was also another way to keep them from going to the mainland at a time when the maintenance of a white monoculture was seen as imperative.

The people increasingly came to understand that their education did not allow them to know 'how much they could get for trochus shell so that the Protector wouldn't be able to bluff them'; 'We had no education to check the scales, we knew no arithmetic, subtraction, addition. If we brought up 5 or 7 tons and the price was, say, £155 per ton, we might get, oh, £5 or £6? Just pocket money.'[6] There was a sense of powerlessness about their lives. Subsequent to the 1936 seamen's strike, on 23 August 1937, the first inter-island conference of Torres Strait Islander councillors was held. An old Masig woman remembered her father's concern at that time for the future of all Torres Strait Islanders: 'We cannot go see him. He tried to get away, plan something for Torres Strait. For six months by himself in his own place, he sit down all day thinking.' One of the outcomes of the conference was that the councillors made known to the Protector their continued dissatisfaction with the standard of their children's education. They wanted them educated 'to the stage at which they could check over their earnings with their employers'.[7] A new Scheme of Work was introduced but it was directed towards 'improved natives', not full citizenship. It certainly did not meet the people's aspiration for knowledge to 'go anywhere from school outside'.[8]

> We must maintain our education services despite war conditions and ... such maintenance is an integral part of our national life.[9]

Government rhetoric on the mainland called for increased education services because it was envisaged that, after the war, there would be a 'new order' in which white children would grow up to play more important roles. Torres Strait Islanders also hoped for a postwar order in which their children would be employed in a wider range of skilled jobs and be free to go to the mainland, if they so desired. These aspirations, however, were dependent on what the people called 'proper schooling'. Thus, the women's efforts, no matter how insignificant to outsiders, were important to them: 'When the war started, everything broke off because we cannot do anything. [Then] some of these parents, they tried to teach their children ... they wanted to get rid of this war and put the kids back into a proper school and carry on their education.'

The situation with regard to schooling was met in a variety of ways by the various island groups. The Masig people got organised relatively rapidly. A signaller recalled that the school was 'up and running' there when he arrived in March 1942. Ned Mosby, who had been the assistant to the white teacher, was in charge of the school, helped by Bugun Mosby. They taught the children the three Rs and a little history and geography. Formal schooling was not resumed quite so quickly elsewhere and the curriculum on some communities was even more basic. On Mer, for instance, the school was closed until August 1942 but, in the interim, mothers gave their children lessons. When classes did resume, they were not without many interruptions. One woman recalled: 'I was schooling at that time when the planes came over and we just dropped everything and rushed to our home and into the bush to hide.' On Badu, too, schooling was intermittent: 'We came from the bush to school and when we saw a plane our parents made us stay home. There were lots and lots of planes. We just stayed there in our bush houses, we don't go further, stayed close, just played underneath the trees.' However, when the war was not 'too strong', more regular schooling was possible. A wartime student living in the bush estimated that he walked several kilometres to school, but thought 'it was not far when you knew the island; when you don't know the island it seems a long way.'

Although Masig Islanders returned to their bush houses at dusk, they were around the village during the day and this made it easier for children to attend school. It was a very different story for the people from Poid, who were widely dispersed in the bush. Mothers were afraid to let their children out of their sight for long. One mother said: 'We cannot teach the children, we had no school. We cannot come out because the army won't let us come out ... We had a very hard time ... We cannot school them because we are frightened and we had different camps in the bush.' Nevertheless, other mothers and older sisters gave the children schoolwork to do. Late in the war, when they were able to leave the bush, the women set up shelters on the beach at Kubin while they built a new village. It was then that the children resumed regular lessons but, because the school house was in the old village at Poid, they too had to make a long journey on foot through the swamps and bush. 'It was a long way and we had to run to get to school on time. We walked and played coming back, there was plenty of time then', a former student reminisced.

On the Top-Western Islands of Saibai, Dauan and Boigu, the children attended classes in the school houses for the entire war period. However, because of their close proximity to the southern coastline of Papua into which area the Japanese eventually infiltrated, lessons were interrupted often by the sound of the *bu sel*. According to a former student, while the older boys were not put off by such disruptions, 'the younger kids were not sort of interested in school, they were frightened'.

Some St Paul's mothers were too afraid to let their children go to the village and family members again assumed responsibility for the children's schooling: 'We stopped in different patches in the bush and somebody in the family would teach the children. What we had was a slate for something to write on and we had only a few books to read. They took books from the school and used them.' Another recollection was: 'Our parents they taught us what they knew.' Later, these children too walked long distances to classes: 'School was in the village. An island girl taught school. She had never trained. She was there to help the white teacher before; and when she went away the island girl ran the classes.'

Mabuiag women recalled what happened to schooling there. One said: 'We were just outside in the bush now and we cannot come over to the village, we don't because of the war. There was no schooling. Some of the parents ... got little experience in their heads but they just taught them what they knew'; another recalled that in her family 'no one gave the kids any school'. A former teacher explained what happened to her during the war: '*Baba* Turner, he sent me to Yam Island 1939, 1940 ... I go to Purma 1941, 1942. Then that same time the war started and I came back here to Mabuiag and I taught in the bush. Later, we came out of the bush in the daytime and came to the primary school.' These testimonies indicate that the women on Mabuiag did respond differently to schooling the children during the early wartime period when there was great fear for everyone's safety. Undoubtedly, there were mixed responses on other communities. On Nagi, with its one extended family community, it fell to the eldest girl in a family of ten children, who had boarded at the convent school on Thursday Island, to teach her younger siblings: 'They got me to teach out there. I taught what I knew, I made these kids know how to write the letters A B C and count.'

On Purma, there was so little protection on this tiny coral cay that it was unthinkable to allow the children to go to the school house in the village in broad daylight. Consequently, the school remained closed and the storekeeper supplied the women with 'paper and pencils and things like that ... and they just helped the children during the day'. With no school supplies being shipped to outer Torres Strait, the Purma women were lucky to have these materials. A Meriam woman recalled that all they had were 'slates and they got their pencils from the sea — a piece of coral'. On Ugar, the population was no more than thirty-five in 1942. Sam Passi, the storekeeper/teacher there, taught until there were evacuations to other communities because of the island's extreme vulnerability. Charlie Turner, the one white government teacher who opted to remain in Torres Strait, visited the islands at great personal risk. A Nagi woman recalled: 'He used to come around and stay there to help the island teacher.' He was, to the people, 'teacher, nurse, helping out in everything and he was the medical man'.

The signallers also assisted the women whenever they could, although for two men to keep a day and night surveillance of their area demanded a great deal of time. They helped the women on Mabuiag to eventually re-open the school in August 1942. On Saibai and Erub, a former signaller recalled: 'We recruited senior girls who had a few grades at school and the Islander priest helped.' This was another way for them to participate in the island people's system of reciprocity. Even so, it was the women and a handful of island men who bore the brunt of responsibility until late in the war. Years later, Bleakley acknowledged this: 'All credit must be given to them for the able way in which they "held the fort", ensuring that ... the children's education carried on as well as could be expected.'[10]

It is important to understand that, while the women did not make it clear in their testimonies that their efforts at schooling the children were politically motivated, this was indeed the case. As already shown, they were hard-working women with few hours to spare. Moreover, in the absence of their colonisers, without government support and in their extremely dangerous location, they had every reason and opportunity to abandon schooling in that early period of fear and uncertainty. But the majority of the testimonies suggested that the children were receiving some sort of schooling during that time. That the women had such concern about their children's schooling is even more remarkable when it is recalled that state schools in far north Queensland were closed for the first eight months of the war. Moreover, there were complaints that children in these areas were 'running around the streets' and, as one local council suggested, 'losing all opportunities of education ... so vital to their upbringing'.[11] Torres Strait Islander women did not want their children to miss even the most basic educational opportunities.

In September 1944, PR Frith returned to supervise the children's schooling on the three Top-Western Islands. Hope spread as word of his return was passed on to other communities. It seemed that the war must be coming to an end and the children would finally get 'proper' schooling. However, until late 1944, the Queensland government gave the people no indication that their children would receive a postwar education which would enable them to participate in the state's economy and society other than as a 'lower caste' on their communities. Indeed, the Director's strong stand on the soldiers' pay and the women's allotments suggested he had no intention of raising the people's status after the war.

For their part, the TSLI men took every opportunity to express their dissatisfaction with the education their children received. In late 1944, the Queensland Governor was petitioned for 'university education' for their young people.[12] This was undoubtedly in response to a greater understanding of higher education the men gained from white soldiers with whom they served or who came to the islands. George Mye, a teenager at the time, recalled that his talks with signallers about university education had a lasting effect on him. Councillors also took every opportunity to press claims for 'proper schooling'. Several leaders spoke with the Governor during his visit to Badu in 1943 about 'higher education both Secondary and Rural, including Domestic Science'.[13] In August 1944, the newly elected councillors discussed education with the Director at the inter-island conference held on Masig. Subsequently, a unanimous resolution calling for a 'higher standard of education than previously applied' was passed.[14] Moreover, they agreed to a scheme to be set up immediately after the war for the secondary education on the mainland of at least an elite group of children. This, it was hoped, would open the door to university education for some and ultimately the people would have their own professional people. As an old woman remarked in 1988: 'If we had done scholarship it might have brightened up our education, our outlook on things. Probably we would have had our own doctors and lawyers and things like that.'

By late 1944, the Director himself conceded that wartime events in Torres Strait had brought about an 'unprecedented psychological change in [the Torres Strait Islanders'] outlook and demeanour generally'.[15] Their 'growing experience of civilised life beyond their own borders', Bleakley subsequently wrote, had made the 'rudimentary instruction' they had received 'while content with simple village life' obsolete:

> Higher education [was] the natural request of a race desiring to progress. The primary education hitherto provided was too limited and dependent on the availability of teachers applying for the positions. Experience showed that such teachers were often unsuitable.[16]

Bleakley was wrong in his assessment of the people's former satisfaction with their colonial status. Moreover, he was obviously unconscious of the irony in his use of the term 'civilised life' when Australia was a nation engaged in a vicious war of survival. In late 1944, the then Director supported the proposal that 'selected children should be given secondary education in schools [on the mainland] willing to accept them'.[17] But, in a dominantly white Australian society still grappling with the place of Indigenous people, how realistic was that solution likely to be?

As it happened, island children were not able to attend high school in Torres Strait until one was opened on Thursday Island on 24 January 1966, and they did not go to the mainland for their education in anything like reasonable numbers until the early 1970s.

'Without proper medical help'

Immediately after the evacuation of the white teachers, some of the younger women took responsibility for and distributed whatever supplies of western medicines became available. Even so, during the worst months of the war, the women were forced to rely heavily on their own bush medicines.

Like other traditional Melanesian people in the South Pacific, the health of the Torres Strait Islanders was tied to their supernatural beliefs. These beliefs gave them a sense of security in a world with the usual human share of illness, accident and death, and made them confident they could control individual and community health. After colonisation, the earliest white government teachers concluded that death, to these people, particularly during epidemics, was the result of 'sorcery' rather than the disease. In 1989, a Meriam woman said, 'You know, we still believe in *puripuri*'. Another recalled the war years: 'People died from island sorcery — *maid* men. These ones worked hypnotism, they killed a lot of people during the war. Sometimes they killed babies. They can kill you and they can tell you you are going to die. You get sick and die.' She knew about these things from her own experience:

> My big mother, father's eldest sister, she had twins, two girls, and the *maid* men killed my auntie and one girl died, one was still alive. The trouble was the lump [the afterbirth] wouldn't come out and my big mother she cried and cried with the pain. My father and my mother knew who the *maid* men were, but they didn't talk about it. My grandfather told them. Very bad, eh! My mother, she died before the war on Dauan by *maid* men too.

However, their practices were not all malevolent. They were also medicine men in the most positive sense of the term: they could heal the sick. Moreover, there were lay people in all Melanesian societies in the South Pacific who had their own 'custom medicine' to deal with sickness.[18] Torres Strait Islanders referred to such as bush or island medicines. They were used without special supernatural powers. A Badu man recalled that all sorts of bush medicines had been passed down for generations: 'Older people told us what to do when we were sick.'[19] According to an old Erub woman: 'At that time we had no hospital and our parents looked after us with bush medicine.' Therefore, bush medicines were traditionally important and they continued to be so after white intervention.

Nonetheless, in all Melanesian groups, outsiders attempted to eradicate such practices. The missionaries in other Melanesian groups saw education as the answer, whereas in Torres Strait the government outlawed them. 'It was a crime to use bush medicines. That was forced on them by the Protector', a Torres Strait Islander leader recalled. However, while the colonisers were unable to stop the passing on of this knowledge, there was no total rejection of the new. In Torres Strait, an old woman recalled: 'We got medicines from the government teacher but we still use island medicine — still using it now, they do you good.' The present perceptions of some Torres Strait Islanders are that, in those early days, the government had frequently been unable to meet their medical needs. For instance, during the influenza epidemic in the early 1920s: 'When people got that flu they died like nothing, no help, nothing.' In a malaria epidemic on Saibai in 1934, supplies of quinine ran out and the people turned to blood-letting to release the 'pain and heat' from their bodies.[20] So, they resisted the government's prohibition on the use of bush medicines because, as an old couple recalled: 'When the law said not to use bush medicine, what will happen if they take away that medicine, we the people won't know what to do.' An old man remembered the situation on smaller communities: 'They lived without really any assistance. Doctors never came around in the early days in government patrol boat, never for medical ... My father and mother never got medical treatment.' Even when there was some improvement in health services in the 1930s, the people remained unwilling to throw away an institution that had worked for them for generations: 'Bush medicine was one of the things that kept our people.' Ironically, on the mainland, many white mothers sought professional medical help only as a last resort, but they used their own home remedies without fear of reprisal. It was the war that enabled the Torres Strait Islander women to use their bush medicines just as freely.

At the beginning of the 1930s, there were improvements in the government's health care system. Nonetheless, removal of seriously ill patients to the Thursday Island hospital posed problems.

Frequently, the only means of transport was in the people's sail-powered luggers:

> Sometimes you steadied the patient and got there all right. Sometimes they got worse and when the wind dropped you had to float along, follow the tide. When the tide was going to that island because you follow it, okay, but when it came from that island, you have to anchor and wait for the tide to turn.

From Boigu, one man recalled, the voyage took 'one and one-half days. If there's no wind, you don't go. It was very sad, people died.' It is little wonder that the people wanted better health services on their communities.

In early 1942, only a few Torres Strait Islanders had a basic knowledge of western medicines from experience gained in the cottage hospitals and from first aid lessons taught at the Mabuiag teachers training college. Occasionally, a young woman was asked to help the white teacher and she was given a shallow insight into the practice of western medicine. An old Kubin woman recalled working for Mr and Mrs Armstrong: 'They did the medicine. I was working in the house and when people came from the village and they were away, I did it.'

After the bombing of Nurupai, the government's stock of medical supplies on Thursday Island was hastily transferred to Badu for distribution among the outer island communities. Curtis, and Turner worked against almost impossible odds to get supplies to them. Not only did civil communications between islands become extremely difficult and dangerous, there were the enormous problems with the flow of cargo from Brisbane. The young women who took charge of and distributed basic western medicines, such as painkillers, cough mixtures, disinfectants and bandages, were untrained. Reflecting on this, an old leader said: 'It's bad enough to pick up someone from the road to teach my kid, but when you take someone from the road, not trained, and put him in charge of medicine, you are playing with the lives of my people.' Bakoi Baud, the teacher on Mer, combined her role as teacher with that of the island 'nurse'. She held sick parades before school every morning. On other islands, checking the people's health meant going long distances into the bush. A Badu woman recalled: 'I was the nurse and had to go round with medicine to those villages here in the bush. I went all day and they gave me something to eat.' Someone remembered that the teacher on Poid went from 'this camp to another camp' in the bush, supplying medicine to the sick.

Some help came from the army, although Colonel Langford had few men to spare for at least the first two desperate years of the war. When the army signallers arrived on the communities, they advised the councillors that they had medicines and basic medical skills. Basic indeed! According to one signaller:

> We did a two-hour crash course in medicine and surgery and all those associated matters and I can recall the senior army medical officer telling me that we could probably handle most emergencies and thinking to myself, 'Well, I'm aged nineteen and no medical skill'. To demonstrate the point, he said to me, 'Just take a sample by opening your comprehensive book [on medical matters] at random and we'll see what it's all about'. This I did, and the chapter was 'Complications of Childbirth'. 'Try another', said the SMO [Senior Medical Officer], and this turned out to be something like 'Surgery following Major Shark Bite'.

They had arrived with their book on basic medicine, Dettol, castor oil, acriflavine, cascara, aspirins, a generous supply of bandages and adhesive plasters as well as scalpels and sutures and 'a bottle of Tolly's [Tolley's] Three Star Brandy'. In cases of extreme emergency, radio contact was made with army doctors on Thursday Island who assisted with diagnoses and treatments. A Mabuiag woman had her arm bitten off by a shark and, while one signaller received instructions over the radio, the other attended to the woman's injuries. On another occasion, a signaller likewise treated an old man with a bladder obstruction. A child's wrists were reset with splints made from the wood of a butter box, and a boy's scalp was stitched. Despite their youthfulness and inexperience, the signallers were called on to handle many such emergencies.

The smaller communities were again disadvantaged because they had no radios. Someone had to row a dingy to a larger island for help, although the people on Purma received some assistance from the medical personnel on an American warship which frequently anchored off the island: 'They had doctors and people on board. If we had to be treated they told us to go down to the *Challenger* and get treated.'

Army officers listened to the TSLI men's various concerns for their families: 'They worried about everything, even if they didn't have cotton in the store.' Their health was of great concern. A St Paul's man reported that his pregnant wife had written that she was having premature pains; she was subsequently visited by an army doctor. While he was there, the doctor saw the ageing James Morrison and told him: 'See that you rub your damper and sweeten your tea with Vegemite to keep you strong.' The doctor was obviously unaware of what the people could obtain from the store: 'We never heard of Vegemite before the war.' Another soldier applied for leave to help his pregnant wife who was not well enough to cut firewood, wash clothes, work in the garden, cook food, look after two young children and walk long distances each day to get water and firewood. However, when the women had their babies, they looked first to their old midwives.

Childbirth had always been women's business in Torres Strait. Their midwives were locally trained: 'The old women said to me, "You must try to deliver babies", and I went to learn. We sat near the old one and trained from her.' Another woman said she watched her grandmother at work but was unable to be a midwife: 'My fingers were too fat. You have to have long thin hands to get the baby out.' Midwives had their own bush medicines: a poultice of wongai tree leaves would be placed on the woman's stomach to give relief during labour; or

> if the baby was cleared but that lump [the afterbirth] was still inside ... we always used the bush medicine. You break this grass, smash it well, and put it in a banana leaf, put it in the ashes and wait for one hour and take it out and the midwife tied it over the tummy to smash that lump. That's all the medicine they had. Nothing from TI.

Sometimes women delivered their own babies: 'Some women were lucky, some were unlucky like when it was time for the birth and she was in pain, lucky if she had a midwife close and if no one was there, she just cleared it herself.' The government respected the women's birthing customs until about 1935 when the decision was made to bring mothers into the Thursday Island hospital if a difficult birth was anticipated. But sea travel in sail-powered vessels could result in death:

> From Erub and Mer we lost a lot of our people, the women gave birth halfway. There were just sailing boats. Sometimes it was calm and they had to row the dinghy and tow the boat and the women just died. I saw how we lost our people. It was so sad to sit there and know what was going to happen.

However, from the Thursday Island hospital records, there is no evidence that women were confined there during the war. One woman recalled that a lot of babies were born at that time, but little detail was voluntarily offered by the women on the subject. Did the old women find it too painful to talk about their suffering in childbirth? Perhaps, for that generation, it was still a subject for the inner circle of island women.

Confinements during wartime frequently took place in huts in the bush. On St Paul's, and undoubtedly other communities, some women ignored the danger of leaving the bush to have their babies in their homes. The midwife, who had to come on foot, might not get there in time or there might be no midwife on the island to call. For instance, a woman on Nagi gave birth prematurely in the bush without a midwife. While it was extremely dangerous to do so, the mother and baby were transported to Badu in a dinghy to get Mrs Curtis' help. The mother died but the baby survived on milk collected every day from nursing mothers in the different bush villages. A Ugar man took no chances; he rowed a dinghy to Masig about a month before his wife was due to have her baby and returned with the midwife. An old storekeeper remembered his sister-in-law died in childbirth during the war: 'She gave birth ... and the women were there trying to do what they could to help her. She was just there all day, until four or five in the afternoon. The baby was delivered and the mother died.'

The signallers and Charlie Turner were sometimes called to help with deliveries, something unacceptable until just prior to the war, 'definitely no men were present when the women had their babies', although a white teacher on Mer in the 1920s claimed he delivered babies.[21] The women gave no reasons for the wartime breaches of the tradition that childbirth was women's business. Once the women began to go to the Thursday Island hospital and were attended by male doctors, the way must have been paved for them to feel freer about white male attendance at births. Perhaps because these men were white, they were not seen as bound by the usual cultural expectations, particularly in the women's desperate wartime circumstances. Moreover, there was a suggestion that a shortage of island midwives pertained during the war. The Protector's perception in 1935 was that,

> as the women get more European ideas, childbirth is becoming increasingly difficult. When the birth is normal, the native midwife is good; when complications arise, she does not know what to do and is afraid to do anything on her own initiative, for if her treatment fails she is blamed for everything that has gone wrong.[22]

The women's testimonies certainly did not indicate that this was the case. Their recollections were that their midwives were very capable women. However, because their white colonisers had persistently devalued the people's knowledge, it is understandable, particularly once the outsiders interfered with their birthing practices, that trainees might have been hard to find. They would have found it difficult to pit their knowledge against that of their colonisers, who presented themselves as superior beings with superior knowledge. Indeed, an army officer found that, on Badu in 1944, there was only one old midwife practising and she suggested that it had been almost impossible 'to secure a good learner'.[23]

On the withdrawal of the Department's personnel, the army had given the Director assurances that it would 'watch the interests of the Department in caring for and protecting the civilian Islanders'.[24] This was a difficult undertaking to fulfil in the desperate and chaotic circumstances which pertained in Torres Strait during 1942 and most of 1943, and so their help was of necessity intermittent. In May 1943, however, island councillors expressed to the Governor their concerns: the people were 'without proper medical help of any sort, and ... several on Badu had died for lack of that help'.[25] Shortly afterwards, when the Queensland Public Service Commissioner and the Director visited Badu, they too were made aware of the health problems of the people and the difficulties experienced in getting the most basic supplies, whether medical or otherwise, to the outer islands. In response, two officers were sent from Brisbane in July to assist Curtis in the administrative work. However, it was not until November 1944 that there was anywhere near enough staff on Badu to do the work with reasonable efficiency. Meanwhile, the transmission of medical supplies through the Badu store to the outer islands remained unreliable.

In September 1943, a sixteen-bed hospital was set up on Badu to serve the Western Islanders. Mrs Curtis was appointed matron. Then, in October, a dressing station was established on Masig in readiness for the opening of a hospital to serve the Central and Eastern Islanders. It was opened in December. The army freed sail-powered vessels to carry people from other islands to Masig for this momentous occasion. One woman said that there was so much excitement about the opening that those travelling to Masig 'didn't even think about the Japanese shooting at the boat'. A TSLI man recalled: 'We were happy ... there was turtle and fish for feasting and island dancing.' What the hospital meant to mothers was expressed in a letter written by an island woman to her son in the TSLI, telling him that sick children could now receive hospital attention and dental care.[26] Torres Strait Islanders had good reason to be happy about the opening of the two hospitals. While they had not lost faith in their own remedies, they realised that they would now have easier access to the western medicines and treatments they had come increasingly to rely upon as a consequence of outsider intervention in their lives.

Having their own hospitals also meant that, for the first time, some young women received training and experience in western health care institutions. An old Masig woman recalled that she was only seventeen when the hospital opened. She took a job there as a cook until she realised that perhaps there were benefits in becoming a nurse: 'I joined to be a nurse because I might learn something for my children.' The Masig hospital was the training institution: 'Nurses from every island came to train. They learnt from Mrs Curtis ... then they chose whether to be a nurse.' The training was basic: 'She did all the injections but she taught them how to make beds and bath people.' A Badu woman recalled that 'every fortnight when the doctor came out he gave us lectures'.

In the wards, however, a new experience was the very personal side of nursing white servicemen who were dropped off from naval convoys transporting troops to New Guinea. The old Masig woman recalled: 'They passed through, they felt sick mostly when they got lumps in the groin [a symptom of a septic wound].' She was the youngest nurse on Masig and Turner told her to bath them: 'I was scared, they were big tall men. They said, "Miss ... when you come, just pull the pants down and do your job".' She thought Turner gave her the job because he 'had that silly idea that the older ones have this dirty thought, so I had to bath those fellas'. What Turner had in mind is not certain. Did he think that a seventeen-year-old was too naive to get 'dirty thoughts'? If the older ones were more likely to be provocative, he may have thought that the men would respond and miscegenation might occur, something white Australia was strongly opposed to.[27]

Despite their inhibitions, however, most of the young women adapted well to their new work environment and some excelled. Bugun Mosby took charge of the hospital on Masig during Turner's absence on leave in early 1945, in recognition for which her wages were raised from £3 10s to £10 a month.[28] From these basic beginnings, Torres Strait Islander women, like Bugun and Timena Tamwoy, also on Badu, and Bakoi Baud on Mer, might have expected that after the war they would be able to further their nursing careers.

The hospitals were run under difficult circumstances and improvisation was often the name of the game. When the Masig pantry was down to a 'few Red Cross supplies', Turner bartered for food with passing American warships.[29] Matron Curtis frequently looked to the army for medical supplies. Overcrowded wards were common; for instance, in January 1944 there were thirty-nine patients in the sixteen-bed Badu hospital. Basic equipment, such as sterilisers, was lacking, increasing the potential for the spread of disease. The communities without hospitals also had desperate medical needs. Finally, the Director conceded that something had to be done for these people: 'They [could] not be left indefinitely to their own resources.'[30] Medical aid centres (MACs), or medical aid posts (MAPs) as they became known after the war, were set up on Erub and Mer. They were subsequently expanded into cottage hospitals with beds for two or three in-patients and, after it proved impossible to recruit white nursing sisters, John Pau and Bakoi Baud, respectively, were put in charge. Mrs Frith became matron of a small hospital set up on Saibai to serve the three Top-Western Islands. On the remaining communities, medicines continued to be dispensed by untrained Torres Strait Islander teachers. These were non-prescriptive-type medicines but, as suggested previously, their distribution was not without risk. It was not until the last stages of the war that someone was sent to the islands to instruct those who dispensed seemingly harmless medicines.

The army's role

When Mrs Curtis called for a determination of the people's health in mid-1943, she expressed the opinion that those left on the outer islands were suffering from diseases, such as tuberculosis, anaemia, scabies and hookworm, to a 'greater degree than before the war'. In the first army medical reports completed in May 1944, tuberculosis, malaria and deficiency diseases were stated to be the 'outstanding prevalent diseases'.[31]

Tuberculosis (TB) was first introduced into mainland Australia from convict ships. It spread throughout the country. Torres Strait Islanders contracted the disease from the outsiders and it became an ongoing problem for the Protector's Department. Dugong oil was the remedial and preventative antidote. A Masig woman recalled that, as children, they 'had to line up every morning and get a cup of that oil'. In the 1944 army medical surveys, concern was expressed about the non-segregation of TB patients. An attempt to secure building materials and suitable equipment to provide segregated accommodation failed, so patients were housed in a separate ward in the Badu hospital and treated by Mrs Curtis: 'She treated that TB with dugong oil, rubbed them with dugong oil and made them sit in the sun and let it get in. Some survived.' Others did not: 'A lot of people from the Central Islands, from Poid, came to Badu, a lot of people died of TB. Plenty of people were buried there from various islands.'

Malaria, too, had been an ongoing problem in prewar Torres Strait. It prevailed during the northwest monsoon, especially on Mer, Erub, Boigu and Saibai, but how much more serious the incidence of it was when the army made its survey is difficult to know. Dr Elkington, the Commissioner of Public Health, surveyed the islands in 1912 but no further report on malaria was made until the 1944 survey.[32] Prewar insecticide campaigns had not been successful on all islands and during the war they were virtually impossible to carry out. Moreover, it is highly unlikely that island women were given drugs like quinine and atebrin to hand out; medical opinion was that they should be administered under medical supervision. Thus, an increase in the incidence of malaria was possible and likely.

The survey teams concluded that malnutrition amongst the people was related to a diet imbalance brought about by the women's 'neglect' of their gardens. It was also suggested the people lacked protein foods (fish, dugong and turtle); the average diet, the army concluded, consisted of 'rice, white flour and canned foods'; 'little fishing' was done and the women's gardens 'seem[ed] to be few ... Instead of ... living on fish, turtle, dugong, cocoanut [sic], taro, potato, an attempt was made to procure everything from the store.'[33] This was an outsider perspective, one framed by military men with their own white, middle-class values and little or no understanding of the Torres Strait Islanders' beliefs about the causes of sickness and death or even their methods of gardening. A Torres Strait Islander leader revealed that his people were unaware of the connection between diet and health until much later:

> These yaws and all that, it was common ... I was talking in council and said, 'What's happened? We don't get these things any more ... sores on the kids' legs and heads.' Yes, vitamin deficiency maybe. As soon as we drank from that milk scheme, all these things disappeared.

The army teams also seem to have had no idea of the women's stringent economic status prior to the survey or that rice, white flour and canned foods were, for the most part, in short supply or absent altogether from store shelves. Furthermore, the army men did not take into consideration that, under prolonged wartime conditions, it had been very difficult for the women to maintain their gardens at the same level of productivity as had been the case before the war. On the Central and Western Islands, too, gardening had never been the major occupation of the women as it had been for those on the Eastern Islands. Moreover, during the worst period of the war when the women were told to keep away from the shoreline and their boats were beached or impressed, they were not always able to get enough fish for their families' daily requirements.

Perhaps what was even more damaging to the credibility of the outsider perception was that the army admitted that it had been impossible, in the time allotted and with the men available, to do a proper health survey of all of the islands. Colonel Robinson, in concluding his summary of the medical reports, stated that a complete survey of the people's health would have been a 'huge task' requiring several medical men over a period of twelve months, something beyond the army's medical capabilities and manpower resources. He further stated that it would be 'dangerous to draw conclusions from the evidence available'.[34] Yet the army did, and damning ones too.

The argument is not that the army was wrong in its assessment or that the women were right when they said that they worked hard in their gardens and that they bought little from the store: 'We were eating mostly bush tucker and we were healthy'; 'That's why we were so healthy, we never had anything sweet to eat or drink.' The contradictory evidence comes from two defensible positions, in contemporary social theorist Jean-Francois Lyotard's words, two incommensurable language games.[35] Moreover, if the women had a simplistic view of their situation, so too did the white observers. The matter was too complex to lay the blame for the people's health during the war at anyone's feet. And how much it had deteriorated was impossible to say with any accuracy in the absence of thorough prior and wartime surveys. Nevertheless, the army surveys demonstrated the validity of the Torres Strait Islanders' dissatisfaction with the western health care on the islands.

It was still a year before the Japanese surrender when the Inter-Island Councillors Conference was held on Masig in August 1944 at which a comprehensive scheme for postwar medical services, designed by Major GR Beattie, the army's most senior medical officer on Thursday Island, was presented for approval. Beattie made it clear that he was prepared to recommend his scheme as *'essential* [emphasis added] for the Torres Strait District'. It envisaged fifty-bed, fully equipped hospitals on both Badu and Masig, with midwifery wards, labour rooms and special wards for infectious diseases, as well as nurses quarters and doctors residences. Young local women would be trained in these hospitals to double-certificate level to provide a pool of qualified nurses for the main hospitals, cottage hospitals and MACs. It was envisaged that Torres Strait Islanders would also train as doctors on the mainland and then return to the islands. To meet the needs of tuberculosis patients, a separate sanatorium would be provided, with annual radiological surveys of everyone. The scheme extended to the provision of improved housing because Beattie was concerned that the incidence of tuberculosis could not be reduced if the 'present habit' of sleeping huddled together, with all doors and windows closed because of a continued fear of *puripuri*, persisted. He believed that 'appropriate education' would dispel these fears. This was the essence of Beattie's revolutionary health scheme for Torres Strait.[36] The councillors expressed their unanimous approval of the scheme and also agreed to the imposition of a tax on all wage earners to help defray the cost. Thus, after two generations of Queensland government administration, a scheme to meet the health needs of the island communities was designed by an army doctor.

The councillors' acceptance of Beattie's scheme gave the people every reason to believe that a standard of health care more in line with what whites received on the mainland would be implemented after the war. It was not long after the war, however, that the hospitals on Badu and Masig ceased to operate, and almost insurmountable barriers for decades to come prevented island women gaining full nursing qualifications. Anything like an appropriate health scheme was not instituted in Torres Strait until 1991.

Chapter 11

Breaking down barriers

In August 1942, Prime Minister Curtin sounded the warning that, although the threat of imminent attack no longer existed, the enemy was, nonetheless, 'waging a war to the death' and the allied forces had the gigantic task of pushing him all the way back to Japan.[1] To finance Australia's role in this, Curtin launched his £100 million Austerity Loan campaign and called the people to support it to the fullest: 'every selfish, comfortable habit, every luxurious impulse' had to go.[2] His government introduced initiatives towards this end. Suburban housewives with large families were immediate victims. Already juggling food and clothing coupons under difficult shopping conditions, and perhaps holding down a job as well, they were further inconvenienced when meat, grocery, milk, greengrocery and bread deliveries were prohibited. It was a common sight to see them, like 'tired packhorses', lugging home the family supplies, stretching to the limit that wartime invention, the string bag. With his 'selfless sense of duty', Curtin led Australia through the greatest crisis in its history.[3] Nonetheless, his impassioned plea for individual self-sacrifice on the part of all Australians was ignored by many and a thriving black market emerged. Taxes were placed on entertainments and one meeting in every four was cut from the racing calendar, a sacrifice only a nation of gamblers would appreciate. However, it proved easier to stop delivery carts than to deter crowds and investments at the race tracks where records in both were recorded. The majority of Australians considered some relief from their oppressive wartime environment imperative.

They were heady days for young mainland women. Wartime demands for their labour enabled many to break away from the controlling influence of home. They had none of the worries associated with the housewife's lot and fun and excitement were not hard to find. Australian and American troops constantly passed through cities and towns on their way to the front and they looked for female company. The influx of 120,000 American troops by June 1943 impacted quite dramatically upon the conservative Australian society.[4] Entertainment in America was a seven-day phenomenon, so Australian cities and towns were dreary places for US servicemen on Sundays, but the idea of introducing Sunday entertainment was strenuously opposed by the Australian Council of Churches: to 'scrap' Sunday, the president declared, would be to damage the soul of the country.[5] Nonetheless, the government finally allowed Sunday dances, theatres, films, concerts and sports for the entertainment of troops and their friends only.

With so many troops passing through the north, Townsville was an exciting place to be. There were dances every night: 'The Americans had a lot of dances ... and we'd get ... invited', a woman from that city recalled. In Sydney too: 'It was dance, dance, dance all the time ... There was a lot of laughter, a lot of talk. Everybody seemed in a hurry to live.'[6] Of course, the inevitable happened, some Australian women fell in love and married American men, although the thought of a daughter's emigration marred the family's happiness. Rural mothers were less likely to have to face this scenario: young men were a rare sight in the country and at dances women were partnered by teenage boys or older men.

The social lives of many mainland mothers, wives and fiancées of absent servicemen were not so exciting. Without childminding centres, women with children had respite only if grandparents or friends assisted. Older women found companionship amongst peers with whom they did voluntary or paid work. Moreover, there were women all around the country for whom social life had lost its attraction. They had loved ones in prisoner-of-war camps, listed missing or lying wounded in a foreign hospital. Other women's lives were devastated by news of a death.

Fifty years on, it is difficult to recapture and relate to the emotions of a nation of people facing the realities of war, more so for those who know the Pacific War as an historical fact only. However, one thing is evident from the oral histories of wartime women: there was a spirit of urgency about living. It was not a time for too much personal planning for the future: people snatched at happiness.

In Torres Strait, with their heavy wartime responsibilities in providing for large families in unprecedented circumstances of fear and uncertainty, it was somewhat surprising to learn that a spirit of fun was no less imperative. They feasted and danced and there was a good deal of socialisation with the white soldiers who came to the communities. Moreover, young women married with hope in their hearts, even though they knew the time with their husbands would be short. The men would return to Thursday Island where their brides had no idea what might be happening to them. Like their mainland counterparts, island women also grasped for some relief from their oppressive wartime lives.

'Work and play together'

Remote from the mainland, Torres Strait Islander societies had no sophisticated entertainment facilities, such as dance halls, theatres, sports grounds and race tracks. Indeed, the island people's institutions of work and play were not compartmentalised like those of the white mainlanders. Play was totally compatible with the working lives of the island people. It was, according to one old man, 'a life of doing something, work and play together — we laugh and sing while we work'. There were council, or public, days set aside for work in the communities, which was done without wages. 'All the village worked together, men and women, not one would stay away', the late Jerry Anau wrote. On the completion of large village projects:

> The women always prepared food; it is also an important custom that those who come together to work should eat together

afterwards. Along with that custom went the dancing, a brief celebration to share joy at the achievements of the day. In the same way, house builders were not paid in cash; they helped each other in their turn. When a house was complete it was a time of great rejoicing, a feast would be held.[7]

Much of women's work was team work, whether working with the men on house-building, with other women on public days, preparing feasts, building fish traps or plaiting matting walls for houses. During the war, the signallers observed the women working in groups and described the gatherings as 'sort of social occasions'. The cooperative spirit associated with their traditional work ethic was in contrast to that of the industrialised western world. Nonetheless, colonisation seems to have made inroads into this custom by 1942.

Perhaps, with more talk about freedom in the late 1930s, there was a reaction to the government by-law which made attendance at council days obligatory. It provided punishment for those who did not attend: 'Then you have to clean the street ... public day, everybody work ... [if not] they give you hard punishment.' Despite the women's extenuating circumstances during the war, the Meriam court reports reveal examples of this. On 19 June 1942, five women on Mer were charged with 'not being present on a public day'. They were found guilty and given two days imprisonment, during which time they cleaned weeds from the village square. On 29 October 1943, another ten women were charged with 'not cleaning their street'. They were more fortunate, being discharged with a warning from the council.[8] A Meriam woman recalled that she and her friend failed to attend a public day because they had been asked to clean the signallers' house. No reason for their absence was disclosed to the court and their punishment was 'several days work in the village'. It was only when the signallers spoke to Marou that this was waived. A former store worker talked about seeing something better for herself when store work became available to more young women. She said: 'When I grew up seeing those women doing that work, I said, "I'm not going to do that. I'm going to get a job".' But such work was available to only a few women. However, after 1942, other younger women also began looking at their roles in a more independent light. Their war experiences were expanding their horizons.

Feasting and dancing

Traditionally, it is believed, religious dances were performed for special occasions only; for instance, the men danced at death and initiation ceremonies or to celebrate the seasons and turtle harvest time. Secular dances were held on less formal occasions and women could participate in these. Their dancing, however, was seen by the LMS missionary teachers as offensive to Christian sensibilities and the people were encouraged to adopt South Sea Island dances.[9] Conversely, feasting was not considered offensive, so with the new dances it was incorporated into celebrations on the Christian calendar. Feasting and dancing added richness to island culture and it maintained a sense of social cohesion which was particularly important during the war when the future seemed so uncertain.

The women made it quite clear that there were many occasions, both religious and purely social, when feasting occurred despite their stringent economic circumstances and fear of Japanese attack. Traditionally, men and women worked together to prepare feasts. The men did the harder manual work, like building the earth ovens or *kapmauri*. Nevertheless, the women were self-reliant. One old woman claimed proudly: 'I can dig the *kapmauri* like a man. I can climb coconut trees to get the leaves for the *kapmauri* food.' They carried heavy loads of fruit and vegetables from their gardens, and caught fish, crabs and crayfish. A female turtle might be captured on the beach and eggs collected from her nest. On the Top-Western Islands, the women sailed in the long canoes with the old men to get dugong. On Nagi and Badu, the women hunted wild pigs and dressed them: 'We butchered them, stabbed them in the throat and get the blood out ... We get the hot water and peel the pigs clean, open them up and cut all those things out that are bad and burn them.' Pig was *kapmauried* whole, or a Filipino dish, called *dinaguan*, was made with selected portions cooked in the animal's blood. The younger women prepared the food for cooking under the watchful eyes of the older ones whose softly spoken words or facial expressions ensured the job was well done. *Kapmauried* foods included turtle, dugong, fish, pig, yams, sweet potatoes, pumpkin, *sop sop* and damper.

It might be wondered how such feasts were possible given the desperate economic circumstances. Torres Strait Islanders had little money even before the war, but large feasts were either community or family efforts. Every household shared whatever local produce and store goods they had, even if that meant going without afterwards. A former signaller described a wartime feast on Masig:

> The food was set out on a very long coconut-leaf mat with Barney Mosby at the head of the mat, myself in the place of honour first on the right and Max [the other signaller] on the left. Island councillors and elders were near the head of the table ... together with the police sergeant and police constable. The older ladies stayed in the background, keeping an eye on the proceedings and supervising. The younger ladies had the job of making sure there was plenty to eat and drink ... The men at the VIP end of the table seemed to have a personal serving lady ... The males ate for quite a long time. The ladies busied themselves and hovered in the background ... Prayers were said. After the males adjourned to the beach under the big almond tree ... and once out of the way, I fancy the ladies and children got stuck into the good things to eat.

This particular feast was not in celebration of a religious or any regular social occasion. It was occasioned by a very stressful wartime event early in 1942 and demonstrates how the women grasped at any opportunity to lighten their lives. The island's cutter, the *Masig*, was long overdue. Perhaps Japanese gunners had seen the little cutter and had strafed it. The village lads kept a constant watch for it from a large sprawling almond tree near the water's edge. One day their cries of 'Sail ho, sail ho' resounded throughout the village as they pointed out to sea. The women ran to the beach, plunged into the sea and waded towards the boat until the water was up to their armpits. Everyone was crying for joy. It was then that the women declared their intention to make a feast in celebration of the safe return of the men. Shortly after the feast, however, a great sadness again fell over the community: the little cutter and its crew had been ordered to leave the island. The memory of that day has remained with a signaller: 'I can remember the picture of Elda [the skipper] leaning out from the transom of the *Masig* as he sailed the vessel away ... The tide was full and I can still see the island ladies and girls up to their necks in the sea, waving to the crew as they left ... for Palm Island.'

On another occasion, the women on Mer decided to make a feast to celebrate the arrival of the army vessel *Reliance* carrying Major Keith Colwill, the officer in charge of army signals. The feast was held after a day of uncertainty and fear. The *Reliance* had mysteriously left the island. Allied aircraft kept flying overhead and everyone was concerned. But all was forgotten when the feasting and dancing began.

Welcome home feasts were held when the men returned to the communities on annual leave. At the sight of the boats, the women ran to the shore and waited as they drew nearer. There was weeping: 'The men were glad to be back with their family and the family was glad to receive their sons. Everyone came and cried ... That war had never happened before, it was a very bad day when it started.' The soldiers paraded to the village square before going home to be with their families: 'We stayed with our mothers, fathers and sisters ... all the boys were here now and we were happy.' Shortly, everyone was feasting, 'mothers, wives, sisters, brothers, grandmas and grandpas'. Men and women danced until dawn. But their happiness was short-lived: 'We had leave for two weeks ... it was a happy time. When we went back it was a hard time.' These sad separations were yet another price being paid for the freedom they hoped for when peace returned.

Wartime weddings were clearly special times and old women reminisced at length about them, recalling the smallest details. One woman said she had had no plans to marry until her parents negotiated the wedding with the young man's parents when he came home on leave: 'The families agreed together that we were going to be married. We were there when they talked about it.' They were engaged at ten o'clock and married in the church at three in the afternoon. Despite the haste, the old woman told how they all wore wedding regalia and that a big feast was prepared, 'enough to feed the whole village'. She remembered, too, that the present-giving custom was maintained: 'The people came around, they gathered and shook hands with the couple and gave ... presents, money or whatever. All the island did this — everyone on the island.'

On some communities, church weddings were impossible and there was less formality:

> The men wore army uniform. The girls only wore ordinary dresses. We could only use one lamp and we were holding it near the wedding couple and the rest walked behind. They had a small feast and six o'clock in the morning they went back to camp. There was no dancing.

Marriages were conducted in the bush on Moa at the height of the danger. Relatives did their best to attend: 'Some came by dinghy or you walked ... Another family cannot come ... because they were frightened of the enemy.' At the height of the war, couples on St Paul's who wanted a 'proper wedding' risked the danger of leaving the bush to go to the church in the village. Church weddings were important, as was the wedding regalia: 'The wedding was very nice ... I wore a white dress and I had a bridesmaid, my cousin-sister [daughter of her mother's sister]. My husband wore his army uniform ... we feasted and danced until dawn.' In December 1943, a Masig couple celebrated their wedding with all the trimmings a day or so after the opening of the hospital on the island: 'It was a big wedding. All the people stayed to celebrate with the newlyweds.'

While young island couples married despite what the future might hold for them, a Purma woman remembered how the reality of their situation could not be totally forgotten: 'Weddings were really sad times, people were crying.' Everyone knew that a dark cloud hung over them and that caused sadness, but marriages brought families together and babies were born. Marriage was a sign of hope for the future.

Socialising with the outsider

Wartime feasting was one of the avenues which helped to break down barriers between island women and white soldiers. Invitations to feasts had always been extended to white visitors before the war but it was the men who, generally, had hosted the guests. The war gave the women greater responsibility in this respect. A Mabuiag woman recalled that, when a navy boat anchored off the island one July 1, the women told her old father: 'We want to invite all the sailors.' The captain agreed. She said the sailors spent all day on the island; they feasted and danced and slept there that night: 'It was a happy day.' The Badu women were just as hospitable to the air force men who operated the radar station on Mount Kamat. The location made them invisible to the women on a day-to-day basis but, as one woman recalled: 'We always invite them when we have a feast.' Years after the war, Keith Colwill recalled the hospitality he received from the Mabuiag women: 'I can remember a very cordial welcome ... the farewell we were given was one to be well remembered. The cries of "*Ya-wah* [goodbye]" across the water to our ketch were very impressive.'[10] Some of the older men on the communities invited servicemen into their homes for meals. Marou was one. However, his wife refused to depart from her customary role in the presence of strangers; when she was invited to eat with her husband and his military guests, she replied: 'I can't eat with them.'

Some of the younger women, beginning to see their lives in a new light, probably found it easier to discard that role. A Meriam woman, in her late teens at the time, said she felt quite comfortable about her father inviting signallers to their home for supper: 'They played the guitar and I cooked a cake and ... put the tablecloth on the mat ... They taught us games in the moonlight, like hide the handkerchief ... card games, coon-can, five hundred, twos and threes.' Young Badu women learned to play the game of 'hookey' from the radar operators. The women taught them island dancing. The signallers were very young in 1942 when they were suddenly torn from families, jobs and education. Older women played special roles in the lives of some of these men. One recalled that he was made to feel very comfortable in his new environment because of the status he was given in one family: 'Barney and his wife became my adopted father and mother. It was a fairly disorganised arrangement but they kept a weather eye on me and used to make sure, when there was a feast, I would sit at the top of the table and ladies were elected to look after and serve me.' His adoption into this island family reflected an old custom in Torres Strait, one which could be extended to respected outsiders.

There is no suggestion that all of the women socialised to the same extent with the white servicemen; some said: 'We had nothing to do with them.' Why this was so, they did not say. Perhaps some women, because of their fathers' status in the villages, were in a better position to get to know the white men. However, those who socialised with these men obviously gained in confidence in their presence. The stereotype of the white colonial masters who maintained their social distance and superior caste status was being broken down by Torres Strait Islander women and young mainlanders thrown together by the accident of war.

Many changes were occurring in the lives of the outer island women, which a short time earlier would have been inconceivable. Nonetheless, there was no disruption to the very strict observance of the Sabbath on the outer islands. The people were, by their own designation, 'very religious ... Sunday is a day of rest, do nothing, no fishing, gardening'. They had made Christianity their religion and they complied with the church's teaching on the holiness of the Sabbath. There was no suggestion that the white soldiers were less than content to also attend church: 'Every Sunday they came to church with us and they made friends with us and mixed up with us and we got to know each other.' In this way, the women had another avenue of socialisation with the outsiders.

On their small wartime communities, young Torres Strait Islander women did not break free of parental supervision to the extent that many of their mainland counterparts did. Two Masig women, who were teenagers during the war, explained that they had 'a very tough mother' who kept them from getting into trouble: 'We never had boyfriends ... our parents don't like us to run around, we must be where the father and mother are.' Parents knew the consequences of even a hint of immorality by their children. The possibility of this was not avoided because of the war: 'For a breach of any by-law you would go before the courts ... Young soldiers came home and there is immorality. They come home in uniform and the bloke thinks he can do what he likes. He says, "I'm in government uniform", but not here you can't.' An old woman recalled:

> During army time there were problems and the island courts still continued. You must be careful about getting into that trouble because when you get into trouble you are finished for couple of months. They punished you by hard work, put you in jail on the island. They were hard, those councillors. They made everything straight ... and they kept us from trouble.

However, even with the strictest island parents, any socialisation between the white servicemen and their daughters carried with it the potential for romantic attachments. But these young women were not free to marry the white men: 'That time we were not allowed to marry or love a white man; that was not allowed — we cannot like a white man.' Marriage between a Torres Strait Islander woman and a white man, indeed with any outsider, was subject to the Director's approval and this was unlikely to be given.[11] Before the war, a Meriam woman was refused that permission when she asked to marry a Japanese man. Nevertheless, the law did not stop some young women from seeking romance with the soldiers. 'Some of the girls styled [presented themselves attractively] for the white boys', but were told they 'cannot marry the white ones'. Late in the war, a white employee at the Board's store wanted to marry a young Badu woman: 'One white man, he liked me because I cooked for him. He asked me to marry him. Mr O'Leary was the Protector and he said, "She's no half-caste, she's full native". I am full native, so he said, "No".' As she told her story with a half grin, she gave no indication she thought it had been unfair of him to refuse permission. It is doubtful that women of that generation would have expressed a political opinion on such a matter. They had been conditioned to believe that they had no option but to accept the decisions of the Director. Thus, while many younger Torres Strait Islander women were breaking away from some of the restrictive customs, parental control and paternalistic legal constraints still determined who they married.

The war years were particularly hard for the old people; it was hard to run to safety and some thought it did not matter what happened to them. It was more important to save the young ones. Nonetheless, they made important contributions to the family's well-being. The old men left on the islands, like their warrior forebears, were always on the alert to protect the women and children, as was demonstrated on Mer when it was thought that the Japanese had landed. The old women mended clothes and helped with food preparation. And it was suggested that it was the old women who carried on the tradition of telling stories to the children. Storytelling, an old priest explained, was 'the thing that we should do ... sit in the one place on mats, drawing our children and grand-children to us for the evening chat where you might tell them a story'.[12] A Saibai man recalled this tradition:

> Storytelling is usually done at night-time. We have mats set outside on one side and, whichever way the wind is blowing, we have the fire in front of the wind. The fire is also used to light the father's smoke, twisted black tobacco wrapped in banana leaf. The mother is at one end of the mat, could be weaving a mat, and I will be in the middle of the mat, rolling around or listening to father telling the story and of course we will have people from other houses, other relatives, to take part in the storytelling.

Lizzie Nawia remembered that, during the war, 'plenty of old ladies told the children stories all around Torres Strait'. At night, as everyone huddled together in their stuffy overcrowded bush and village homes by the gentlest flicker of light from a burning strip of calico, the children listened to the old women's stories. The nights brought no relief from their fears: 'So, we told them the stories to make them quiet', Lizzie commented.

Peace

John Curtin's successor, Ben Chifley, proclaimed to the nation on 15 August 1945 the advent of peace. People in cities, towns, hamlets, isolated farms and remote Aboriginal and Torres Strait Islander communities, wherever they were, rejoiced. 'They hugged in the street and kissed people they had never seen', a New South Wales woman recalled, 'they just went wild ... it was wonderful, and sad of course, terribly sad'.[13]

In Torres Strait, peace was announced, appropriately enough, by the ringing of church bells. An old woman recalled that, on Badu, when peace came they heard the bell. Nobody knew who rang the bell and they [returned to] the village and that was the end of the war, the bell rang. When the bell rang, the message came and it was peace.

For those still in the bush, it was time to go home:

The noise of the bell went into the bush. When it came to peace and the war was finished, everybody in the bush said, 'What's that bell ringing at twelve o'clock for?' After that we had to carry things, coming out from our bush houses ... People came out then.

It was also time to feast: 'When the war was finished they told all the people and the people started coming back to the village. We had a big feast when the war was over.'

In the cities and towns, there were the victory marches. People crowded into the streets, hung from windows, climbed trees and scaffolding, and children sat on older family members' shoulders to watch the columns of marching men and women and to shower them with confetti and streamers. The TSLIB men marched proudly with their compatriots on Thursday Island. A small group of boys from Mabuiag and Saibai had been recruited a month or so before the end of the war to train in the army camp on Thursday Island as bugle boys, just for the parade through that town. They too marched proudly with their fathers, uncles and brothers. Later, the hospital ships returned to mainland Australia and crowds again lined city streets, this time more subdued, to welcome home busloads of wounded servicemen and women on their way to army hospitals and rehabilitation centres. There was indescribable pain for the women left mourning.

At the end of the war, no Torres Strait Islander woman was left to mourn a loved one killed in action. They did not see their men march for victory; they just waited for the day of their return to the islands. A veteran remembered how glad the men were to be back with their families: 'Everyone came and they cried. Nothing like the war happened to them before — it was a very bad time.' But it was all behind them. They were happy now and more feasting and dancing began: 'What a joy it was when families were reunited again. The islands became alive with feasting and dancing. The terrible war days were over.' And, in the spiritual sense with which they entered the war, so too did they see its conclusion: 'When the war was finished we praise God and were so happy that the tears rolled down our faces.'[14]

Kapmauri (*amai*) or earth oven

Feasting on Badu, c1935 (courtesy John Oxley Library)

Anglican church, Badu, built 1935

Wartime wedding in Torres Strait (*Walkabout*, 1 February 1946)

Chapter 12

Reflections

> It is not difference that immobilises us, but silence, and there are many silences to be broken.[1]

This history is based on the interpretations of old Torres Strait Islanders of their present recollections of the women's experiences during the Pacific War. However, while the silence about this historical episode has been broken, there remain many gaps in its presentation — incidences not recalled and the accounts of people who have died since the end of the war. Nonetheless, contemporary social theorist FR Ankersmit reassures historians that no amount of historical evidence constitutes a magnifying glass on the past; whatever the evidence, it bears no more than a 'resemblance to the brushstrokes used by the painter to achieve a certain effect'. Indeed, evidence, as he sees it, 'does not send us back to the past, but gives rise to the question of what an historian here and now can or cannot do with it'.[2] Thus, on the basis that certain contemporary social theorists see historical data as affording other interpretations of the past rather than pointing to a past reality, this interpretation presents as meaningful and authentic an account of the women's experiences as was possible for an outsider to achieve after a lapse of almost fifty years.

While the recollections of the old island people are central to this history, the inclusion of the eurocentric discourses of the author and other outsiders was unavoidable. The insider testimonies are set in the context of outsider interpretations of the people's own history and culture and the Pacific War and its consequences for all Australians. Moreover, under the internal colonial rule of the Queensland government, the people's treatment as second-class citizens was implicit in many of their testimonies. Thus, throughout, their recollections are also put in context to give a broader understanding of what that status meant for them. This intertextuality affords not only Torres Strait Islanders but also outsider readers a greater understanding of the uniqueness and poignancy of this Indigenous group of Australian women's wartime experiences.

One of the aims throughout the collection of the oral histories was to allow the people to talk about what was uppermost in their minds. Moreover, I felt that it was important for them to retain some control over their own knowledge, and so substantial use of the island voice is made. However, as indicated, this history is not a totally insider interpretation: it is at best a partial inversion away from a totally eurocentric interpretation of the Pacific War episode. A total inversion becomes possible only when an insider takes full responsibility for authorship.[3] Nonetheless, to avoid impinging to any greater extent upon the people's testimonies, there is no intention in this final chapter to draw definitive conclusions about what the Torres Strait Islander women made of their wartime experiences. Their words tell that story. What follows are intended as reflections, only, on their oral testimonies.

There were some similarities in the experiences of the women who were evacuated and those who remained on their island communities. All had been denied opportunities which would have broadened their understanding of the world beyond Torres Strait. Thus, they entered the war years with fears which were very much related to what they termed their 'innocence'. It is also probably true to say that the majority, if not all, of the women, if given the choice, would have preferred to remain in Torres Strait and face whatever they had to face. In early 1942, their innocence of their situation and of the destructive potential of the machines of modern warfare would have justified such a decision. They were confident that they could maintain their own safety. Those who left on the *Ormiston* went with reluctant hearts. In the case of the outer island women, it is highly unlikely that they would have welcomed an evacuation order, even though the men were favourably disposed to such a move. For all of these women, an initial reaction might have been that to endure the war in a familiar environment was preferable to relocation in an alien one.

Initially, the evacuee women were apprehensive about the mainland. Racist attitudes very soon became apparent. Nonetheless, it seems that, whether young or old, the women adapted in their own ways to the mainland. For the majority of the Hammond Island women, the ultimate demonstration of this was their willingness to remain on the mainland when the opportunity finally arrived to return home. The dream of returning home was too strong, however, for most of the TI women, perhaps because they knew they would not be returning to be controlled by any government or church institution, and probably with the hope that things would be different.

The women who stayed on the mainland saw for themselves and their families an improved lifestyle. For the few Hammond Island women who returned, there was the separation from the family members they had left behind. They were to see the mission community reconstituted as new families swelled their numbers. Both the Hammond and Thursday Island women were overwhelmed by the devastation of their islands. On Thursday Island, young women's employment opportunities took a turn for the better; no more scrubbing floors for whites, they took positions as shop assistants and clerical workers with higher pay. Higher wages for seamen also raised family expectations. However, the trauma of war did little to rid the island of the 'coloured thing'. But, looking back almost in disbelief, an old woman expressed what all of the evacuee women must have felt in their hearts: their evacuation had been 'a really big experience'.

The women who were left on their small outer island communities can be counted among those in northern Australia who had 'an experience of the crisis different from that of the rest of the continent'.[4] In early 1942, mainland women feared what the Japanese were going to do to them; island women remembered

Japanese men as their friends. Their fears were of guns, planes, submarines, mines, men in uniform and their own inability to speak 'proper English', and even the roles they were accustomed to play in the presence of strangers engendered fear. Fear was 'the problem'. Its only antidotes were faith and prayer; prayer 'camouflaged' everyone from danger.

What was uppermost in the women's minds after fifty years, or what they were willing to share with outsiders, were, generally, positive experiences which had impacted on them in ways related to their responsibilities as wives, mothers and daughters. This is evident in their recollections about faith and prayer, of strong feelings when their men were taken away, how they kept their families safe, fed and clothed, schooling the children, management of health care and the sorts of social outlets available to them — weddings, feasting, dancing, entertaining white soldiers.

The anger expressed when recalling the recruitment of almost all of their able-bodied men went right to the core of the women's emotions, despite the time lapse. Taking them away when the women needed them most, it seemed, had been harder to bear than their desertion by the government. Furthermore, recollections of recruitment were of guns, uniforms, their own powerlessness, great fear; the method of the men's recruitment was wrong. Such pain was personal. Furthermore, they were losing their men when the future was more uncertain than they could ever have remembered it. It was, however, the men who expressed their disgust, even anger, about what they saw as the abandonment of the women by their white administrators. Overall, the women's testimonies suggested a good deal of acceptance of their wartime lot. Whether this was so in 1942 may be conjectural.

The steps they took to ensure their families' safety were related to the women's role as carers. What a eurocentric author might have considered equally, if not more, worthy of recall were their coast-watching and other activities in collaboration with the signallers; these were more in tune with the 'heroic' acts which fill history books. The world of the island woman of that generation centred on her family, so that the things she did for them personally were indelibly written on her mind; family was and still is of paramount importance to the old women. Moreover, the enemy's activity in

Torres Strait had been the signallers' responsibility, so the women's contributions to any broader defence measures may have seemed less worthy of recall, perhaps even irrelevant, in their contemporary memories of the episode.

The women maintained that their main sources of food had been the result of their own hard work. Basic store goods were constantly in short supply, or completely absent from store shelves. Efforts to supplement their food supplies with bush tucker and seafoods were affected because of the danger of being seen and by the loss of their boats. This made it 'very, very hard to feed all the kids'. It was hard also to keep everyone clothed. The few clothes they had were constantly mended; not a scrap of material was wasted.

However, despite the women's statements to the contrary, outsiders criticised them for their neglect of their gardens which, it was claimed, resulted in serious sicknesses. In the context of what is known about prewar health in Torres Strait and indeed on the mainland among poorer families and outsider lack of understanding, to lay the blame on the women was too simplistic. Moreover, for almost two years, the government gave the women virtually no medical support. The women relied heavily, therefore, on their own outlawed bush medicines, while not underestimating the importance of western medicine. Without training, they again took on a caring role and distributed whatever medical supplies were received. Only when the hospitals were set up on Badu and Masig in late 1943 did they receive any basic training for their part in the western health care system.

According to one woman, most mothers had 'little experience in their heads' but they taught the children what they knew, hoping for a quick end to the war so that they could get the children back into a 'proper school and continue their education'. They knew 'proper schooling' was basic to their aspirations for a new deal after the war. They were obviously motivated by this fact.

Because most of their recollections related to the harder side of what they made of their experience, it was refreshing when anyone spoke about dancing and feasting, or socialising with the white soldiers. Their recollections of these things and a signaller's remark that the women 'carried on as if there was no war on' might be interpreted to contradict everything they said about their fears. But rather than being contradictory, the women's efforts to find some relief from their oppressive situation were complementary to those fears. They saw the need, just as their mainland counterparts did, to grasp whatever moments of happiness they could. While these occasions resulted in the breaking down of barriers between the two cultures, inter-racial marriage laws were safeguarded: 'You cannot marry the white ones', they were reminded.

The women's recollections of the return to peace were of bells, God's mercy, their prayers, the return of the men and tears. In the end, peace for them was not the result of the superior strategies, forces and arms of the allies; it had been God's work. Many of these old people still have a deep sense of the spiritual about all that happens. Nonetheless, they had realistic experiences of the physical aspects of modern warfare. The politics of it all was, perhaps, another matter.

Evidence from other sources revealed outsider interpretations of the negative aspects of the women's experiences. They were not pursued with the women because I wanted them to tell their stories without the pressures associated with an interrogation. Nonetheless, I was curious about the nature of the gaps in their recall. Some light was thrown on the matter by a Saibai nun who, although only a baby during the war, said she had given a lot of thought to why the old women had been so silent about much that had happened then:

> Probably it was very sad for them to think about their troubles and their failures to look after the family while the men were away. It is a natural way for a human being to do that. They don't want to look back and talk about things that were unpleasant to them.

Perhaps the women did not talk about their sicknesses because they felt that in some way they had failed in caring for their families, particularly as outsiders had told them they had. It can also be understood that old people who still embrace their custom of reciprocity would find it hard to recall the divisions which occurred on St Paul's and probably other communities as a result of the self-interest of the more affluent. Their silence on matters of controversy with whites might also be related to a long conditioning of outsider disrespect for their knowledge. Thus, if they had been asked to comment on specific adverse archival evidence, they may still have been reticent to test an outsider reaction to their interpretations. They may have remained silent because it was only the positive side of their experiences which stood out for them after so long, as an old nun who recalled the evacuation of the Hammond Island women said was the case for her. The outer island women's stoicism in face of the inevitable and what they saw as their special care of their families seem to have constituted the best side for them.

Speculations aside, however, what remains certain is that there is never just one reality to any historical episode: all evidence is only partial, as it was in this inquiry. There is always the potential for reinterpretation and this interpretation certainly does not constitute a last word. A Torres Strait Islander's version of the episode would undoubtedly produce a more culturally attuned and comprehensive interpretation of the women's wartime experiences.

Nonetheless, an account of the Torres Strait Islander women's 'really big experiences' and the 'hard times' they experienced during the Pacific War has been finally recorded. The account expands the historiography of Torres Strait Islanders and enables all Australians to gain a broader view of this nation's involvement in the Pacific War. It also raises the question of how valuable the outer island women's lives were to the government in 1942. Moreover, just as the history of the Delany sisters is not solely for Black American readership, the histories of these Torres Strait Islander women are histories for all Australians. And, as such, they can only help to break down the barriers which have kept white Australians ignorant of not only the experiences of this Indigenous group of Australians but also their own.

Notes

Chapter 1 Introduction

1. Delany and Delany 1993.

2. Patai 1988, p 3; Cruikshank 1988, p 198; McGrath 1988, p 172.

3. Nakata 1993, p 334.

4. TSIRECC 1992, p i.

5. *Torres News*, 18–24 August 1989, p 30.

6. Nakata 1990, p 5.

7. Erub Islander, Early History Workshop, videotape made by Pro-Octa Productions Pty Ltd, Thursday Island, March 1987.

8. Saibai Islander, Early History Workshop, March 1987.

9. Kosker 1928, p 54.

10. Moresby 1874, p 3.

11. Haddon 1935, p 112.

12. Cited in Sharp 1984, vol 2, p B99.

13. Ganter 1994, p 84.

14. Beckett 1987, p 13.

15. Cited in Sharp 1993, p 189.

16. Sharp 1993, pp 211–18. After the strike, a Department of Native Affairs (DNA) was set up with a Director as its head and Local Protectors.

17. Petition, Torres Strait Islanders to Governor of Queensland, 13 April 1944, TR12257, Bundle 140, QSA.

18. Ankersmit 1989, pp 145–48.

Chapter 2 'We didn't know we would be evacuated'

1. Douglas 1886, p 76; Gill 1876, p 200.

2. JF McMahon to author, undated (about September 1989).

3. Teleprinter message, Department of Navy to Department of External Territories, 30 January 1942, M41/1/9, A1608/1, AA (ACT).

4. Telegram, Collins to WJF Riordan, 30 January 1942, 82/713/58, MP508/1, AA (Vic).

5. Cairns Council, Minutes Ordinary Meeting, 20 January 1942, p 3, Cairns City Council Archives.

6. Memorandum, JR Halligan to Department of Interior, 2 February 1942, M41/1/9, A1608/1, AA (ACT).

7. Cited in Reynolds 1989, p 205.

8. Telegram, Forgan Smith to Prime Minister, 17 February 1942, M41/1/9, A1608/1, AA (ACT).

9. Forgan Smith to Prime Minister, 25 May 1942, M41/1/9, A1608/1, AA (ACT).

10. Telegram, Prime Minister to Premier, 26 February 1942, B470, Premier's Department Archives, Brisbane.

11. Gaffney 1989, pp 14–16.

12. Foley 1986, p 52.

13. RM Retallack to Prime Minister's Department, 1 March 1942, Part I, B470, Premier's Department Archives.

Chapter 3 The mainland experience

1. Rowley 1971, p 117.

2. Franklin 1976, p 122.

3. Markus 1987, p 84.

4. Queensland, House of Representatives, *Debates*, vol 174, 1939, p 467.

5. See note 2, p 123–25.

6. See note 4, p 458.

7. Cited in Markus 1987, p 87.

8. Summers 1977, p 416.

9. War Cabinet Agenda, 24 January 1942, M41/1/9, A1608/1, AA (ACT).

10. Telegrams, on Japanese internment action, 1941–42, 8 and 15 December 1941 and 6 January 1942. (All in Q39362, BP242/1, AA (Qld).)

11. *Courier Mail*, Brisbane, 19 April 1945, p 3.

12. Beckett 1987, p 221.

13. See note 4, p 498.

14. Berndt and Berndt 1987, pp 21 and 164–69.

15. Queensland, House of Representatives, *Debates*, vol 175, 1945–46, p 48.

16. SH Davies, Bishop of Carpentaria, to the Premier, 13 September 1946, 46/2598, A431/1, AA (ACT).

Chapter 4 'It was all of a sudden'

1. Sharp 1992, p 29.

2. History of Hammond Island, undated, Aboriginal Education Unit, Department of Education Archives, Brisbane.

3. Bleakley 1961, p 295.

4. See note 2.

5. DW McCullagh to Father Provincial, 21 August 1940, Catholic Archives, Sydney.

6. Minister of Health and Home Affairs to Acting Premier, 17 March 1942, Aboriginals General, 42/2345, QSA.

7. Teleprinter message, 30 January 1942, A1608/1, AA (ACT).

8. Sacred Heart Mission, undated.

9. Father Provincial to W Flynn, 5 March 1942, Catholic Archives, Sydney.

10. Mangan 1989, p 46.

11. WH Flynn to Father Provincial, 1 August 1942, Catholic Archives, Sydney.

12. JM Docherty to Father Provincial, 31 May 1943, Catholic Archives, Sydney.

13. JM Docherty to Father Provincial, 7 April 1943, Catholic Archives, Sydney.

14. AG Nicoll to Commonwealth Investigation Branch, 20 November 1944, C58616, A367/1, AA (ACT).

15. Memorandum, Ban on Employment of Asiatics and Coloured Men by Sanitary Contractors, 18 July 1945, 45/6423, A317/41, QSA.

Chapter 5 'Leave the Islanders where they are'

1. 'Coastal Evacuations', *Townsville Daily Bulletin*, 7 August 1941, p 4.

2. Spaull 1982, pp 10–11.

3. 'Victorian Education Plans', *Townsville Daily Bulletin*, 11 December 1941, p 5.

4. Hasluck 1970, p 138.

5. Lockwood 1966, pp 184–85.

6. Tyler 1986, pp 1–3.

7. Thornell 1986, pp 105–11.

8. 'The Aussie Pearl Harbour', *The Bulletin*, 18 February 1992, pp 39, 44; Spaull 1982, p 14.

9. Ngabidj 1981, pp 138–39.

10. Lt-Col R Bolton to Director, 12 March 1942, CA753, Item Q25356, BP242/1, AA (Qld).

11. Wilson 1988, p 9.

12. See note 7, p 110.

13. See note 4, p 132.

14. Horner 1982, p 183.

15. P Pearson, Early History Workshop, March 1987.

16. Petition, Torres Strait Islanders to Governor of Queensland, 13 April 1944, Bundle 140, TR12257, QSA.

17. Report, Governor of Queensland, 28 April 1943, p 2, Gov/93, QSA.

18. Hall 1989, p 36.

19. Memorandum, Under-Secretary to Auditor-General, 11 April 1944, AUD/W129, QSA.

20. Director to Under-Secretary, 30 March 1944, p 1, AUD/W129, QSA.

21. Ingui et al 1991, pp 78–84.

22. Lawrie 1983, pp 6–9.

23. Passi 1986, p 58.

24. Cited in Sharp 1993, p 3.

25. Cited in Griffin 1976, pp xxv and 33.

26. Cited in Sharp 1980, p 36.

Chapter 6 Enlistment and the quest for freedom

1. Markus 1990, p 189.

2. Hall 1989, pp 8–16.

3. Sharp 1984, vol 1, p 241.

4. Minute Paper, 4 April 1941, 274/101/328, MP508/1, AA (Vic).

5. Colonel i/c, AMF-NC to Military Board, 29 November 1940, p 1, 275/701/293, MP508/1, AA (Vic).

6. See note 2, p 34.

7. Report ... on Employment of Natives in the Army, 19 June 1944, p 1, 628/1/1, AWM54, AWM (Canberra).

8. Robson 1939, p 220.

9. Minute Paper, 4 April 1941, 275/301/328, MP508/1, AA (Vic).

10. Major-General Jackson, AMF-NC to Military Board, 29 April 1941, 275/701/328, MP508/1, AA (Vic).

11. 36 Meriam men, 4 from Erub, 18 from Moa and 3 from Badu. Colonel AM Forbes to Military Board, 22 August 1941, 275/701/383, AA (Vic).

12. Meriam men 61, St Paul's 13, Badu 6, Ugar 1, Mabuiag 9, Erub 7, Poid 7, Yam 1 and Moa 1. Colonel AM Forbes to Military Board, 30 October 1941, 275/701/393, MP508/1, AA (Vic).

13. Premier to Prime Minister, 5 December 1941, 10/719/23, MP508/1, AA (Vic).

14. Bolton to Director, 12 March 1942, CA753, Q25356, BP242/1, AA (Qld).

15. Cited in Hasluck 1970, p 39.

16. MacArthur 1964, p 152.

17. Hasluck 1970, pp 120–21 and 283–84.

18. 'Port Moresby Now Vital to Australia', *Courier Mail*, 18 December 1942, p 1.

19. See note 2, p 12.

20. W Nona, Early History Workshop, March 1987.

21. P Pearson, Early History Workshop, March 1987.

22. See note 21.

23. See note 2, pp 38–39.

24. Lowah 1988, p 75.

25. History of women on Thursday Island during the Second World War, HE Palmer, 19 March 1991.

26. See note 21.

27. Beckett 1987, p 63; Hall 1989, p 37.

28. D Ober, Townsville, 1990; report of Director of Native Affairs for twelve months ended 30 June 1943.

29. Brigadier Lt-Gen Legge to LHQ, 23 July 1943 and 15 September 1943, 506/5/10, AWM54, AWM (Canberra).

30. Report, Medical Conditions, 22 May 1944, Bundle 140, TR1227, QSA.

31. See note 25.

32. Cited in Sharp 1984, vol 1, p 244–45.

33. See note 2, p 66.

34. See note 21.

35. See note 32.

36. Thompson, Impressions, 805/7/1, AWM54, AWM (Canberra).

37. Beckett 1987, p 65.

38. Report, Army Intelligence, week ending 9 January 1944, 628/4/5, AWM54, AWM (Canberra).

39. Recommendations, Melbourne conference for altered rates of pay, 24 April 1944, A/122257, QSA.

40. Minutes, conference (undated), 628/1/1, AWM54, AWM (Canberra).

41. Report, Employment of Natives, 19 June 1944, p 1, 628/1/1, AWM54, AWM (Canberra).

Chapter 7 The enemy at the front door

1. Report, EM Hanlon, 1 February 1941, 82/713/13, MP729/6, AA (Vic).

2. Long 1952, p 33.

3. Clark 1969, p 236.

4. Tyler 1986, pp 1–6.

5. Cited in Moles 1979, pp 101 and 108.

6. Cited in Copeman and Vance 1992, p 8.

7. Horner 1978, p 46.

8. Piper 1987, p B2.

9. TISHSS 1987, pp 12–14.

10. Queensland, *The Year Book*, No. 5, 1941, p 31.

11. See note 9, p 13.

12. Report, Rev Godfrey Gilbert, January 1942, OM.AV/150/2, JOL, Brisbane.

13. Audiotape TSIMA, Riza Morrison, Townsville, 11 May 1986.

14. Cited in TISHSS 1987, p 38.

15. Sharp 1993, p 36.

16. John 1982, pp 91–95.

17. Hoyt 1975, pp 5, 11, 31.

18. See note 17, p xiii.

Chapter 8 Fear and faith

1. Crowley 1974, p 464.

2. Millar 1978, pp 91–95.

3. See note 2, p 100.

4. Cited in Millar 1978, p 102.

5. Warner and Seno 1986, p 90.

6. See note 1, p 465.

7. Bleakley 1961, p 272.

8. Report, Governor of Queensland, 28 April 1943, p 2, Gov/93, QSA.

9. Peel 1946, pp 8 and 115.

10. Beckett 1987, p 63.

11. Cited in Sharp 1984, vol 1, p 10.

12. Langbridge 1977, p 24.

13. Report, John Douglas, 6 August 1885, *QV&P* 1885, vol 2, p 1084.

14. See note 11, pp 189–90.

15. Cited in Sharp 1993, p 143.

16. Cited in Sharp 1984, vol 2, pp B63 and B77.

17. Thaiday 1981, p 10.

18. See note 16, pp B77–78.

19. Jukes 1847, pp 160, 166, 172.

20. Gill 1876, p 207.

21. Mullins 1989, pp 5–6.

22. Lama Anagarika Govinda, cited in Happold 1971, p 43.

23. McKernan 1980, pp 24–32.

24. 'Archbishops Deplore Apathy to Religion', *Courier Mail*, 16 February 1942, p 3.

25. 'Japan's Threat to Church', *Courier Mail*, 9 March 1942, p 4.

26. 'Clergy Call to Courage, Faith', *Courier Mail*, 16 March 1942, p 5.

27. Whiteman 1983, pp 65–66.

28. Haddon 1904, p 257.

29. Fuary 1991, pp 190–91.

30. Singe 1993, pp 58–67.

31. See note 27, p 74.

32. Sharp 1993, p 29.

33. Haddon nd, pp 37–41.

34. See note 28, pp 321–22.

35. Moore 1989, p 29.

36. Orrell 1969, p 24.

37. Done 1987, p 104.

38. Lee 1983.

39. Minutes, meeting 1 May 1931; Reports, Mothers Union, July 1933 and June 1939: Anglican Diocese of Carpentaria, OM.AV/12/2, JOL (Brisbane).

40. History of women on Thursday Island during World War Two, HE Palmer, 19 March 1991, pp 7–8.

41. Minutes, Mothers Union 25 September 1940, Anglican Diocese of Carpentaria, OM.AV/12/2, JOL (Brisbane).

42. See note 32, p 116.

43. Cowan 1993, p 52.

44. Bishop's letter, Thursday Island, January 1942, p 74, Anglican Diocese of Carpentaria, OM.AV/150/2, JOL (Brisbane).

45. News of the Diocese, Thursday Island, January 1942, pp 74, 79–80, Anglican Diocese of Carpentaria, OM.AV/150/2, JOL (Brisbane).

46. Report, Godfrey Gilbert, January 1942, p 80, Anglican Diocese of Carpentaria, OM.AV/150/2, JOL (Brisbane).

47. Bayton 1965, p 106.

Chapter 9 Hard times

1. Long 1973, p 291.

2. See note 1, p 290; Odgers 1957, pp 38–40 and 116.

3. Cited in Connell 1988, p 85.

4. 'Rationing of Clothes on Monday', *Courier Mail*, 9 May 1942, p 1.

5. Director to Under-Secretary, 15 May 1945, pp 1–2, AUD/W146, QSA.

6. Beckett 1987, p 64.

7. Australia, House of Representatives 1941, *Debates*, vol HR166, p 620.

8. See note 7, pp 360 and 435.

9. See note 6, p 103.

10. Bleakley 1961, p 305.

11. Statement, Grainger Smith, 14 March 1942, A/15997, QSA.

12. Report, Army Intelligence, 9 January 1944, 528/4/5, AWM54, AWM.

13. Report, Protector's Accounts, 30 April 1942 to 11 January 1943, p 22, AUD/W129, QSA; Report, Director's Accounts, 1 October 1944 to 31 December 1945, p 38, AUD/T141, QSA; Report, Director's Accounts, 1 January 1946 to 4 February 1947, p 29, AUD/T141, QSA.

14. Report, Director's Accounts to 31 December 1945, p 38, AUD/T141, QSA.

15. AR, Director to 30 June 1946, *QPP* 1946, vol 2, p 1040.

16. Director to Under-Secretary, 30 March 1944, p 1, AUD/W129, QSA.

17. Report, Protector's Accounts, 1 May 1945 to 30 April 1946, pp 2, 4, AUD/W153, QSA.

18. Statement, Darnley (Erub) Island Councillors, 3 March 1942, p 2, A/15997, QSA.

19. Director to Home Secretary, 28 September 1944, p 2, Bundle 140, TR1227, QSA.

20. Report, Protector's Accounts, 16 September 1943 to 30 April 1945, pp 12–13, AUD/W146, QSA.

21. McKernan 1983, pp 49–51.

22. Cited in Keesing 1991, p 76.

23. Encel et al 1974, p 18; Allport 1984, p 18.

24. Keesing 1991, pp 36 and 188.

25. Summers 1977, p 414.

26. AR, Director to 30 June 1945, *QPP* 1945–46, vol 2, p 1077.

27. AR, Accounts Director of Native Affairs to 30 June 1946, *QPP* 1946, vol 2, p 1040.

28. Nietschmann and Nietschmann 1981, p 62; Passi 1986, p 37.

29. Haddon 1904, p 210.

30. History of women on Thursday Island during World War Two, HE Palmer, 19 March 1991.

31. Complaint, Namok and Ware, 30 October 1943, 628/4/5; Minutes, Conference AAG and ors., nd, 528/1/1. (Both in AWM54, AWM.)

32. Hall 1989, p 43.

33. Notes for leave recommendations, 22 November 1943; Report, St Paul's mission, nd. (Both in 628/4/5, AWM54, AWM.)

34. Reports, Army Intelligence, 5 December 1943 and 26 December 1943; Report, Saibai leave personnel's request, 3 November 1943, pp 1–2. (All in 628/4/5, AWM54, AWM.)

35. Report, St Paul's mission, nd, 628/4/5, AWM54, AWM.

36. See note 32, p 53.

37. Reports, by army survey teams, 12–30 August 1944, Bundle 140, TR1227, QSA.

38. Ankersmit 1989, p 142–43; Osborne 1995, pp 28–29.

Chapter 10 'The people had to do it'

1. Connell et al 1983, p 15.

2. Bleakley 1961, p 299.

3. Badu Islander, Early History Workshop, March 1987.

4. St Paul's man, Early History Workshop, March 1987.

5. Orr and Williamson 1973.

6. Ganter 1994, p 72.

7. Queensland, Legislative Assembly 1939, *Debates*, vol 174, p 499.

8. Cited in Williamson 1994, p 165.

9. Cited in Spaull 1982, p 9.

10. See note 2, p 288.

11. Minutes, ordinary meeting, Cairns Council, January 1942, Cairns City Council Archives.

12. Petition to Governor, 13 April 1944, Bundle 140, TR12257, QSA.

13. Report, Governor of Queensland, 28 April 1942, p 4, Gov/93, QSA.

14. Minutes, Councillors Conference, Yorke (Masig) Island, 19 August 1944, p 3, TR1227, Bundle 140, QSA.

15. Summary to Minutes of Councillors Conference, 11 September 1944, Bundle 140, TR1227, QSA.

16. See note 2, p 289.

17. Director to Secretary, 28 September 1944, Bundle 140, TR1227, QSA.

18. Whiteman 1983, p 353.

19. B Nona, Oral History Unit, James Cook University (Townsville).

20. AR, Aboriginals Department, 31 December 1934, *QPP* 1935, vol 1, p 986.

21. Orrell 1969, pp 22–23.

22. AR, Aboriginals Department, 31 December 1935, *QPP* 1936, vol 1, p 1036.

23. Reports, Army survey teams, Survey Badu, 11–13 August 1944, Bundle 140, TR1227, QSA.

24. Director to Under-Secretary, 15 June 1944, p 1, Bundle 140, TR1227, QSA.

25. Report, Governor of Queensland, 28 April 1943, p 3, Gov/93, QSA.

26. Report, Army Intelligence, 12 December 1943, 628/4/5, AWM54, AWM.

27. Loos 1993, p 17.

28. Reports, Army Survey Teams, Badu, 12–13 August 1944, Bundle 140, TR1227, QSA.

29. Report, Col. GN Robinson, 22 May 1944, p 2, Bundle 140, TR1227, QSA.

30. Director to Under-Secretary, 15 June 1944, p 2, Bundle 140, TR1227, QSA.

31. Director to Under-Secretary, 22 September 1943, p 1; Report, medical conditions, Robinson, 22 May 1944, p 5. (In Bundle 140, TR1227, QSA.)

32. Mackerras and Sandars 1954, p 4.

33. Report, Medical Conditions, Robinson, 22 May 1944, pp 2–4, Bundle 140, TR1227, QSA.

34. See note 33.

35. Osborne 1995, pp 34–35.

36. Suggested Scheme for Organisation of Medical Services in Torres Strait Area, Major GR Beattie, 31 August 1944, pp 1–4, Bundle 140, TR1227, QSA.

Chapter 11 Breaking down barriers

1. Cited in McKernan 1983, p 168.

2. Cited in Hasluck 1970, pp 270–71.

3. Adam-Smith 1984, p 335; Long 1973, p 114; Crowley 1974, p 464.

4. Penglase and Horner 1992, p 169.

5. 'Protest by Churches on Sunday Sport', *Courier Mail*, 22 May 1942, p 5.

6. Cited in Copeman and Vance 1992, pp 52–53.

7. Anau 1990, p 14.

8. Court reports, Murray Island 1938–45, Department of Family Services and Aboriginal and Islander Affairs, Brisbane.

9. Haddon 1890, pp 362 and 365; Beckett 1987, p 43.

10. Colwill to Burge, 10 June 1949, p 2, 425/6/15, AWM54, AWM.

11. See Section 21 of the *Torres Strait Islanders Act 1939* and Section 19, subsection (1) paragraph (a) of the *Aboriginals Preservation and Protection Act of 1939* (Qld).

12. Peter 1990, p 32.

13. Connell 1988, p 133.

14. Cited in Sharp 1984, vol 1, p 245.

Chapter 12 Reflections

1. Lorde 1984, p 44.

2. Ankersmit 1989, p 146.

3. Osborne 1995, pp 22, 28–32, 95–100.

4. Hasluck 1970, p 132.

Bibliography

Adam-Smith, Patsy 1984 *Australian Women at War*, Thomas Nelson, Melbourne.

Allport, Carolyn 1984 Left off the Agenda: Women, Reconstruction and New Order Housing, *Labour History* 46, May, 1–20.

Anau, Jerry 1990 Working Together, Helping Each Other. In Rod and Judy Kennedy, with the people of the Western Torres Strait, *Adha Gar Tidi: Cultural Sensitivity in Western Torres Strait*, Summer Institute of Linguistics, Darwin, 17–19.

Ankersmit, F.R. 1989 Historiography and Postmodernism, *History and Theory* 28(2), 137–53.

Bayton, John 1965 *Cross over Carpentaria: Being a History of the Church of England in Northern Australia from 1865–1965*, W.R. Smith & Paterson, Brisbane.

Beckett, Jeremy 1987 *Torres Strait Islanders: Custom and Colonialism*, Cambridge University Press, Sydney.

Berndt, Ronald M. and Catherine H. Berndt 1987 *End of an Era: Aboriginal Labour in the Northern Territory*, Australian Institute of Aboriginal Studies, Canberra.

Bleakley, John William 1961 *The Aborigines of Australia: Their History, Their Habits, Their Assimilation*, Jacaranda, Brisbane.

Boigu Island Community 1991 *Boigu: Our History and Culture*, Aboriginal Studies Press, Canberra.

Clark, Manning 1969 *A Short History of Australia*, A Mentor Book, New York.

Connell, Daniel 1988 *The War at Home: Australia 1939–1949*, ABC Enterprises, Sydney.

Connell, R.W., D.J. Ashenden, S. Kessler and G.W. Dowsett (eds) 1983 *Making the Difference: Schools, Families and Social Division*, George Allen & Unwin, Sydney.

Copeman, G. and D. Vance (eds) 1992 *'It Was a Different Town': Being Some Memories of Townsville and District 1942–1945*, Thuringowa City Council, Townsville.

Cowan, James G. 1993 *Messengers of the Gods*, Bell Tower, New York.

Crowley, F.K. (ed) 1974 *A New History of Australia*, William Heinemann, Melbourne.

Cruikshank, Julie 1988 Myth and Tradition as Narrative Framework: Oral Histories from Northern Canada, *International Journal of History* 9(3), November, 198–214.

Delany, Sara and A. Elizabeth Delany with Amy Hill Hearth 1993 *Having Our Say: The Delany Sisters' First 100 Years*, Kodansha International, New York.

Done, John E. (compiled by Barbara Stevenson) 1987 *Wings across the Sea*, Boolarong Publications, Brisbane.

Douglas, Hon. John 1886 The Islands of Torres Straits, *Queensland Geographical Journal* 1, 70–83.

Encel, Sol, Norman MacKenzie and Margaret Tebbutt 1974 *Women and Society: An Australian Study*, Cheshire, Melbourne.

Foley, J.C.H. 1986 *Timeless Isle: An Illustrated History of Thursday Island*, Torres Strait Historical Society, Thursday Island.

Franklin, Margaret Ann 1976 *Black and White Australians: An Inter-Racial History 1788–1975*, Heinemann, Melbourne.

Fuary, Maureen Majella 1991 In So Many Words: An Ethnography of Life and Identity on Yam Island, Torres Strait, PhD thesis, James Cook University, Townsville.

Gaffney, Ellie 1989 *Somebody Now: The Autobiography of Ellie Gaffney, A Woman of Torres Strait*, Aboriginal Studies Press, Canberra.

Ganter, Regina 1994 *The Pearl-Shellers of Torres Strait: Resource Use, Development and Decline, 1860s–1960s*, Melbourne University Press, Melbourne.

Gill, Rev. W. Wyatt 1876 *Life in the Southern Isles: Or, Scenes and Incidents in the South Pacific and New Guinea*, The Religious Tract Society, London.

Griffin, James (ed) 1976 *The Torres Strait Border Issue: Consolidation, Conflict or Compromise*, Townsville College of Advanced Education, Townsville.

Haddon, A.C. nd *Head-Hunters, Black, White and Brown*, Watts & Co, London.

—— 1890 The Ethnography of the Western Tribes of Torres Straits, *Journal of the Anthropological Institute of Great Britain and Ireland* 19, 297–437.

Haddon, A.C. (ed) 1901–35 *Reports of the Cambridge Anthropological Expedition to Torres Straits*, 6 vols, Cambridge University Press, UK: 1901 (vol 2), 1904 (vol 5), 1907 (vol 3), 1908 (vol 6), 1912 (vol 4), 1935 (vol 1).

Hall, Robert A. 1989 *The Black Diggers: Aborigines and Torres Strait Islanders in the Second World War*, Allen & Unwin, Sydney.

Happold, F.C. 1971 *Prayer and Meditation: Their Nature and Practice*, Penguin, Harmondsworth, UK.

Hasluck, Paul 1970 *The Government and People 1942–1945*, Australian War Memorial, Canberra.

Horner, David Murray 1978 *Crisis of Command: Australian Generalship and the Japanese Threat 1941–1945*, Australian National University Press, Canberra.

—— 1982 *High Command: Australia and Allied Strategy 1939–1945*, George Allen & Unwin, Sydney.

Hoyt, Edwin R. 1975 *Blue Skies and Blood: The Battle of the Coral Sea*, Paul S. Eriksson, Inc, New York.

Ingui, Abia, Ishmael Banu, Jacob Matthew, Ganalai Matthew, Charlie Gibuma, Melezina Gibuma, Aggie Pina Matthew and Isobel Tom 1991 Traditional Warfare. In Boigu Island Community, *Boigu: Our History and Culture*, Aboriginal Studies Press, Canberra, 78–84.

John, C.H. 1982 *Reef Pilots: The History of the Queensland Coast and Torres Strait Pilot Service*, Banks Bros & Street, Sydney.

Jukes, J. Beete 1847 *Narrative of the Surveying Voyage of H.M.S. Fly*, vol 1, T. & W. Boone, London.

Keesing, Nancy (ed) 1991 *The Home Front Family Album: Remembering Australia 1939–1945*, Weldon Publishing, Sydney.

Kennedy, Rod and Judy Kennedy with the people of the Western Torres Strait 1990 *Adha Gar Tidi: Cultural Sensitivity in Western Torres Strait*, Summer Institute of Linguistics, Darwin.

Kosker (pseud) 1928 Women's Work in the Torres Straits, *The Australian Woman's Mirror*, 26 June, 52–55.

Langbridge, John William 1977 From Enculturation to Evangelization: An Account of Missionary Education in the Islands of Torres Strait to 1915, BEd (Hons) thesis, James Cook University, Townsville.

Lawrie, Margaret 1983 Death of the Head-man Alis, *Torres Strait Islanders* 4, 6–9.

Lee, Erna 1983 *Mary Sumner and the Mothers' Union: A Brief Account of the Story*, Assembly Press, Brisbane.

Lockwood, Douglas 1966 *Australia's Pearl Harbour: Darwin 1942*, Rigby, Adelaide.

Long, Gavin 1952 *To Benghazi*, Australian War Memorial, Canberra.

—— 1973 *The Six Years War*, Australian War Memorial, Canberra.

Loos, Noel 1993 A Chapter of Contact: Aboriginal–European Relations in North Queensland, 1606–1992. In Henry Reynolds (ed), *Race Relations in North Queensland*, James Cook University, Townsville, 4–39.

Lorde, Audre 1984 *Sister Outsider: Essays and Speeches*, Crossing Press Feminist Series, Freedom, California.

Lowah, Thomas 1988 *Eded Mer (My Life)*, Rams Skull Press, Kuranda, Queensland.

MacArthur, Douglas 1964 *Reminiscences*, Heinemann, London.

Mackerras, M.J. and D.F. Sandars 1954 *Malaria in the Torres Strait Islands*, South Pacific Commission Technical Paper No 68, Anton Brienl Centre, Townsville.

Mangan, Jim 1989 *To Hear To See To Speak*, Jim Mangan, Kingaroy, Queensland.

Markus, Andrew 1987 Cherbourg. In Bill Gammage and Peter Spearitt (eds), *Australians 1938*, Fairfax, Syme & Weldon, Sydney, 84–88.

—— 1990 *Governing Savages*, Allen & Unwin, Sydney.

McGrath, Ann 1988 Born or Reborn in the Cattle, *Meanjin* 47(2), Winter, 171–77.

McKernan, Michael 1980 *Australian Churches at War: Attitudes and Activities of the Major Churches, 1914–1918*, Australian War Memorial, Canberra.

—— 1983 *All In! Australia during the Second World War*, Nelson, Melbourne.

Millar, T.B. 1978 *Australia in Peace and War: External Relations 1788–1977*, Australian National University Press, Canberra.

Moles, Ian 1979 *A Majority of One: Tom Aikens and Independent Politics in Townsville*, University of Queensland, St Lucia.

Moore, David R. 1989 *Arts and Crafts of Torres Strait*, Shire Publications, Aylesbury, UK.

Moresby, J. 1874 Recent Discoveries at the Eastern End of New Guinea, *The Journal of the Royal Geographical Society* 44, 1–14.

Mullins, Steve 1989 Torres Strait 1864–1884: A History of Occupation and Culture Contact, PhD thesis, University of New England, Armidale.

Nakata, Martin 1990 Constituting the Torres Strait Islanders: A Foucauldian Discourse Analysis of the 1989 National Aboriginal and Torres Strait Islander Education Policy: Joint Policy Statement, paper presented to AARE annual conference, Sydney.

—— 1993 Culture in Education: For Us or For Them? In Noel Loos and Takeshi Osanai (eds), *Indigenous Minorities and Education: Australian and Japanese Perspectives on Their Indigenous Peoples, the Ainu, Aborigines and Torres Strait Islanders*, Sanyusha Publishing, Tokyo, 334–49.

Ngabidj, Grant (as told to Peter Shaw) 1981 *My Country of the Pelican Dreaming: The Life of an Australian Aborigine of the Gadjerong, Grant Ngabidj, 1904–1977*, Australian Institute of Aboriginal Studies, Canberra.

Nietschmann, B. and J. Nietschmann 1981 Good Dugong, Bad Dugong; Bad Turtle, Good Turtle, *Natural History* 90(5), New York, 54–63, 86–87.

Odgers, George 1957 *Air War against Japan 1943–1945*, Australian War Memorial, Canberra.

Orr, Kenneth and Alan Williamson 1973 *Education in Torres Strait: Perspectives for Development*, Australian National University, Canberra.

Orrell, John (ed) 1969 Unpublished Diaries of A.O.C. Davies: Pasi — A Story of the Islands, Technical and Further Education College Library, Cairns.

Osborne, Barry 1993 Education in Torres Strait: Past, Present and Future. In Noel Loos and Takeshi Osanai (eds), *Indigenous Minorities and Education: Australian and Japanese Perspectives of Their Indigenous Peoples, the Ainu, Aborigines and Torres Strait Islanders*, Sanyusha Publishing, Tokyo, 222–36.

Osborne, Betty (Elizabeth) 1990 In the Midst of War: A Lone Teacher in Torres Strait, *The Educational Historian* 3(3), 1, 7.

—— 1990 The Forgotten Evacuation, BA (Hons) thesis, James Cook University, Townsville.

—— 1993 'Looking at the New Light': Torres Strait Islanders and the Pacific War, 1942–1945. In Noel Loos and Takeshi Osanai (eds), *Indigenous Minorities and Education: Australian and Japanese Perspectives of Their Indigenous Peoples, the Ainu, Aborigines and Torres Strait Islanders*, Sanyusha Publishing, Tokyo, 52–66.

—— 1995 Our Voices: Torres Strait Islander Women in a War Zone 1942–1945, PhD thesis, James Cook University, Townsville.

Passi, Dave 1987 From Pagan to Christian Priesthood. In G.W. Trompf (ed), *The Gospel Is Not Western: Black Theologies from the South West Pacific*, Orbis Books, Maryknoll, New York, 45–48.

Passi, George 1986 Knowledge, Education and Self-Management: Autonomy of Torres Strait, Master's thesis, University of Queensland, Brisbane.

Patai, Daphne 1988 *Brazilian Women Speak: Contemporary Life Stories*, Rutgers University Press, New Brunswick.

Peel, Gerald 1946 *Isles of the Torres Strait*, Current Book Distributions, Sydney.

Penglase, Joanne and David Horner 1992 *When the War Came to Australia: Memories of the Second World War*, Allen & Unwin, Sydney.

Peter, Father John 1990 Sitting on the Mat of an Evening — Helping Our Children. In Rod and Judy Kennedy, with the people of the Western Torres Strait, *Adha Gar Tidi: Cultural Sensitivity in Western Torres Strait*, Summer Institute of Linguistics, Darwin, 32–33.

Piper, R.K. 1987 The Forgotten Air Raids on Horn Island, *The Canberra Times Saturday Magazine*, 3 October.

Reynolds, Henry 1989 *Dispossession: Black Australians and White Invaders*, Allen & Unwin, Sydney.

Robson, R.W. (comp and ed) 1939 *The Pacific Island Year-Book*, Pacific Publications, Sydney.

Rowley, C.D. 1971 *Outcasts in White Australia*, Australian National University Press, Canberra.

Sacred Heart Mission Thursday Island nd *Our First 100 Years: 1884–1984*, G.K. Botton, Cairns.

Sharp, Nonie 1980 *Torres Strait Islands 1879–1979: Theme of an Overview*, La Trobe University, Melbourne.

—— 1981–82 Culture Clash in the Torres Strait Islands: The Maritime Strike of 1936, *The Royal Historical Society of Queensland Journal* 11(3), 107–26.

—— 1984 Springs of Originality among the Torres Strait Islanders, 2 vols, PhD thesis, La Trobe University, Melbourne.

—— 1992 *Footprints along the Cape York Sandbeaches*, Aboriginal Studies Press, Canberra.

—— 1993 *Stars of Tagai: The Torres Strait Islanders*, Aboriginal Studies Press, Canberra.

Shnukal, Anna 1988 *Broken: An Introduction to the Creole Language of Torres Strait*, Australian National University, Canberra.

Singe, John 1993 *Among Islands*, Torres News, Thursday Island.

Spaull, A. 1982 *Australian Education in the Second World War*, University of Queensland Press, St Lucia.

Summers, Anne 1977 *Damned Whores and God's Police: The Colonization of Women in Australia*, Penguin, Harmondsworth, UK.

Thaiday, Willie 1981 *Under the Act*, North Queensland Black Publishing, Townsville.

Thornell, Harold (as told by Estelle Thompson) 1986 *A Bridge over Time: Living in Arnhem Land with the Aborigines 1938–1944*, J.M. Dent, Melbourne.

TISHSS (Thursday Island State High School Students) 1986 *Pearling in the Torres Strait*, Thursday Island State High School.

TISHSS (Thursday Island State High School Students) (eds) 1987 *Torres Strait at War: A Recollection of Wartime Experiences*, Thursday Island State High School.

TSIRECC (Torres Strait Islander Regional Education Consultative Committee) 1992 *Ngampula Yawadhan Ziawali: Education Policy for Torres Strait*, Queensland Aboriginal and Torres Strait Education Consultative Committee, Thursday Island.

Tyler, William 1986 *'Flight of the Diamond': The Story of Broome's War and the Carnot Bay Diamond*, Hesperian Press, Carlisle, Western Australia.

Warner, Peggy and Sadao Seno 1986 *The Coffin Boats: Japanese Midget Submarine Operations in the Second World War*, Secker and Warburg, London.

Whiteman, Darrell L. 1983 *Melanesians and Missionaries: An Ethnological Study of Social and Religious Change in Southwest Pacific*, W. Carey Library, Pasadena, California.

Williamson, Alan 1994 *Schooling the Torres Strait Islander 1873–1941: Context, Custom and Colonialism*, Aboriginal Research Institute Publications, Underdale, South Australia.

Wilson, P.D. 1988 *North Queensland World War II 1942–1945*, Department of Geographic Information, Brisbane.